Overlook

Joel

That was the night I decided to quit. Remotely. From the comfort of my bed. No need to haul the meat of myself down there. My absence would do just fine.

But there it was. The old belly womp of anxiety. Professional remorse? Or maybe just the residue of my grade-school conditioning. The Pavlonian drilling of bells and tedium, the ass-death of extended sitting.

God. The look on my manager's face, tasting the lemons of my fortitude.

My non-presence would be a ghost haunting the office, a form of supernatural anti-matter. At 8:15 I'd be considered late. 9:45 and I was an official defector. The manager would call around ten and I'd ignore it or, better yet, answer and remain silent. My chair would be mecca, silently observed by the pallid, the frumpy, the shiny and robust alike. Even Sarah, the turtle-built middle-aged woman who diligently tracked her water consumption and steps, would parade the aisles adding big digits to her wristlet pedometer consuming upwards of an extra liter in my name and honor.

I was under the assumption that all great men slept on their backs, mighty and supine, staring at shadows on the ceiling before drifting off into powerful dreams, visions that altered history. I squeezed my eyes shut as my body begged to lie prone, face down like a peasant in a ditch. This was how I usually slept, sprawled on my belly, collapsed as a broken casualty of the day. A dot of green light beamed off the smoke alarm. I saw it every night, the dot, and vowed to cover it. This was something of a ritual, my own form of dilapidated prayer.

A sheep formed in my head—yes, the old ghastly cliché. It emerged spontaneously from my lower brain, the part responsible for baser, wordless thoughts. The grazing beast stood in my mind's eye, old and dumb, chewing with nothing in its mouth. I couldn't tell if the sheep's mechanical chewing was a sign of faith or pure stupidity, but it kept on, thoughtlessly blinking to celebrate every successful chew. I guided the animal toward a fence and it leapt over with ease, clearing it victoriously. Another sheep came down the pike and leapt, also clearing the fence. This was good. Controlling this mental flock was the first step toward successfully sleeping on my back. I geared up the next creature. Its shoulder twitched and striated to ward off a pesky fly.

A car door slammed outside my house. A woman yelled and another door slammed. The sheep fell short and impaled itself on the fence, the rest scattered like mad, the weak trampled by the strong. I got out of bed and slumped over to the window, cracking the blinds to see what was going on.

Snow.

It had started secretly, accumulating behind my back. I was glad to catch it in the process, to be in the know. Abrupt shifts in scenery due to weather, snow in particular, can weaken my sense of reality. I stood and watched the crystalline flakes tumble as the wind cut eastward, scooping the fallen snow and hurling it back into the sky. A blanket of resurrected powder shimmered in the air, glistening under the urine-colored streetlights.

One of the arguing girls hiked her jeans up and prepared for action. I didn't recognize her, but I knew the other one. It was Brenda's sister,

Lynne. I watched as she rage-kicked John's chain link fence to ready herself for battle.

God, I liked Brenda.

Lynne was chubby and vaguely rough-looking in the face. Due to a nagging heroin problem, she crashed with Brenda on and off in the house they grew up in. It was across the street and two houses down. Theirs was one of those drastic sister situations where one was markedly prettier than the other. Actually, no, where one *was* pretty and the other simply wasn't. Though, in Lynne's defense, she did exude a sort of primitive sexuality, a sense of teenage defiance carried into her thirties. Admittedly, there were times when she'd occupied some of my darker masturbatory fantasies, called upon in circumstances of dire need. Mostly related to the sad endeavor of drunken self-pleasure. Masturbation that was more a means of quelling the aching, atmospheric crush of genuine soul-loneliness. On three separate occasions I'd called her to mind: once under a bridge, once against an abandoned shopping cart, and finally, on top of a pile of trash bags full of donated clothing, experiencing an abrupt wave of nausea immediately after each time. The shame, the self-disgust, it was so thick, so putridly dense that I swore off masturbating for a period of ninety days soon after having read somewhere that it was supposed to be helpful in terms of building confidence and self-esteem. Anyway, Lynne lived with Brenda off and on, whenever she needed to get "sober", which could be described more aptly as a court-ordered hiatus from drugs.

The house, from what I gathered, belonged to their aunt. Their mom defaulted on the mortgage and the aunt bailed them out. Their mom wasn't a fuck up. She had cancer—breast, I believe. The aunt was supposed to sell it back to the daughters after the mom died, but never did. Lynne was too fucked up. And Brenda, the one taking care of Lynne, wasn't exactly clean either. She was nothing like Lynne though;

Lynne was *majorly* fucked up, you could tell by looking at her. She always wore these comically shrunken outfits, the garb of a blossoming junkie. Stuff sold on discount racks that gave warnings about attitude, or being in her way, or (my favorite) the "*I CANT BE HELD RESPONSIBLE FOR WHAT MY FACE DOES WHEN YOU TALK*" t-shirt. She had this one getup that always got me. It was this combo of neon-green spandex pants and a black and gold generic sports jersey. The jersey simply said SPORTS across the chest. No specific game or player. Just SPORTS. And the back said HUSTLE, like it was her last name, with 24-7 written below as if demonstrating some undying work ethic. The whole ensemble ended up coming off as some kind of hyper-whorish active wear, like if Lululemon made a separate clothing line for getting fingered on the bus.

The wind shifted the snow. It swirled in a magical, dancing whoosh, iridescent over the girls as they fought, both oblivious to the natural spectacle around them. Lynne was losing, jammed against the very fence she kicked to start the fight.

The other girl. Who was she? Maybe I'd seen her around, but it was hard to tell. A lot of the people in the neighborhood shared a common facial structure—the archetypal mug of poor white Americans—a set of beady little eyes seated on a hook-nose, perched on top of a permanent sourpuss—a face with a structurally built-in sneer that even in its resting state was mean-looking and shrunken-in as if pinched by God before being hurled into the universe. A face specially designed to drink efficiently from a hose or to spit really far.

Lynne clung to the fence and threw a donkey kick, which was expertly caught by her opponent. The woman popped Lynne's sneaker off and beat her with it.

The porch light flicked on. Brenda materialized through the grey mist of winter storm, out from the snow-reflected aura of light. She ran down the sidewalk, gaining roughly fifty feet of steam, and bulldogged the woman off her sister and into the snow, which erupted on impact, sending a light powdery splash into the current of moving air, the invisible river of wind all around them. The woman scrambled, tussling with Brenda to get back on her feet, but Lynne, now up and moving with her sneaker re-attached, got behind her opponent and held her arms, forcing her to her knees. The woman squirmed, but Lynne held her still. Brenda took two steps back and kicked her in the forehead.

A cop car appeared at the top of the street, moving in that slow predatory crawl, the one right before pulling people over, right when you look in your rearview and think, "me?"

Red and blue lights tumbled through the winter sky as the car careened over the freshly laid snow.

The lights poured through my window, colors washing through my room in oblong sweeps; I scuttled out of the reach of their glow. A small but very convincing portion of my brain theorized that the lights contained intelligence and could report back. I closed my eyes but I could still see them through my lids. Breathing was a task. The thought of a heart attack crossed my mind. I tried to make myself yawn to get a full breath.

There were sixty-three plants of Skywalker OG growing in my basement, days away from being harvested.

The wind kicked up, making an airy cat noise against my screen. People murmured, doors shut, more murmurs. My heart skipped a beat and gurgled in my throat. Then, after what seemed like forever, doors shut again. Cars were started. Headlights hit my wall and stretched before disappearing.

They were gone. Everyone.

I crawled back into bed and laid down on my belly.

Brenda

The sound of Lynne puking echoed down the hall in a way that made me think her head was inside the toilet, inches above the water.

I sat up in bed, stewing in my usual morning state, crushed under a thousand pounds of accumulated disappointment, like there was a beam running from my head to the ceiling and I was responsible for physically supporting the house.

My thigh alerted me to the fact that it was bruised as I bent to grab some Tylenol out of my purse which rattled like a maraca from all the pills. I popped it into my mouth and scanned the room for something to drink. My phone buzzed and lit up. Tons of texts and missed calls. I stretched and grabbed it off the charger. The Tylenol started to dissolve giving off a chalky, chemical taste. I gathered my spit and swallowed it. My empty stomach panged.

Hungry was good. Hungry was normal. Normal was the goal.

The light inside the fridge was dim, but still irritating. Maybe it wasn't so much the light as what was inside: sliced bread mashed in the bag, a jar of strawberry jelly dotted with crumbs and chunks of butter, a two-liter of diet coke pinched and hunched over, little packets of fast food condiments littered randomly around the fridge, and a mysterious brown stain that looked like Russia on a map. An empty ketchup bottle hung out of the shelf on the door like it was debating whether to jump or not.

I spiked it in the trash, purposely rattling empties to irritate Lynne as she continued vomiting above me.

Luckily, there was some peanut butter in the cabinet. I scraped the last of it out and spread it onto my toast. The heat made the peanut butter all wet and runny, oozing out of the sides. I licked it off my finger, feeling horny for some reason. It had been forever since I had sex and it was starting to bother me...weird how that worked. I wouldn't think about it for months, and then out of nowhere, it'd be the only thing on my mind. I think it had something to do with my birth control, which I only really took because of my fucked up periods, gushing and scary from the very first one. My mom's and Lynne's were light. Figures.

I sat at the table eating my shitty PB&J (strawberry jelly instead of grape) sipping flat diet coke as I listened to my sister continue to deposit her soul into the toilet above me. My twenty-fifth birthday was in a month and I wanted to do something fun, get away for a while. Plans scrolled through my head as I chewed, imagining myself celebrating in different places: clubbing in Atlantic City, tanning in Miami, gambling in Vegas, skiing in Vermont.

I rolled a ball of chewed up sandwich around my mouth as I thought about the fact that my party plans required friends; and I had exactly *zero*. When did it happen? When did I lose my friends? The closest thing to friends I had were the people I bought pills *from*, the people I sold pills *to*, and my sister, who didn't really count. There were times, usually at night, where I'd get so lonely that my head would get heavy. My body would vibrate with this feeling, like everything was going to be wrong forever. Laying there thinking about the billions of people in the world and how there wasn't a *single* person for me. My life as a bad banana, seen and skipped at the store. I'd get this feeling, a low-voltage charge, an electric pulsating swirl, like there was a garbage disposal where my heart was supposed to be.

All that bullshit people told me when I was a kid, all that "you-can-be-whatever-you-want-to-be" stuff, died in me long ago. Everything felt so flexible when I was young, so open. And then I got older and it was like there was cement around my feet, impossible to move or change until finally I was stuck. All I could do was be *in* it, be in my life, prisoner of a pre-existing situation. Shipwrecked.

My dad left when I was six. I was playing with Barbie on the carpet. We had a dog then, Barney. A hopelessly untrainable mutt. He was lying with his face between his paws watching me play. Barbie was a nurse taking care of a stuffed elephant who had chicken pox. I was laying on my belly, freshly over my own chicken pox, the little dots drying and falling off me, and something in the carpet made me sneeze. I closed my eyes to get ready. My parents yelled in the kitchen as my face exploded in a mist of spit. The ground shook as their fight carried into the living room, but I couldn't hear them. I was stuck briefly in the pinged silence of my sneeze as another loaded up. My eyes bulged open under the full weight of my mom as her heel dug into my back as she tumbled toward the coffee table and made a face I'll never forget, like she was sorry.

Shards of glass crunched underneath her as she kicked and wriggled, her body moving like a stomped bug, trying to make sense of what happened. I got up to help but was brushed to the side by one of my dad's rough hands. I exaggerated my fall and landed on the dog. Barney growled and stood up as my dad opened the door. The sun came in and hurt my eyes. I remember wanting to hide, to move out of the light. Then he left, Barney did too. I can vividly remember the way he ran out after my dad. It was like he was sneaking. Never saw him again, Barney I mean. I saw my dad. Once or twice, but not on purpose.

I stood at the sink, struggling to wash peanut butter off my plate as it protested, clinging to the plastic in slick oily swirls. There was a small spot of wallpaper coming loose where the ceiling met the wall. I tried to look away, but it was hard. The kitchen was covered in the oldest, ugliest wallpaper. The background color was this creamy white that'd decayed into a yellowish-brown. Across it were interlinked diamond-shaped boxes, a blue and green plaid design. Inside the plaid boxes were different illustrations: drawings of geese, blocks of cheese, pieces of wheat, tractors—shit like that. Apparently whoever designed it had a serious hard-on for farming. Between the wallpaper and the puke-colored carpet, I felt like I'd somehow gotten stuck in the 70s.

Breakfast was over. Time to organize pills, sort the orders for the day. I counted by twos, sliding different pills across the coffee table into a system of piles. The table was old and heavy. The top all nicked up from Lynne chopping lines on it. Some spots still held the original glossy finish, but the rest of it was faded and dull. My mom's brother, my uncle Stevie, gave it to us after my dad left.

I finished counting the Xanax and set them to the side. They were all the same football shape but had different colors. Blue for 1mg, peach for .5mg, and white for .25mg. I took two bottles of ten-milligram Percocet out of my purse and set them on the table. The yellow ones. Everyone called them bananas. There were supposed to be forty-six left and I wanted to check and make sure.

Lynne called me from the top of the steps. "Hey, Bren."

I scooped the pill bottles off the table with my arm, letting them fall into my purse. The Xanax got stuffed into a bag and mixed between the different strengths.

Lynne trudged down the steps, lifting her arms as each foot hit the ground. She moved her head like a snake as she came toward me, trying to see what I was doing from different angles, see what I was hiding.

"Whaddya got there?"

I zipped my purse and picked it up as I sat up on the couch from the floor. "Nothing, just some addies."

"Let me get one."

"Nope."

"Whatever. I hate those things anyway."

I grabbed the remote and turned on the TV. Extreme Realtors was on. A young couple in matching sweaters buying a house in Arizona. Two gay men.

"Can you help me find my earring?"

"No."

"C'mon, Bren, it's the one mommy gave me! Fuckin' bitch knocked it off my ear last night."

One of the guys was short and pudgy and the other was tall and lean. Upon looking closer I noticed their sweaters didn't exactly match like I thought. I thought they were the same exact sweater, a mutual purchase. But no. They were both the same blue, but the pudgy guy's sweater had an argyle pattern. Un unflattering pattern for the fat. The tall skinny one seemed to be aging naturally while the short pudgy guy looked artificially young. The camera panned to a wide view of the street and all the houses looked the same; white stucco with those clay Mexican roofs. The gay guys' realtor was a blonde lady who looked like an alien. Every time she walked them into a room she'd say, "Ta-da!"

"BREN-DA."

Lynne held my coat. She was wearing a leather jacket that looked like it belonged to a large man; I didn't bother asking. I didn't really ask her about anything anymore. Lynne grabbed the remote and shut off the TV. The show collapsed into a single line of light and disappeared.

"Fine, but you gotta do me a favor."

"What's that?"

"Go upstairs and see how much toilet paper we have left."

"Are you serious?" she asked, glancing at my purse.

"Yeah, I am."

Lynne sighed and walked up the stairs, stomping up each step for maximal bratty effect. I shoved my purse under the couch and threw on my coat. I heard a cabinet slam upstairs and then Lynne's heavy footsteps squeaking the floor above me. Her feet appeared first and then slowly the rest of her body as she came down the steps, suspiciously wiping her nose.

"Good you told me to check because we're fresh out."

"Really?" I asked.

"Uh, no," she said, unironically giving me a cold look as she slugged down the steps, "you just bought some yesterday, remember?"

I put my jacket on and opened the door, pulling my face away from the light. Flecks of snow blew in and sparkled, settling on the carpet before turning to water. My sidewalk was shoveled clean.

"Who shoveled our walk?"

Lynne pinched me and smiled. "Probably your little boyfriend."

"Who?"

"John, dummy."

"Ew," I said, meaning it.

Lynne pushed me out of the way and walked outside. I followed her, squinting in the glare which, by the way, wasn't doing Lynne's non-made up face any favors. The drugs were taking their toll. All the bags and wrinkles, the red blotches; She looked twenty-eight going on forty.

"Shit, I'd suck his dick," she said, dusting her sneakers off on our white fence. "Dude's got money."

"Yeah? And would you be willing to play stepmom for his piece-of-shit kid?"

Lynne blew in her hands and rubbed them. "Who, Figgy? Sure. I'll suck his dick too."

"Jesus, Lynne, he's *fourteen*!"

"Yeah, well, speaking of which, here comes the "Statutory King" himself."

Blocking the glare, I saw Eddie Hayden knocking some snow off the rusty 'For Sale' sign in front of his house. He waved and wobbled toward us down the icy street. He was a retired cop in his seventies who'd been kicked off the force for having sex with an underage girl. My mom hated him. She said he was disgusting and told us to stay away from him when we were little. He didn't seem that bad though, aside from the little girl stuff. And actually, he was *really* nice to us, especially after our mom died. He bought our groceries and everything. It was kinda weird.

"Hey, ladies," he said, carefully choosing his steps on the snow.

I waved and smiled. Lynne spit on the ground.

Joel

I sat on the edge of my bed, iguana-eyed in the morning light. Saliva rose from my sub-mouth, the bump of flesh under the tongue that reminded me of Sally Burton's vagina. She had one of those harsh, unwelcoming ones, angular and convex. Her genitals were tough, seemingly from another time or era. An heirloom of feminine ruggedness dating back to when women dug into the dirt for worms and bugs and squatted to give birth in fields. Back when they crapped babies and got on with it.

I swallowed. My mouth tasted awful.

My phone buzzed on my dresser, moving in bursts toward the edge. I thought about not answering it, possibly never answering it again.

It was Sagar, the frat kid I planned on selling all my stuff to. He was a dentistry student at U Penn. Indian kid. Pretty nice dude, kinda flamboyant, but wasn't a dick. I'd have to front him everything (annoying since I knew he was rich) but whatever. Giving him ten pounds at twenty-nine hundred per? I wasn't really in a position to complain.

I answered the phone:

"Yo."

"Hey, Joel—"

"Dude, chill with the names."

"Oh, right."

I peeked out my window. The sky was a soft, pale blue. The clouds were thin and wispy. The world outside: a ruined civilization of snow. My old neighbor, Eddie Hayden, was outside talking to Lynne and Brenda, who I was surprised to see conscious and mobile. He wore a light windbreaker and black ushanka-hat with the flaps up. A Nerf football blew along his shoveled path, moving in eccentric, ill-fated circles. The front end was missing, possibly bitten off. It was one of those footballs with a built-in whistle that howled if perfectly spiraled.

John Cork, the ex-military guy who lived across the street, rumbled down the sidewalk behind a snow blower clearing the way for all the neighbors. It was mostly older people on the block.

"So, when do you think—"

"Two weeks max."

I rubbed a finger along the blinds. They were incredibly dusty. Every inch covered, except where I rubbed, the spot now clean-looking and new; a glimpse into what my life could be. A world beyond the dust and wasted time. I rubbed my big toe along the baseboard. They weren't as dusty as the blinds.

"Shit," said Sagar.

"What?"

"I'll be in India."

"Fuck. How long are you gonna be there for?"

"I don't know, it depends. A month, maybe two."

"Fuck, dude."

"Can't you just set it aside?"

"I don't know, man. Let me call you back."

I threw my phone onto the bed and continued to rub the dust. It was on the walls, the dressers, the floor.

***

I descended my basement steps in a stiff, sideways shuffle, one creaky foot at a time. I paused, toeing the cold cement floor, testing it like a hesitant swimmer. My sock scraped across the cement as I stepped down, reminding me of childhood. I used to get in trouble for ruining my socks. They were no match for our basement floor and I knew it. I'd run back and forth between the walls, barely lifting my feet. Then later at school, I'd stick my toe out of one of the holes when I got changed for gym class, thrilled at the thought of people thinking I was poor.

I squinted from the bright purplish light of my metal halides as I walked along the little rows of plants. Bushy green stalks with purplish hues brushed my knees as I passed, poking out of the scrog netting.

The plants were connected by a tubing system rigged to deliver CO_2. They sat in five-gallon buckets that rested on thick pieces of wood. The wood buffered the roots from feeling the cold floor. Roots hate the cold. They stop themselves from growing if they detect it, thus shrinking overall plant size, thus shrinking output and yield, thus reducing my little nut of money to start over, move somewhere else.

I couldn't wait to tell my dad, show him the cash and split.

The lights slowly intensified as the plants swayed under the gentle force of multiple box fans. I snipped a bud off one of the weaker plants. Figured it would be fine for Sip. Sip didn't know shit about weed, he just liked to sell it. I stopped dealing with him as soon as I found Sagar. Sip was more of a coke, crack, and pill guy, which I found unsettling. He wasn't a junkie, he was just nuts. He used to smoke crack right in front of me—only on Fridays, which was perverse since he'd say TGIF before lighting it up—and I'd sit there, holding my breath in fear of the secondhand crack smoke, having massive panic attacks on the way home thinking I somehow ingested it. Almost like the time I unknowingly held a sheet of acid in my hand for thirty seconds before my cousin knocked it out. I thought I was going to start tripping and lose my mind like one of those urban legends; every hometown's version of the kid who thinks he's a glass of orange juice and people are out to drink him.

The bud I snipped was a beauty, a true show pony. It was moist and fragrant, glimmering in all of its raw and uncured glory as I spun it between my finger and my thumb, a little green disco ball in the light. I wanted to deal with Sagar, but waiting another month on top of the month (or possibly two) it would take him to sell the shit was out of the question. Sip would be COD. I could leave right after.

Walking toward the steps, I noticed a rusty water stain on the basement's grey cement walls. It triggered something, one of those deep body memories. Strange how a simple slab of concrete could stab my subconscious so effectively. To think of our past being stored in the world around us, lurking in inanimate objects.

My dad comes down the basement and sees me playing with my action figures. I'm making green plastic army guys fight along the one-inch drainage channel that scores the perimeter of my basement. It's supposed to prevent flooding but never works. The inch-deep trench is just an expensive home for big hairy spiders. Whoever dies in plastic battle has to sit in the channel. The dead left to be devoured by giant, ditch dwelling spiders. Spiders with hair. I explain it to my dad and he says, "Aren't you a little old for action figures?"

That's when I started running in my socks.

***

My Ford Ranger rocked to a stop behind Sip's house. He had one of those places right off Roosevelt Blvd., off 5th St. towards the Northeast. The same squat rowhomes as my street, only somehow shittier, with wider streets and double, maybe triple the number of people outside at any given time. If there was one place I hated more than Roxborough, this was it. A mob of little kids crossed the street, smacking each other, laughing as they dodged retaliation. They moved as a group toward a single destination, pulsing in chaotic activity as they went. Old people stared at me from their porches, turning heads as I drove by. I was the only white person in a twenty-block radius so I kind of stuck out.

Sip's neighborhood was a cluster of Southeast-Asian immigrants who'd mixed into the inner city among poor black people and Puerto Ricans. They mostly came during the 70s and stuck around. It wasn't the *worst* part of Philly, but I still had to be careful. The murder rate (as defined by the city) was low-medium, orange according to the crime map's official color coding.

Sip was in his back alley smoking a cigarette when I pulled up. I couldn't miss him. No one could. A forty-year-old Asian guy in a baby blue velour suit cannot be missed. He guided me into his back-alley driveway with infuriating care, waving his arms like an air traffic controller; as if he was worried I'd run over his frozen hose or rusty barbecue grill. He motioned me forward, squatting to keep a close eye on what my tires were touching. My head bumped and rocked as I drove up the four-inch lip of concrete that led me into his driveway.

Sip ditched his cigarette and closed the crooked chain-link fence around my truck. The fence scraped the ground as he pulled it. There were arced lines in the concrete from these scrapings. Sip kicked his frozen hose out of the way and smiled.

"Wassup, doo?"

"Hey long time, man."

Sip looked down each end of the block and threw his head towards the door. He bent down and picked a gun off the ground. A nine-millimeter pistol he'd stashed behind a rock. It was standard procedure for him to have a gun on him whenever leading me in or out of his house.

We went up a set of creaky, Jenga-like steps and stopped as he struggled with his back door. There was a malfunctionary riddle to the lock. He leaned in with his shoulder and pulled back as he twisted. I imagined every house around here held a similar kind of puzzle, a mystery buried in the unique entropy of each individual structure.

The door opened and led into the kitchen. There was a pot boiling on the stove with an unidentifiable smell. Maybe an entire animal— skin, hair, and nails. The floors were spotless, but the counter space bordered on the edge of chaos: jars filled with bright-colored sauces and pastes, hand tools, soggy vegetables in plastic bags, loose change, screws, an old outlet plate. There was a bar of soap stuck to the kitchen sink. The soap was dirty.

We made a left out of the kitchen and entered the living room.

"Chill one minute, doo."

He gestured me towards a musty brown armchair in an *unbelievably* clean space where a very old Asian woman sat perfectly upright in a dining room chair watching TV, an old black-and-white western. The TV was old, a cube-shaped relic of the past sitting on an even older entertainment center. The walls were adorned with pictures of children, school photos mainly. The rug was white with considerable nap. The legs of the chair pressed down into the rug. The old woman turned to us, detaching her vision from the TV. Her hair was cut in a square bob, bangs high and straight. She said something to Sip in Cambodian. Sip sighed and stormed off. The woman readjusted her posture and went back to the movie. Next to her was a metal ashtray, one of those ones that stemmed off the ground. A piece of furniture just for smoking. The woman produced a cigarette and lit it. She puffed it once and set it down into the ashtray. She pointed up at the shelf above the TV and muttered something, a command. I sat up straight, on high alert, trying to figure out what she was saying. She muttered again, stretching her arm out even further, quickly gaining annoyance. I stood up, panicked, looking around the room. The woman turned to me and grunted. I put my arms out to either side, signaling confusion. She rolled her eyes and got up. I followed her to the entertainment center against the wall, a maze of shelves that contained the heavy old TV, last of the non-flat screens. A cowboy took an arrow to the chest and fell off his horse. The woman reached upward, specifically wiggling her fingers under a jar. I reached up and grabbed it, happy that my height was useful to this woman. I stood humbly, presenting the jar with a strange reverence. *Was I being extra humble and reverent because she was Asian?* She snatched the jar and sat down, grunting as she dug. It was filled with candies. I took my seat but remained at attention, figuring I'd have to put it back for her. I don't know why, but It was very important that I pleased her. She grunted again and raised her arm, a tiny candy rustling in her bony fingers. I stood up, nervous and unsure. She waved her arm and turned around, holding the candy out to me. I thanked her and sat, inspecting it. The wrapper bore the mystical markings of Asian lettering. A language of cool tattoos, I thought as I opened the candy and put it on my tongue. It tasted like lamb and apples.

Sip's eyes bulged as he re-entered the room. He charged the old woman and raided the jar of lamb caramels, rapaciously plundering to the bottom. Candies detached and fell from his grip with every slap from the old woman as he extricated his hand; A rugged gunman reared his horse into the air behind them, blasting his guns into the black-and-white horizon.

I got up and followed Sip.

***

Sip's room was in the basement. It was Scarface-chic and ridiculous. White tiles ran throughout from bed to bathroom. His bathroom, which you could see into through the French doors, had a Jacuzzi instead of a shower and a cheap, almost plastic looking chandelier hanging over the tub, slightly askew to the left. Outside the bathroom was a Bowflex 900 with clothes hanging off like an old willow tree. A black four-post bed sat to the other side against the wall. Its silk sheets were blood red and its pillowcases a mismatched ensemble of various animal prints. Pictures of X-rated porn, rappers, and various political guerrillas lined his walls. There was a projector mounted in the ceiling, beaming a blown-up feed of a Catholic mass onto the huge screen.

"What's good, doo?" he asked, giving me a handshake that morphed into a hug.

"Loving the set-up, man. I, uh—are you watching the Church Channel?"

"Hell yea, doo, I get baptized last week. Are you Christians?"

"I don't know man. Kinda trapped between the stories, I guess."

Sip eyed me while rolling a blunt, "Stories?"

"Yeah. Like little mermaid king in the sky making people in a garden versus the other one, the one where we're all just like space dust, sentient remains of a universe that somehow exploded itself into existence out of nothing."

Sip wet the tip of his finger and fixed a stray edge, "That's crazy doo," he said, obviously not paying attention.

I took my jar out to show him what I'd been growing. My arm glowed with the images of mass. An older woman got communion directly to the mouth on my forearm as a plug-in air freshener sprayed cinnamon-scented mist. The smell made me nauseous.

"This is only a sample. It still needs time."

Sip opened the jar and brutally flattened the bud. "Smells good, but too fuckin' wet. Wet shit gets moldy, doo."

I took it back and put it in my pocket. "Yeah, man. It's not ready yet. It's still growing."

Sip's eyes popped open, "Oh shit, doo! Das your buds? I didn't know you grow! C'mere!"

We walked past the Bowflex 900 and into his bathroom. Sitting in the Jacuzzi were three very weak, very sickly weed plants growing in tiny Styrofoam containers in the tub. UV desk lamps sat on the edges, bent to hit the plants at different angles. One of the lamps was duct-taped to the tile wall.

"Da fuck is wrong wif these? So shitty."

I bent down, pretending to inspect them as if the answer wasn't totally obvious. I didn't want to make him feel dumb. "Well, dude, these, uh, these lights aren't enough. You need—"

"Fuck that, man! Internet said UV light is good!"

"Yeah, well you need advanced spectrum LEDs. See, UV can get, like, a seedling started, but to actually grow weed, you need the full color spectrum of the sun. Really metal halide or—"

"Doo, enuff. I get headache about this shit. I just see how it goes."

I nodded.

"So, how much you gonna have?" he asked me, walking us back into the bedroom.

 Hoping for around ten or fifteen pounds once it's done. I still gotta dry it out and cure it, so it won't be ready for a few weeks."

"How much you want?"

"I don't know, I was thinking like twenty-five hundred a pound."

"I take all for twenty-three."

"Fuck, man."

"Hey, my doo, it's just bidjaniss."

"Twenty-four, but you gotta have the cash up front."

"Always my doo."

***

We stood in Sip's backyard and chatted while he smoked another cigarette. His gun was clenched, pointing to the ground. A different mob of little kids came down the alley on their bicycles. Two of them did wheelies and gave us the finger. One of the kids in the group didn't have a bike. He had to run to keep up. Sip picked a bottlecap off the ground and threw it at them, spinning it the way people throw seashells into the ocean.

"Oh, shit, almost forget—" Sip pulled his phone out and leaned against my truck. "Download this app."

"What is it?"

"Sig-nerz."

"Sig-nerz?"

"Yeah, doo, for text. Shit's double encryptions."

"Wow...wait what does encryption actually do?"

"I don't know, doo. Blocks cops and shit from seeing message. Also, lets you set auto delete. After five minute, message gone."

"Cool," I said, getting in my truck. "I'll definitely have to download that."

Sip nodded as he ditched his cigarette and opened the gate, pushing it with his gun. My phone vibrated; It was my mom. I silenced the call and pulled out.

Eddie

I watched the girls through my breath as they approached. They were still young, still beautiful—both staggering in their own right. Brenda was athletic, fiery, and fit, attractive by modern standards. Lynne, however, seemed designed for another time. She was short, plump, and decadent, with a frame built more for copulating and feasting, something like a Roman senator's prized concubine. I tipped my hat and nodded.

"Come have a look at this, ladies."

Brenda tugged her sister in my direction, the middle of the cul-de-sac. I led them toward my house, waving them on as I went.

Roxborough is an interesting part of Philadelphia. It's laid out like a suburb, but still technically in the city. Overlook Road was the street we all lived on. The side that Brenda and John lived on butted up against the woods, the cul-de-sac did too. Across the street where I lived didn't. There were just other houses behind those ones and more houses behind them until they hit the river. After the river was a highway, then eventually more houses. The "woods" near our street weren't very dense or big, just an undeveloped parcel of land some guy was waiting to sell once the market got better—which I guess is what all woods are really.

I parted some of the shrubbery, nothing fancy, just some standard holly crop-cut twice a year into living cubes. The flatter the better when it comes to bushes. Nothing wrong with a little order. There, between the tamed vegetation, a medium-sized pit bull shivered in the snow, snake-curled with its head resting near his tail. Its brindle coat was flecked with orange and brown. The mutt's eyes were sad and pathetic, cringing with animal fear.

Brenda cooed and bent down as her sister looked around, seemingly disinterested by everything in the world at once.

"Tried to get him inside, but he won't come in. See that vent right there? That's the dryer vent. Left that thing on for some warmth. One hell of a tough sucker though, I'll tell you."

"Let's bring him inside!"

Lynne stretched her face in disagreement.

"That thing? No way, Bren."

Lynne continued to look around. All the time with her, the looking around, the chronic shiftiness and her perpetual casing. It was the drugs, if I had to guess.

"Here, give him a treat," I said digging in my pocket.

Brenda snatched the treat from my hand and held it in her palm. "Hey, little guy. C'mere. Hey," she cooed.

John Cork rounded the corner with his snow blower and shut it off. He dragged it backward and put it in his front yard. His metal gate clanked against the post, pinging in the cold hollow air.

"Whatcha guys find, a snake or somethin'?" he asked from across the street.

Lynne smacked her sister, "Ohh, Brennie, here comes your man."

Brenda shook her head. She was engrossed in the dog, slowly gaining its confidence as it sniffed the treat.

John Cork jogged until he was ten feet from us and stopped. He was wearing Carhartt overalls and a matching tan jacket. His hands were bare, insulated by layers of dead skin cells. They were permanently chapped and lifeless, systemically cracked and calloused. He stood a moment and admired the sidewalks he cleared, the network of walkable land he'd opened with his machine.

"You forgot one," I said pointing to Joel's house.

John clasped his hands and rubbed them. "You know he didn't go to work today, right? Took a *snow day.*"

He looked good standing in the street. He seemed well adapted, almost painted into his environment. His being, if you will, matched the houses perfectly; The squat brick structures that sat shoulder to shoulder, grimly inspecting each other from across the street. There was an aggression in their plainness, a brutal mediocrity that suited John well.

He leaned into our little gathering and whispered, "I heard, and keep this between us, but a buddy of mine works at PECO and said he was out inspectin' pussy-boy's meter. Apparently, he's been drawin' some major amps, enough to make PECO think it was broken or something. Turns out—"

The dog snarled and snapped as Brenda got closer.

"Careful!" I told her.

Brenda backed up. The dog stood and bared its teeth.

John pushed me out of the way and got between the dog and Brenda. The dog lunged forward and barked. John didn't move.

"Go get your gun, Eddie."

"No!" Brenda screamed.

"Alright, John, let's take it easy here. The animal people are on their way."

The dog hopped forward on his front paws and growled. Hair rose along his back. His teeth glistened with saliva. John threw a hand to the left and rushed to the right, tackling him by its neck. The dog reached back to snap at John and missed. John, pausing to note the clap of the dog's teeth, punched it in the ribs and held him down, somehow choking the dog despite his thick, musclebound neck. Brenda grabbed the collar of John's jacket and tried to pull him off. I turned to tell Lynne to call for help but she was gone.

Joel

I pulled up to a red light on Henry Ave. The streets were sufficiently plowed. Salty, shiny, and black, a direct contrast to the walls of snow on either side. The sun hung high in a perfect blue dome, buttoned at the very top of the three-dimensional horizon.

My phone buzzed again. A text message from my mom.

HEY JOEL ITS ME YOUR MOM DON'T FORGET YOUR FATHERS RETIREMENT PARTY IS TONIGHT YOU BETTER COME!!!!!!!!! CALL ME BACK LOVE YOU SWEETIE. –MOM

I had planned on getting incredibly stoned and watching nature documentaries for the guts of the day; and now I'd have to scale back since I'd be around old people later that night. It was my own personal policy not to be high around the aged. I didn't like it. For reasons both aesthetic and philosophical. Like the time I was halfway through eating a buffalo wing and realized I was chewing an animal's severed limb. It was the same with old people. Seeing them inhabit the ground they were about to be under, always sitting as if inside of a waiting room. Totally detached and clueless. Pre-embalmed in nose-pinch perfumes from distant epochs. Their physical closeness to the life beyond was wildly unsettling for me, doubly if I was stoned. I envisioned my mom's Aunt Sally eating a buffalo wing and shuddered.

There was also the issue of interrogation by relatives, the "so-what-have-you-been-up-to's" and other morbid forms of gossip foraging. I needed to be sharp to withstand the inquisitive assault, erect a wall of evasive responses, to safeguard the gooey core of my apparent loserdom and illegal enterprise.

I hit a left on Ridge, drowning in the realization that Mr. Levy would be there, the head honcho at ABM, the company I valiantly no-showed. Mr. Levy and my dad were relatively chummy. Loosely connected through charity golf tournaments. Somewhere on the back nine of a memorial-day weekend game he and my father decided I'd be a good fit for ABM and that was all it took. Condemned to my cross of corporate drudgery without even being *asked*. How could two sunburnt geezers drunk on low-carb beer ask anyone anything? Who is more certain than them?

For approximately eighteen months, I sat in a big square room with white walls. The room smelled exactly like artificial vanilla bean via a vast network of strategically placed plug-in air fresheners. Cubicles stretched across a grey industrial carpet in long, disorienting rows, populated by a world of people seemingly dressed for funerals as they baked under rectangular fluorescent lighting in a way that eerily reminded me of my basement. Bordering the cubicles were slightly-less-sad, glass-walled offices, display case exhibits of defeated middle managers hunched over their computers. The people around me all looked one of two ways: sickly and grey or violently healthy, robust to the point of concern, greasily sheened and oddly exuberant. And there was always someone moving; haunting the lanes of cubicles, all with the same look: someone who walked into a room but forgot what for.

I resolved to go to the party no matter who was there. To start this new chapter of my life on my own two feet, facing anyone who opposed me, retirement party or not. I was fueled, I believed, by my new practice of non-ejaculation, which I was roughly six days into—and having (what I also believed to be) an increase in certain low-key cardio episodes, arrhythmias basically, as a result of which. Possibly from all the excess animus kundalini. But that was just a theory.

***

I pulled up on Overlook and parked. There was a small gathering at the end of the cul-de-sac. Brenda and Eddie were yelling at my neighbor John as he wrestled a whimpering dog. All of the sidewalks were plowed but mine.

Eddie waved me down like he was shipwrecked. "Call animal control!"

I got out of my truck and ran over, pulling out my phone. "Is that like 911?"

The dog flailed against John, who was holding it in a chokehold.

"I don't have a choice, Eddie! I gotta use force."

Brenda grabbed John's shoulder and pulled. "Get off him, you fucking psycho!"

I took my jacket off and wrapped it around my arm, "Quick. Give me yours too."

Eddie hesitated, "I–I don't want to catch a chill out here."

Brenda took her coat off and threw it to me. She was wearing a blue thermal shirt with no bra that I remember. An exhaust of steam trailed out from her little rose petal lips as we officially made eye contact for the first time. Her cheeks were flushed from the cold; living dots of red that faded into her pale skin.

Eddie smacked my shoulder, "Go!"

I held my cushioned arm out and budged John, "Look out, man."

John turned around at me, annoyed. Him and the dog had the same bulging eyes, wild and dangerous. "*You* look out, faggot."

"C'mon, John," Eddie said, slightly embarrassed.

"I can't let this mongrel go!" John insisted, "He'll retaliate."

"I'm gonna stick my arm out in front of his face. When I do it, let go."

"What are you nuts?" asked John, still squirming with the dog.

Dogs go for the first thing they see, it's how they work."

"Where the hell did ja get that from?" asked John as he readjusted his grip. The dog squealed and cried.

"Cesar Milan, I saw him do it last night."

John laughed at the sky, "Oh, right, the Chihuahua wrangler, nice. Eddie, get the girl out of here. I'm gonna contain the situation."

Brenda hit his shoulders. "I swear to God John, I'll burn your fucking house down if you hurt that dog!"

"Hey, that Cesar Milan knows a lot about dogs. He's got his own brand of treats and everything. I mean, they don't just give that to anyone," Eddie chimed in.

John rolled his eyes. "Jesus, fine, I'll let go. But so help me God, if it turns on any of us, I'm killin' it...clear?"

No one agreed.

I stuck my arm in front of its face. "Alright, when I say when."

John sat up. "Wait, shouldn't I say when? I'm the one holdin' the fucking thing."

The dog lurched back and bit his finger. "Ow!"

Eddie took off, galloping toward his house.

I stuck my arm out and the dog chomped down on the jackets. Its jaws squeezed with tremendous force as it stood squat and muscular, whipping its head to either side. John went to kick the dog and hit me in the back by mistake.

Brenda pushed him. "Fuck, John!"

He spun past Brenda and assaulted the dog with an overhand fist, dropping to his knees as he delivered it. My arm was starting to hurt. I secretly cheered John on as he went up and rained down on the dog's back again. The dog froze. Its jaws loosened as he darted his eyes to the side, looking at John. Stepping back for a kick, John lined his boot up at the dog's face and swung his leg. The dog let go of my arm and lunged for John's other leg as Brenda tried to hold him back. I dove forward to stop the dog. The world spun and scrambled as we fell, merging into a confused tangle of limbs.

I ended up half on top of Brenda and half on top of John. The neck of her thermal was stretched, showing a scratch on her chest, the top of her left breast, the part that could almost be a muscle. She thrashed, pushing me off. I could smell her breath: peanut butter and decaying carbohydrates. I pushed myself up, nonsensically apologizing as I offered to help her to her feet. She declined and rushed back toward the dog. John had triumphed over it, squeezing its neck from behind in the same sleeper hold as before. Eddie stood in front of it with a taser. He aimed and pulled the trigger. A little line shot out and stuck in the dog.

Brenda stomped the ground and stretched the sleeves of her shirt as she closed her eyes. Eddie pulled the trigger again. There was no sound. No buzz either.

"Where'd you get that piece of shit from?" asked John, dusting the snow off his pants as he got up. He was still looking at the dog, watching as it panted on its side in the snow, tongue hanging in exhaustion.

Fig

The tile floor was cold on my socks. It was new, barely a few weeks old. My dad put it in himself. He said it was supposed to be warm all the time because there were little pipes of hot water underneath. He was a contractor. His company was Cork & Son, which pissed me off since I thought it meant I had to work for him when I got older. He took me to jobs with him on the weekends and I hated it. All the dust and shit. It made my snot black. It sucked. The only fun part was when we got to throw stuff out the window and watch it break in dumpsters, or that one time when I found porn in this old guy's bathroom. He had it hidden behind a plaster wall. I showed it to these two Mexican guys who were working for the plumber. The one Mexican asked to see it and never gave it back. His friend laughed as they walked away.

Thank god for wrestling. It was the only thing keeping me from having to work with him on Saturdays. Even if he didn't have a job going, he'd be working on something else, usually around our house. He'd been going nuts renovating everything: new tile, oak floors, walls painted with this shit from Holland he never shut up about.

My dad got all of his ideas from those gay ass girl-shows he watched on HGTV. They were the worst. Some dumb lady smiling at a poor family, asking them if they liked the new lights and counter tops, like *that* was what they needed, like they still weren't gonna be poor and shitty after she left.

I switched the cigarette to my other hand and clenched it. My other fist was too sweaty. I asked my dad why my hands sweat whenever I held something and he said it was because I was afraid of losing it. There was a picture of us on the fridge. Me and my dad. My mom had been cut out of it. You could still see a tiny slice of her shoulder if you looked close. She was wearing a white sweater.

The door jerked open. My dad knocked the snow off his boots and came in. The smell of cigarettes instantly filled the house. I moved away from the fridge and headed out the door.

"Hey, dad," I said, trying to squeeze by him.

"Not so fast," he grunted.

He unlaced his boots and kicked them off. They made a hollow knocking sound against the drywall and fell dead, instantly forming a pool of melted snow on the tile. He went to the fridge and cracked a beer can. A silver bullet, his favorite. My dad leaned against the countertop and stared at the cabinets while he wrapped his finger in electric tape.

"What happened to your finger?"

He bit the tape off the roll and spit in the sink. "God damn dog out there bit me."

I rushed to the window, almost forgetting about the cig. "There's a dog outside? Where?"

"Don't worry about it."

I parted the curtains, flexing my head to see down the street. Just cars covered in snow. "Where's the dog, dad?"

My dad slammed his can on the counter. "Damnit! You hear what I said?"

I stopped and turned around, almost at the door. The cig was sweatier than ever.

"Yeah."

He pointed his can of Coors Light at me. "*Yeah?*"

I scratched my head with my non-cig hand. "Yes."

My dad nodded in approval and continued on. "You noticed these cabinets stickin' or actin' up at all?"

I shook my head even though I knew exactly what he was talking about. The middle cabinet, the one with the bowls and plates, would clink when I swung it open. I think the hinge was messed up or something.

"No?" he asked, walking over to the exact cabinet I was thinking about. "I feel like this one here needs to go." He jerked it open and shut.

"Why don't you spray the hinge with some WD-40 or something?"

He shook his head and took another sip of his beer, swallowing as he replied. "Because that's how niggers fix stuff. Are we niggers?"

I shook my head.

"I'm gonna need your help tomorrow. Thinkin' about ripping these cabs out and puttin' in some new ones. Whaddya say, huh?"

He came over and punched me in the arm that was connected to my cig hand. I squeezed, bending the cigarette and making it crooked.

"Yeah, dad. No problem."

He cocked his head and studied me like he was deciding if I needed another punch on the arm. I looked back at him, right in the eyes so he didn't smack me in the head. I got in trouble for not looking him in the eyes. I also got in trouble for looking him *in* the eyes too. It was hard to tell where to look sometimes.

"I'm going to Brian's. I'll be back for dinner."

My dad raised his beer can, like we were doing a cheers, and nodded. I turned around and opened the door.

***

The sun was bright. Not a cloud in the sky. It looked like they all fell and smashed into the ground, every inch of which was covered in snow except for a small patch where my dad left the snow blower in our front yard. The heat must've melted it. The grass around the carburetor was mashed and dead looking, like gelled hair on the day after. I hated gelling my hair, but my dad always made me do it before school dances. He said it would get me pussy. Every Friday night my dad would gel his hair and go to The Thirsty Bulldog. He never brought a girl back, but he did come home in the morning a couple times. Only like three times that I know of.

I crunched and squeaked across the ground, looking for the dog he mentioned as I rounded the side of my house toward the woods. A chunk of snow slid off my neighbor's roof and exploded. I hopped the fence in my backyard and climbed down the retention wall my dad had built. Rocks stacked in big metal cages that held the ground from moving. I didn't understand it, though I figured I'd know how to stop the ground from moving when I got older, became a dad. I looked around for the dog one last time and then hopped down the last section of wall.

The woods looked like a place out of a fairy tale. All the trees were bearded with wet heavy snow, bending like they were sighing. I breathed out and moved my head, trying to spell my name in the air with my breath. No luck.

There were some older kids about fifty feet away, hanging around the fire pit. One guy coughed and rolled around on the ground, hitting his chest as the others laughed. They were smoking out of a soda can. I tucked the cig behind my ear as I took a seat on an abandoned tire, deliberating whether or not to join them.

Maybe they'd be cool and would think I was cool since I had the cig behind my ear and wanted to smoke pot out of their soda can. Or, they'd be dicks and punch me, take my cig, possibly even call me a fag for wearing winter gloves.

I crouched behind the tire and launched a rock in the air towards them, running down the hill toward Brian's before it fell, touching my ear now and again to make sure the cig was still behind it.

I kicked the side of Brian's house to get the snow off my shoe. The house was a rancher with a cement front porch that you had to step up onto. Brian's dad, Mr. Babinski, did it himself so it came out all rough and crooked. The rest of the house was nice though. It was small but clean. Clean in a good way. My house was clean like a hospital, sad clean. They had nice pillows and pictures of coffee mugs and cinnamon candles. The only problem with Brian's house was his mom. She was a fucking bitch.

The door opened.

Mrs. B came outside holding a stretched-out trash bag in her yellow kitchen gloves. The bag dripped, darkening spots on the cement as she moved. She was short and thick and had these huge fucking tits—I mean *huge*. She set the bag down and folded her arms across her chest like she was trying to block them, but it only made them stick out more. She readjusted her arms and eyed me up, almost smiling. The bag leaned against the house in a very sad way. It looked sick and bent over like people I saw on the corner sometimes. Mrs. B had a big nose but in a good way. It gave her face this foreign look. Like European or something. I don't know how Brian could deal with such a hot mom. It must've turned him into a pervert.

"Whatcha got there, Figgy?" she asked, lining up her nose with the crack of her big tits like she was looking down a rifle.

"Nothing, Mrs. B, whaddya mean?" I asked, reaching around my head—and then I felt it. The cig. Fuck.

Brian, the fucking pussy, finally appeared in the doorway. He looked more like his dad than his mom. He had the roundest, most bland face. He wasn't fat or skinny, in-shape or out. He was just normal, *extremely* normal. One of his uncles told him he'd make an excellent private eye since his face was so forgettable and it bothered Brian a lot. His mom told him to ignore it and that he was handsome. He even asked *me* if *I* thought he was handsome. I could have fucked with him so bad for that, but just let it go. He was too messed up from it, messed up from all his plainness. Still, him asking me if I thought he was handsome was gay as shit. I should have punched him or something.

"See ya," Brian said as he slid past his mom.

She put her arm out like a toll booth, stopping him in his tracks. Brian crashed into her arm, and those nugs got to jiggling.

"I-I found it in the woods, Mrs. B, I swear!"

She snatched it out from behind my ear and held it up in the light of the sun, squinting at it. The cigarette was crushed, crooked to the left. She looked sternly back at Brian. "And did you know about this, mister?"

Brian melted.

She pulled out her phone and pointed it at me, "I'm calling your dad."

The sky sharpened. The sun got unbearably bright. My head pulsated and throbbed. Saliva rushed my mouth in warm globs as everything seemed to move further and further away, Brian, his mom, the house, the woods—all of it. The world felt different, new, but familiar. The opposite feeling of waking up and realizing it was just a bad dream. The familiar crush of trouble.

Brian stood next to his mom, hands by his sides as he stared at his sneakers. They were brand new, a mix of loud neons: bright green, construction orange, and a super gay pinkish color around the toe. I kicked a small rock toward him. It bounced and veered into the snow.

Brenda

Eddie hiked his pants and squatted to pull his taser out of the dog. It laid there with its one eye open. The other was against the snow. He had a brown face with a white spot over his eye, sorta like the dog from Little Rascals. Only his coat was brindle, a dead leaf tiger-stripe camo. I scooped his big square head from out of the snow and lifted his body. He was heavier than he looked.

Eddie moved toward me, careful on the snow. "No, no. Leave him be. The animal people—"

"The *animal people* are gonna kill him."

I adjusted my grip under what I guess were the dog's armpits. His stubby little legs clung to my neck. I could feel it, the cling. Its little nails digging into my skin. Needing me. I could have cried.

John's truck roared toward us in reverse. His diesel engine was loud. Thick black smoke assaulted the air. He hopped out of his truck and lowered his gate.

"Hey," he yelled over his engine to Joel. "Throw him in the bed. I'm taking him to the pound."

John's phone rang in his pocket, somehow louder than his truck. He dug his hands into his pocket and silenced it.

Joel, ignoring John, petted the dog. I squeezed the sun out of my eyes, trying to see if Joel was smiling or not; I couldn't tell. His face, with the sun behind it, was like an illuminated potato, glowing and blank. His hands were warm though. I felt them when he touched my wrist by mistake. They were soft but not clammy or gross.

John came barreling towards us through the snow, roaring over his engine. "Sorry, Brenda, but I'm not letting that thing—"

His phone rang again. He stomped the ground and took it out of his pocket.

"Yeah."

He extended his arm out to the sky, cupping his hand like a king who'd just been betrayed. He leaned on his cab, head down on the plastic liner as the rest of his body slumped in defeat. Slouched in resignation, he nodded in acceptance of whatever he was hearing.

Joel nudged me and talked out the side of his mouth, "What's that about?

The smell of Winterfresh gum carried in his breath, the whole visible cloud of it. It reminded me of vodka and high school dances. One of those things where you're driving to the shore and smell the ocean, the salt and fish and bird shit smell that somehow reminds you of your mom's 80's hairdo, the poofy bangs and big square glasses.

I shrugged in reply, letting our shoulders touch. Joel didn't necessarily lean in, but he also didn't move away. We sat like that for a second, letting our jackets rub.

Eddie came to my other side. I smelled his breath before he got there. One of those hard white throat things that smells like a dead person. His jacket touched my shoulder and I moved.

He whispered, "Better get that mutt inside while you can."

John hung up and smacked his truck with two hands. He jogged around to the driver's side, arms outstretched like he was choking the air, and hopped in. His engine roared as he pulled away, that rattling industrial sound of diesel. A blanket of black smoke hung where he'd been.

The dog was getting heavy.

I turned to Joel, "Here. Help me get him inside."

Joel hoisted the dog up on his shoulder. There was something strong about the way he moved. It was also kind of effeminate and uncoordinated, but there was something to it, like he was oblivious and didn't care. Joel patted the dog's drooling head, rocking him like a sleeping toddler. I opened the gate and ran ahead to get the door for them, knocking my sneakers against the concrete steps to get the snow off.

I opened the door.

Lynne was belly down on the living room floor, her arm slithering under the couch. An ample amount of back fat laid in the open, white and unprotected. I ran up and slapped one of her love handles as hard as I possibly could.

"*Owwww!*" She screamed from under the couch.

I tried to double back to shut the door but it was too late. Joel was already inside, kicking off his shoes. He watched as Lynne thrashed around the floor, causing a mini-earthquake that only affected the couch cushions. The dog, who I guess had been startled by Lynne's yell, jumped from Joel's arms and smashed on the floor. He tried to get up and collapsed.

"Fuckin' Christ, Bren! I'm down here looking for the *remote!*"

I turned to Joel, "Hey, can you put him downstairs?"

He nodded, carefully choosing his steps around Lynne's body that was still somehow stuck under the furniture as he re-scooped the dog and disappeared into the kitchen.

Lynne crawled out from under the couch and sat against it on the floor, pulling her shirt down indignantly. The bag of Percocet was in her hand. "Thought you didn't have any of these?"

"Oh, don't you fucking dare!"

Lynne narrowed her eyes into little slits. "I'm *sick*, Bren. God forbid I need a little help from my *sister* to get clean."

"Lynne, no!"

Lynne opened the bag, dumping almost every single pill into her mouth. I bent down and slapped her across the face, freeing the world of yellow pills into the air. She belly-crawled across the carpet, picking pills off the floor and shoving them in her mouth. I grabbed her by the hair and pulled her toward the steps. She got up to her feet, smacking my hand as she chewed.

Joel walked back in the room, "His name is Roger. He's got a tag and everything—", he stopped, taking us in. "Everything okay?"

I shoved Lynne's head toward the steps. "Get the fuck out!"

Lynne picked another pill off the ground and put it in her mouth. "Fuck you, Brenda. You're no better than me, *drug dealer*." She ran up the steps, covering her bright red face as she licked her molars.

Joel bent down and started cleaning up.

"Stop. Please don't."

Joel, ignoring me, put the rest of the pills back in the bag. They were all soggy, pitted with tiny holes from Lynne's saliva.

"Wanna see the dog?" he asked, wiping his hands off on his jeans. "He made a little bed out of your dirty laundry."

The ceiling shook. Lynne came barreling down the steps, eying the pills on the table.

"They're *better* not be any dog here. I'm allergic, Bren."

"What? Since when?"

Lynne opened the door, letting in the sound of squealing brakes and the low rattle of aftermarket speakers, a horrible storm of distorted bass and screeching metal. Some shitty Dodge Neon rocked to a stop by the gate. Speakers rattled the trunk giving it that hummingbird look of constant movement. The driver lowered his tinted window. I knew him. Some piece of shit I went to high school with.

"Is that fucking Donny Falzone? And who's he with? The other guy looks homeless!"

Lynne tried to shut the door and I stopped it. "Oh, please. Don't act like you give a shit now." She jogged to the car and hopped in the back seat.

The guy riding shotgun, the homeless looking kid, hung out the window on his forearms, staring off. He was white with ratty dreadlocks.

Lynne pulled the rear door shut dramatically with two hands and the car zoomed off. The exhaust, sounding like metal going through puberty, whined. The grainy bass of the speakers lingered in the air.

Joel scratched the back of his head and looked around. After what seemed like an eternity of awkward silence he asked, "You, uh, want to come for a jog with me?"

"*What?*"

"Just figured it'd be nice to, well, you know."

"I got a job interview. Plus, I *hate* jogging

"Going legit, huh?"

I tried to punch his arm, but missed, catching the edge of his shoulder with my pinky knuckle.

"Fuck you."

"Where's the job?"

"Quizno's."

"Wait, that's the one that *wasn't* disgraced publicly for an underage sex scandal, right?"

"Yup. They don't fuck kids and they always toast the roll."

Cork's truck roared back down the street, that wet diesely rattle. We watched from the window as he opened the door and ripped Fig out of the seat. Fig, propelled by what looked like a judo throw from his dad, tumbled and caught himself, narrowly avoiding John's boot as it kicked in the direction of his running ass.

Fig

I stumbled across the yard, juking to avoid my dad's slaps and kicks as he chased me toward the front door.

"Get inside!" he gritted through his coffee-stained teeth.

My shirt was wet and smelled like coffee, clinging to my chest in cold, wet blotches. My left arm, the side that was closest to my dad as he drove, pulsed with pain. My left knee burned with scratches. My hair hurt like it had been pulled.

I tumbled through the door and spun through the hallway, washing up on the kitchen floor. My dad pulled a chair out from the table. It was a dining room chair, one with a cushion under the butt and everything. It got demoted to a regular kitchen chair after my dad smashed the other one when I got in trouble for mooning a girl at school. She wasn't retarded but had something else that was similar.

"Sit."

I sat down, staring at my feet. My dad smacked me in the head.

"Look at me!" He pulled his pack of Marlboro reds out of his jacket and slid one out. He held it in the light, all dramatic and shit. "You wanna smoke, huh?"

"No—"

He smacked me in the face.

"Shut up!"

He put a cigarette in my mouth and lit it. I looked up at him, afraid to move or breathe.

He nodded. "Go on."

I inhaled deep and slow, blowing out the smoke in a neat little puff without coughing. I'd stolen cigs about ten times before and was pretty used to it by now.

My dad scrunched his face as he watched me, "Smokin' that thing like you done it before, Figgy."

"No, sir," taking another drag.

He pushed his cheek out with his tongue. The bridge of his nose crinkled above his lips, somewhere buried in all of it was a look of twisted amusement. Somewhere, deep in all the wrinkles, the ingrown hairs and stubble, he seemed *excited.*

My dad walked over to the cabinet he'd been messing with earlier that day, clicking it open and shut. He'd installed most of a subway tile backsplash a few weeks before. Two yellow wires stuck out from the blue outlet box, bent and crooked. The one looked like a lightning bolt. The other just looked like a yellow wire.

"You were supposed to help me throw these GFI's in," he said, as he straightened the wires, tugging them roughly. "C'mere—no, no. Keep the cig in your mouth. A real man works with one in there."

My dad's eyes opened wide as I flicked the ash into the trashcan and got up. The smile hidden in his scowl became more noticeable, more intense, sucking the other parts of his face into it like quicksand. He muttered something under his breath and pulled a razor knife out of his pocket.

"C'mere," he said, facing the wall. Blue smoke streamed off the tip of his cigarette, blocking the light of the high hat above us. My cig was burnt halfway. The smoke was getting in my eyes. I wanted to take it out.

He ran the knife down the outside of the wire and opened up the casing, peeling it like a banana. He untangled the three wires inside. White, black, and a naked copper wire.

"Here," he said, facing the wall. "Come do the other one."

I stood next to him, drowning in the smoke of my cig, accepting the knife from his hand as he stood behind me and took my wrist.

"Hold the wire tight. Now, take the razor, and remember, always cut away from yourself. Yup, just like that."

The blade felt good as it slid through the casing. It felt like I was doing something important for once. Not just sweeping up dust piles and throwing out pieces of drywall. I thought maybe he was ready to start treating me like a man now, judging by the way I smoked cigs and all.

"Great cut."

My dad took the knife back from me. He pulled back on the yellow casing and cut it away. My wire also had the same three wires sticking out from the inside, the black, the white, and the one bare one. He skinned the black and white casing, giving each wire an inch of exposed copper.

"Dad?"

"What?"

"Is it true that Mexicans can't do electrical?"

"Shut up." He patted his pockets and looked around. "I need you to pull some more wire up from the basement. Here actually, let me see something." My dad pulled a drawer open and shut it. He opened another, digging through batteries, a hot glue gun, a couple marbles— finally pulling out a roll of duct tape. "Hold still. I'm gonna make sure you get a good grip," he said, rolling the silvery tape up all the way up around my wrists.

I puffed my cig and nodded. It was tiny now, stinging my nose and watering my eyes.

He bit the end off the tape and set it on the counter. I tried to move my arms but couldn't. He taped them tight as shit, all the way up to my elbows, making it look like I was part robot.

"Alright, I'm gonna go downstairs. When I say pull—"

"Wait, why do you gotta go downstairs?"

"I gotta make sure the wires come up smoothly, check for snags."

I nodded. My dad opened the basement door and disappeared down the steps. His boots clunked down on the wood with every heavy step.

I stood there, arms tight and ready to pull. I wanted to pull hard when he called, show my dad how strong I was. After about thirty seconds I got bored and looked around. I saw the empty fruit basket on the counter, a black wire container. He bought it a month before and filled it with a bunch of healthy shit. Every morning before work, he'd stop and grab an apple, sometimes even popping it up in the air with the inside of his elbow. There was something about grabbing fruit out a basket that made him happy. I'd sit there eating my cereal, watching him try to hide his smile, whistling as he left the house. But after a few days the fruit started going bad, his basket of happiness slowly rotting, dying before his eyes. I watched in the morning as he stood in front of the basket, desperate and overwhelmed, grabbing two or three things before he left: soggy pears, a withered clementine, and some camouflaged bananas. He started forcing the fruit on me too. There was fruit in my cereal, fruit in my lunch, fruit after dinner. After three days, and a close call of almost shitting myself at wrestling practice, I decided to act. I started that night, going outside and throwing pieces of fruit off the back deck.

Something vibrated in my skull. A quiet buzz that I could somehow hear inside of myself. The buzzing noise spread into a feeling. I convulsed and then it went away.

I spit the cigarette out and yelled. "Dad!"

The breaker clicked from downstairs. The buzzing noise came back. I couldn't breathe, and then I could.

"Dad! Stop! Please! I won't steal another cig I swear!"

The buzz came back, taking my breath with it. My brain clicked and hummed. I saw myself standing over the deck, cocking the rotten pineapple back with two hands, releasing it as my dad came out the basement door carrying a cast iron trap for the slop sink. I could tell by the way he was walking, his slow thudding steps, that the pipe was heavy as fuck. I tried to pull back, but it was too late, the pineapple was in the air, sailing in the deadly slow motion of a ball heading toward a window, the big green leaves fluttering on top like a parachute. It caught my dad in the back, square between his shoulders, putting him into a running fall, dropping the cast iron trap and tumbling over it.

The buzz stopped. I got ready for another, but it didn't come. Something spilled downstairs, something small and metal. A coffee can of bolts or something. I heard drawers open and shut, then the *tap* of his hammer. Every five seconds like clockwork. *Tap.* There was this drawing table in the basement that he hammered tiny nails into whenever he got mad, nails he could get all the way in with one hit.

I tugged my hands back, horrified at the idea of being stuck like this for an hour. One of the tiles bulged, making a tiny hairline crack. I pushed back against the wall with my duct-tape robo-arms, but it was no use. The crack was there for good. I took a deep breath and closed my eyes as the hammering got harder, more intense.

***

I sat in bed rubbing my forearms as I looked out the window into my backyard. My dad was outside unloading tools from his truck into the shed. Fucking duct-tape killed my arm hairs. I had a couple that were getting curly too.

My dad kicked through the sloppy, melting snow, carrying tools across the yard. His face looked blank and squinted like he was trying to see something a thousand miles away. He got like that sometimes. You could see it on his face. His mouth would hang in a circle and his eyes drilled straight ahead, like a movie was being projected all around him, something only he could see. And he'd be like that for *hours.* I first noticed it after the pineapple hit him in the back. After he came up the stairs and beat my ass in the kitchen, he went into the backyard and unloaded his tools like a zombie, just like he was now. Brian told me that his dad said it was called *stress disorder.* Something you get from killing too many people in a war.

I planned on enlisting the day I turned eighteen. Anything to get the fuck out of here. Plus, that's what my family did. Pretty much all of them. My dad's dad and all the dads before them had all been soldiers at one point in their lives. My dad even told me about our great-great grandfather Cornelius Cork, how he went around the southwest after the civil war and got paid to exterminate Indians. My dad said Cornelius would roll into the barracks with big burlap sacks full of scalps dragging behind his horse. The army would pay him per scalp.

He even told me another time, when he was drunk, that anyone who hasn't seen death isn't a man.

My dad banged his workout bag against the shed to knock the dust off it. *Yes yes yes.* I watched him walk across the yard, going around the house where I couldn't see. I tried to count the seconds before his truck started up. I figured twelve. It ended up taking sixteen. He was going to work out and wouldn't be back for at least an hour.

I got up and ran into his room, salivating at the thought of watching porn on his iPad and jerking off with the volume cranked all the way up. I loved hearing that shit. The moans and stuff.

His room was neat. Bed perfectly made, carpet vacuumed, not a speck of dust. I always tiptoed around in there, even when he was gone. It was a reflex or something. I seized the iPad off his nightstand and hit the power button. A little red battery flashed on the screen.

"*Fucker!*"

I dug around his room, careful not to disturb his shit. My dad had a sixth sense for telling when I'd messed with his stuff. I lifted a few books, slid out some drawers, moved some pictures; the charger was nowhere to be found. I sighed and slumped against the window, pissed I'd have to use my imagination. And then, like it was God talking to me or something, I saw her—my neighbor Brenda getting changed in the window. I couldn't believe it. The luck of it all. She had pants on, but no shirt, and was undoing a black strapless bra. She unhooked the bra and walked away, just out of my view.

I smacked the windowsill, "Fuck!"

A pair of camouflage binoculars fell from the windowsill, landing directly on my big toe. My toe pulsed and throbbed, keeping a perfect rhythm with my boner. I grabbed the binoculars and ran downstairs. I could get a better look from the woods.

John

I held the wheel with my knee and lit a cigarette as I pulled away. Fuckin' boy had me riled. But it wasn't no big deal. Boys raise hell. It's what they do. Shit, I was a *motherfucker* at his age. I cracked my window to thin the smoke. The cold air felt good on my face. I exhaled a drag from my cig in a neat little stream and took in some of that cold, clean air. I liked winter, hated the summer. Hot weather made me feel off, kinda fucked up in general. A sense of shit goin' wrong, all the bad possibilities.

I tried talkin' to one of those military shrinks once, but it was worthless. All she did was nod and say, "uh huh" or "hmm." The stuff I was telling her (and I barely told her shit) was *light*. I didn't, or actually *couldn't*, mention any of the real shit. Like the time we caught that one sandnigger hotshot wrapped up in that *bacha bazi* business, which is "boy fucking" in their bullshit wing-ding ah-la-la-la-la language. Some of those rich motherfuckers in the Middle East, the scum we had to work with and protect, loved that shit. It was like a status thing for them to get the most handsome boys and dress them up like girls, make them *dance*. The stuff was beyond gay and offensive, it was fucking *foul*. And we'd lay there, fresh from patrolling, sometimes killing, though a lot of times not. There wasn't a whole ton of action over there. We'd come back to sleep at the base, get a night's rest, which was hard enough with the *heat*, and we'd hear these cymbals clappin' and music playing, little tranny boys dancin' as those old faggots hooted and hollered in that dirty goat language from the main diaperhead's tent. Made me fucking hurl. One night, before we transferred to another base, me and a few guys—I think the higher-ups knew but turned a blind eye—we snuck into that sick fuck's tent and held him down. One of the guys in our company grabbed his dirty, uncut cock and squeezed it in his hand. Told that fuckin' camel monkey that he'd cut it off if he didn't stop fucking around with those little boys. The guy tried to scream and I covered his mouth. His gross, warm tongue pushed against my palm, I'll never forget it, as my buddy ran the tip of his blade down the side of the boy-toucher's disgusting dick, givin' this guy somethin' like a paper cut on his unit. Told him it'd bleed if he put it into a little kid's ass. *Could you imagine if I told the pretty little shrink about that?* Would've fried her little wig. Melted her fancy headshrinker degree hangin' all neat and proper on the wall. No way. Just had to give her the old dog-and-pony, yammerin' about how "the people I killed haunted me" yadi ya and all that bullshit. Tellin' her about that red mist coming off a human target after hitting it— hairspray we called it—and how it bothered me, even though I loved it. I loved seeing that shit come off those fucks. It didn't matter what I said anyway. The talkin' was just a formality, dinner before the blowjob. The Government has to *pretend* they aren't just sendin' people over, ruinin' their minds and lives, and giving them drugs to shut them up and forget.

And those pills, that Celexa shit she gave me? Worthless. Didn't do nothin' but glaze me over. Made me feel like I was behind a sheet of glass. Turned me into a dickless zero. Sent me mentally far, far away. Dumb bullshit pills from a lady who doesn't have a clue. I didn't go over there and serve my damn country to be stuck in a pill-trance for the rest of my days; I did it to give my family a better life. But when I got back it was all fucked up. Everything. Me. My wife. My son. Everything was shit.

I sped down Kelly Drive, lookin' around, disgusted at the people I saw: men in spandex suits joggin', women pushin' their eight-year-olds in strollers, people walkin' their stupid fuckin' dogs. All of them soft as fuckin' ice cream. Sittin' up at night in their big, pillowy beds watchin' TV, laughin' at some faggy comedy news show pushin' their bullshit liberal agenda as if some fuckin' comedian has *any* clue what's goin' on in the world. And all these fuckin' dudes in spandex bicycle suits, laughin' and scoffin' their heads off, while guys like me crawl around on the floor, killin' the fuckin' monsters under their beds as they sit and watch some over-educated, candy-pants liberal talk about how *evil* this country is. The fuckin' host, some twenty-five-year-old Jew kid, parrot for the network, sayin', "Maybe we should stop *bombing* them and actually get to *know* them," as the studio audience goes wild with applause, stunnin' guys like me since I, for one, *did* get to know them. They would have cut that pussy's head off *just for bein' a Jew.* And he wants us to be nice to them? Get the fuck out of here. That's just that shit people say for ratings. Bullshit for the TV world. A fake world with everyone lost in the glow of the tube, lost in the fantasy of it all, millions of fat pussy Americans sittin' on their asses, the glow of pure bullshit flickerin' across their faces while they feed on the nonsense— pop stars, home makeovers, wife makeovers, bar makeovers, my internet girlfriend is a boy, cunt wives of Miami and wherever the fuck else—just so they don't have to deal with their actual lives or the real world around them. Give them a million dumb shows to watch and tell them their vote matters and they're happy...fuckin' morons.

And I'm not pretendin' to be some kind of hero for goin' over there either. There's nothin' noble about what I did, I know that. I killed motherfuckers for money over there. I killed those sandniggers to send my boy to college, just like our country did it for the oil. And I'm not ashamed of myself, or America. We did what we had to do, which is exactly what the world is: people doin' what they got to do to get ahead. It's been what's happenin' from the beginning of time, and it ain't ever gonna stop.

And everyone thinks all the troops are walkin' around feelin' bad about it. Like we all lose sleep over those dead Iraqi kids and shit because that's what people see Mark Wahlberg doin' in the movie. *Oh, those poor soldiers! All distraught and feelin' bad about the people they fucked up, all the death they caused, haunted by the screams comin' out of the shacks they plowed over, never forgettin' the look on that guy's face who showed them the pictures of his family, beggin' for his life*—all that movie bullshit.

Truth is, I liked killin', and I know a lot of other guys who did too. I'll admit, I didn't at first. The first time, I puked. I'll never forget. I was inside an operative's house, Al Qaeda, I believe. It was supposed to be a little snatch and grab, but it turned into a firefight. Me and my team—there was five of us—were getting ready to bust in. It was my turn to be first and I raised my leg to boot this bullshit door down and shots came from the mountain, literally the second I busted in. It had to have been a trap.

So I kick through the door and roll in. My team's outside pluggin' jockeys, so I'm alone. The fuckin' moment I bust in, this no-dick desert-retard comes at me with a dagger. Just like those ones you see at flea markets, blades dealt strictly in nerd-to-nerd transactions, somethin' for virgins to guard their parent's basements with. The guy came from the right and knocked my barrel to the side, screaming some mumbly-jumbly bullshit. He hacked at me and missed. I hit the wrist of his knife hand up with the butt of the rifle and cranked his elbow with my other hand. Next thing I know, I'm pushing that nerd-knife right into his gross, hairy belly. I even jacked it up and over like they showed us to make a big hole. All the blood came spillin' out and me and this crazy fuck are face-to-face, almost kissin' distance. Two strangers in the most intimate situation of them all. It didn't feel real until his blood soaked through my gear. Everything got warm, almost sexual, but nothin' gay. More of a power thing. He didn't just die then and there either. He stood there, clutching my arm, his stinkin', dyin' breath hot on my face. His eyes got all cloudy and red, and right before he went, soon as his grip was starting to loosen, I spewed up my lunch. The guy collapsed over and died in a pool of his blood mixed with my semi-digested burger and tots, bile and shit.

That's when I saw his boy peek out from behind a chair. He must've seen the whole thing. I let go of the knife and watched it fall to the ground like it was in slow motion, and I looked up at the boy, the sandnigger's son, and boom, his head exploded, just like that, up and into the air. One of my guys shot him. Said the kid was holdin' a grenade. Fixed on blowin' us both off the map so he could suck all those virginal titties up there in raghead heaven. I walked out of the house in a daze. That sun, that big hot fuckin' sun pierced my eyes. I tried to look at it, stare at it, give that big ball of gas my vision. I made it barely twenty feet before noticin' that kid's ear was stuck on my shoulder. I peeled it off my vest and threw it on the ground. And I-shit-you-not, a stray dog came out from behind a rock and gobbled that motherfucker up. Shit. Heaven fell out the sky for me that day. Started questionin' God and everythin', wonderin': maybe we are all just a bunch of monkeys killin' our way to the top before we die in the dirt like dogs. Maybe there's nothin' after this life but bugs and worms. Personally, I'd rather be a member of the spirit world and live forever, but who's to say that's the case? I wonder about that sometimes.

I pulled off Kelly Drive and into the park's gravel lot. The snow had mostly melted leavin' little brown patches of muddy dirt here and there with dotted yellow spots where dogs pissed. The sky was startin' to pale on the horizon. Wispy clouds settlin' in the sky after an otherwise clear day. I opened the door and swung my heavy boots out onto the gravel. I had done some cement work not long before. Added a pound to each shoe. A gust of cold air hit my face and saliva rushed my mouth as I unzipped my workout bag and put on my sneakers. I hadn't been back here in a long time, hadn't let any steam out in a while. These trails were an infamous hangout for junkies, tweakers, and other shit like that. I liked to come back here. Raise some raise hell on them. Fuck that Celexa, all I needed was some silver bullets and to whip some ass from time to time. The only cure for anger was anger. Gettin' that shit out onto someone else.

Joel

I ran along the park's gravel path; It was cold, but not unbearable. The air ran through my nostrils, crisp and refreshing as I motored along, breathing, keeping my fingers loose like my high school track coach showed me. I turned a bend, dropping my head and picking up steam as my heart fluttered in several empty squishes of air. I froze, holding my hand to my chest, and worked to breathe slowly as waves of doom flowed through my body making everything feel cold and tight. My stomach pulsed with acidic twinges, that licked-battery feeling of anxiety—I worried I was having a heart attack.

I went to a cardiologist once to get it checked out. He told me arrhythmias were "actually quite normal and that I shouldn't be worried" with no follow-up or anything, which pissed me off considering it was also "quite normal" for people's hearts to explode in their chest in the middle of exercise. Otherwise, why would they have those Frankenstein machines in gyms? Plus, I *knew* people it'd happened to, loosely, but still, people's uncles and stuff.

I burst into a sprint, into what might have been the lamest, most watered-down suicide attempt ever, pushing along in my jogging gear, daring the cosmos, god, atheist non-god, whoever to take me then and there, to explode my heart if it was to be exploded. I kept running, faster and faster, thinking about my corpse disintegrating into the ground, my loaned molecules dispersing back into the Earth, going back into the cycle of matter as parts of what was once me was sucked up by the root of a tree and redistributed toward the production of a flower. "*I could totally be a flower*," I thought as I picked up the pace, reveling in this new existential breakthrough.

My heart fluttered again and I immediately stopped. I put my hands over my head and breathed, mentally nulling and voiding any heroic cosmic dares, begging any offended parties for mercy.

I had a real bad episode at CVS a couple weeks before. I was holding a drink and a bag of chips, ready to check out, and my heart started beating all crazy, real fast, then real slow. Fast again, and back to slow. I ran out of the store, chips in hand, thinking this was it—the big one. I pictured myself collapsing on the sidewalk, the automatic doors opening and closing in robotic confusion as the bag of baked, heart-healthy chips tumbled ironically about my corpse as it was stepped over by impatient strangers scurrying about, hurrying to enjoy their lunch breaks, unaware of their steadily beating, non-arrhythmic hearts.

I stood off the trail, bent forward in the slushy grass, trying to catch my breath as I rubbed my chest in a layman's attempt at monitoring my own cardiac activity, more or less petting my breast as I mused over the fact that I had unknowingly stolen the bag of baked chips on the day of my last attack. Something about that made me happy.

Two scraggly-looking homeless dudes busted out of the tree line and ran by. One of them was so close that he brushed my shoulder as he blew past me. I jumped back, a delayed startle, smelling the boozy body odor emanating from their skin. They didn't even look at me. I honestly don't think they even *saw* me, they were too scared.

There were woods alongside the trail, a shallow stretch of ratty Jack Pines, dregs of the Evergreen family. They went back a few hundred feet and butted up against a metal chain link fence that kept people from wandering onto the train tracks on the other side. When the ground wasn't covered in snow there were patches of grass scattered off the trail between bald spaces of dirt, roughly, in the ratio of water to land on earth with the grass being land. During certain seasons, the bald spots of dirt would get covered in fallen pine needles, which gave the ground a padded feeling, almost in an enchanted kind of way. There were a few other types of trees too, but they were temporarily dead from winter, so I couldn't tell what kind they were.

The evergreen sap rubbed off, sticking to my hands and face as I slithered through to see what was going on, what those dudes were running from. I could hear something, but it didn't sound like much, a crazy homeless guy talking to himself if anything. I parted the evergreen's sticky branches and poked my face out, letting them settle back around my head like some kind of a Tolkienesque man/tree hybrid.

I almost shit myself when I saw him.

My neighbor, John Cork, had this chronically skinny black guy on the ground, pummeling the back of his head from a mounted position. The poor guy was on his hands and knees, crunching in on himself, trying to buck John off, but it wasn't working. There was a small crowd, about six or seven homeless people sitting by their makeshift tents, huddled around various trashcan fires, watching. One of the vagrants, an older white guy with a ponytail and a toothless, sucked-in face was visibly nodding out. The rest were blank looking, uninterested.

Cork got up and brushed himself off. He kicked the guy a couple times and wiped his mouth. Cork's bottom lip was cut and a little swollen. He sucked his fat lip and spit as he stood over the guy, out of breath and panting. One of the fires popped and crackled, sending a flaming ember into a death spiral toward the ground.

"You had enough?" Cork asked the man, clutching his fists.

One of the homeless onlookers picked a cigarette butt off the ground and put it in his mouth. I'm pretty sure the guy next to him was smoking crack or meth, using one of those scary looking stem things. Another one got up and meandered off. Cork booted one of the steel drums they were using for their fire and knocked it over; Sparks and embers hissed in the snow.

I struggled with cold hands to get my phone out of my pocket as I sucked my face back within the needled confines of the tree. I mapped my escape route, figuring I'd get some footage, before hightailing back to the truck, but then heard another voice.

"Fuck you, dude!"

I poked my head back out of the branches and saw Cork in someone else's face now, someone younger. The kid looked like one of those millennial deadheads, someone who got a little too far into the hippy scene and ended up on heroin. Your classic wooked-out fader.

The hippy kid, via Cork's angry shove, flew against his ramshackle tarp-tent, compromising the already shoddy structure. The patchy blue canopy came crashing down, swallowing him and his belongings—an unstrung acoustic guitar and some clothes. The kid wriggled out of the wreckage and got back on his feet, glowing in the spilled fire.

"Hey, what the *fuck* man? What's your fucking deal?"

Cork walked over in a cold, surgical fashion and grabbed the kid by his dreadlocks. The kid tried to resist but crumpled under the force of Cork's arms.

"Get off! Get the *fuck* off!" he shrieked.

Cork, focused and silent, pulled the kid's face down toward the spilled fire, over the roasting chunks of wood and cardboard peppered with melted and unidentifiable beer cans. Satisfied by the kid's operatic crescendo of screams, Cork flipped him over, pulling his face away from the fire, and began roasting his dreads. The horrible smell of burnt hair hovered about the camp, forcing the dead-eyed spectators to cover their mouths and noses. Some even got up and walked away.

As I hit record and zoomed my phone camera in on the kid's face, a sense of familiarity crept in, a sense of knowing. Slowly, I recognized him as he kicked and pleaded. He was the passenger in the car that Lynne hopped into earlier that day. Looking at his face as he struggled in the grips of my neighbor, twisting between contortions of anger and pain, I wondered if it was the ugliest I'd ever seen in my life: big nose, wandering eyes, open mouth of crooked teeth—sorta like it was put on after the fact, like a human Mr. Potato head.

"Please!" the kid wailed. "I'm *sorry*, please!"

"Shut up," Cork commanded.

The kid kicked and writhed on the ground over the soggy dead leaves, crying and holding his hair. He looked like a worm that had just been cut in half with a shovel. "No," he pleaded. "Please!"

Cork, satisfied by the hippy's display of mortal fear, lifted him off the ground by his collar and threw him into the molten barrel. A hellish mix of fiery wood spewed about the encampment, first catching some cardboard which lit up an old pile of dirty clothes. The flame crept toward an old two-by-six, one that was holding up another one of the makeshift tents. The lumber caught, spreading among the blankets and papers around it. The kid rolled off the barrel and laid on the ground, nursing his burnt head with his dirty hands.

A sense of boyish wonder smeared across Cork's face. His body turned to go, but his eyes were still glued on the growing flames, watching them dance back and forth, this way and that, groping the land for all things combustible. Burn or die. That is the true nature of fire. Finally, he turned around and took off, headed in my general direction. I stuffed my phone in my pocket and jetted to my truck.

Brenda

A stampede of tiny orange balls spilled out of the Adderall capsule as I cracked it on my desk. A few stragglers rolled off the side, but I saved them with my hand, which had been ready in the spot they were gonna roll to.

I hated these ones, fucking time release bullshit. They were such a pain in the ass. They had this clear gel coating on all the little balls, and the coating was different for each one, some thicker than others. That way, it released the drug in little bursts over time—which is why they were called time release. So what I had to do, since I personally preferred the *now-release*, was crush every little ball and separate all the gel coatings so I could snort it.

After the Adderall was crushed and ready, I separated the hill of orange powder into five neat lines and snorted one (smallest one first was always my policy) and checked myself in the mirror. I looked like shit. My outfit, my hair, my face—everything looked awful. I looked tired and ugly. Little wrinkle lines already forming at twenty-six. Probably from worrying about my fucking sister all the time.

My heart picked up as I assessed my outfit; navy-blue slacks and a white button-down blouse. Ugh. And my room was a *mess*. I snorted another line off my desk and looked back in the mirror. One of my blouses, my red one, was lying button-side down on my shitty area rug with an outstretched arm like it was crawling through the desert, reaching for help.

I snorted another line.

I was *so* not looking forward to my interview at Quiznos, answering those dumb questions like: "So, why do you want to work here?", which, duh, obviously it was because I fucked off in school, my dad left, my mom was dead, and I was a piece of shit, but I couldn't say that. I had to feed them *lies*, the bullshit they wanted to hear. Fake-nice with a fake smile, as I sat across from some guy who probably paid for blowjobs at strip clubs while we talked about our passion for sandwiches. All for what? A barely livable wage?

I snorted the last two lines, wiping my nose as I unbuttoned my white blouse. The urge to clean my room was insane. I zipped through my hangers for a different shirt, a blue one. I needed some flair, a pop of color. I threw on the blue blouse, checking myself from different angles as I cupped my boobs, boosting them with my hands. I let go and watched them jiggle back into their normal position. The white blouse landed next to the red one; It looked like it was telling it to give up.

I suddenly got the feeling of being watched, one of those sixth sense things. I turned to the window to shut the blinds and sure enough saw John's son, Fig, lying on his belly at the edge of the woods looking right into my window with binoculars, digging his little boner into the snow.

I flew down the steps as I buttoned my shirt. Lynne was lying on the couch watching 'Lizard Lick Towing', yelling at the screen. Her stomach hung out the bottom of her tank top and jiggled as she cheered the repo team on.

"Where you goin'?" she asked, eyes stuck on the TV, words falling out of her mouth like shit.

I'd just cleaned the coffee table that morning and it was already a mess. Riddled with the dust of crushed pills, empty wild cherry Pepsi cans, tiny airplane liquor bottles, and blunt guts. Part of her face moved toward me for a second, like she was going to say something else, but her eyes pulled her back toward the TV.

***

Fig came walking nonchalantly out of the woods, using the binoculars to look at trees and shit around him.

"Yo! What the fuck?"

"What?" he asked, looking at me through the binoculars from barely five feet away.

I went for him, but he dipped left. I grabbed his wrist. My nails dug into his arm and he slipped out, letting the binoculars settle on a string around his neck. Fig braced himself, bouncing, like a boxer feeling out his opponent and wiggled his eyebrows at me like this shit was some kind of game.

"Whatever," I said, turning around to go home. "Have fun jerking off in the woods."

As soon as I started walking away, Fig jogged past me toward his house, examining his arm where I scratched him, looking back every few feet to make sure I wasn't going to chase him. I stopped, giving him a second to get comfortable and then turned around and tip-toed behind. I wound up, and with a running start, right as he was messing with his front gate, smacked him right on the side of his head.

Fig

I swam past Brenda's bitch slaps and got double underhooks around her waist. I didn't want to hit her. My dad would destroy me if I hit a girl. I just wanted her to stop swinging at me. That first punch was no joke.

I readjusted my grip. "Fucking stop and I'll let go!"

Brenda's tits mashed against me as she wriggled to get free. Maybe that's part of the fuss about hitting girls, how it's kind of pervy. I clamped my hands together behind her, locking my underhooks but leaning my dick away to give her some space.

"Brenda, seriously, just stop."

She spit in my face and kneed me square in my nuts.

I had about four seconds before the pain kicked in—that fucked up, achy nausea of getting rocked in the balls. I swung around her back and put her in a headlock, or guillotine really. I felt bad for choking her, but I had to. I couldn't take another shot to the sack.

She twisted one of her arms free and dug her nails into my back so I whipped her around and tightened up the lock. Every time she scratched, I tightened, until finally, she couldn't breathe. She started getting weaker and weaker, and then someone grabbed me.

I threw my leg back to get them in *their* nuts but missed and hit his shin. I still had Brenda locked. The guy pulling me off was like, "Dude! Let her go!" as he dug his fingers into my pressure point, the one behind my elbow. I let go of Brenda and turned around. It was that guy Joel. The guy my dad didn't like.

"Get off me, you fucking *faggot*!"

Brenda came from behind and clocked me in the head so hard that the world turned purple and green. I was off balance from Brenda's cheap shot, not paying attention, and somehow, she tripped me and got on top of me. Joel might have pushed me too. I blocked a few of her hits and then all I tasted was dog shit.

***

I sat there drooling on the curb. Numb. Cold. In shock and out of breath. Wanting to puke but couldn't. Joel yelled something at Brenda and she snapped back at him. Their words seemed far away, in a language I didn't understand. Laying in the street in front of me, right between my legs, was the dog turd I spit out, lying all wet and slimy. I inhaled the cold air, feeling it hit my throat as spit rushed out of my mouth in big heavy strings. The ghost of the dog turd haunted my mouth. The rough, stale-marshmallow texture of that outside layer, how it was all cold and crumbly when I accidentally bit down, opening the gooey middle—like peanut butter from hell. I could still *feel* it in my mouth, *taste* it. I leaned forward and puked. More thick white strings of cold-weather saliva bounced from my mouth like bungee cords. I couldn't swallow. The spit kept rushing out. Dog shit. All I could smell or taste was dog shit.

"Fuck my dad, I'm gonna beat this bitch's ass," I thought, getting back on my feet.

Joel blocked a couple of my punches while Brenda stood behind him clocking me when she could. He kept saying, "Chill out, man!" while he held my shoulders, trying not to touch me. He was stronger than he looked, but my dad still would have kicked his ass.

"Dude!", he kept saying over and over.

Brenda reached out from behind Joel, right as I was starting to get past him, and got me good, a hook right in the temple. Joel, still holding me, pushed her away.

"You too!" he barked.

Joel looked at Brenda, who was breathing furiously and mad at us both now and waved his hand across his chest to tell her her shirt was open. She crossed her arms and covered up.

"Just go home and clean up," Joel said.

"Cleea uh? I haa huccking shi ih aye outh!", I mumbled, trying not to gag.

My dad's truck pulled up, and for the first time, maybe ever, I was happy to see it. I went to wipe the sweat off my face but just smeared more dog shit. I bent over and puked again. The sun was setting behind him, a half circle in the blue and orange sky.

My dad slid out of his truck the second he opened the door and jammed his hands into his jacket pockets. He walked over with his chest out and put a sneaker up on the curb. His eyes darted back and forth between us. It was clear he meant business.

"What in the name of fuck is goin' on here?" he asked, rolling his head in travelling circles as he spoke. His hair was stiff with wet sweat and he smelled like a bonfire.

Joel's face paled, so scared he could hardly talk. All he could do was nod with his hands up like he had no clue, like he didn't even know where to begin. Brenda, on the other hand, immediately got all loud and bitchy.

"I'll tell you what happened. Your fucking little pervert son was peeping in through my window while I was getting dressed!"

My dad's eyebrows shot up in surprise. "Whoa, whoa, whoa. *Peepin'*?"

"Daa, she puh fuhhin shi ih aye owth!" I tried to explain.

My dad's forehead wrinkled as he pinched the top of his nose like he'd just come down with a monster headache. He cracked his neck and massaged his temples, muttering under his breath. He pointed at Joel through his jacket pockets.

"And what was *your* involvement in this whole ordeal—Jason, right?"

"Um, yeah, yep, sir. Um, no, Joel." He replied.

I puked again.

My dad cut his eyes away from Joel to watch me puke. "What the fuck *happened* here?"

Joel played with his hair like a girl, keeping his eyes away from my dad's. "To tell you the truth, sir, I didn't see the whole thing. I was pulling up and I saw Fig choking Brenda. So I got out of my truck and ran over to help."

My dad switched back to me, his anger in my direction now. "Figgy? Is this true?"

I tried to plead my case but couldn't. I couldn't even talk. My dad stared at Joel and then at his gay little truck, his Ford Ranger. He tightened his lips like he was really thinking.

"And where'd you say you were coming from?" he asked Joel.

Joel got all weird and stuttered. "M-m-me? Wh-where was I from-coming from?"

My dad and Brenda both looked at him like he was retarded.

"Yeah," said my dad. "That *is* what I asked."

"I was, uh, just...running some errands," Joel blurted out.

My dad stared at Joel for a moment and said, "Errands? Where? The woods?"

Joel might have shit. "Wh-what? What woods?"

"You got pine needles all over yourself.

Brenda cut in, raising her hand like some bitch from Jerry Springer. "Who cares about *pine needles*, John? Your pervert son was peeping in my window. I was fucking *naked*."

"Sheh was't ak-ed, she hah a bra ohh!" I blurted out, instantly realizing I'd rolled the boulder over my tomb, diming myself into oblivion.

My dad grabbed the back of my neck and threw me toward the house. "Get inside, ya fuggin jackass! Go!" he yelled, booting me in the ass with his sneaker, which came in with some speed compared to his work boots. His foot connected directly with my butthole, which hurt in a weird and empty way. Not a good feeling.

I got up off the ground and ran to my house, holding my burning ass with one hand and my eyes with the other.

Joel

Fig's expression was wooden and stoic, scrunched under the atmospheric pressure of a boy who didn't want to cry, lips pursed, eyes flat and intent. He marched off, perhaps seeking the warmth of a shower, where he could silently merge his tears in the water, like they were the shower's and not his.

Meanwhile, Brenda and John's argument had escalated into a full-blown legal discussion. The classic white-trash debate over who-could-sue-who-more-and-why, both puffing themselves up with advanced legalese in an attempt the scare the other.

"Okay, for one," Brenda began, pulling back on her index finger with the other hand. "Fig was trespassing—"

"Whoa, whoa, whoa—" Cork cut in.

"No! You fucking let me finish, John. He was *trespassing*, he was on my property, *harassing* me through my window, which is technically *espionage*."

"Espionage?" Whaddaya think, you're the fuckin' president or somethin'? Jesus!" John stepped back, holding his arms out like he was on a cross, stunned. "How about we talk about you *assaultin'* my son? Huh?" he said pointing.

"He assaulted me first!"

"He's a fuckin' minor, a kid! And you not only assaulted him, you shoved fecal matter, dog fecal matter, into his mouth, which is, at the very least, a Class-1a felony, attackin' with biohazardous waste. It's technically *terrorism*!"

"Terrorism? Fucking *terrorism*, John?" Brenda looked around like she was entertaining some invisible jury. "And you say *I'm* trying to act like the president? Well, sorry, because that would be *you*. Fucking terrorism? Get out of here."

Cork waved his hands, blocking Brenda's words. Anyone looking from a distance would have thought he was fanning a fart away from his face.

"Enough!" he said.

Brenda shot her eyes to the side and exhaled hard out of her nose, somehow sweating in the cold. She seemed somewhat satisfied.

Cork looked up into the sky, mumbling inaudible vows of revenge at the setting sun, and then focused his attention on me. "Alright, so just for the record—sorry, Jason, right?—well, close enough. So *you* broke it up. Correct? Okay, and once you pulled my boy *off* her, *she* came back—lemme finish—and-and just so we're clear—she came back and, you know, jammed fecal—dog fecal matter into my son's mouth? Is that the course of events here? I just wanna know."

"Sure did," Brenda cut in before I could respond.

John's bottom lip stretched under the force of his tongue as he looked back out into the sky, an otherworldly majesty to his gaze, looking to the clouds as if he saw gods prancing atop them. We stood in a mutual silence and waited until John returned his hardened visage back to earth, nestling his thumbs deep into his belt loops. He turned to address us but changed his mind, deciding to spit into the street instead. It went far, almost clear across to the other curb. I wondered if hooking his thumbs into his jeans had anything to do with it.

Mustering a feigned diplomatic grace, John bid us adieu and marched off toward his house, his breath visibly trailing out of his chapped lips, the vapor of curses and threats.

Lynne breezed by us in Brenda's grey Hyundai. There was music coming out of the car; It sounded canned. Only drums and vocals leaked out of the windows. Some top 40's dance hit, a song about someone's love being a drug, turned all the way up. Lynne bopped her head along to the rhythm, checking herself in the fold-down mirror as she zoomed past.

Brenda ran at the car with a surprising burst of speed. "Lynne!"

Lynne blew two stops signs and made a left on Silverside. The car disappeared.

Brenda stood in the middle of the street, her body caved and slackened, shoulders beyond round. Her arms dangled by her sides like they were both asleep. She, from my angle, looked like one of those starving kids on TV, slumped and vacant-eyed, devastated by the world.

"Everything okay?" I asked, perched on the little strip of grass above the curb that bordered the sidewalk and the street.

Brenda's crushed posture morphed into a frenetic pacing as she patrolled a small stretch of blacktop, smacking her forehead and cursing. A momentary mental breakdown for sure. I stood and watched, not exactly sure what to do with myself.

Brenda stepped up on the curb and headed right toward me with the exact speed of a person about to kick someone's ass. She had her arms crossed over her chest and was wincing in the wind.

"Does it look okay? My sister just took my car and I—fuck!"

"Can't you call her?"

Brenda shook her head. "Her phone's out of minutes."

"Where did you need to go? I could probably give you a lift."

Her face, at first, suggested she was pissed, as if I shouldn't have offered to drive her, but then it changed, almost melted, into a bemused smirk, like she'd just gotten an old joke, one she heard as a kid and never understood. She shook her head. "Um, a job interview, which I'm *way too late* for because I was fighting a child." She punctuated her response with one of those quiet laughs, expelling excess irony from her system.

I persisted, hoping to cheer her up. "Well, better late than never. C'mon, I'll take you."

"Thanks, but uh—" She held up her dog shit-covered hand to my face, a little closer than I would've liked, giving me full backstage access to both the smell and visual component of smeared dog shit. It was horrific. Another animal's shit mixed with sweat and grass and gravel and blood. Just the sight of it, all the little pieces of sand and twigs and tiny shards of broken glass mixed in there—disgusting.

I moved my head away. "Well if you need anything or whatever, let me know."

My phone rang. I picked it up without thinking. "Hey, mom."

I gave Brenda the "give-me-a-minute" finger and stepped away. "I know, I know. I've been...yeah, I got your message...I know it's tonight...I mean, Mom—Please. I'm busy. I *am* busy. I'm helping my friend right now. She's gotta get to a job—Uh huh..."

I gave Brenda a polite smile, nodding my head to the rhythm of my mother's concerned ramblings as I rolled my eyes, "What? No, she's my *neighbor*. We're—Look, I'll see you there, I gotta go."

I hung up, surprised to see Brenda biting her bottom lip as if to prevent a smile. She held her dog shit hand out in front of her like a vaudeville performer. "Was your mom seriously asking about me?"

"No, no. I have a party to go to, this thing for my dad's retirement. I don't know, she's just being weird."

"How?"

"It's like this perception she needs to uphold since all her friends' kids are married, have kids and real jobs."

Brenda bent down and wiped her shitty hand off in the snow with a casualness that I found disturbing. She stood back up and continued her barbaric hand-washing with a chunk of icy slush. "So what, are you like taking a snow day?"

"No. I quit."

"Today? You quit today? When?"

"I didn't formally resign or anything-"

"Oh, so you just didn't show up."

"Yeah, which come to think of it, my manager hasn't even called yet."

"Probably just assumes you couldn't make it because of the snow—actually no. Maybe the whole place is closed! Ha! You might still have a job!"

"Shit, you might be right. Maybe *all* the chairs are empty."

"Huh?"

"Nothing. Eh, it's probably for the best. My dad's friend, the guy who runs the company, the one I somehow failed to quit, he's going to be there and it would have been super awkward to see him."

"So," said Brenda, "your mommy's worried you don't have a date?"

"Please-"

"I'd go. Probably gonna be some banging food there."

"Seriously?—I mean yeah," I responded, dumbfounded. "Tons of banging food. Crab and lobster, stuff like that. We can smoke some weed and head over there if you want."

"Weed?", Brenda scoffed. "Jesus. I haven't smoked weed since I was like fifteen."

"Yeah, well I only smoke weed when my meth dealer is out of town."

"Really?" she responded, inquisitive but not shocked.

"Jesus, no. I've never even seen meth.

Brenda shook her head and laughed, "Good. Grab a bottle of wine and meet me at my house at 8. And you're obviously driving."

Fig

I laid there watching my ceiling fan; trying to focus on one of the blades as it went around, not letting it get sucked into the swirl of the others. I showered twice and must've mouth-washed ten times. I even swallowed some in case any of the dog shit got into my stomach.

I could hear my dad showering, that rainy sound of water behind the wall. We had two and a half bathrooms: one in his bedroom, one in the upstairs hallway, and a half bath downstairs next to the kitchen. I hated shitting in the downstairs bathroom. My dad for some reason always waited until the last possible second to go, and the few times I'd used it, he'd come trudging up the basement steps and jiggle the handle. And instead of just going upstairs, he'd bang the door and freak out at me, saying I was hogging up the half bath with a dump. He had this idea that the half bath was only for peeing and washing your hands.

The other bathrooms, the full ones, had showers instead of bathtubs. We might have had a tub when my mom was around, but I can't remember that far. The furthest back I can remember is me and my dad showering together when I was really little. Both of us wore bathing suits so it wouldn't be gay.

I hated the look of my room. The walls were sky blue with borders of sports balls stretched across. They were like stickers or wallpaper or something. Some of the blue paint was lighter in spots where it had gotten patched. I had two dressers, one for summer clothes and one for winter stuff. The winter clothes dresser had all my wrestling trophies on it, all eight of them. There was a track ribbon on there too. I ran track once and came in third in the hundred meter. The other dresser, my summer one, had a bunch of random shit on top of it: Swiss army knife, signed football by arena league QB Tony Randall, a rock I found, and now my dad's camo binoculars.

The shower stopped.

My dad still hadn't chewed my ass out about the whole Brenda thing yet. I'd never gotten in trouble while already being in trouble and was preparing for what might come as a result. I'd strategically put my wrestling sweatsuit on, the Roxborough Indians one, hoping he'd notice it while kicking my ass and take it easy. The last thing he'd ever want to do would be to sideline me from an ass-kicking. He loved that I wrestled. It was the only thing I did that made him happy.

He was still in the bathroom slopping around. I heard him opening drawers, running the water, and the buzz of his electric shaver. I thought about grabbing my Swiss Army knife—just in case. Pervs and people who hit women were high up on my dad's shit list. There was an old man on our block, Eddie. He was a perv. They took his badge and everything after he did stuff with a young girl in the seventies.

After a few minutes, the noise stopped from the bathroom. My dad's footsteps treaded lightly on the carpet toward my room. My feet went numb. He opened my door with a couple of light knocks and came in. I adjusted the way I was sitting to make sure he could read my shirt.

He sipped his silver bullet and set it down on my nightstand, right next to the arena league football, stooping down to check his brutally gelled hair in the mirror that hung on the back of my door.

"So you perved out *and* fought a girl today, huh?" he asked as he tamed an un-gelled straggler that was reaching for the light.

"Dad..." was all I could reply.

He raised his hand, not like he was gonna hit me, just for me to shut up. "Relax, he said, beer coming off his breath. "Pretty sure you learned your lesson there with that dog shit." He winced like he could taste it.

I nodded but still didn't trust him. It might have been a trick. My dad was good for telling me to go to my room and then booting me in the ass as I walked away.

He lifted the glass case off the arena league football and held it in his hand, squeezing his fingers around the laces. He looked me in the eye and pumped his arm like he was about to throw it. "Shit, do ya want to end up like Mr. Eddie across the street?"

"How old was the girl?" I asked.

"Not old enough."

My dad dropped back like a quarterback in the pocket.

"Truth is—he fucked up. Just like you did today, only he was a man, and that shit doesn't fly when you're older."

He tossed me the ball and took another sip of his beer. "You wanna know how to get girls?" he asked, looking at his hair in the mirror again.

I nodded, desperately wanting him to get out of my room so I could jerk off. I never got the chance to earlier and was even hornier from seeing Brenda's bra.

"First off, what's rule number one?"

"Always gel your hair," I replied.

"Exactly. Shows a woman you're disciplined. It's especially good for a kid your age since you don't have any shit, ya know, like a powerful job or somethin' they can get horny for. So you gel your hair. Into a spike preferably, but there's nothin' wrong with a slick back either."

My dad's hair was styled in some kinda combination of both.

"So you go someplace nice, somewhere in a shoppin' center or somethin'. Like the Thirsty Bulldog."

He sipped his beer and burped. A little wet burp that sounded like it hurt.

"Then, make sure to establish rapport with the bartender. That way they greet you by your name. Girls pick up on that kind of thing. Oh, and get there early so you can sit at the bar. Facin' the door preferably." My dad paused to sip his beer again. "It's tough to hold court while you're standin' off to the side like a weirdo. Plus, havin' a seat at the bar makes you somethin' like a tollbooth operator. The girls gotta get through *you* to wet their beaks. The price they pay is conversation. Usually, when they come up to get a drink, I'll just turn around...Actually, Figgy, get up. I'll show you."

I set the football down on my bed, wishing he'd came in here and kicked my ass instead of doing whatever this was.

"Yup, now get behind me, actually no, come from the other side. I'm gonna sit on your bed. Yup, like that. Ready?"

I pulled my hoodie down to cover my sweatpants. I wasn't hard but definitely wasn't soft either. Luckily, my dad had his back to me. He fumbled his hand around my dresser looking for his beer. "Okay, approach the bar."

"Wait, isn't this a gay bar since we're both men?"

My dad spun around and held the back of his hand threateningly toward me. "Stop messin' around, Fig! I'm tryin' to teach you some important shit. Now do it again. And, this time—no gay talk." He shuddered as he spun back around and sipped his beer. "Givin' me the heebie-jeebies."

I approached my bed with the speed and excitement of a person at a funeral, fixing my sightline on the back of my dad's mushy head. Even his neck hairs were gelled. "Do you think Brenda's pretty?" I asked him.

My dad whipped his head around. "Damnit, Fig, forget it. And no, no, I don't. Wouldn't touch that girl with a ten-foot pole."

My dad snatched his binoculars off the dresser and headed toward the door. He flicked the lights off and slammed it shut. I stood in the dark a few seconds. The door opened and the light came back on.

He grabbed his beer off his dresser and pointed it at me, the binoculars gripped tightly in his other hand. "Fig," he said, squeezing his eyes so hard that his face muscles twitched and trembled—it was the hardest I'd ever seen him think. "There's gonna be a woman in your life—everyone gets at least *one*—but there's gonna be a girl that comes outta nowhere that's so fuckin' pretty and smart, with skin like she's been layin' in a tub of butter her whole life, good smellin' hair and a body shaped like a guitar, and she's gonna set her sights on *you of all people*, right? The guy fartin' in his sweatpants and pickin' his boogers, and it's gonna stun ya. Like seein' God himself. And little by little the veil will slowly drop. You'll start to notice just how truly fucked up she is, and how it's not really *you* she's after as much as the idea of all your time and attention, and if you're not careful she'll roll through your life like a god damn hurricane, wreckin' everythin' you know. And you'll think you can help her but, fuck." My dad opened his eyes, stroking a bead of condensation from his beer. "She'll just suck you further into her chaotic twirl, her never-ending dance of drama, a confused, directionless shuffle until you're so spun out on *her* that you don't even know yourself. It's like they rip somethin' outta you that you never knew you had till they took it. And, and, you just..." He trailed off into his aluminum beer can as he finished it and then crushed it in his hand. The whole thing looked like some ancient gypsy ritual for containing the evil of the future.

He turned the light off and shut the door. "Remember what I said."

I laid in the dark for a while, thinking the hot nurse at my school, Ms. Green, wishing she'd twirl me into her tornado of chaos or whatever the fuck my dad was talking about. His truck started and faded down the street. I got up and put my sneakers on. Figured I'd get some energy drinks from the gas station or something. Not like he was gonna be back anytime soon.

Eddie

The setting sun hung over Juniata Park like a punctured egg yolk. The sky, which for most of the day had been cloudless and blue, changed into a pool of melted sherbet, shades of pink and orange, blue turning white on the horizon. Clouds rolled along, soft and puffy, frayed and wisped on the edges like torn cotton. The scene above, of course, in total contrast to the hellhole of a neighborhood I was doing surveillance in. Everything around me was crooked. The power lines, the houses, the sidewalks. And the constant noise, the high-pitched whoops and incessant laughter. One argument starting as another ended. I don't know how anyone lived in this goddamn nightmare of a place.

Someone knocked on my car door, startling the daylights out of me. Two young cops stood on either side, one of them chewing gum with his mouth open like a hotshot. My gut burned with self-hatred for letting these bums sneak up on me.

"Alright, buddy," said the one on my passenger side. He rapped my window as he smacked his gum, a loud Italian looking kid.

The other cop, a guy with short blonde hair who I thought I recognized from before, waved the other off. He tapped my window gently, motioning me to roll it down. I lowered it, not all the way, just enough.

"I'm down here on a private investigation, boys."

The gum-chomper sneered. "They gave *you* a license?" he asked incredulously

I ignored the young wop and held up the picture, one of those 8x11 graduation shots. "Looking for this kid. Clay Hart. Some rich brat from the main line that's gone the way of the spike. His family told me he might be down here copping off the *Puertoriquenos*."

"C'mon, Ed, we *talked* about this," the blonde cop said.

I adjusted my cap and stared straight ahead. "It is within my rights to—"

"Eddie," said the Italian one, "you really gonna feed us that YouTube lawyer horseshit?"

The other cop motioned to the Italian one. "Please...Mr. Hayden. We got a couple *actual* stakeouts going on right now. You sitting here is jackin' us up. Spookin' the hay-zooses."

I held the picture up to the window again and shook it. "Okay, so, either of you gobs seen this kid or what?"

The wop chimed in, "Eddie, if I tell you something about that kid, do you promise to get the fuck outta here?"

I nodded.

The wop leaned in and squinted at the picture, chomping his gum harder as he focused. "Judging from what I see there, I'd say...he's a bit too old for you."

I jerked my door open. I wanted to get out and tear that little jackass to shreds, but the other cop kept his weight on it from the outside.

"Get the fuck off my car!" I yelled.

Another cop car pulled up. Two black cops, a man and a woman.

"Everything cool?" asked the lady cop.

The blonde Swedish-looking officer stepped away from my door to address the others. "Yup, all good. Just consulting with one of our people real quick."

They nodded and got back in their car.

The Swede leaned back into my door. "Let me see that picture again."

"Why? You got something smart to say like your greasy friend here?"

"Hey, fuck you!"

"Mario, stand down. I got this."

"*Mario?* Good god you *are* a little gin-ball, aren't you?

Mario rocked the side of my car. "Fuck you, you old pervert."

The Swede leaned in uneasily. "Let me see that picture."

I pulled it off my passenger seat and held it up.

"Do you mind?"

I rolled my window all the way down and handed it to him. He held it up, the picture glowing in the golden light of sunset and studied it.

"Wait here," he said.

He went back into his car and punched some buttons in his computer. I watched him, all the while figuring this was one of their tricks. I figured he'd pull off with the picture and the dago would give me the bird. But after a while, he got out, carrying his mobile computer, looking from side-to-side as he walked. He was a good cop, alert at all times.

Leaning back into my car, he slid his computer onto my lap.

"That's a more recent photo. Someone caught him outside the liquor store on Ridge a few months ago buying booze for high school kids and brought him in. I can't print this off, but figured I'd let you look at it."

The picture of Clay was totally different. Long, dreaded hair instead of his short, graduation crew cut. His face was sallow and sunken in, acne streaking across his forehead. He looked like he'd somehow devolved, a weird process of reverse evolution into a more Neolithic strain of man.

"I can take a picture of it with your phone," he offered.

"No need," I replied, tapping my temple. "It's stored. I never forget a face."

***

Candy's apartment was a mess. Sad really. Her roof leaked down the walls and the place smelled like mold. There were barely any windows, and the windows she did have were blocked up with pillows, blankets, newspaper—anything a whore could get her hands on to keep unwelcome eyes where they belonged.

I adjusted my legs to get comfortable and my foot hit a pizza box that felt like it had a slice or two still in it.

"You almost done, baby?" she asked me.

"Yeah," I said, sitting up, readjusting my body in the chair. "The old boy's got miles on 'em. Takes him a second to warm up."

Candy gave her mouth a break and used her hand. A bit of bubbled saliva built around her bottom gum, occupying space that used to belong to three teeth. "Yeah, well, forty dollars is for short stays and this is becomin' a long one."

"Can I, uh, touch your, uh—"

"Nawww, baby. That's how shit be goin' around."

Candy put my dick back in her mouth and shuddered at the thought of venereal disease.

The mass of floppy flesh I was trying to pass for an erection fell limp. Candy stopped moving and trapped it in her mouth, unsure of what to do.

 "Hey, uh, don't sweat it. I can always come back some other time."

Candy didn't argue. She popped up off her knees and went into the bathroom. She came back out with a hot towel that smelled like rubbing alcohol. "Wipe yourself down baby. Throw it wherever when you're done."

Candy flicked on her porch light and said something. It had gotten dark out and I missed what she said. I could hear fine. I just couldn't comprehend. It was always the same feeling with this whore business, the same drowning inside of myself sensation whenever I reemerged into the world, something like a fish out of water until I reached my car, which of course, *of course* had some young punk leaning against it. I beeped my key to let him know. The shame swelled; a tsunami of shame. What's the feeling? What's the *exact* feeling I'm describing? It's like losing at blackjack while you're jerking off. Think about that, combining those two feelings. The kid got off my car and ended his call. He looked me up and down as we passed each other, with an expression that suggested he wasn't exactly a fan of my existence.

I got in my car and started it, push button. Christ. Another thing I didn't understand and couldn't afford. I don't know when it happened. When I got so old and out of touch. Almost like I blinked one day and there I was. A person from the old Testament living in the New. Alone and over my head in debt at *seventy-three*. How I ended up owing my mortgage company so much goddamn money I'll never understand. All the refi's, reverse mortgages—these were things they offered me. They offered me cash and I took it. And now they wanted to kick me out?

I took another look at Clay's picture, then I looked at my hand. Old and wrinkled and poor. Christ.

Joel

I swerved my truck away from a pothole as I pulled into the liquor store parking lot. It sat in a little shopping center beside the river. There was a movie theatre, a nail place, a pizza place, the liquor store, and a shitty little bar. The Thirsty Dog Saloon or something. I sat there, soaking up what was left of my car heat as I eyed the liquor store's modern glass front, a soft light emanating from within. The sky had gotten dark and the temperature was dropping.

I got out of my truck and squeezed against the wind. The asphalt was cold and tight, appearing almost blue under the salt film left by the plow truck. I heard someone whistle and yell.

"Yo! Hey buddy! Yo!"

Another loud whistle.

I glanced over my shoulder, hoping it wasn't for me.

John Cork hiked the waist of his jeans up and hurried over. He moved naturally, unaffected by the temperature. It was like we were inhabiting two completely different environments. He had on tight black jeans and a leather jacket. A prominent butt-chin dangled from his stubbly face as he flashed me a crooked smile. His hair was shiny and wet, gel-plastered onto his head.

"Yo, Jason."

I didn't bother to correct him. Actually, I liked that he didn't know my name. "John, right?" I asked, my teeth chattering.

"That's me," he said, pausing to flick the ash off his cigarette as he looked at the ground. "Hey, just wanted to say, and I don't know what your involvement is with that girl, but, fuck man, she's trouble. *Shwew*."

"What do you mean?" I asked, watching an old man shuffle into the warmth of the liquor store through its sliding glass doors.

Cork petted his plastic scalp, attempting to gather information from his warped reflection that came off my truck windows. "Well, shit," he said, finally leaving himself alone. "I don't know how else to put it other than she's fucked up. Her and her sister—whole family, really. It's a shame. They've been fucked up a long time, and well, point bein', you're better off stickin' your dick in somethin' else. Nothin' worse than a chick with a habit, buddy. Believe me," he said, chewing his gum with intense force as he studied my face.

I clenched my jaw to stifle my chattering teeth. "Wait, you think she's a drug addict?"

Cork measured me with his eyes, "You seen her sister. Stone cold junkie. You think some of that isn't funnelin' down to old Brenda? Shit, I mean, what's that saying? If you hang around the barbershop long enough, you end up gettin' a haircut. Know what I mean?"

"I don't know, I could see Lynne, but Brenda? She doesn't look like someone who's on drugs."

"Yeah, neither did my ex-wife." Cork pulled an airplane bottle of Jameson out from his jacket pocket. The lid crackled as he twisted it open. He downed it, holding it up and extra second to ensure he'd drained its contents. He whipped his head over toward my truck. "That's yours, right?" he asked, emitting a boozy warmth to the air. That whiskey smell in the cold outdoors. It reminded me of going to high school football games.

I nodded in reply.

"Use it for work?" he asked.

"Uh, yeah. Every day."

"Where'd you say you were comin' from today?" he asked, narrowing his eyes.

"W-what do you mean?"

"When you broke up the fight. You said you were comin' from somewhere."

"Shit, man, I don't even know. I was working. They got me all over the place sometimes."

Cork tilted his head like a curious dog. "Thought you were runnin' errands."

"I mean, yeah, that's what I meant. I had to run to FedEx to print something for my client's new logo...it's for a pitch tomorrow, and then I went to Wal-Mart for some other shit. Why, what's up?"

Cork spun the tiny neck of the liquor bottle between his thumb and index, rolling it back and forth. "Just curious."

He checked his reflection one last time and walked off.

***

The moon was full and bright, etched in streaks of unreflecting grey. Gusts of bitter air assaulted me from every direction as I set off wine in hand across the cul-de-sac toward Brenda's house, a voyage of roughly one-hundred feet. I was prepared to switch hands midway, giving my right a break from the elements at the exact moment that I reached the center of the paved circle. Reaching my point of interest, I put the plan into effect, sliding the reasonably priced bottle of Cabernet into my left with speed and precision as I sheltered my pre-frostbitten right in the vaginal warmth of my coat.

My frontal cortex pulsed and hardened, informing me that the weed muffin I'd eaten before showering had fully passed through my liver and into my bloodstream. Unfortunately, judging by the surrealistic, syrupy goo that seemed to be coating the contents of the world around me, the muffins turned out a little stronger than I'd anticipated. I glanced nervously toward Cork's house, hoping he didn't catch me walking to Brenda's after our little talk. A lone light illuminated one of his second-story windows, triggering a strong sense of digestive unease. The rest of the houses on the block quickly followed suit, transforming under the power of my stoned imagination into shelters for spying neighbors, a network of people intent on watching me blunder my way to what might have been a date. I thought about the cemetery down the street, it was only half a block away. I wondered if all the bones rotting in the nearby dirt emitted a sort of psychic radiation, a broken-life feeling hanging in the air, making everyone around here feel a *little* shittier all the time.

As I opened the gate leading into Brenda's yard, expertly switching the wine bottle again, the thought that she didn't want me to come over dawned on me.

"Maybe she was just being polite? Maybe I was supposed to decline her offer to come as my date but didn't out of some flagrant social retardation." I knelt down in a panic, pretending to tie my shoe as I deliberated between two horrid scenarios. The first, being Brenda's unwanted guest. The second, and possibly more sinister, was being some psycho who'd walked across the street just to turn around and go home— though it dawned on me that I could pretend-rummage through my pockets and act like I'd forgot something, giving any potential nosey neighbors a visual reason for my retreat.

Brenda's porch light flicked on, opening a third, and possibly *most* disturbing, scenario, the apocalypse in terms of imaginary social blunders: Brenda *seeing* me walk across the street, fake tie my shoe, see me *see* the light come on, and then run back to my house, pussying out altogether.

I walked to her door and knocked.

Horror spread as I stood on the doorstep, realizing what I'd just done. The rhythm of my knock, several authoritative thumps, must've scared Brenda, her being a drug-dealer and all. So I knocked again, this time lighter, with a touch of fun and sass. The classic det-det-da-det-da, det-da. Wallowing in the aftermath of my double-knock, I questioned my physical positioning on her front steps. There were four in total. Concrete steps with what could only be called a hand support system since it was too flat and wide to constitute as a rail. I was on the top step, possibly a bit too close for comfort, so I stepped down. The second step was a bit better, but still felt odd, like I was being indecisive about coming in. The thought occurred that I could stand on the bottom, off the steps altogether, and lean against the hand support system in a cool, detached way, possibly even faking a phone call—

The door jerked open.

Brenda stood there looking at me like I was a Jehovah's Witness, beyond uninterested in my arrival. Her hair was dripping wet from the shower. Her shirt, a wife-beater tank top, was damp in spots, highlighting the parts of her body she missed with her towel. She and her house gave off a synthetic bouquet of lotions, sprays, and fresheners to an almost dizzying degree.

"Hey," she said, still showing no discernible emotion regarding my presence.

"Hey," I replied coolly from the second step.

"You gonna come in?" she asked, fixing her hair.

"Yeah—I mean, I wasn't just going to barge past you. I was waiting for you to like, ya know, invite me in."

"What, are you like a vampire or something?" she asked, motioning me into her place. "Get in."

I walked into her house and was hit by more smells: candles, perfume, baby powder, possibly even those little baskets of scented paper scraps and fake pine cones that people kept on their toilets—all these things bombarded me, adding "lightheadedness" to my laundry list of ailments.

She whipped her head down, and in one perfect motion, wrapped her wet hair in a blue towel that was riddled with bleach stains.

"Sorry about the towel. I thought you were gonna call before you came."

"Oh, *fuck*! I totally spaced. I'm so sorry."

"Relax, it's not a big deal. I was just saying...about the towel," she said pointing up.

"Well, if it's any consolation, I like the towel. I like how you put it on your head."

Her brow collapsed into sarcastic disbelief. "Yeah? Any other weird fetishes I should know about?"

The wife-beater had a small hole in the breast, giving me a glimpse of her black bra. The bra's shine led me to believe that it was satiny.

"No," I said. "Pretty much just wet, towel-wrapped hair and minor mommy issues, if you'd care to explore those."

Her face went up in a friendly sneer, not a laugh or smile, more like a visible approval of my joke. "So do you, like, need a formal invitation to sit too?" she asked, pushing the scent of her gum to my nose, classic bubblegum.

I ignored her question, opting to look around her house instead. The wallpaper, carpet, furniture, all gave off a very 70's vibe. Partridge Family hues of orangey-browns and vomitous-greens dominated the motif. I found it unsettling but wasn't sure why.

"Sorry about the mess," she said, excavating a gravity-defying pile of mail and magazines off her ancient coffee table.

I sat down on the couch like it was my idea and not hers. "Nah, please. I'm a slob too."

One of her black bra straps popped out of her shirt while she bent over to grab a piece of mail off the floor. "I'm actually pretty clean. My sister's the fucking pig."

She rolled her shoulder back as she came up, popping the bra strap back into place. There was a meditative quality to her movement, a thoughtless auto-femininity that inspired a sense of awe, a sort of horny reverence within me.

"What's up with this table?" I asked. "And where's the dog?"

Her coffee table was *old*. I could tell. It was dense, heavy in a way they didn't make them anymore. Easily a couple hundred pounds. The top was separated into two sections; both stained a deep cherry hue, trapped under a thick, shiny layer of polyurethane. The grains of the wood seemed to have been traced out with eyeliner, dark and enriched, looking like the top of an old man's cane. Bordering the table's edge were these carved-in designs, all barbarically ornate, whittled-in Celtic weave patterns that blended into linked leaves like Caesar's crown. Other unidentifiable shapes and patterns ran down the legs which finally merged into the table's feet that were carved to resemble some sort of hoof.

Despite the table's glorious craftsmanship, it looked like a turd. It was dinged and slashed, water-stained, and chipped in spots. Razor nicks everywhere across the top. There was this one scratch that stuck out. It looked like someone started carving a swastika but changed their mind.

She shrugged her shoulders, fanning through her mail. "The table? I dunno. One of my uncles did a job for this rich family out on the main line and they said they didn't need it anymore. And the dog's laying in the basement where you left him. He won't move."

"Yeah, it can take rescue dogs a week or two to warm up."

"Don't call him that."

"What?"

"*Rescue* dog."

"Why?"

"I don't know, I just think it's gross."

I decided to change the subject.

"Dude, this table looks so *old*."

"Thanks," she said sarcastically, taking a break from her postmaster duties.

"No, I mean like a genie lamp. *Mystically* old, like it's cursed. Like it can only be moved by some dark ritual—a satanic ceremony of uncles aligning their beer bellies to the north, all saying horrible racist jokes at the exact same time to move it. And whenever one of them dies, all their earthly weight gets trapped inside, making it harder and harder for the next generation of uncles—"

"Are you fucking high?

"Not really," I lied.

"Well can you get it together? My mom's about to stop by."

"Shit, really?"

"No, just kidding. She's dead."

"Oh, fuck, I'm really sorry, I—"

"Eh, don't be weird. You want a beer or something?" she asked. "Maybe some alcohol will calm you down."

"Why? Do I seem nervous?" I asked nervously.

She shook her head and laughed, amused by my discomfort.

"How about you let go of that wine and I'll start us out with that," she said, taking it out of my frozen right hand. "What time do I have to be ready by?"

"Whenever," I replied, staring at her shoulders. They were slender and soft, appearing clay-like and malleable. I imagined myself resting my chin on them and kissing her from behind. I've always had this weird habit of fantasizing about marriage on the first date, playing our whole lives out in my head minutes after meeting.

"It's not whenever, it's a party. It has a beginning and an end. What time does it start?"

"Nine," I replied, thinking of our first-born son.

"Jesus," she said, looking at the time on her phone. "It's already 7:45! I still gotta do my hair."

I sat up. "We don't have to be there exactly when it starts. It's called being fashionably late. Plus your hair looks great."

"Yeah, fashionably late to your dad's retirement party, real cool. And thanks, I'm glad you like the towel on my head."

Wine bottle in hand, Brenda disappeared into the kitchen. Her other hand stuck out to the side in a sort of stopping motion, like she was trying to push something about me away. Her butt sashayed in her sweatpants as she moved.

I looked away from her butt and focused on the table, diverting my sight in order to stave off the quickly forming erection that stormed my jeans at the sight of Brenda's three-dimensional movements, thinking maybe my anti-masturbation thing wasn't such a good idea. Instead I imagined the table's apparent fall from grace, imagining a humble villager crafting it for years in his quaint artisanal lair, whittling his heart out as he obsessed over every aspect of his final masterpiece, his magnum opus, wholly unaware of the day when his table, his four-legged Pinocchio, would take a horrible turn, somehow inhabiting a cruelly wrong space, like a parking lot seagull.

The only thing that remained on the coffee table, since Brenda took the mail, was a driver's license. It had an indent in the middle of it, a dime-sized bubble protruding out of the surface. I peeked into the kitchen to make sure Brenda wasn't coming and picked it up. The bubble was a clear sign of drug abuse. My friend's license was like that, he was an addict. He'd put a pill in the middle, under the license, and press down, grinding until the pill became powder. Angling the card slightly to deter the glare, I was relieved to see Lynne's pudgy face staring back at me, her eyes vacant and muted, the standard soulless mugshot of bureaucratic photography.

"Whaddya doing?"

I slid the license back onto the table, guiltily smiling at Brenda as she walked through the dining room holding bright-colored plastic tumblers filled with water and ice. One pink, one green.

"Just admiring some official PennDOT photography."

"Yeah, well, don't," she said. "Driver's licenses are private."

I got up to help, offering to take the burden of my personal tumbler from her hands. She stopped, looked at me, and stepped around, setting the cups down on the coffee table—no coaster. I smiled to make amends. Brenda returned my smile with a neutral expression, her lips formed in a perfectly straight line as she nodded her head to signify that my smile was noted but wouldn't be returned.

Standing gave me a brief chance to check out her dining room. She had one of those big glass shelves, a fancy cabinet that people kept chock-full of fine china and expensive bullshit in case the Queen of England showed up unannounced for supper. Though I noticed her cabinet didn't have any fine china or crystal knives or any of that stuff, just a bunch of framed pictures and a striking amount of glass knick-knacks, the quantity bordering on eerie. And all the knick-knacks were dolphins. Little glass dolphins.

I took a seat, now looking around the living room, and discovered *even more* of them in here, secretively scattered on various surfaces— some on the shelves between pictures, a few on top of the entertainment center. There was even a little dolphin on the underpart of the coffee table that I had been resting my foot on, the discovery of which startled me.

Brenda snatched the remote off her coffee table and leaned her whole body into the button, like she *needed* the TV to be on. I didn't blame her. Everything was tense. The silence itself heavy, compressing, like the area of carpet that was crushed under the table's tiny hooves.

Light from the television washed over us. A spandex-clad and tightly pony-tailed woman materialized out of the formerly dead screen with news of a "new and revolutionary" workout program, which consisted mainly of jumping jacks and push-ups.

Brenda flipped through the channels. The workout lady disappeared and gave life to a troubled crew of Alaskan Fisherman, who evaporated into a group of young black kids doing some new dance, which turned into news coverage of an active war zone. It was shot in thermal imaging. Red and green blips, like a video game.

"Whaddya wanna watch?" she asked.

"Whatever, I don't really care."

Oddly, she settled on the news. The thermal warzone was replaced by a stern-faced reporter out on the scene of a homicide. Some little black girl had been hit by a stray bullet and died in the street while jump roping with her friends. A group of ladies cried around the mother of the child. The very stern and slick-haired reporter stood solemnly by, wearing fancy leather gloves and a four-hundred-dollar ski jacket. The reporter held a microphone to the girl's father as he broke down, crying into his hands. All the while, the reporter continued working the mic, moving it under the crying father's face as he twitched in spastic grief, capturing the gut-wrenching audio like a pro. There were people piling candles and teddy bears all around a telephone pole close to where the girl was inadvertently slain.

"Is this a plasma?" I asked Brenda.

"Yeah, I think," she replied, finally making eye contact. "Why?"

"I heard they get screen burn."

"What?"

The news cut to a terrorist attack. One hundred and fifty-eight people killed by a suicide bomber in North Africa.

"My uncle told me about them. The screen, for some reason, I don't know how, captures an image and burns it into the screen. I think if you pause it on something too long, the shadow of the image gets stuck, like a broken Etch-A-Sketch or something. My uncle said Alex Trebeck's face got burned into his."

"That's weird," said Brenda, totally uninterested.

"Yeah. Could you imagine if every time you vacuumed you had to look at that guy crying over his dead daughter on your screen?"

A different reporter was covering a story about Muslims being mistreated in the United States.

Brenda, ignoring my question and now visibly angry at the news, fell back in her seat in protest. "Oh, *fuck them*." She said.

I knew who she was talking about but pretended I didn't.

"Who?"

Brenda's face squeezed together, collapsing in an exaggerated disbelief of my naiveté. She had a few scars and indents, little ones, on various spots on her face. Childhood nicks and scratches. I always liked that, girls with little scars on their faces.

"*Muslims*, that's who. Why don't they go cry to the other Muslims who're blowing everyone up?"

The news switched to a pre-commercial break teaser, something about a deadly batch of fentanyl-laced heroin that we'd have to stay tuned to find out about.

I shifted in my seat. "Uh, yeah. I guess I can see what you're saying. So, do you want to smoke some weed?"

Brenda measured me up. "Oh, I'm sorry. Are you one of those easily offended PC types?"

I pulled the bag of weed out of my pocket and started rolling a joint. "Not really," I replied.

Brenda lifted her leg, and with the grace of a samurai woman, folded it under her butt. She leaned into me a little, rocking back and forth to get comfy. Her tank top dipped, opening a new horizon of cleavage which receded as she sat up. "No? So what do you think then?"

I shrugged, licking the joint. "I don't know. I guess I don't really care enough to research it or anything. But I mean, I *get* where the clear majority of Muslims who *don't* go around killing people are coming from. And I also get where you're coming from about them not speaking out against ISIS and shit—I just, I don't know. Who the fuck really knows what's going on over there anyway?

"That's a bullshit response." Brenda started skipping through the channels.

"I mean, it's not that I don't care. I do. I care about people. I want people to be happy. And I think if everyone just focused on each other rather than themselves, the world would be better off. And yeah, radical Muslims should stop blowing shit up—but guess what—so should we. No one straps a bomb to their chest and destroys a mall for no reason. I'm sure the US isn't totally innocent in all of this."

Brenda stopped flicking through the channels. "Innocent has nothing to do with it. You live here, this is your team. Every country wants our spot so they try to fuck us up. That's all there is—it's all just bad people fucking with each other and we're the poor fucks who have to deal with it."

I shook my head. "It's not that simple."

Brenda readjusted her leg and scooted toward me. "Well then, explain it to me," she said, moving into the field of unoccupied space between us, her body heat now a palpable reality to be sensed and biochemically registered on my part. Her breath smelled like gum mixed with the dry white stuff on a toothbrush. She had five freckles on her chest and one in the middle of her neck, right where an Adam's apple would have been on a guy. The smells—lotion, shampoo, perfume, conditioner, candles, hand-sanitizer, and deodorant— swirled, reducing the quality of my thoughts to a thin, low-hanging fog. I didn't care about the other stuff anymore. Terrorism, bombs, murder, inequality—all the world's ills had taken a back seat to this erosion of personal space, that tractor beam feeling.

She looked at me from her new spot on the couch, supporting her head by the palm of her hand, like a kid bored in detention. The towel, now a cotton Tower of Pisa, tilted.

"Well?" she asked, from her new territory on the couch.

Sixteen years of schooling and not a single fucking iota of applicable knowledge. All I had was mush about "being nice" and the "golden rule." I sat there, blabbering a sort of intro to my non-answer, and it struck me—all of my core beliefs, my entire mental essence, was nothing but a hollow construction, a papier-mâché of vapid idealistic conclusions I'd arrived at while really high. I felt duped, betrayed by all my wordless stoned epiphanies. I couldn't explain any of it. I just knew we were supposed to be nice, but even that was stupid.

I threw my hands up. "I don't know, I'm too dumb."

Brenda's neck craned back slightly, her mind working, trying to construct a quick insult or a smart-alecky remark, but something else happened. A facial computation error. A smile.

"You're a fucking nut," she said, smacking my arm. Her shoulders bounced as she laughed and then she popped up. "Oh, I think the wine's cold now!"

Brenda came back with a frosted bottle of Cabernet and set two mugs down on the table. She took the towel off her head and shook her hair out. It was still wet, bogged in rows of crimpy brown clumps darkened by moisture.

She filled the mugs to the brim. Mine spilled over.

"Oops," she said, wiping it away with her finger and licking it off. "Here, sip yours down so we can cheers. We'll drink this bottle and then I'll get ready."

I ashed the joint and passed it to Brenda. "You want us to drink the whole bottle?"

She pinched the joint between her slender fingers, inspecting it like a long-forgotten artifact. She took two hits and coughed. "*Hoockh*, where'd you *get* this shit?" she asked, holding the joint back out for me to take.

I shrugged. "Friend of mine."

Brenda, holding her throat and still coughing, raised her mug to mine. After we toasted, she drank greedily, continuing to nurse her trachea. I sipped my wine. It was ice-cold with a gelatinous texture. Cup over face, she watched me, using her other hand in a lifting motion, telling me to drink. I raised the cup back to my lips and relaxed my throat. The cold wine flowed in, somehow converting into a tingly warmth in my chest. We set our empty mugs down on the table. Brenda poured them full again. The bottle was over half empty.

"Damn, you can really drink, huh?" I said.

She scrunched her face. "Seriously? We're just drinking some wine. And, honestly, no, I'm not a big drinker at all. I only drink wine sometimes."

"Oh, I was just saying. Judging how you drank it and all."

"What's that supposed to mean?"

"Nothing," I said, arching over to suck some wine off the surface before lifting the mug. "Just, you know, you're drinking fast. Reminds me of college."

"Wouldn't know about that," she said. "Never went."

"Yeah, I only went for two years and then I stopped."

"Why?"

"I don't know. At the time...I just felt like—a piece of coal."

"Coal? You quit college because you felt like coal?"

"Yeah, I felt like I was *fueling* this system, something I hated and despised on a deep level. All the buying and selling, the bosses and commercials, the strange obsession of mass production and consumption. I didn't want to be part of it. I don't know, I just started hating it. Hating everything. The teachers, the students, myself. I used to sit in those classes and watch my peers give their presentations, young kids jacked up on hot caffeinated liquids and business casual dress, and I'd imagine them igniting into flames, spontaneously combusting under the force of the market, escaping as a gasp of steam from an industrial whistle."

Brenda sank into the couch. She held her mug in two hands against her lap. She raised it to her lips and slowly sipped.

"I'm sorry. Just drink it however you want. I feel like a dick now."

"Huh?" she asked.

"I was saying about the wine. Just drink it—"

"I'm fucking *stoned!*" she burst out. "Is this how you felt when you came in here?"

I rubbed my mug, hoping to somehow warm its contents with the friction of my hands. "Yeah, a little," I laughed.

"Fuck," she said, looking around her house with a mask of terrified awe. She picked her wine up and toasted me again, spilling it on her lap. Covering the crimson stain on her sweatpants with one hand, she raised her mug to her lips and drained its contents. I followed suit, drinking mine in several labored gulps.

"I'm, like, *super* high," she said, wiping her mouth. Her teeth were highlighted purple, dark stains edged her gums.

I hit the joint two more times and licked my finger to put it out. She refilled our mugs again, eliminating the bottle altogether. I pushed mine away. My head was already swirling.

"You have to give me a second. I'm really not—"

Brenda lifted the mug and put it in my lap. She let go, forcing me to grab it. My erection, which was reawakened thanks to the mug, stirred under the surface of my jeans. I was fully hard now—no negotiation.

Brenda stood up. "I feel like the couch is sucking me in! You ever get like that when you're high? Like the couch is sucking you in? That's normal, right? Holy shit! This has happened before! On this *exact* couch!" She paced along the coffee table and stopped. "Did you notice that picture of JFK?"

"Where?"

"The one hanging in the dining room. Look."

I got up and checked it out. There was a small picture of JFK, a kind of presidential headshot hanging on wall next to the glass case. It was drastically off-center, favoring the right side of the wall. "Yeah, so what?"

"My mom put it up! Oh my God, am I one of those weirdos?"

"Which kind?"

Brenda stopped pacing and addressed me head-on. "Like, one of those people who lives in a house filled with a dead person's stuff. It's creepy, right? Oh my God, am I *creepy?*

I walked over and grabbed her shoulders. "It's okay. You're just a little stoned. Let's—"

"Ew!" Brenda jumped away.

I followed Brenda's eye line to the crotch of my jeans, dreadfully remembering the denim-clad erection that was now protruding out into time and space. "I'm—I know it's—I swear it has nothing to do with death or grief or anything like that, I promise."

Brenda's eyes widened.

"No, no, no. Sorry—it, it's from when you pushed down on my crotch with the mug. It's a biological—you have to—it's actually very normal," I stammered.

Brenda stood, overwhelmed, leaning at an awkward angle as she minced her socks into the rug. Her heels pistoned minutely, reducing crumbs into nano-crumbs deep within the carpet floor. "I'm sorry. I-I can't go," she said. "There's no way—" she stopped as if suddenly nauseated. "Why did I even *agree* to go?"

"You didn't actually *agree*," I said, sitting back down on the couch. "You offered." I smacked my lips in an effort to determine the state of my mouth. It was dry, coated with that gross alcohol feeling, like I'd swallowed a bunch of baby powder.

Brenda turned her back to me to study the picture of JFK. The dog barked downstairs and my heart skipped a beat. All the good smells from before were gone. All I could taste or smell was wine. It was more of an oily feeling than a baby powder one. Strange that we drink flammable liquids to relax, I thought.

"Look, I get if you don't want to go. Shit, I wouldn't either if I had a choice. It's gonna be brutal."

A plug-in air freshener sprayed its chemical mist, a pseudo-tropical odor that reminded me of sunscreen. The mist fell directly onto Brenda's head as she stood transfixed by all her bequeathed décor.

"God, the old ladies," I continued, "it's so sad. Seeing them sitting there like time travelers. Always nodding their heads too. Did you ever notice that? How old people grab your arm when they talk to you? It's like they're trying to drag you back into the past. And my *dad*...Jesus, I don't feel like hearing his shit."

The thermostat ticked and the heat kicked on. The low hum of forced air whooshed behind some unidentifiable spot of the wall.

"What's your dad's deal?" Brenda asked, sitting down like nothing ever happened.

I stopped, half-thinking to question the radical shift of mood, but decided to leave it alone, picking up my mug of wine and sipping from it instead. Brenda looked right at me. Her eye contact was precise, penetrative in a way that I wasn't very comfortable with. The mug made a satisfying knocking noise when I put it back down on the table. Heavy glass against heavy wood. Very nice. Complete in a way.

"I don't know. He's just, like, thinks he's the shit, or something, because he kept the same dumb job for so many years. I just—you'd have to meet him for yourself. It's hard to explain."

"Do you think he's disappointed in you?" she asked, sipping her wine.

I forced a laugh. "*Think?* No, he's made his disappointment abundantly clear, trust me. I mean—" I picked the half-smoked joint up off the table and lit it up. "This is going to sound weird."

"Weirder than you trying to comfort me with your boner?"

I shot her a sideways glance, "I'm serious."

She nodded in reply.

"Okay, so you know how you're basically just a mix of your mom and dad?"

"Yeah. Now that you mention it, I *have* heard something like that before. Something about a sperm and an egg, right?"

I ashed the joint and coughed, passing it toward Brenda but she declined. "No, really. It's like, I'm a man, but I exhibit more tendencies from my mother if that makes sense. I have similar mannerisms, thoughts, views, we both get really bad anxiety attacks, and I don't know, but I think it may be confusing for my dad, like some crazy sexual Freudian shit he doesn't understand that plagues his subconscious to the point where he *just doesn't like me* but is really battling this primordial attraction to the woman he sees inside me, my anima, I guess, but doesn't know why, and all these years he sublimated his hatred into his stupid job at Evermore Tires, which was basically his way of conquering his own psychological—"

Brenda pulled the joint out of my mouth. She finished her wine and dropped it into her mug. The orange, incandescent tip gasped and went grey in the purple liquid.

"Or, maybe your dad just thinks you're a loser because you sit around and smoke pot all day, concocting these sicko, paranoid theories. Please tell me you've never told him that, that whole *thing* you just told me?"

I shook my head. "No way, it would blow his mind."

Brenda curled up against the couch. "I'm gonna be honest, Joel."

We were far apart now, mentally and physically. My boner totally dead, record-breaking in terms of flaccidity and inertness.

"The only reason I agreed to go to your dad's party, which—" she checked her watch—"has definitely started about an hour ago, was because of my ADHD medicine. I took a little too much before my interview."

"Really?" I scoffed. "ADHD?"

"What the fuck's that supposed to mean?" Brenda sat up perfectly straight, folding her hands across her lap as if our weird date had somehow become a high-powered business meeting.

I dusted my jeans in preparation to leave. "Nothing, I just, I don't know. I haven't met many *adults* with ADHD and honestly, Brenda, if you want to do Ritalin or Adderall, that's your business, I'm not John."

"John-the-fuck-who?" she asked, clearly incensed.

"Brenda. I think—"

"Who, Cork over there? Has John Cork been talking shit?"

"Brenda, no, please, he hasn't, I was just saying. He seems like a tight ass who *would* be against drugs and stuff. I'm just letting you know I'm not like that."

Brenda leaned back, eyeing me incredulously. "Yeah, well, that's pretty weird considering we've—me and John—have had some pretty intense *discussions* about him going around spreading rumors about me being a drug addict. And here you are bringing him up in that *exact* context." She leaned forward again, folding her hands in that business-like manner. Her breasts dangled—no that seems too meat-like and graceless—*rippled* forward through the opening in her shirt, abandoning the safety of her bra due to the change of gravity from the new tilt in her bodily axis. "What the fuck did he say, Joel?" she said punctuating every word with a slap to the back of her hand, thus propelling the ripple.

"He just said your sister's a drug addict, nothing about you I swear!"

Brenda got up and grabbed her coat.

"He's not home, if that's where you're headed."

"How the fuck do you know?"

"Because I saw him at the liquor store. He was headed into that bar next to it, the place near the movies."

"The Thirsty Bulldog?" She grabbed her purse. "Fine, I'll just go there then."

Blood rushed to my head as I stood up off her sofa. My heart palpitated twice. I patted it reassuringly and stepped in front of the door. "You can't go," I said.

"Sorry, but I'm not going to your dad's stupid ass party, now fucking move."

I dug into my pocket for my phone. Brenda shifted her weight to the left, bracing her face into an expression of gross disbelief. I think she thought I was doing something with my dick.

"Trust me," I said, still fumbling around in my pockets. "Just hold on a second."

Brenda crossed her arms.

I pulled my phone out and opened it to the video. "Here, go ahead. It's from earlier today."

The front door burst open as Brenda grabbed my phone. Lynne stumbled in behind the guy who'd picked her up earlier that day, the dude with the greasy hair. Her meaty arms clung around his skinny waist from behind.

"The hell are you and gay-boy doin' in here?" she asked, laughing. Her speech was shaded with a somnolent gurgle. Her eyes drooped dumbly.

The guy straightened up and shook my hand, doing his best impression of a sober person. "Donny Falcone, bro."

Brenda's eyes opened wide. "Holy fucking shit! Is that John? Check it out, Lynne. Restart it."

Lynne grabbed Brenda's wrist and pulled the phone close to her face. Her permanent squint melted into motherly concern. I stood over their shoulders and watched. The footage was shaky and a bit grainy, but it was unmistakable: Cork roasting the evil hippy's dreads over the fire. The audio was off, thank God.

"*Hoo-lee* fuckin' shit! Donny, call Clay," Lynne muttered. "Fuckin' call 'im right now."

Donny came over and put his hand over Lynne's, moving the phone to his face. Brenda pulled her hand out of the pile and got behind them to watch as Cork threw Clay into the blazing steel drum. The camera focused on a bag of pizza-flavored Combos melting—and then shook violently as I must have started to run. The screen went black.

My phone buzzed and lit up. My mom was calling.

Donny grabbed my shoulder. "Bro, send me that video. Bro!"

I snatched my phone and headed for the door. My head pulsed in crushing pumps of panic. Feigning calm and naturalness, I held my vibrating phone out to the thunderstruck trio and nodded, signaling that everything was cool and that I just needed to take this call from my mom and it was no big deal. Donny and Lynne were locked in creepy eye contact as if engaging in an opiate-induced telekinesis. My heart palpitated, a bad triple quiver. Brenda searched my face as I turned around and stepped out into the cold.

Brenda

Cold air ripped through the room as Joel slammed the door. Donny clenched his teeth and muttered something to Lynne; She nodded and sat down. The heat kicked on and hummed.

"You gotta get us that video, Bren."

I smelled Donny's cologne as he walked past me, pulling a bag of pills out of his pocket and digging a few out. He dropped four pills, little blue ones, onto the table. They bounced and rattled on the wood as he crashed down next to Lynne. "Lynne's right, Brenda. Either dude sends us a copy 'cause he *wants* to, or he sends it 'cause he *has* to. Know what I mean?"

"No, actually, I don't know what you mean. And what the fuck are those? Lynne, get that shit out of here. I have company."

Lynne picked one of the pills up and held it in her fingers. "Thirty-milligram oxycodones, Bren. Clay's got a pill connect from the hospital. He went after John—I can't fuckin' *believe* it was Cork, Jesus!—he went after John beat his ass and got an assload of scripts. I mean *everything*, Bren."

"Yeah, bro," Donny agreed. "Clay's the man right now. He's gettin' everyone money. He'd probably make a straight up trade with you. A couple scripts of thirties for that video."

Lynne reached under the couch and grabbed a rusty set of pliers. She put her license over each pill and cracked it into powder, separating the coatings as she went along. She stretched the blue powder into two long lines with her driver's license. Donny rolled two twenties and handed one to Lynne. They went down and vacuumed the powder off the table.

I peeked out the window. Joel was gone.

"So much for being sober, huh?"

Donny nudged Lynne and went to the kitchen to rinse his nose out in the sink. Lynne sat back and sniffed everything as far up into her brain as she could. The thermostat clicked and the heat stopped.

"Yeah, yeah, yeah," Lynne mumbled through her stuffed nose. "Ol' Saind, Brenda." She pulled a tissue out of her jacket and blew. "Seriously, Bren," she said from behind the tissue, "two scripts of sixty thirties, that's like three G's."

"What's he even gonna do with it?"

Donny walked back into the room inspecting the twisted paper towel he'd been probing his nose with. "Where should I put this?"

"Um, how about the trash?" I said annoyed.

"Where is it?"

Lynne went to get off the couch and then stumbled back and fell. Donny started cracking up.

"Yo! I tried to tell you about those thirties. Shits are legit. I *told* you," he said, clapping his fist into the back of his hand.

Lynne, a little embarrassed, got up and grabbed the napkin from Donny and they both disappeared into the kitchen. I went back to the window and parted the curtain. Joel's living room light was on.

Lynne came back and grabbed her ID off the table.

"You gotta tell them somethin' by tonight, Bren. Or they're gonna roll up on gay-boy."

***

A cat darted out from under a parked car and pounced on an empty bag of chips as the wind blew it down the sidewalk. I kicked a nerf football out of my way and wrapped my coat around myself. What was left of the snow glistened under the moonlight, web-like patches of ice up and down along the sidewalk from where the plow came. There was a pile in the cul-de-sac, a dirty-white mountain full of leaves and gravel.

Joel's gate whined as it opened. His house was the only one on the block with a bricked-in front yard. The lady who lived there before him was this crazy old woman. She built four-foot brick walls around the front and back. John told me she had him paint her basement floor pink when he was younger.

I opened Joel's storm door and knocked on the one behind it. My knuckles felt like they could shatter in the cold. The hum of the TV quieted. Things shuffled around and stopped. The door unlocked and opened in a sudden, paranoid swing.

Joel stood in the doorway wearing a sweatsuit. He looked down at his dirty socks and mumbled, "Sorry I just—I don't want problems with Cork."

I barged past Joel and went inside.

His house was warm and comfy, but it stunk. It smelled like weed mixed with a dirty sponge. Joel's eyes were red and puffy like he'd been crying. A bird hopped along the screen of his huge 70-inch TV. He was watching one of those nature shows on Discovery.

"Yeah, well, I wouldn't worry about Cork if I were you."

Joel sulked across his parquet floor looking beyond pathetic in his sweatsuit. "You saw what he did!" he whisper-screamed. "Imagine what Cork would do to someone he *actually* had a problem with."

I moved a blanket out of my way and sat down. He had one of those wraparound couches. It was black, made from fake leather. The part of the blanket I touched was a little crusty, but it could have been a burn.

"True, but that kid he beat up, he's connected to some pretty serious people and apparently they're gonna come looking for *you* if you don't give them the video."

I rubbed my hands off on my jeans.

"Who? That hippy? The kid he beat the shit out of? Yeah right."

"Clay's a junkie, Joel. He's all tied in with coke and dope dealers. Bad fucking people."

An eagle swooped down on screen and grabbed a field mouse in its talons, rising back into the blue sky as it flapped and flew away. The shot faded, zooming in on rings of light coming from the sun until it all become this abstract blob that cut to a dog food commercial.

"Hey, do what you want. But you should probably just give the video to Clay. Let him and Cork fight about it. It's not like Cork will know it came from you."

Joel chewed on his remote. He put a hand down his sweatpants and stared at the TV. "Remember how I told you I saw John outside that bar, the Thirsty Dog?"

"Thirsty Bulldog, yeah, why?"

"Yeah, bulldog, whatever. He kept grilling me about where I was before your thing with Fig. You know, before I broke it up."

"Can we not mention that ever again?"

"Okay, well, either way. It's like he *knows*. The whole thing's bugging me out. And now, my fucking mom—"

"Oh, shit! The party. Get some clothes on, c'mon."

Joel shot me a curious look, like I was dumb for even bringing it up.

"My anxiety's through the roof."

"Oh, come on."

"I've been fighting off a panic attack since I took that video, and now I have a gang of evil hippies to worry about? Do you know what they do?"

"Who?"

"The GDF?"

"What the fuck are you talking about? No."

"There's this nationwide gang of evil hippies, the Grateful Dead Family, who bum around from festival to festival selling K, molly, acid, weed—mostly psychedelic shit, but they also dabble in coke and pills—real drugs. And the way they handle, I guess, conflicts, you could say, is they spin people out on huge doses of acid, which, as much as I hate to admit, is the perfect revenge. Totally evil."

Joel watched as I dug through my purse. I found a bottle Xanax and dumped one out.

"Here, this should help."

"What is it?"

"It's Xanax. 1 milligram."

Joel recoiled in disbelief. "You want me to pile a benzo on top of weed and alcohol and then go to my Dad's retirement party, which I'm already two hours late for?"

"You drank two glasses of wine."

"Three."

"Oh, don't be such a pussy, here!" I grabbed some of the loose change off his table and split the pill with a dime. "This is *half* a milligram. It's like drinking *one* more glass of wine. Unless of course you're a thirty-year-old man who is still too terrified of his parents to go to some family party—"

"I'm not scared of my parents," he said, snatching both halves of the pill off the table and popping them. "I'm just careful about what I put in my body. I have a sensitive system."

"Spoken like a true pussy."

The TV zoomed out to a wide shot of the African Serengeti. A group of birds flew into the neon sunset as I wondered about the spot on Joel's blanket, the crusty one I had touched.

"Go get changed so we can go."

"Wait. I thought you said—"

I stood up and pushed him toward the steps. "Go!"

***

Joel came back downstairs after what seemed like forever wearing a pair of jeans and a plaid button-down dress shirt that, for some unknown reason, had leather patches stitched over the elbows. He smelled like that shitty natural deodorant mixed with the stuff they spray on yoga mats.

"You look like an English teacher."

Joel dug his heel into the ground and hit a spin. Drops of water flew off his wet head and splattered on his big TV, causing this weird inner-rainbow effect as they slid down.

"A sexy ass English teacher," he replied.

He stopped before heading toward the door, holding his two index fingers up as if he'd just remembered something important and headed into the kitchen. The refrigerator whooshed opened, something banged on the counter, and then a bag rustled. Another whoosh and it shut. Joel came back into his living room with puffed out cheeks, chewing.

"I thought you said there's gonna be food here?"

Joel smiled disgustingly, showing chunks of soggy crumbs stuck to random spots on his teeth. "Iz a wee muffin," he said, stoned eyes crinkling as he smiled.

"Jesus." I ripped the keys out of his hands and opened the door, flinching as freezing air ripped across my face.

Joel pushed by me and walked outside. "The cruel winds of outer space," he muttered.

I shivered, fumbling with Joel's stupid key as I tried to unlock his truck. Joel, licking the last of the muffin from his teeth, smiled at the stars. The sky was deep, velvety purple, brightened from the moon. The wind threw my hair wildly.

"Don't you have one of those beepy things?"

"What, a key fob? "

I finally popped the door open and got in. The inside of his truck was somehow colder than outside. I brushed some sunflower seeds out from between my legs and stomped my boots down on empty water bottles. Joel peered in from outside, fogging his window on purpose like a dick. I reached over and opened his door, so he'd get in.

"No," I said, trying to start the car, "a key fob's one of those things people attach to keys, like a decoration."

"I thought that was a key*chain*."

A graveyard of water bottles crinkled under his feet as he pulled his seatbelt across and clicked it in. Every possible warning light was on and his truck *reeked* like weed.

"Jesus, Joel! This thing's about to explode."

"Just need her to get me to California and I'll be okay," he said, lovingly tapping the dash.

The engine turned over after a few cranks. It knocked and rattled. A belt whined and stopped. Joel picked some of the water bottles up and stuffed them behind the seat. I picked some of the trash up from the driver's side and followed his lead.

"You'd be lucky to make it to Pittsburgh."

Joel shrugged as we pulled off.

"Seriously, though. Your house? Your car? You're a fucking mess, dude."

"I'm depressed," he replied, tracing a happy face in the foggy window.

We made a left and pulled out past the cemetery. The graves were all old and broken, leaning in different directions like bad teeth. They were especially creepy tonight as the blotches of surviving snow, which had hardened into ice, now reflected the moonlight back on them.

"Just because you're depressed doesn't mean you have to live like a piece of shit."

"Yeah, it does, it's the whole point of being depressed."

I turned right on Ridge and stopped next to the Speedway gas station, lifting my hand off the wheel to check the gas as I waited for the light. "You know you only have a quarter tank, right?"

Joel waved me off. "Plenty. This place isn't far."

"You're not supposed to go below a quarter tank in the winter. The cold air—moisture or whatever, gets into your tank and fucks up your car."

"Are you sure you're not confusing moisture with *time*? I mean—" Joel tapped on the glass. "Holy shit! Is that John's *son*? Look!"

The Speedway's glass doors burst open behind Fig as he tore down the street. The store was owned by an Indian family. A Grandfather, father, and son. They were the only people who ever worked there, except for the rare occasion when one of their wives would fill in, but that was usually not the case. The middle owner—we called him #2— chased behind Fig. His silk shirt flapped violently in the wind as he took off, fast as his leather dress shoes would allow.

A truck hit its air brakes, letting out a deep *whomp* as Fig darted across the street. A chorus of horns sounded, a hair-raising melody of different makes and models. Fig cleared the street and headed for the woods. #2 stopped on the edge of the sidewalk. He leaned over and panted, pressing his hands against his knees. His Bluetooth earpiece blinked rapid-fire bursts of urgent light.

Fig sprinted up a hill and disappeared into the woods as the light turned green.

"Oh my God," I said, hitting the gas. "What do you think he did?"

Joel shrugged. "Probably stole something. Hey, uh, can I get one more of those things?"

"You sure that's a good idea? You already seem a little fucked up."

"Fucked up? No, I'm in party mode. Make a left here."

"Party mode?" I looked at Joel through the rearview. "Are you serious?"

Joel pointed. "Turn right."

"Ugh, please tell me we're *not* going to the Elks."

"Thought it was a Moose lodge." Joel rolled his bottom lip out in thought. "Must have my deer-themed bars—"

"I'll make you a deal."

"Up here—"

I searched my purse with a blind hand, splitting my attention between the road. "Yeah, I know where it is. How about I give you the rest of my Xanax for the video? Here, there's like six left."

I pulled into the Elks parking lot and killed the lights. The building was a tan, windowless square with filmy glass doors. Rusted metal cages covered the windows and the weather stripping stuck out in spots. A dark water stain ran down from the top left, starting where the gutter was severed near the roof. The door's glass glowed with expired light, trapped and stained by time, the decades of tobacco smoke. An older woman with short spiky hair stood outside in an orange vest. She was waving us up to park somewhere else. Ignoring her, I pulled the pills out of my purse and parked between a lopsided conversion van and a Mercedes station wagon.

"Do we have a deal?"

Joel pulled his phone out. His head dropped, chin to chest, neck fat bulging in a way that wasn't exactly flattering. His eyes hung half-opened as he ran his finger across his phone screen.

"This little video here?" he giggled. "Of course."

"Dude, there's no way you're this—" I checked the bottle of Xanax, they were the two-milligram bars, not the ones I thought.

He leaned in for a kiss and was abruptly stopped by the palm of my hand. The spiky headed woman in the vest threw her hand in the air and approached the car. Joel threw his phone onto the seat and opened the door. The interior light came on.

"1-2-3-4 is the password. And thanks again for the ride, Brendini."

He kissed my hand as he slid out of the truck on his stomach, landing in a froggy squat. I grabbed his wrist. "Joel, hold on!"

He pulled his arm away and started to walk off, straight toward the lodge's dim glow, traveling in odd, shuffled steps. The lady in the vest grabbed one of her glowstick things and held it up to see what he was doing. Joel's hands were in his pockets and he was looking at his feet, head bobbing as he went along. I got out and zipped my jacket, splitting my attention between Joel and my phone as I sent myself the video. The wind yanked the driver side door and slammed it into the side of the station wagon. I grabbed my purse and got out, ramming the door shut with my shoulder, using my entire body against the force of the wind as I texted my sister.

300 ills for vid. Will send when they're in my hand.

"Joel! Wait up."

I got closer to the door's mustard light and looked inside my bag. The one-milligram bars were in another bottle, jammed behind my coin purse and under some crooked tampons. The woman in a vest approached. Under the vest, she wore a leather jacket and baggy cargo pocket sweats. Some of her teeth were missing and the rest were barely worth keeping, tan and swirled with stains that reminded me of a countertop pattern.

The doors opened. A short, older lady with an impossibly big head came outside clutching her husband's arm. The couple shook when they walked, moving in a mutual vibration, crushing their bodies together in the cold.

The old man waved at Joel, his arm moving in slow tics like it was under an invisible strobe light. "Ho! Is that Joel Jr?"

Joel kissed the old man on his cheek and walked inside.

Fig

I tripped over a rock and rolled down a hill of dead sod, into the new neighborhood that my dad hated, one of those yuppie developments with Lego-looking houses. My dad said if he wanted to he could break into these places with nothing but a razor knife. Slice the vinyl siding, kick through the plywood and sheetrock and kill the whole family—of course only if he wanted to. I thought about the trucker who honked his horn when I ran out in the street. My dad told me about truckers. He said most of them are freaks who can't get along in society, crazy sexual deviants who do gay stuff with each other off at those turnpike rest stops.

Some skinny husband came out of his sliding glass doors. One of those young dads with a beard and tattoos who carried his baby in a papoose like one of those ladies from national geographic. The same guy that always bitched at me for cutting through his yard.

"Hey, can you please—"

I picked a rock up off the ground and launched it at his house. "Fuck off!"

It was getting dark—or purple really. Night was starting, but not officially. The neighborhood's windows lit up, one at a time, reminding me of fireflies in the summer. It let me get a look inside of the houses. They all looked so warm and comfortable.

I saw a family sitting around a table. All of them eating a big dinner, surrounded by huge plates of food. Sides galore, maybe five or six options. The mom stood by the side of the table dumping what looked like big spoonfuls of mashed potatoes on everyone's plates. The dad waved his arms in the air telling a story and everyone laughed—dad, mom, and two kids.

An old dog got up off their back porch and started barking his head off, some dumb slobbering lab. I let it get close. I whistled and cajoled it over and then kicked it right in the snout before running into the woods.

I finally got to me and Brian's secret spot. We set it up last summer. Perfect location. Right in the middle of the woods between our houses and halfway up the hill, which was awesome since no one could see us. There were a ton of bushes and a shitload of thorns on each side. In the middle of the thorns was this little clearing. Inside that was this dilapidated old cottage with only two walls left. They weren't that high, just about four feet. Our fort was right in the corner of the mossy "L" shaped walls. Me and Brian dug a hole and lined it with trash bags so our shit didn't get wet. We covered it up with some junk plywood and kicked leaves over it so people didn't notice.

I lifted the plywood and rummaged through our stash. We had a few porno mags, a couple of M-80's, bottle rockets, matches, a condom, a silver necklace I stole from the mall, a pair of cheetah panties Brian found on the ground, and some other shit. I moved the panties to the side and found the little corncob pipe I'd discovered under the bleachers at our school. One of the older kids told me that the black shit in there was res and we smoked it. Me and Brian tried smoking some other shit with it, too. Nothing crazy, just like tea and coffee. Stuff we found around the house.

I flipped my empty paint bucket over so I could sit. It landed with a hollow thump on the cold ground. It was nighttime now, just like that. It snuck right by. Which always threw me how it does that, gets dark all of a sudden. I took a couple deep breaths and blew into my hands to warm them up. I was nervous to smoke the stuff I stole from the gas station.

The one was called *Spice* and the other packet said *Salvia 40x*.

I didn't plan on stealing them at first. My original plan was to buy three energy drinks with the change I took from my dad's jug. I was going to chug them and run around the woods. I liked to get hyped on

Monster and karate kick baby trees down. The best was when some of the bigger trees got dry rotted. The branches would explode.

I opened the one that said *Spice* and dumped some into my pipe. It took me a couple tries with the match since the pack was old but I finally got it to light. The smoke was harsh but it tasted good, like air freshener. My first inhale was light, real pussy-ish. I exhaled and hit it again—this time breathing harder. I kept hitting it until it felt like my throat was on fire and then I coughed.

At first, I thought the stuff was bunk. I didn't feel high at all. But then, after I don't know how long, I looked up. The moon was gone from the sky. Everything was pure black. I panicked, thinking it had disappeared. Then my mind went blank. I tried to think about whatever I was thinking about before but couldn't remember. I started to nerd out, thinking I'd forgotten everything I ever knew and then, out of nowhere, the clouds parted. I saw the moon and remembered what I had been thinking about; It was the moon.

I thought about some of the wrestling moves my coach showed me the day before and all these different combinations came to me. It was weird how they all just popped into my head. I sat, trying to think what a thought *actually* was, which was hard since my thoughts about thoughts were trapped inside of other thoughts.

My body felt light, like I was in one of those dreams where I floated when I jumped. I moved around my little fort in the woods, pretend wrestling, attacking an imaginary opponent. I wanted to wrestle someone so bad, practice these new moves. I would have knocked up for Brian, but it was late and there was no way I was going to face his mom like this. I'd end up having to wrestle my dad instead. This made me giggle, the thought of my dad wrestling me instead of kicking my ass.

There was a pressure building in my head, like someone put a bike pump in my ear and pumped it a hundred times. I noticed the pressure went away when I moved, so I started to run. Fast as I could, just to keep my head from exploding.

The shrubs and trees glowed in the moonlight. Not to sound gay or anything, but they seemed alive. Obviously, I knew from science class how plants are living things and how they had to soak up photosynthesis and shit, but they seemed alive in a *real* way. Like how people are.

I ran faster and faster, hopping over rocks and exposed roots. It made me feel like an Indian—not like the guy at the gas station, a real one, the badass kind. I understood why they called themselves animal names like Running Bear or Screaming Wolf. It made sense to me. Everything made sense.

I made it back to my spot and sat on my bucket. I packed my pipe with more of the spice and smoked the whole thing. I wanted to feel like this forever.

When the second round of spice kicked in, I was ready. The pressure came back, but I let it be. Sitting on the bucket, I folded my hands and closed my eyes. I could see things with them closed, squiggles and shit, blue waves of light bouncing around in my head. Eventually, the lights and squiggles faded and everything went black. It took me a few seconds to realize that everything went black because I had opened my eyes and was looking at the sky. I laughed. I'd never been this fucked up before. I closed my eyes and the blue waves came back. They formed into shapes, even changed colors. Indian animal names and how I wanted one. I got real quiet, hoping the woods would give me my own name. My mind, for the first time ever, was blank. There was absolutely nothing going on. It was like I was dead.

A while passed.

I tried to think of some of those wrestling moves, but they were like a dream I couldn't remember. I pulled out the other packet that said "Salvia 40x." I blew out the ash and stuffed some of the new stuff into my pipe, hoping it would be a little stronger.

The smoke from the salvia was way harsher than the spice and it tasted horrible, like a burning rubber band. I wanted this high to last longer so I kept hitting it over and over until I couldn't breathe. I coughed so hard that I fell off the bucket. I tried to get up but couldn't. My body was too heavy. The bucket tilted and fell over. I was on the ground but still felt like I was falling.

The trees stretched and bent away from each other, shooting all the way up into the sky. The stars vibrated, moving around like the blue squiggles I saw behind my eyelids. Then I felt something around me, like a ghost or spirit lurking in the woods, and fought to sit up but I was still too heavy. I could barely move my head.

And then I saw it: An old Indian warrior running through the woods, darting between the trees.

The warrior's neck stretched out from the tree, all the way to where I was laying. He had big yellow eyes, a long tongue, and sharp teeth. His body ran out from behind the tree and joined his head. He dug through the ground like a dog, kicking dirt between his legs, finally ripping a knife out of the ground like a plant, roots and all, with chunks of soil shaking off and crumbling against the earth as he raised it into the sky. His face grew angrier. It started to change and contort, blurring in and out of focus, finally settling into someone I recognized—my dad. He grabbed my shoulders with one hand and drove that dirty knife into my chest. I tried to yell but nothing came out. I was frozen. Moonlight bounced off the blade and lit my dad's face. I couldn't see anything else, just my dad's wrinkled, twisted smile—a real one. He spoke, but his words came out as total gibberish, something that sounded like an old dead language. I didn't know what he was saying, but from the look on his face I could tell he was *proud*. It seemed like he was telling me everything he'd always wanted to but couldn't—and then he stopped, realizing I couldn't understand him. He pulled the knife out of my chest and thrust it into his own.

I finally came to, shivering on the ground. I don't know how long I'd been lying there, but it seemed like years. Everything looked fuzzy, like the world was made from the soft side of Velcro.

Standing on shaky legs, I slid the plywood over the hole, kicked some leaves to cover it over and started walking up the hill toward my house. I felt as if I was in a foreign country. Everything looked *off*.

John

The Bulldog was jumpin'! Glasses clankin', people hootin' and hollerin'. Every spot on the bar was taken with plenty of folks millin' around the sides. A bunch of soft-lookin', long-haired types fiddled with their tangle of cords and instruments on stage. The drummer rapped his snare and yelled something to one of the security guys. There was a huge Gadsden flag hung up on the wall behind the band. Hell yeah.

I leaned forward on the bar and lit a cig. Took a nice hearty drag. Feels good after a couple. It's nice to watch the smoke rise, up toward the fog of other cigs, how when it gets closer to the fan it dips down and then zips up into the blades, mixing in with the smells of the kitchen before being shot out into the world.

The Bulldog was perfect, built like a bar should be. It was a square box of wood-paneled walls. Popcorn ceilings painted jet black with Christmas lights strung along in intersecting rows. Seven flatscreen TVs playing five different games. A take-out six-pack fridge with none of those faggy craft beers. Neon beer legos scattered across the walls along with funny signs. They said stuff like:

According To Chemistry, Alcohol is a SOLUTION!
And:
No Shirt. No Service. No Exceptions.
(Unless you're a lady 'cause then you drink for free!)

The clientele was typical in terms of what you'd expect. Guys with cut-sleeve neon shirts, repairmen in blue button downs, drunk grandpas—each with noses bigger and redder than the next—sickly lookin' office types, and girls with puffy bangs and dry skin. Of course, there were some other types, skinny tree guys with tattoos and bushy beards, the kind that made you wonder what the fuck happened when you looked at them.

It was all a guy could ask for. My only gripe was the bands. They used to be okay. Mainly buddy bands. Workin' guys coverin' hit songs. People knew the lyrics, the girls got to dancin'. Perfect. Everyone wins. But lately, they'd been bookin' these hippy bands. A bunch of fat forty-year-olds stoned out of their gourds banging on instruments like they were in a god damn garage with no one watchin'. Which of course attracted every two-bit wastoid in the tri-state area. They'd come and watch these burnouts cover Grateful Dead songs and other loser music, thirty-minute songs with no words. Had all the decent women glued to their seats while the scummier sorts twirled about like drug-crazed dodos. No time or rhythm, just pure chaos.

I think the change in musical bookings had something to do with the owner's new girlfriend. Ron owned and tended the bar. And as weird as he was—he had an earring and wore shorts all year round—I still admired him. Men who tended and oversaw their own business with pride were a dying breed. I could appreciate that. His new girlfriend, however, was another thing. One of those insufferable hippy kinds. She wore long patchwork dresses with thin, unnecessary scarves. Weird hats. Sometimes even shirts with illusions that messed up my eyes. She looked like a goddamn cross between a hobo and a witch. She had the body of a snowman and a face plainer than water, dead eyes and reoccurring acne. But, she did have somethin' goin' for her. Yup. One *crucial* thing—her birthdate. A whole twenty years after Ron's ex-wife's.

I stubbed my cig in the ashtray and dropped it in an empty plastic cup someone left on the bar. The z-shaped cig hissed in an inch of blue liquid. One of those fruity drinks. I sipped the spits of my beer down and wiggled the bottle at Ron. He acted like he didn't see me and served one of the freaks instead. I closed my eyes and took a breath to calm my thoughts. There were some bad ones spinnin' around about old Ron now, denying a vet's hard-earned pilsner for some piece of shit do-nothing's whiskey.

When I opened my eyes she was standin' there, Ron's girl, lookin' worse than ever. Lookin' like she hadn't slept in years.

"Coors light?"

I drummed my knuckles on the bar and nodded. "Yes, ma'am."

Two blondes came into the bar. Philly-U babes, no doubt. It was easy to tell when college chicks entered the Dog. The one girl pulled her hair out of her face and pointed at the band. Her friend nodded and looked around, clearly in awe as her eyes devoured every inch of the undiscovered watering hole for alphas. Probably her first time in a *real* bar, seeing *real* men drink *real* beer, a needed departure from her male peers—mushy-dick liberals drinking wine and cider. Her eyes hardened as she continued to sweep the room. It was all too clear what she was after. The one nodded to her ditsy friend and they approached, settin' up shop just two fat drunks down from me.

I nodded to the hobo-witch.

"Yeah?"

"Send those ladies two blackberry brandies. Tell 'em they got a secret admirer—and then point to me."

The girl groaned. "Ugh. Please reconsider."

"Excuse me, Stevie Nicks?"

She rolled her eyes. "It's just so— disgustingly *mannish*."

I pulled another five out of my wallet. "Ok, ok, I get it. A shot of blackberry brandy for you too. Don't want you feelin' all hurt and left out."

"Oh, Jesus. Please."

The hungry blonde looked my way and smiled. People were gettin' closer to the girls, a whole mess of jokers sucked into their orbit as we locked eyes. Scores of bong-brained weirdos hoverin' like flies, puffin' their bird-chests and talking a little louder than normal as they drifted under the gravitational force of true beauty, polluting the scene with their rank smell of pot and body odor.

"Just send 'em the goddamn shots, will ya!"

I slid a cig out my pack and lit up, grinning through the veil of smoke as I watched my plan kick into action. The sourpuss, to my absolute delight, forced herself to smile as she bestowed my gifts upon women much more attractive and lovely than her. And the girl's faces, oh how they lit up! The one I had my sights on beamed and looked away. Shy, but definitely ready, I thought as I swiveled my seat toward them and spread eagle, tippin' my cap and noddin' as the bartender stormed off. The girls giggled amongst themselves and downed the shots. The hungry blonde wiped her mouth and slid off her stool, headed right in my direction. I stubbed my cig on the bar and dropped it into the plastic cup with the other beerlogged butts as I prepared, straightenin' my shoulders and touchin' my hair.

Someone patted my back from behind. I didn't even bother to turn around. "Not right now, buddy."

They patted me again, this time a little harder.

"Dammit, what part of—"

The kid from the park stood grinnin' behind me. He was wearin' one of those Jamaican snow hats over his singed dreadlocks, big baggy corduroys, and a tattered sweatshirt. His head was wrapped in gauze. He seemed cleaned up, but still ugly as ever. His left eye was black and bruised and a gash ran down the bridge of his crooked nose. Another kid stood to his left. A young dago. Skinny with slicked back hair— mousse, not gel—wearing a velour sweatsuit and a pair of Timberland boots.

I swung around on my stool. "Sorry, boys. Maybe try the Purple Parrot down there in Center City. Might be more your speed."

"What, dude?" asked the dago, more like a threat than a question.

"It's a fag bar.

"Yeah, I know—"

The blonde tapped my other shoulder. "Hey, thanks for the shot. What was that?"

I swiveled back. "That, lil' miss thing, was a double of blackberry brandy. A token of my appreciation for decidin' to grace this hippy pigpen with your beauty. Helps cut down on the smells these crystal-sniffers tend to put off."

The dago shot his mouth off. "Don't get it twisted, bro. I ain't no fuckin' hippy."

I excused myself from the blond and turned around. "Hey, bud. I'm pretty sure there's a sign on the front door that clearly states you're not allowed to be wearing timberland boots in here. Oh, and is that a sports jersey I see under your gay little sweatshirt?"

"Yeah, aight."

The blonde put her little hand on my shoulder. Her touch was soft, gentle beyond anything I could understand. My insides floated as her hand slid across me.

"Hey, be nice!" she said as she moved past me toward the two mopes to my left. Colors exploded in my head as her tight butt rubbed my knees.

The band started its first song and the place exploded drowsily. Even the bartender girl threw her hands up and shook her frumpy self to the pitiful attempt at rhythm. The weed smell increased ten-fold.

"You good, Donny?" asked my blonde angel.

I was shocked. "You actually *know* these derelicts?"

Donny nodded. "Let's ditch the cop and go outside."

"Who the fuck are you callin' a cop, you wigger?"

The blonde recoiled in disgust. Even my stool neighbor to the right shivered. Pot smoke rose over our silence as the band entered a deeper level of idiocy, entrancing the crowd of burnouts with more of their nonsense. Instruments clanged about on separate agendas like they were all playin' different songs.

"That's *so* racist," she said.

Donny stuck his tongue out behind her head. "Yeah, bro, *so* racist. C'mon, let's go."

"Maybe you're right," I said getting up out of my stool. My feet hit the ground and sent tingles up my legs. Red spots floated in my field of vision. My legs felt strong, but unbalanced, like my center of gravity was changin' by the second. "But, I'm not about to let you wander off with that knucklehead druggie and—"

The red dots merged into a blob. The liquor bottles, people's skin—everythin' was red. Except the ceiling. That was more maroon. Suddenly, I felt top heavy, like a tree getting' hacked from the bottom. My legs quivered and I crashed into the bar. The people around me laughed as I pulled myself back onto my stool.

Donny snorted as he walked outside with the blonde, his voice trailin' off at the door. "Yeah bro, how about you worry about whatever *you're* on. Dude can't even walk, and he wants to tell me how to live *my* life!"

Ron's girlfriend waved and smiled. "Hi, Clay."

The hippy smiled. "Hey, Sammy."

Sammy narrowed her eyes, giving me a bratty look as she slid a whiskey in front of Clay, her lips pursed in smug satisfaction, a victory of sorts. Clay nodded and sipped lightly. Samantha lingered, lookin' back and forth at us.

I snuck a foot to the floor to test it. It felt like I could bust through the tile, all the energy in my legs, but I still couldn't move. It was horrible.

Clay leaned over. "That's the Datura kicking in."

"Who?"

"Jimson weed," offered Samantha. "One of a witch's many tricks."

Ron came behind the bar to mess with the icemaker. He slid the plastic door open and bowed into the steaming ice below. His foot was tappin' to the rhythm.

"Hey, Ron."

Ron pulled his head out of the ice. "Yeah?"

He stood in front of the ice machine with his arms danglin' by his sides, lookin' back and forth between me and Samantha and then at Clay. The band was louder than ever. Distortion. Echo. Wah-wah. The whole spread.

Ron, still standin' there like an ape, said, "What's up?"

Samantha yelled over the noise. "He's drunk, Ron. We're letting him sober up before he goes home. He just freaked some girls out and fell."

I tried to speak up but my tongue was tied. It felt enormous in my mouth, fat and swollen. I stuck it out to check, but it looked normal. I wanted to tell him, let him know his girlfriend was guilty of reckless endangerment, corruption, and first-degree poisonin', but couldn't get it out. Evil wordless thoughts churned through my head as I watched Ron snuggle up to his little bruja and share a giggle. They stood shoulder to shoulder, drinkin' me in with their stoned, lazy eyes. I couldn't believe it. Old Ron. Stoned to the bone. Hostin' these derelicts in a bar that was supposed to be for good, hardworkin' men.

Clay slid his seat next to mine. "You know, I'm willing to forgive your unwarranted attack on me today—"

I tried to reply but only drooled. Clay took a napkin and wiped my face.

"I'm—oop, stay still. There you . I'm sure you've heard how important it is to forgive and all, but do you *really* understand it? The act of internalizing someone else's negative energy and removing it from the world? Absorbing and transforming that hate, that vitriol into love? It's alchemy of the highest order." He dropped the napkin in the cup with my butts. "I could've had her slip you a thousand hits of acid instead of that baby dose of Datura. Could you imagine being the disgruntled vet who finally lost his mind in some shitty strip mall bar? Getting carted out of this—" he looked around to find the words. "this, this impossibly sad establishment while babbling incoherently? Babbling like that forever? Imagine how embarrassed your kid would be, God."

Bubbles formed around my lips. "*Doan.*"

Clay's ugly face lit up like a jack-o-lantern as he leaned into the light. "Don't what?"

I snatched the napkin out of the cup, wiped my face, and stared him in the eyes. "Mesh wid my fambly."

Clay smiled and nodded as he sipped his whiskey. "Yeah, well, I got family too. Not like your family. Not a family-family. Mine's more of a network, I guess. A group of people—people with a single-minded focus. A very determined bunch, you know?"

"You mee a gan?"

"A gang? No. I prefer...hmm—more like a *cooperative*."

I pushed my spiked beer forward onto the little groove for empties and shook my head. There was a feelin' in my chest. A pressure. A dull glow. It was the same feelin' I used to get right before kickin' in a door or loadin' up a mortar. It was *excitement*. I was amped to the gills but couldn't fuckin' move. It was bizarre. "Cut da shich. Whaddya whan?"

The band coalesced into a puddle of colors as I wiped my eyes. They were twitchin' like crazy.

"Guns," he said simply. "I need you to sell me some guns."

Donny came back inside with the blonde, both laughin' and rubbin' their noses. She hugged Donny and rubbed Clay's back. Her friend, still ponied up at the bar, finally looked away from the band, realizin' her girl was back and had scored. She arched her eyebrows up and down from across the bar. A kind of facial Morse code for: did you score?

"See ya, guys!" the blonde said to Clay and Donny, her smile fadin' as she saw me. She turned around to take another route, detourin' around some fat creep in suspenders so as not to get near me. Her disgust changed back to gleeful excitement as soon as she reunited with her slam-pig of a friend. The two threw some dough on the bar and split.

"Yeah, an wha if I dawn whanna?"

Donny rubbed his nose and tapped Clay. "What'd he say?"

Clay held a finger up to Donny. "Do you know what the punishment would be for attacking a bunch of peaceful citizens and setting fire to their encampment?"

I shrugged.

"That's like first-degree terrorism," offered Donny.

"Actually, no, it's multiple charges of assault, which can carry up to five years—"

I rolled my eyes. "Woo-dee-fuh-hin-woo."

"Yeah. I agree," said Clay, a little irritated. "A little assault, right? No biggie. How about arson with the intent to endanger life? Huh? That can carry a life sentence. And since it was on so many people? Yikes, minimum's twenty-five years."

"Yeah, but isn't that terrorism since it was so many people at once?"

I took the bottle back off the bar and held it in my hands. I thought about crackin' them but my arms were heavy, stuck, like I was in a dream. "You doan have no proof."

Clay reached for my pack. "You mind?"

Donny knocked his arm. "Grab me one."

Clay slid two cigs out. He passed one to Donny and lit his. "You seeing any dots or anything?"

"Wha?"

"Dots," Clay said, flittering his fingers in front of his face.

I nodded.

"Are they red or black?"

"Wha the fuh?"

Donny dragged his cig. "Answer the fuckin' question, dickhead. Clay knows a lot about this shit."

I eyed Donny and turned to Clay. "Reh. An teh yuh boy ta wahchit."

"Really?" Clay seemed impressed, watchin' me intently as he took a long drag on his cig, "Interesting."

"Wuh?"

"Gimme some," said Donny. "I wanna know what color I see."

Clay waved Donny off and continued on. "I spent some time in Mexico studying as an ethnobotanist, my Terrence McKenna phase, I guess."

"Huh?"

"Eh, this guy, he's like, I don't know... Anyway, this group I studied, the Yaqui, they believe that people who see red are—eh I'm trying to think of how to translate it— strong and violent, the power-hungry type."

"Ya-kee?"

Donny cut in. "Yeah, dude, these old-ass Mexicans Clay studied 'broad with, ancient hobbit-lookin'motherfuckers. Seriously, dude, I'm talkin' like this tall," he held his hand in comparison with a bar stool, danglin' the cig out of his mouth. His cell phone lit up in his pocket and he pulled it out.

"Holy fuckin' shit, bro! Gay boy gave up the vid! The one with this nutso attackin' you! We got him, dude!" Donny put his arm around my neck and blew his cig off the side. "You're toast, bro."

Clay came from behind and snatched the phone. "Jesus, man."

"What?"

"What do you think? Use your head."

"You callin' me dumb or somethin'?"

"I didn't say you were dumb. I said use your head, meaning I know you're more intelligent than that."

"Whatever, dude. Just show him. We *got* him!"

Clay clenched his teeth and shook his head. "No, Donny. We don't *got him*. There's no video here. Just a text saying you-know-who has it and won't release until we trade."

"Lemme see that." Donny grabbed his phone back, shaking his shoulders like he was trying to get something off them. His cig went up towards his eyes as his chin sank lower and lower into his chest. His face glowed blue in the light of his phone screen. Squinting through the smoke, he wiped his forearm across his sweaty brow. "Fuck. You're right. She needs—"

Clay shoved Donny's arm. "Dude!"

Donny crushed his butt in the ashtray. "What? She? Gay boy? Really? You think that's givin' shit away? You're paranoid, bro."

Seein' them bicker made me feel a little easier about the whole thing, set them in the amateurish light they deserved. Clay seemed smart, but at the end of the day? These were just a couple of dope fiends set to task by one of their bigger, badder dealers to secure themselves some firepower. I slid into a brief fantasy about using these two dopeazoid numbskulls to get to their dealers and blazin' the whole lot of them, right in their crummy apartment. Do the world a favor.

I grabbed Clay's arm. "How bow you tuh-guy? Reh ar blah?

Clay smiled and stopped squabbling with Donny. He scratched his face, inhaling deep through his nostrils, absorbing the smoke, the noise, the light—seemin' real at peace with everythin' all of a sudden. Just a big act. He closed his eyes and nodded. "I saw red as well."

"Yeh?"

I picked my beer up and chugged the rest. Just to let them know who they asked to the dance. Show them I didn't give a fuck. Didn't give a fuck about them or their gay little potions. Matter of fact, I was startin' to feel pretty good, horny as a goat too.

Clay, seeming impressed, smacked my shoulder and got up. "You know where to find me."

I pulled him back into the seat next to me. My hands felt strong, like I could rip one of his arms off. I collected spit and stretched my tongue. "Whuh-t's ta stah me fruh—ehhh—killun' you two and bein' duh-n wih it?"

Donny looked at Clay. It seemed like the idea *never* even occurred to his dumb ass.

Clay just smiled coolly, naturally, freeing his arm from my grip. "That's a great question, something I've pondered myself. And I really, really hope it doesn't get to this. It would just be so ugly for the both of us, you know? Because I don't want to die. And, to, I guess, not die, or really, insulate myself against your particular brand of fury, I've preemptively shared some information with a few of our, eh, people, I guess, for lack of a better term. Just a couple things about your little Jimmy. Or, Fig, right? That's what you call him? Fig? Wrestler? Up for states this year, I hear." He arched his eyebrows as if he was impressed. Clay set his half-smoked cig down in the ashtray, makin' sure to balance it so it didn't fall out. A ribbon of smoke twirled off the cherry-lit end up into the exhaust as he exhaled out of the side of his mouth. "Point being—if something happens to me, something happens to your son. Something particularly nasty."

"Ehhhh," I said stretching my tongue out. It was starting to feel normal. "Like what?"

Clay picked his cig back out of the ashtray. He held it to his lips to take a drag and stopped, rolling it between his fingers, dashin' it around as he spoke. "Granted this is absolutely plan X, you know? I really, really don't want to pull the cord on—"

"Spit it out, faggot."

Clay tapped his ash on the bar and blew it off. "Your son would be dosed with a *Biblical* amount of LSD. When? Not sure. But trust me, it would happen. And could you imagine? Good god, the *fear*. Fear that defies mortality and targets the *soul*. Matters of eternity. Fuck, man. They'd have to strap him to a bed *forever*. It's all they can do with a person like that. Sedate them into oblivion."

Donny, regaining his bravado smacked my arm. "Or ya can just sell us a couple of guns, right? I don't know. Seems easy to me."

Clay put a hand on my shoulder, rockin' it in a familiar friendly way. "Of course, I'd much prefer we trade peacefully. Shit, man, hit up a few of your old army buddies. I'm sure they'd like to make some cash as well, seeing how badly this country fucks their soldiers over. It'll be good for everyone."

He stubbed his cigarette neatly, flattenin' the tip in the ashtray. He smiled and patted my shoulder. I shrugged him off.

Joel

The murky streetlight pin-holed through a gap in the blinds, illuminating a bic, an empty water bottle, and a sock lying limp on the parquet floors. My hand brushed the wet spot where my head had been, sliding damply across the couch's sweaty leather.

I unzipped and wiggled out of my jacket, pulling the sweater over my head and unbuttoning my dress shirt. My t-shirt was soaking wet, stuck to my body as I tried to rip it off. An internal hurricane of anxiety thrashed me, squeezing my innards. Every square inch of my skin was prickly and on alert. I stood up and paced, guided by the weak light of the cable box. Turning on the overhead lights was out of the question. It would destroy me. Something dug into my leg as I moved. I pulled what felt like a watch out of my pocket and bent down to inspect it in the glowing time of the box. I was right. It was a gold watch—a Rolex.

I stretched the gold strap in my fingers, trying to replay the night. It was there. The memory was there, but it was broken. A shattered pile of events. Brenda. My mom. Great Aunt Dottie. My hot cousin Tracey from Ohio who I was surprised to see and possibly hugged twice. The toast I gave my dad.

"Oh God."

What I said was irreversible. I'd be shunned forever. No doubt about it. I actively fought to repress the memory but it came barreling through—the looks of their faces, expressions of unanimous disgust; me holding the watch up for everyone to see, rambling over my father as he calmly sat and looked back at me, his face reading, *why?*

"*This,*" I'd proclaimed to the gathering of drunken uncles, tipsy, red-faced wives, distracted toddlers, and grimly bored teens, "this is Evermore Tires' ironic sneer at my father. A cruel joke played by the soulless warehouse that stole his life, his *time...*only to give it back to him in gold!" I looked dramatically at the watch. "It's all in there, dad, all your best years. Might as well slip it on your wrist and hop in the casket. That's the whole point of it, right? To look good at the fune—"

Someone grabbed me, maybe my uncle Benny, maybe Brenda. I don't know.

Another memory: crying outside while talking to my dad, his neon-lit skin under the square streetlights above. A thin cable wire hanging off a telephone pole, rattling in the wind. My uncle Steve and Aunt Becky coming outside to smoke a cigarette and moving away. Their hushed whispers. Brenda pulling around in my truck, uttering an apology to my dad that I couldn't understand. Why was my dad being such a dick to her? Brenda's tight-lipped stare as she pulled off, the cold air rushing faster and faster through the window. Her warm shoulder. Touching her breast. Her slap and shove. Feeling crumpled against the side of my door. The frigid glass of the passenger window slowly warming from my cheek. More cold air, coming in faster and faster, ripping my steam to shreds as I exhaled a cigarette.

My fingers smelled like nicotine, a burnt, minty note from the menthol. My mouth was dry and sour. It tasted like the internal process of decaying chemicals. I fumbled around the dark for a light switch as the floor seemed to slant downward. My balance was fucked. I slapped, not flicked, the lights on, detonating a latent ache in my frontal lobe, which was now throbbing. I shut the light off and headed for the door.

The outside world was cold and peaceful, a frozen suburban desert. The sky was crisp and sharply dark, contrasted by the stars as they pulsed and flickered, as if interfered with by some mad cosmic scientist on the edge of the universe, thoughtlessly meddling with the power supply. There were clouds around the moon. The parts that touched it glowed.

I leaned against the concrete steps as my headache subsided, tagging in the familiar melancholy that often ensued a family gathering. The frozen concrete felt wonderful on my face, the trapped sand-papery pebbles digging into my cheek. There was something true about its solidity, something to be learned from this petrified slab of goo.

A twig snapped as someone moved in the shadows, crunching their way across Brenda's frozen chunk of Earth. The lurker had an unsettling bob to their gait, the erratic shuffle of a wandering crazy person.

"J-j-joel?," said the figure as he stepped into the light of the street.

Fig, now identified as the lurker, bobbed along, not necessarily toward me, but in my general direction. His lightless eyes hung vacant, fixed in a thousand-yard stare. He got to the middle of the cul-de-sac and stopped. An airplane blinked red across the heavens above him.

I opened my gate and walked toward him. "Dude, you okay?"

He stood shivering in his wrestling sweatsuit, the knees of which were soggy, stretched by mud and moisture. His cheeks were red, the rest of his face a shade of vampire white. A single shiny line of snot ran down his nose. I got closer and saw his pupils. Two dilated black holes.

"Dude, what are you on? You're wasted."

"How can you tell?"

"Your eyes man. What did you do?"

Fig pulled two packets out of his pocket and marched toward my yard with the solemnity of a church boy, placing them on the altar of my brick half-wall. I followed him, re-establishing myself within the bounds of my laughable courtyard and leaned on the other side like I was his bartender.

"What is this stuff?" he asked, tapping them with his hand.

"This one is that legal weed bullshit people smoke on probation and the other is salvia. Which one did you smoke?"

"Both."

"Shit."

"Why? Is that bad?"

"I mean."

His face, and then body, sank against the wall. "Is this one," he pointed to the salvia, "supposed to be stronger than the other one?"

"Yeah, dude, way stronger. Plus, you don't know what's in it. All this shit's made in these sketchy labs in China. Big evil warehouses that play techno 24/7—"

A diesel engine roared in the distance.

Fig whipped his head around to locate his father's truck. His feet shuffled underneath as he frantically groped the wall. It was like each part of his body had a different plan. His eyes bulged as he smacked my bricks. "*Fuck!*"

Halogen aftermarkets set the street aglow. I grabbed the back of Fig's sweats and hoisted him over the wall. "Get inside. Go!"

Fig scurried through my yard like a rat, squeezing his body through the barely opened door. Meanwhile, John's truck lumbered up the street in a series of awkward jerks. He attempted to parallel park, raising his back tire up on the curb and coming off. His engine rattled and roared, incredibly loud at this time of night. I reached into my pocket to check my phone. My soul ached at the sight of four missed messages from my mom; no doubt all of which were in CAPS LOCK with hundreds of exclamations. John re-attempted his park job, this time coming in front ways. His front passenger tire went up on the curb and gnawed at the mound of frozen snow erected by his blower. He backed up and pulled forward again, mounting the ice with his all-terrain tires, his black Ford cocked and gleaming in the moonlight. It reminded me of one of those truck commercials where they climb rocks and drive in the desert.

The door opened, and John hopped out of his truck. Spotting me, he decided to cross the street and come over. His walk was somehow meaner, more intense. The collar of his work jacket was disheveled, one up one down. This particular Carhartt jacket was brown instead of his usual oil-spotted tan, which led me to believe it must've been his "going-out" work jacket. He raised two fingers to his face and touched his lips as he crossed the street, tilting his head and exhaling up into the sky, arching his back in a way that reminded me of John Travolta in Grease.

"Joel, right?" John jumped over a pile of ice-crusted snow and onto my sidewalk.

"Yup."

He raised his fingers to his lips and inhaled, holding them down by his side in a peculiar way. His eyes were unblinking and wild. Crazed. He exhaled a cloud of breath directly into my face and lifted his fingers to his lips again to breathe in. It dawned on me: he was smoking and imaginary cigarette.

I tried to break the very strange ice.

"How was the bar?"

"The bar—" John laughed, blown away by the weight of the word. "The *bar* was, well, it was the bar, same as ever, the same desperate situation."

"The old human mating grounds, huh?"

John leaned against my wall, still puffing away at his fingers. His eyes squeezed tight as if he was getting down to the butt of his imaginary smoke. A flicker caught my eye as I turned around, horrified to see my upstairs bedroom light come on.

John tapped the packets his son left on my wall. "Is this that boner shit they sell at the gas station?"

"Uh, yeah, I think so. Someone must've left it there. It's not mine."

The familiar din of canned radio hits filled the street as Donny pulled up in his junky Neon, his subs vibrating at a semi-respectful frequency in the trunk. The passenger door opened and Lynne came stumbling out. She took a few steps and crashed into her sister's white picket fence.

Donny got out of the car and helped her up. Looking over his shoulder, he noticed us and dropped her.

Lynne, toppled in the snow, spotted us and yelled. "Look! It's Psycho Cork and his sidekick, Gay boy!"

Donny got back in his car and made a spastic three-point turn, frozen in a scared stare toward Cork, who was tilting his head curiously like a dog, looking back between me and Donny.

He pulled next to us and stopped. "You have 'til tomorrow, bro," he yelled and skidded off.

Brenda came out to collect her fallen sister.

"Alright John. I'm turning in," I said, turning to walk inside.

John hopped the snow bank, impregnating my little brick fortress with ease. He grabbed my jacket with inhuman strength and pushed me into the sapling that was planted by my landlord. The young tree bent under his tremendous force.

"Gay boy, is it?"

"What? What are you talking about?"

"You sure about that, *Gay boy*?"

"Dude! What the fuck?"

"Heard you've been takin' videos."

"What? No, John, I swear."

His stubble dug against the side of my face as his hot, boozy breath invaded my air supply.

"They *drugged* me."

My gate creaked open. Brenda smacked John's back with her little fists.

"Get offa him!"

We went further into the tree, pushing the poor sapling beyond its limits and snapping it in half. I fell back in the snow. John came down on me. A machine of grinding denim. The lifeless tree hung forward, still connected by a strip of fresh bark.

Then my face felt really hot. I caught a blow to the gut as I hobbled blindly, led by Brenda's soft hand.

"Stop it, John!" she yelled.

The air got spicy again, choking me. My throat, eyes, nose— everything tingled and burned. "Arggh! God damnit!" I couldn't understand what was happening.

I heard my gate clank shut as I bounced up and down through my yard, wondering if that's what blind people saw when they walked, a never-ending darkness bouncing up and down inside their heads. My storm door let out a tin rattle and I was back in the warmth of my house, pushed for some reason. The push sent me sprawling back onto my sectional. My face landed in the same sweaty wetness from earlier.

"Do you have any milk?"

"Milk? Really? What the fuck, Brenda? How's he know?"

"It'll help with the pepper spray. And, I don't know. Maybe Donny told him? I really don't know."

My eyes burned like hell. "Top shelf in the fridge.

Her feet tapped off and then returned along with her voice.

"What the fuck is this?"

"What's what? I can't see!"

"*Almond* milk?"

"Brenda, not right now. Not really in the mood to take flack about my dairy issues."

A wet and very cold paper towel soaked in almond milk wiped across my eyes.

"Does that help?"

"Yeah," I lied, blinking to reactivate my vision. It was blurred but serviceable. My eyes were puffy and hot, my throat warm. "What the hell happened?"

"John was kicking your ass—"

"No, I mean at the party—oh and about John. What the fuck, Brenda? He *knows*!"

"How? I haven't even sent them the video yet."

"Yet?! To who?"

"Donny and Clay. You said I could have it, remember?"

"What?! No! I don't remember... I don't remember anything—except for my speech. I remember that."

"Oh, God," Brenda cackled.

"It's not funny!"

Brenda rubbed my back. "Would you relax? Everything is fine. Your family just thinks you were a little drunk. I smoothed it over. Don't worry."

"Please, it's already hard enough going to those things and now—"

"Hard? Joel, you have a wonderful family. What could possibly be hard about that?"

"I don't know. I just…I feel like they think I'm a fuck up. And now—I just…I get so sad at those things. I always have."

"Why?"

"You've *never* felt sad at a family party?"

"My family doesn't have *parties*."

"Well okay, but did you ever want to cry for no reason? That's the feeling I get. Seeing those little pots of meatballs and roast beef, the dips, napkins, and cheese. Something about the effort, all the crockpots, the fact that someone somewhere rolled lunchmeat into neat little tubes. It just overwhelms me."

Brenda leaned against me. "Like when people gather around you and sing Happy Birthday?"

"Oh, *God*, that's even worse."

Fig emerged from my kitchen. His sweatsuit was even dirtier than I remembered. The knees of his sweatpants were abstract bullseyes, rings of mud and water soaked up in the cotton around his knees. The sleeves of his hoodie were pushed up on his arms, making him look mean in addition to being dirty.

"What the fuck are you guys *talking* about?

Brenda propelled herself off me. "Why is Fig inside your house?"

"He told me I could hide. What the fuck are *you* doing in here?" Fig, still mad about the dog shit, fired back.

"Well, no, I told him to come in, but only because he was outside all high on gas station drugs and his dad was pulling up—oh, and by the way, dude, we saw you steal that stuff," I tried to elaborate since his explanation made me sound like a pedophile.

"Yeah, and I saw the weed in your basement, so what?"

"What weed?" Brenda asked, deciding to join me and Fig's close physical proximity, forming a triangle of sorts.

My stomach plummeted. It felt hollow and then very full. Fig's words echoed off my walls, "*weed, weed, weed.*" I watched their faces move in a ringing silence, my reality stunned in a flashbang of sheer panic. Brenda's brow raised into a rainbow of inquisitive arches, while Fig's eyes and mouth opened with wonder, using his hands to demonstrate the size of something. I was in a vacuum, paralyzed in the shadow of looming truth, hearing my voiced detached and far away, words rushing out to swashbuckle theirs, to defend my castle of secrets.

"There's no weed in my basement. You didn't see any weed down there. That's impossible."

"Uh, ok," he said. "Then how come there's like fifty weed plants down there right now?"

Brenda cupped the sides of her head like it was going to explode. "Wait, wait, wait. You grow *weed?*" Her face moved in a sort of calculated wonder or suspicion. I couldn't tell.

Fig raised a bud triumphantly into the air proclaiming, "Hell yeah, check it out!"

"Who told you you could touch my shit?" I asked, walking toward him.

Fig backed away toward the wall as I got closer.

"I should've let your dad kick your fucking ass."

The boyish excitement drained out of Fig's face, his features hardening back into their usual rockish state, mean and cold.

Brenda paced the parquet floors with a hand on her forehead. "I...Joel...I can't. I-I gotta go."

"Brenda, wait." I grabbed her shoulder in a poor attempt to change her mind. "I'm sorry. I didn't mean...you know."

"Oh, so you were just going to keep it a secret then?"

"Well, considering I barely know you, yeah."

She sucked her teeth and laughed. "Okay, well, that's—hmm—that's great. I'll, uh, I'll see ya, Joel."

Figgy, who was still inspecting his little nugget, called after her from the couch. "What's got your pickle-grabber puckered? You sell drugs with your sister."

Brenda let go of the doorknob and whipped around. "My pickle-grabber? And who told you that? Your piece of shit psycho dad?"

"At least I have one!"

I grabbed Brenda by the waist as she steamed toward Fig. Her soft brown hair swayed as she rioted against me. It was like silk on my face. The unmistakable odor of Pantene Pro-V, same shampoo as my mom.

"Get the fuck off me, Joel!" she yelled, hammering me with the pinky side of her fists

Fig sat on the couch laughing. *"Get off me, Joel!"*

Brenda groped around my crotch in a very unloving way, furiously squeezing my jeans in search of testicles. I instinctively pushed her off, sending her tumbling onto my leather sectional. She looked up at me like I hit her.

"Oh, *fuck you*," she said, looking at me before turning back to Fig. "And guess where your dad was today? Out beating up homeless people in the park. Why? Because he's a fucking lunatic psycho. Yup, you're dad's a psycho, and guess what? You're gonna be one, too. Yup, just like him, Cork and Son, psycho-homeless beaters."

"Brenda! Fucking stop!" I yelled.

"Or what? You'll push me again?"

"You were trying to crush my balls!"

"Yeah, well, your dad was a piece of shit and left, so you'll just become a piece of shit one day and leave your family too," Fig chimed in, finally recovered from Brenda's revelation.

"Yeah well your mom left, so where does that leave you?"

"I heard your mom died from AIDS!"

I stood between them, silent, absorbing the feverish blows they launched over me, covering my face and genitals. The flurry of strikes slowly weakened and eventually subsided as the assailing parties lost their breath.

"Please," I begged. "No more fighting. I can't. I really can't."

Brenda squished her face in a mocking smirk. "Oh, *you* can't? I'm sorry, Joel. Is all this *upsetting* you?"

"Yeah, what a pussy."

I snatched the nugget out of Fig's hand. "Fine. Go ahead and fight. Hit each other. Call each other names. That'll solve everything."

"Whatever," said Brenda as she got up and headed to the door.

I grabbed her arm to stop her and she shot me a look, one of those "how-dare-you's?"

I let go. "Sorry, I wasn't—you guys can't just keep fighting like this—"

"Oh, spare us the sermon, Joel." Brenda felt her pockets and then walked back to the couch to grab her phone. "I'm fucking out of here."

I leaned against the door in protest. "Brenda, Please. Hear me out. Just—"

Fig perked up in his seat. "Yeah, Brenda, at least hear the guy out."

Me and Brenda exchanged bemused glances, sharing a mutual smirk over Fig's odd nature. There was something tragically humorous about him, how at fourteen he carried himself like a forty-year-old trash man with a weekend drinking problem. I actually thought she was about to laugh for a second, but she didn't, though she did give in and come sit back on the couch, mumbling a bunch of stuff under her breath, as if explaining her actions for some official personal record. Her and Fig sat on opposite ends of my sofa, literally as far as the couch would allow.

I tried to think of something to say, something to bond us, unite the parties, something to deescalate the situation. I started out vague.

"Whether we like it or not we're in this together now, in a knot of mutual circumstance—"

Brenda let out an audible groan as Fig's attention visibly wandered. Noting their mutual distaste, I changed it up, choosing to address them a little more frankly.

"Ok, whatever. Look, Brenda, you sell drugs. And Fig, I can just go tell your dad about the salvia and let him deal with you. And you guys can no-doubt fuck my shit up since you are now the only other people who know what I do. But, I think if we work together here—"

"Yeah, okay, whatever," Brenda said, brushing the whole thing off. "We all have dirt on each other, I get it. Let me see your plants."

"Well—so that's—?"

"Yeah, dude," added Fig. "No more of your gay speeches, show us your weed."

I didn't exactly appreciate Fig calling my speech gay but was pleased nonetheless. "I can, but, uh, you have to give me a minute. I need to set up the proper lighting. See, the plants are in their dark cycle and I can't just flick on a regular light. Give me a second and—"

Fig's face morphed into a very guilty one. "So it's bad if the lights are on now?

"God fucking dammit, Fig!" I yelled, running towards the basement.

Fig and Brenda made their way downstairs. I had my string of green lights plugged in giving off a real funky hue. The plants swayed under the fans, almost dancing, which combined with the ambiance, extracting a perfectly timed "Ooooh" out of them.

"Doesn't it remind you of that Jennifer Lopez video?" I asked. "The one where she's at that party in the jungle?"

Brenda and Fig looked at me and then at each other and shrugged.

"Whatever. Just try to keep your voices down." I said.

Brenda laughed, "Oh, God. You can't be serious." She turned to Fig. "Shh, don't wake his plants up."

I was more worried about the neighbors hearing them talk through the wall, but figured, whatever, they were getting along. "Uh, yeah, something like that."

I showed them my two growing sections. They were separated by thick sheets of insulation foam boards conjoined by gobs of expanding sealant jutting out from the joints. "The first and smallest section", I explained, "is for my clones. These are clippings from other plants that become plants of their own when I cut them and put them in the gel."

"Whoa! Isn't cloning like super advanced?" Brenda was impressed. She scanned my empty little clone area. "How come you don't have any here now?"

"Uh, well, for sheep, yeah, cloning is advanced. But for plants? Not really. And I don't have any clones since the plan is to finish up and get the fuck out of here so I can live in California where I can grow weed legally and enjoy a nice peaceful life."

Brenda winced.

"What?"

"I should have known."

"Known what?"

"That you actually grow weed considering you kept mumbling about it to old ladies at the party. The same spiel about moving to Cali and everything."

Her statement produced something like a mental kidney stone deep in my left frontal cortex, speeding my heart rate up by at least ten beats per minute.

Fig beamed up at me with a sense of uncanny admiration, "What did the old ladies say when you told them you—"

"You'll have to ask Brenda since you weren't the only one who overindulged in substances of nefarious origins. Apparently, me, you, and your dad bit off more than we—"

"My dad was fucked up too?"

"He was just a little tipsy. Nothing major."

Brenda shot me a look, condensing her brow in a manner that led me to believe she knew I wasn't telling Fig the truth but wanted the scoop later.

"So, anyway," I continued, "this second section is where they come to life. It's where I veg and flower the plants. A lot of growers would have a third compartment so they can have some vegging while other plants flower, but that's too much of a headache. I like to do it all at once."

Fig stood next to one of the plants, comparing his height to it. "Why don't you make them taller?"

"Because they can't get too close to the lights."

"Why?"

"It burns them. Turns the bud all yellow and brown."

I walked over to the plant that Fig ripped the bud from and cleaned the spot with some pruning scissors. The plant he assailed was raw and splayed, much like the poor sapling in the front yard above us.

"Is it gonna die?" Fig asked. He seemed genuinely upset.

I got up off the ground and dusted my knees. "No, it'll actually get stronger, which is neat. See where you ripped off? Now two new stalks will grow in its place. It's how I get them all fat and bushy. It's called *training the plant*."

"How the fuck does that make sense?"

"Yeah, that doesn't," Brenda chimed in.

"Ah, but it does," I said, on some level excited to finally have people with whom I could talk shop with. "The thing about these plants is, if you cut a stalk off, two new shoots will grow to replace the one that was lost, giving you more than you started out with weight-wise. It's an important part of the whole thing, and it's tricky. I gotta bully these plants, stress them a little, but not too much or they die. There's a balance, just like in nature. I gotta simulate *nature* down here. Like, I'm playing God. It's wild."

A silent confusion filled the air.

Finally, Brenda broke it. "So what's up with these lights? Why are they green?"

"The plants need total darkness to rest and produce THC—or technically THC-A—but whatever. They can't absorb the green light. They can only reflect it, if that makes sense."

"Dude, how?" a shocked Fig asked.

"Honestly, I don't know. Something to do with chlorophyll and photosynthesis." I pointed my little scissors at him. "Which is why you need to pay attention in school, so you won't have to learn your science like I did—from nasty old hippies with ketamine problems."

Brenda dusted the top of her head for spider webs. "Anyway, how are we gonna get this guy back in his house without his dad freaking out?"

Fig leaned against my washing machine. His face displayed an almost out-of-body detachment. "I'm just gonna walk in there and let him kick my ass. He'll probably take it easy on me."

"Why?" I asked.

"I've got a tournament tomorrow."

"Oh," said Brenda, "well, that's good."

I pulled a cobweb out of Brenda's hair and rubbed it on my jeans. "Cool out a minute before you go. Sober up. Who knows, maybe he'll fall asleep. He was pretty fucked up when I saw him."

"Really?" Fig asked, oddly proud.

Brenda shook her head. "Nothing sadder than getting drunk at the Bulldog."

"I wouldn't know," I said, turning around and walking up the steps.

Brenda and Fig both laughed shortly after. I'm guessing one of them jeered at the fact that I'd never gotten drunk at the dog bar.

Brenda joined me and Fig on the couch, setting down the glass of wine she'd poured herself out the bottle I'd apparently stolen with the watch. She grabbed the remote and flipped through the channels—

seeking what turned out to be *The Bachelor*. A group of cosmetically enhanced and nutritionally deficient women standing under a tiki-lit gazebo, fawning over some carbon copy douchebag, the physical manifestation of the name Chad. A square-chin dude with a torn and faded backward hat encapsulating his simple mind. His clothes were casual but noticeably expensive. The women, basking in the glow of Super Chad, smiled, twinkling in hopes of becoming the next hollow flash-in-the-pan celebrity, whoring themselves in exchange for the possibility of digitized ascension. To beam their souls through the matrix of fiber optic cables and rise again, anew in the two-dimensional heaven of cathode rays and liquid crystal molecules. To be sucked into the wet, messy folds of a stranger's brain. That was the dream.

Fig smacked my arm. "Dude! I can't believe you watch this. This show's *gay*."

"No I don't—" I said, feeling dumb as soon as the words left my lips.

Brenda exhaled like a horse, vibrating her purple-cornered lips. She wiped her mouth. "Puh-lease, just admit it, you like this show. It's not a big deal."

Fig tapped my arm, motioning us toward the kitchen with his head. "I gotta talk to you."

Brenda kept her face toward the TV, but her eyes followed as we moved.

"Dude, just say it," I told him, halfway across the floor.

Fig looked at Brenda and then back at me. "I need some weed."

"Yeah, dude. No *way*."

"I'm just using it to get better at wrestling. It makes me think of moves and shit." Fig pleaded.

Brenda waved him off. "He'll be smoking crack by the time he's nineteen anyway."

Fig stood there confused. He didn't know whether to argue or thank her.

"C'mon man. You're like twelve. I *can't* give you weed."

"I'm fourteen! And...and ...you have to or I swear...I-I'll fucking tell..."

Brenda, whose face had been concernedly crunched over the voted-off and crying blonde from Texas, narrowed her eyes into slits, studying Fig out of her periphery. She got up off the couch, walked over to the kitchen table, rummaged through her purse, and extracted a little snub-nosed .38.

She pointed it at Fig. "Yeah, you gonna tell daddy?"

I jumped between them, my hand in front of the barrel but cringing away from the gun. "Brenda! Jesus fucking Christ! Stop!"

"I-I-I-I..." Fig was beyond pale.

Brenda held the gun at her side and pushed Fig's temple with her finger. "No one likes a rat."

She sat back down on the couch. Fig was still frozen in front of the TV.

"Move!" she said. "I wanna see the scenes from next week."

Fig slid away from the TV with his back pressed to the screen. He looked like he was walking across a small ledge overlooking a hundred-foot cliff. I followed him into my kitchen.

"She was just fucking with you man." I tried to assure him. "She'd never do anything like that for real."

"Yeah I would," she called from the other room.

Fig's eyes darted toward the living room and then back to me. "Look," he explained, "I'm just trying to use weed to get better at wrestling, and I knew you'd be gay about it, so I threatened to tell. It's just business."

"Yeah, that's actually not business. And plus, the stuff downstairs isn't ready yet, so you'll have to wait."

"You don't have any other weed?" he asked incredulously.

"No, I don't."

"Why don't you give him some of that weed we smoked tonight?"

Fig shot me an angrily disappointed look. I tried to give Brenda a similar one from where I was standing, but she was too absorbed in her show.

"The weed I do have, which I barely have any left, stinks so bad. Your dad would smell it right when you walked into the house. I'll make you some muffins or something."

Fig looked at me blankly. "Muffins?"

"They fuck you up more," said Brenda, gracing us with her presence in the kitchen as she refilled her glass.

"Yeah. Plus, you don't want to be smoking. It'll fuck up your cardio."

Fig stood up and stuck his hand out. "Tomorrow then."

I squeezed his to make a point. "I'll get them to you when I have time. And don't you dare come knocking or do anything stupid."

Fig opened my back door, looking around to see who was outside. He crouched down before walking out. "Tomorrow, Joel. I'm not fucking around." He looked at Brenda, swallowing a lump before he darted out, sprinting toward the burning twilight, the dead earth, the messy leaves and frozen gleaming snow, joining a stream of blowing litter as he pulled his hood up and ran off.

Eddie

The same damn dream woke me up again, one I'd had a hundred times before. I was at a parade thrown by the city in my honor. I was dead. Hundreds of uniformed officers marched along the black limo that held my body. The clouds were dark, hanging heavy in the sky. Big, fat drops fell sparsely but with force, splashing when they hit. A huge float, a replica of me, hovered over the parade, eclipsing the already hidden sun.

In the dream, I was secretly alive, uniformed and walking, trying to blend with my peers who weren't exactly mourning. They seemed more impatient or annoyed. All of them, even the civilians, would look at me, turning their heads slowly, stealing glances but diverting their eyes whenever I looked back. Their faces all held the same confused look, the look given before going up and saying, "Hey, don't I know you?" But they wouldn't talk to me. They'd just keep looking, longer and longer. Glances eventually becoming stares, and then, like all the other times in the dream, my gun would go off and shoot the floating replica of myself clean out of the sky. Everyone would point and say, "He did it!" And we'd all stand still, frozen under the pregnant drops of rain, stuck in an eerie stalemate as my rubber doppelganger withered and fell.

The alarm clock glowed blue: 5:03 AM

I wrestled out of the blankets and sat on the edge of my bed, blinking myself awake. My feet touched down on the winter-tight floors while my hand fumbled around my dresser and poked the speckled darkness in search of the lamp's string. I grabbed it and popped it down. Light overtook my room, one of those newfangled LEDs. Bought the wrong goddamn one at the hardware store just a few days prior and forgot.

The phone rang.

I slid into my slippers and headed down the hallway, mentally preparing to scathe the rogue, early-bird bill collector. The house was brisk, downright chilly. I turned the thermostat up and shuffled through the violet shadowy darkness.

"...and I'll get back to you as soon as possible. Beep!"

"Good morning, Mr. Hayden. This is Orson Hart calling—Oh, bother. It must be ...three, four—very early in the morning. Apologies! I'm on Tokyo time and a bit jet lagged to boot. Anyhoo, in regards to Clay—it was brought to my attention that he washed up at Roxborough Memorial Hospital. Your neck of the woods, if I recall. He was checked in earlier this—or was it last?—yes, this afternoon but apparently vanished before I was contacted. I've learned, and keep this between us—a doctor granted me some Hippocratic leniencies—that Clay was involved in some kind of attack or fire, though, you never know, it could just be one of his stories. My main concern, and I didn't bring this up to the doctors, is that he may have made off with a couple of those prescription pads. He's done it twice before and—Akame kyaramerumakiāto shite kudasai? —and last time, well, he almost went to jail—hai venti!—That being said, I'd like to double my initial offer in hopes you can expedite the process of determining his whereabouts. So...just...good morning and seize the day. And please, please let me know what you find. You have my direct—beep."

The voice-machine cut out, but I heard all I needed. Double the initial offer put me back on top with plenty to spare. I could go down to those mortgage jerks and pay them off, give them a piece of my mind and then some. Between the hookers, the cams, a few bad sports bets, several failed attempts at obtaining a Russian mail-order bride, a mismanaged refi, the market crashing, and that Goddamn Nigerian Prince I met on craigslist, I was in danger of losing my home. I'd also backslid pretty hard on my real estate tax, figuring I'd be dead sooner but to no avail. My only hope was to find the kid or sell my dump. If I didn't do either, I was out on my ass.

I swirled the leftover coffee around the pot peering in, debating whether to microwave it or make a new batch. *Why did the fire sound so familiar?*

I rushed over to my table and turned on the police scanner, remembering how they'd mentioned it the day before. Out in the park, somewhere off Henry Ave. Junkie camp set ablaze, which was nothing new, what with those numbskulls dipping off like they do. A plan formed, establishing a welcome sense of order for the day. Though, my first order of business was to deploy the boys. My balk at Candy's had me a bit tight.

I sat down in front of the computer, squinting as my monitor flicked on. Static garblings of police radio popped in the background and quickly turned to sonic mush. I was already sucked in. Amazing, the stuff on the internet. I didn't see a tit until I was seventeen and here kids could watch a gal getting her butt humped by two guys at once.

I'd also check the hooker ads now and again, see who was new among the pro-ladies. Sometimes I'd pop a blue pill and call them. Rub one out to their voices while looking at their pictures. Most times I couldn't finish, but if I drank enough coffee and got enough sleep, sometimes I could deploy the boys. It was rare, and a dribble at best, but it happened from time to time. Quarterly if I had to guess. And God was it good to get it out! Stuff's poison to the body, cancerous after about a few weeks.

I jiggled myself, slapped it, squeezed the base, tickled the top. Nothing was working. Nothing. My Johnson remained limp, immune to any form of penile CPR. I browsed some videos hoping porn would do the trick, settling on one about a chubby teen babysitter who got caught being naughty on a sofa. I watched through the steam of my coffee as the bald "parent" caught the girl frigging on the couch. The steam wet my forehead as I continued to sip, my gulps growing larger and greedier as I watched the girl's bottom turn pink from the slaps administered by the man. Still nothing, other than a faint urge to pee.

Frustrated, I got up and went to the counter, digging through the little basket that housed my medications. Heart pills, sleep pills, the expired antidepressants I refused to take, cholesterol stuff—and bingo. My Viagra. Last one for the rest of the month. I threw it in my mouth and swallowed it with nothing more than saliva and determination.

Someone banged my door hard, startling me at the counter. A side-fist hammer knock hitting with a uniform consistency—code for the impatient. My door almost jumped off the hinges. *Deh deh deh.* I shuffled to the monitor and powered it down

Peeking outside I saw John Cork bouncing on my steps as he mumbled into the collar of his jacket. It was odd seeing him out there. He'd made it clear on more than one occasion that I should stay away from his house and all, given my history. He was one of the few people on the street that knew about what went down.

I opened the door.

"Hey there, Johnny-boy. What can I do you for?"

"Got a second, sir?"

***

I emptied the rest of the day-old coffee into a mug and set it down on the counter for him. He was rigid, tense and tightly wound, careful in his movements. Something cornered doggish about him. He ran his chapped hands through his plastic-looking hair, alternating one at a time. His eyes darted about, looking around my place, studying it like it was some kind of exhibit.

"Really hate to intrude like this."

"Ah, don't worry, kiddo, don't worry at all. What brings you?"

John Cork sipped his coffee, studying his knuckles as he rapped them on the counter. "Well, Mr. Hayden—"

"Call me Eddie, son."

"Okay," he said, clearing his throat. "I, uh, I think we have some monkey business goin' down around here."

One of those four-by-three, commercial-grade lights hung in the drop ceiling above his head, highlighting a thinning-out situation at the crown of his noggin. The light was one of those big rectangular jobs you'd see in a mechanic's office or janitor's closet. And mine, like the rest I'd ever seen, had that same world of crunchy dead bugs trapped behind the lens. One of them was a giant cricket.

John Cork jerked his head in the direction of Joel's house and then pointed through his pocket toward Brenda's. "Bit of an unholy alliance between Jack-ass and Jill."

"Really? Any idea what they're up to?"

Cork dropped two foil wrappers onto my table. One said Spice. The other said Salvia 40x. "Not sure just yet. Though I did find some boner pills outside of Joel's last...or was that...yeah, last night. Anyway, a kid that young needing boner pills? What's up with that? That's gotta be something, right?"

Light gleamed off the foil packets as I inspected them. "Heh, hate to break it, but these here aren't boner pills. This is some other stuff. Some kind of designer drug they sell over at the Speedway. Stuff kids smoke and jump off the roof."

John shivered in disgust, a little dejected as he sipped his coffee. A brown drop trickled down the side of the mug and was absorbed into his finger as he wiped it clean, "Yeah well, obviously I'm just spitballin', but I know it's not just those two. There's a whole lot of them. There's Lynne, some moron Donny, and then, I guess the ringleader from what it seems, this Clay character."

"Clay?" My ears pricked up.

"Yeah, some smartass hippy kid. Saw him at the bar last night, him and that Donny kid. A real fucking punk.

"What bar?"

"What? Ya know him or somethin'?" John scoffed.

I braced my lower back and got out of my chair. There was a mess of manila folders on my kitchen table piled in a dangerously crooked stack. I slid a folder off the top.

"What's that there?" Cork asked, eying them up. "You, uh—"

"Doing some private work. A rich family out around the main line near Villanova." I slid Clay's picture out. "Is this the kid you're talking about?"

Cork stared at the picture. He slid his chair forward, scuffing the floor. His head tilted like he was trying to move the juice from one side of his brain to the other and slowly started to nod in recollection. "Yeah... yeah. That's him. Hell of an old picture. But definitely your guy." John jerked his neck, cracking it on right and getting nothing on the left. He picked his coffee up and held it in his lap. "Kid's *way* uglier now. You should see him. He's got those dread things. Fucked up teeth too. Uck."

"So, what's he want with you?" I asked, dumping my microwaved coffee in the sink as I set up a fresh batch. An outside gust rattled my windows and sent my hood vent slapping like mad. A jet of cold air snuck in from somewhere.

"I could get rid of that noise for you. A couple of spring-loaded dampers—"

"John, how do you know the kid?"

John set his coffee on the table. "Shit, Eddie, I don't know. He was just—at the bar, they do this kind of hippy night. The music, people—I don't know what's worse. But in this Clay-person comes with his wigger-dago sidekick and totally interrupts me with this little blonde, who, ya know, was pretty into me—Did you know you can't say *wigger* anymore?"

"News to me. So what happened?"

So, I'm sittin' there, workin' hard on this blonde and these two numbskulls ooze into the bar and start their nonsense, sellin' dope to the girl I was chattin'. Donny did the dope-sellin'. Clay's more of a boss-type. She had a friend there with her too. Sittin' on the other side of the bar. Decent tits. And so I gave them some grief, ya know, about sellin' that shit in Ron's bar and...and come to find out the whole thing was just a rouse. Yup. The girls were *plants*. See, what you don't know? And are lucky that I'm tellin' *you*, is that this whole thing's deeper than you think. See, Clay's usin' Joel and Brenda to follow me around and video me."

"Video you?"

"Yeah, like tryin' to catch me breakin' OSHA rules on my jobs. Usin' illegals. Shit like that. And Joel, the little rat fuck, got me on video—a video of me and my son on a roof without harnesses. It was a flat roof, but you know how OSHA breaks your balls about everything, and the fine's like thirty grand, not withstandin' potential child endangerment on my end, which is all I need. I mean, his mom, as you know, isn't in the picture, but who knows? If the court came at me for somethin' like that who knows? And so anyway, the girls leave and Clay and Donny flank me from either side, ponyin' up to the bar, ya know? One on my left and my right and Clay tells me about the video. And my first thought is to crack them on the mop with a bottle, but when I go to move, I'm frozen. Seriously, Eddie, I was stiff."

"Stiff?"

"No. Not like that. I just—they had Ron's knucklehead, hippy girlfriend in on the thing too. She laced my drink with some shit. Some witch stuff. Dah-roar-uh or somethin'? I don't know. Had me in this trance and—I know it sounds crazy, but I swear it's true." Cork drained his coffee and set it on the counter.

"Why you? Is there something they're after?"

"Guns."

"Guns?"

"Yup. Said if I don't give them some guns, they'll expose the video...or worse."

"Worse?"

"Poison my son with LSD."

My member pulsed and slid warm up my thigh, awakening from the Viagra as John washed his cup in the sink, angrily swashing my sponge in hard foamy twirls.

"Christ! Had no idea this Clay kid was such a player. Guns? Drugs?—Leave it. I'll get it later. Speaking of which—" I adjusted my crotch under the table. "I gotta ship off soon. Headed to the park off Henry after sunrise, look into a fire. I think this Clay kid might have been—"

"That was on the news?"

"No, it was on the scan—wait—how'd you hear about that?"

"About what?"

"The fire."

Cork cleared his throat. "Uh, my buddy mentioned it. He's a volunteer firefighter."

"Not here he isn't. Our nozzle nuts have always been on salary," I replied, adjusting my khakis. "Your boy must be one of those county dogs."

"Yup. Upper Darby. It's so close I forget sometimes." He finished washing the mug and set it down on the counter, which he leaned against and folded his arms. "I think we can help each other here, Eddie. Your police mind and my military training? We can bring these thugs down."

"I'll do whatever you want if you can link me to that kid."

John looked around the house nodding as an idea apparently entered his head. "What we need to do is get some dirt on this Joel guy. Start from the bottom and work up."

"Why not start with Clay? Attack the head of the snake. What was that bar you—"

"I can't set up nothin' if the kid doesn't got a phone. He's smart, Eddie. Donny does all his communicatin' and I don't have Donny's number. But Joel? He lives right there. I'm tellin' you. He'll give us Clay. We just need to jam him up. Get some dirt on him. Remember that electric bill thing I was talkin' about?"

I poured myself a fresh cup of coffee and set it down on the table, licking the plaque on my teeth. Forgot to brush in the scramble of things. Yawning, I looked up at the dead bugs. Could've sworn I saw a new one, a rollie-pollie. "Yep, sure do. We'll start with his trash," I said.

"His trash?"

"Yup, that'll tell us if he's doing anything. It's a common tactic used for drug cases."

John rubbed his chin in thought, "My buddy from PECO said high electric bills could mean he's growin' pot. Would make a hell of alotta sense."

"Just grab his bags. I'll take it from there. And try to get a phone number on this Donny guy."

"I knew I could count—"

"Hey, this buddy of yours, how did he come to find out about the fire?"

"Whaddya mean?"

"Well, sometimes the counties come in and help if the blaze is too big, but from what I heard this wasn't anything like that. Plus, the nearest county to help would have been Montgomery, not Delaware."

John shrugged as he walked toward the door. "Beats me. Probably friends with some of the Philly guys. But, hey, I gotta jet, try to get some shuteye. Fig's got a wrestling thing. I'll snag a bag and leave it in my basement. We can check it out when I get home. Probably around five or so."

I nodded from my chair, watching as John twisted the knob. My whistle was screaming, ready to deploy the boys, harder than a goddamn nail.

"Hey, wait, what was that bar again?"

"What bar? The one I saw 'em at?"

"Yes."

"Right over there at Murphy's." John stood pointlessly, lingering for a few seconds. He nodded to no one as he opened the door and walked out into the dawn.

Fig

I slid in through the basement window and shut it, leaving it open a hair. That way it didn't beep the alarm next time I needed to get in or out. The basement was shadowy, everything stenciled in the early morning light. I felt around the rows of tools as I made my way to the steps and crept upstairs.

Guided by weak light from the microwave, the cable box, touch screen shit on the fridge, I snuck through the kitchen and headed for the stairs. Metal keys clanged against the door, clawing inside the lock as it popped open. I tore ass up the steps and breathlessly sped into my room as my dad's fat key ring jingled against the door downstairs, knocking against it, sounding like a metal brush.

I shed my clothes like a snake and hopped into bed. It felt weird getting in all dirty like that, the dry sweat rubbing against my sheets. My dad's boots trudged up the steps in slow, quiet thuds. And then through the hallway toward my room. My light flicked on.

"Figgy."

I didn't move.

"Get up, c'mon." He came over and shook me. His breath reeked of beer, cigs, and coffee.

"What time is it?" I stretched and genuinely yawned.

"Time to get up."

I sat up and rubbed my eyes. The artificial light looked stupid compared to the golden nipple of sun rising off the ground. It made me want to break the bulbs.

"You just getting in, dad?"

My dad was fiddling with something on my bureau. My little swiss army knife. He pulled out the blade and held it in comparison to the width of his four fingers. His face was drawn in a tired frown.

"Whadjya say there, Fig?"

"Are you just getting—"

"Gotta pay the bills to ask questions like that, champ. C'mon, throw some clothes on. I wanna show you somethin'."

We threw our coats on and stepped outside. Dead trees stretched out to the orange and violet sky, rattling in the cold wind. My face stung. It felt like cold glass ready to shatter. My dad tugged me by the arm and pulled me along. The world was moving around me in snapshots, one long roll of film. I was still fucked up from that stuff.

"Where we goin'?"

"Doin' a little secret mission, bud."

We stopped and turned our backs to the whistling wind. It dawned on me that the wind whistled through the gaps in trees and rocks, like teeth. Trees and rocks as the earth's teeth. It blew my mind.

My dad nudged my shoulder. "Look alive. This is serious business."

"What is?" I asked as we crossed the salty street.

"Turns out some people on this block are plannin' my demise."

"Who? Bren—"

My dad smacked my head. "Don't point, you dolt! Just listen."

I purposely stepped on a soda can and crunched it. My dad shot me a look and kept moving. He was walking fast as shit.

"All I can tell you, and this is for your safety, is there's some people out there who want to use you to get to me. Hurt you, you understand?"

"Who?"

"Damnit! What part of 'all I can tell you' don't you understand?"

"Sorry."

"Save your sorries for later. This is war. Do or die time," he said, turning the corner down toward the back of Joel's house.

We stopped at Joel's brick wall. My dad crouched and took a knee, holding out his hands as he interlocked his fingers. "Here. I'm gonna boost ya. Hop over and grab me a trash bag."

"For what?"

"Damnit!"

My dad picked me up by the back of my sweats and dropped me over the wall, into a snowy bush. A large sheet of snow fell off the bush and crashed on the ground sending a cat scampering out from Joel's dryer vent and through the bottom of his gate. I thought I saw my dad try to kick it but wasn't sure. I could only see the top half of his body. Joel's trash bulged out of the top of the can. A lid sat crooked on top, kinda like a cool hat. I pulled the lid off and lifted the bag. Bottles rolled forward and clanked as I walked toward my dad who was furiously shushing me from behind the wall.

I hoisted the bag over to my dad and stuck my foot in the now jacked-up bush to use it as a push off.

Joel's back door opened.

"What the fuck dude!?" He stood on the step in his boxers, covering his cold nipples like a little bitch.

I held a finger up to my mouth and opened my eyes as far as they could go, urging him not to say a word. "I was chasing a cat and it ended up in your yard."

"Chasing a cat?"

"Yeah, for wrestling. Like when Rocky chased the chickens?"

Joel tightened his lips and opened his eyes at me. Urging me to tell him what was going on.

I opened my eyes even wider, letting him know to shut the fuck up and play along. "Go back to sleep before your little morning boner freezes off. Thing's poking out like crazy."

Joel moved a hand from his nipple to his dick—and then back to his nipple as if proving a point. "Have fun chasing cats or whatever you're doing out here. Just, you know, stay the fuck out of my yard."

I pointed to the woods and held up seven fingers.

Brenda

A trash truck rumbled somewhere down the street, hissing and beeping, reminding me of my dream. I was taking out my trash, floating in the air between jumps. Eddie had been floating too, thrashing his body violently in the air. He told me we were just visions trapped inside of John Cork's binoculars and not our real selves. We jumped over the trash truck and looked down as it drove through my cans, and then my house, plowing them into the woods as the world turned upward, giving me and Eddie no other choice than to stare up at the sun. I felt him touching my leg and woke up.

A beam of morning light crept through the gap in Joel's curtains. It hit his wood floor and went off in angles that cut through the shadows. Dust fibers, hairs, and other floaty things spiraled in the rays, heading toward the return vent like they were ascending into heaven.

Joel came back into the room in his boxers, rubbing his hands, shrinking self-consciously toward his dresser to grab some shorts. Finding nothing in his drawers, he decided to lay down, pulling the blankets off my left thigh and elbow. I pulled back and scooted over. Joel wiggled his frigid body over and latched on, muttering under his breath. My mouth was dry and tasted like a balloon.

"What's the matter?" I asked, trying to put out minimal breath.

Joel wrapped his legs around me and shivered, "Nothing. I'm glad you stayed over."

I broke out of his hold and sat up, flinching against his cold headboard. He latched onto me, rubbing his face in my ribs. I felt dumb wearing his clothes. A pair of his sweatpants and what he claimed to be his most comfortable socks. The night before was weird, grade-schoolish really. We started on opposite ends of the bed, slowly inching closer over the course of an hour. Our feet twitching here and there in exploratory wiggles, little cotton feelers traveling under a network of quilts and Egyptian cotton, touching and pressing. Every time one of us flipped to the cool side of a pillow we'd use it as an excuse to slide over, closer and closer, inch by inch, until we were both right up against each other, hearing and feeling each other's breathing and digestion, swallowing spit and everything—and finally his arm slipped under my head, catching my hair for a painful second, and I rolled into him, letting his weight absorb mine, stopping me, like I'd been a rock rolling down a hill, falling with no end in sight and then, *thud*, I was smack against him. Solid. Like I was only gas before. I didn't fall into love but definitely fell into something. Relief, maybe? Maybe I fell into relief. Listening to the whine of his deviated septum, the tranquilizing squeeze of his arms locking me, containing me, slowing something inside me I didn't know was spinning until it stopped. His whiskers scratched against my cheek. That's the last thing I remember before passing out.

"Why didn't you try to fuck me last night?"

"I did," he replied into my rib cage.

"No, you tried to kiss me."

He pulled his face out of my side but continued staring at it. "Yeah, that's usually where I start. Leading with penetration seems like a bad idea."

"There are other things you can do to let a person know," I replied, smacking him lightly.

Joel shimmied his body up and whispered in my ear, "Let's buttfuck"

I shoved him down, hitting him in the back as we laughed. He resumed his original position with his face on my side.

"I just caught Fig in my backyard," Joel said into my rib cage, nibbling a roll.

"What? Ow, stop. What was he doing?"

"I don't know. I don't think he was alone, though."

"How do you figure?"

Joel rolled back onto his pillow and looked up. His dark curly hair fell around his head like a mane. His eyes were a smoky bluish grey. A gross little patch of hair sprung out between his nipples.

"He kept giving me these looks, shooting me signals with his hands."

"Signals? Really?"

"Yeah, I think he wants to meet me back behind your house at 7 am."

"My house? Fuck that."

"Maybe the woods then, I don't know."

A hush fell over as Joel's boner awkwardly protruded out of his boxers. It twitched and grew, savagely fighting the cotton. I slid back down onto my side, eye level with it, laying my face on top of my folded hands in the classic sleeping position. His eyes darted nervously around the room as I stared.

"Getting excited for your secret meeting in the woods?"

"Please, it's purely hormonal. This is the time in the morning—"

Joel let out a startled, breathless gasp as I squeezed his boner over his boxers, rubbing it up and down.

"Suuure," I mocked, "how're your hormones now?"

Joel couldn't even reply. His face twisted in a disgusting mannish expression, almost like he was in pain. His breathing increased with the speed of my hand as he pleaded in creepy whispers for me to stop.

"Brenda. No. Brenda. Please. Brenda! Ughhhhhhh!"

His butt shot up off the bed as he gripped my wrist. He closed his eyes and straightened his body, jolting up and down like he was being electrocuted. After a few seconds he stopped and pushed my arm off. His boxers were splotched with musky goo.

"Brenda! Did I say—"

"You didn't have time to say anything," I giggled, wiping my hand on his chest. "That was like ten seconds—"

"Yeah, well I've been trying this new thing where I'm not supposed to ejaculate! All the testosterone, you know, it builds up. It gives you confidence and energy, and I usually don't finish that fast, but it's been like seven days, and I was around you all night last night and I just think, I don't know, you're really pretty—"

"Yeah, good excuse, quick draw."

Joel's face grew serious. "Really, Brenda, you are. I like your shoulders. They're like bird shoulders. And your eyes too, they're a good match for your face. And how your breath smells good even when it's, you know, a little bad. Oh God, and your butt in those sweatpants—"

I grabbed Joel's dick again, this time under his cold, wet boxers and rubbed it. I slid out of my sweatpants and got on top of him.

"What are you doing?" he asked uneasily.

"I'm building your confidence."

"No, Brenda, wait," he said while pulling me toward him. "Shouldn't we get—"

I lowered myself onto him, letting him grow inside me, moving in little up and down motions. Joel laid perfectly still, staring into my eyes. It looked like he wasn't breathing.

"Brenda, please."

"Shh, just shut up. I haven't had sex in forever."

"But...Brenda. You can't just do this."

"Fine, I'll stop."

"Please don't."

Joel, after a couple wonderful minutes, smacked my ass and lifted me off, emitting another grotesque geyser of semen. Apologizing in breathless grunts, he masturbated himself furiously as string-like projectiles sailed overhead, crashing on his body like mortars.

I grabbed a pillow for cover, peeking only after I felt the bed stop shaking. "Good Lord, Joel! Is it like that every time?"

"I told you. It's because of my—"

"Oh, yeah, your anti-jerking off thing."

"Sorry. I—whoa I feel dizzy—whoa. It's usually not like that." He rolled towards me. "Sorry you didn't get to, you know."

"Joel, stop. It's fine. I *rarely* ever come during my first time with someone."

"Wait, but you have—?"

"Joel..."

"Sorry, sorry."

I playfully bit his nipple and cuddled into his chest as he wiped his stomach with a shirt he dug from behind the pillow. His skin was shiny in the spots he wiped with his shirt. It looked like his torso was covered in saran wrap.

"What's all the stuff floating around?" I asked him.

"You mean like the dust?"

"Yeah, is it really our dead skin cells?"

Joel smiled patronizingly, crunching his chin to look down at me. He wasn't fat but looked like it from the angle. "Yeah, I've heard that too. Kinda neat if you think about it. Like the universe is slowly ripping us apart. Piece by tiny—"

"I'm giving them the tape."

"What? No, you're not."

"Yes, I am," I replied sucking his nipple. My mouth came off with a popping sound.

"No," he said, letting me suck his other nipple for a second before pushing me off. "You're not."

I nestled against him, pressing our bodies together, a squishy interlocking. Joel's armpit let off a funk that I wasn't sure if I liked or not. Getting away from his armpit, I put my head on his shoulder. It was bony and uncomfortable.

"Here are your options, Joel. A, I give the tape to them and make some money. B, they come in here and take it."

"How much money?"

"We're trading. For pills or whatever, I dunno."

"Hmm," he muttered.

"Fine, I'm making like two grand. All depends on how I sell them, really. But, Joel, I'm telling you, those are your options. All the shit you got going on? Better off letting Cork fight it out with those two dummies, not you."

"Yeah, but Cork *knows* I gave it to them. And if those evil hippies are as tough as you say they are, which I find it very hard to believe, then Cork is going to come at me first. I'm the easier target. But...I could give *him* the tape. Make an alliance.

"With who? Cork? He'll destroy you."

Joel tapped his lips with his finger. "Hmm... or..."

He smacked my ass and jolted up in bed, sending me rolling off his chest, "Or you could give them the video, but not let them *have* it!"

"What?"

Joel grabbed his phone. "Hold on. Let me pull up the app."

"What app?"

"Sig-nerr."

"Sig-nerr?"

"Yeah, Sig-nerr. It's double encrypted."

"What's that mean?

Joel wiped his brow as he searched for the app. "Where the hell-? I don't know. I just know it lets you send messages with a time limit."

"And?"

"And you could send them the video, but not let them have it. It disappears after five, ten, or thirty minutes. Let them watch it. Get your money. And it disappears. And then I could go to Cork and tell him what I did and how I'm deleting it. Everyone wins—of course, besides the evil hippies, but we'll let Cork deal with their supposed wrath."

"You mean Signal?"

"Huh?"

"Give me your phone." I took his phone and downloaded the app he was looking for. "It's Sig-*nal*, dumbass."

The streaks of light on the floor were brighter, wider and stretched further into the room. Soon they wouldn't be noticeable at all. I watched some more dust float up toward the vent and thought about sunlight, how it could fill a room from so far away.

"What's your plan?" I asked.

"With what?"

"After this is all done, your weed and shit."

Joel took another sip of water from the bottle on his nightstand. "What do you mean *plan*?"

"I mean overall, with everything. Like how I'm gonna take this money from Clay, get a job, and save up. After a while, I'm gonna start buying houses—I know a lot of old ladies who are ready to sell—"

"How?"

"How what?"

"How do you know so many old ladies?"

"I buy their prescriptions"

He folded his arms behind his neck and looked at the ceiling. His toes wiggled under the blanket.

"I'm going to California."

"Yeah, you mentioned that."

"When?"

"Last night, on the way to the party." I plucked one of his nipple hairs.

"Ow!"

"Don't be a baby. And what are you going to do once you're in California?"

Joel looked around the room. I could tell he wasn't enjoying my questions, which only made me want to question him more. I eyed another hair. "Same thing as now—Ow! Stop!—only legally."

"Yeah? Or what?" I gripped another hair but didn't pull. "And have you thought about the details?"

"Details of what?"

"Um, your plan, which isn't a plan unless you think of the details. Place to grow. Customers. Permits. Rent. Budget. Investment and return."

Joel exhaled quietly through his nose. "I don't plan like that, all the specifics and minuscule detail. My plans are larger, broader. More big picture—scenario-based if that makes sense."

"Yeah, it's called daydreaming."

The air vent stopped, sending our awkward silence into a deeper one. Joel's eyes dulled, frozen in what looked like a negative thought-trance.

"Honestly, Brenda, all you really need to do is make sure you don't starve or freeze to death. Everything else is just shit we invent in our heads. You know what I mean? Like, the other stuff we worry about is just bullshit. Our own weird little fears wrapped up into these bullshit problems we obsess over every day. I try not to live like that. You know?"

I took the bottle of water out of his hand and sipped it. "You done?"

"Done with what?" He snatched it back and drank the rest.

He threw the empty water bottle into his already overflowing trashcan. One of those little ones. The empty bottle hit the top and bounced off, taking some tissue and other empty bottles onto the ground with it.

"Your little hippy speech, the 'all you need is love' bullshit."

Joel sat up and flinched against the cold headboard. "What's that supposed to mean?"

I realized my tits were out and folded my arms around them to cover them since we were apparently in a fight. "Nevermind, just forget it."

"No, please, clue me into this *secret of existence* I'm missing since I'm clearly an idiot."

I grabbed his arm and forced a smile. "Look, just forget it, okay? I was just being a dick."

"No, I want to hear it. Why is what I said bullshit to you?"

"I don't know. You're just making it seem like...like all you need to do is eat and stay out of the rain like we're fucking animals or something. Like everything else is just bullshit that doesn't mean anything."

Joel shrugged. "But it's true," he said, all smug and cocky.

"Oh, okay, so what if your dad came home one day and beat the shit out of your mom right in front of you and then just left forever? You never see or hear from him ever again—actually, no, no—actually you *do* see him...years later while you're working for some fat dickhead at the Sprint store who thinks it's okay to grab your ass and talk about your tits since he's paying you ten dollars an hour and you see him, your dad, and he just ignores you like you don't exist since he's there with his new family, this dead-eyed gypsy bitch and her two rat-fuck kids who have *his* nose. His shitty thick-at-the-top nose and asks your dickhead manager for some help. And the dickhead manager sends them to you. Piece of shit dad. Gypsy bitch. Ratfuck kids. Noses marching toward the counter. And he drums his knuckles and looks, not at his feet, but over you, past you, like the stuff behind you is more important, phone cases and chargers. Not a twinge of sympathy or remorse. He looks through you, past the years, the changes, not even flinching at how much you've grown or anything like that. He just clears his throat and asks about a *family plan*. And you run crying out of the store. And your fucking manager has the nerve to call and say—"

Joel put his arm around me. "Jesus, Brenda, I'm—"

I wiggled out of his embrace. My face squeezed as I fought the tears. My throat tightened. "And then your manager fires *you*!" My chest heaved in short breaths. My face withered. "So...so what then, Joel? W-w-what do I do? Just p-plant some p-p-potatoes and build a fff-f-fucking igloo?"

Joel pulled me into him. I reached around the bed weakly, searching through the blur of tears for my bra. I wanted to leave. I didn't want him to see me cry.

He squeezed me harder, holding his lips to the top of my head as he shushed me.

"Joel..."

I resisted, trying to pull away but he didn't budge. He kissed the tears running down the side of my nose and whispered I was okay. I collapsed and gave in, crying into his chest.

Eddie

I sat in the Speedway's parking lot and watched as the exhaust floated by my window. The wind hit the plume of petrol, breaking it into factions, each moving in their own looping floats, untethering against atmospheric forces beyond anything they could understand, reduced into nothing under the sheer magnitude of the sky.

I opened the door and swiveled out the car. There was a crunch under my sneakers, a scatter of neglected gravel. The parking lot was old, thirsty for a good sealant—a bucket of vaporous liquid with warnings of death and cancer on the label; something serious and toxic. I gripped the cold exterior of my car and pulled the rest of myself out. My tater was still greasy, serving as a reminder of the morning's poor attempt at masturbation. God damn Vaseline will do that.

A primitive system of bells clanged as I opened the Speedway's heavy glass door. The cashier, an old Indian fellow about my age, looked up from the newspaper and then back down. He followed the article with his finger and rested his chin on his hand. His body fell into the shape of a question mark.

I hovered in the area immediately under the cashier, milling around his selection of outdated candy as he stood elevated, boosted by the platform from which he conducted business. There were magazines to my right and a plastic tree of sunglasses to my left. Behind him, hanging from hooks and crooked shelves were different over-the-counter medicines, various toiletries and the like. Above his head was one of those plastic cigarette contraptions.

His counter was oddly barren, directly contrasting the dramatic density of stuff that defined his convenience store and many others. Its surface was free from the hectic mess of energy powders, lighters, water pipes, calling cards, boner pills—even the good faith penny system. There was a strange nudity to the counter, to his lack of merchandise.

The Speedway was one of the last gas stations in the area that didn't hide their employees behind bulletproof glass. This was the sole reason for my patronage. The gas was shitty and overpriced and almost everything in here was expired, but the lack of protection was refreshing and necessary. I remember when those things first started. Men standing behind their own crystalized paranoia, inhabiting some post-apocalyptic trading post.

The Indian fellow stopped reading and greeted me. "Yes, my sir?"

"Cleaned the counter, I see?"

"Yes, but only because of a thief. A criminal brat. So we hide now. Back here. What of do you need?"

The bells jangled. A woman EMT strutted forearm-first through the doorway. Her face was mean and square, serious as can be. Her hair, which only intensified the seriousness of her face, was erected in a severe spike, a battlement atop her head. Her prickly scowl deepened as she got near us.

"Oh, you can go ahead," I offered, "Still looking."

She regarded us suspiciously, eyes darting above her lack-of-sleep-bruises. She was hunched forward with a scared animal puff to her.

"Let me get a tin of Skoal."

"Wintergreen or Citrus?"

"Classic straight."

The man sighed in a friendly way. "I am afraid we do not have."

"Just—" The woman sighed in an unfriendly way. "Fine. Wintergreen."

The man twisted his torso toward the Skoal display. His left arm seemed to float as he pinched the can delicately with his right, handling it like a used Kleenex. There was sensuality in his movement, a sexual pleasure brought on by the transaction.

He addressed me while giving the woman her tin.

"This stuff? Great. I do sometimes, putting a pinch under the tongue until it burns me. My wife loves the smell. Very delicious."

The EMT darted her eyes between us as she pocketed her change and the tin. She mumbled something under her breath and walked off, bells crashing in her wake.

The man arched his eyebrows, signaling he was ready to return to our deal.

"Were you looking into investment of our new e-cigarettes?"

"E-what?"

He reached under the counter and pulled out a little stick, a kind of pen-like contraption, running it under his nose as if it were an expensive cigar.

"What's that?"

"It is E-cigarette technology. Latest edition. Very good for you."

"What's it do?"

"This lets you smoke without fear of death."

The man put his lips on the end and depressed a button. The tip glowed evil blue as he took a shallow breath. He looked defiantly into my eyes, nodding a two-count. Dancing with his head, he gasped a puny cloud of vanilla-scented smoke.

"See? It is very healthy and the best for me. All day I smell like vanilla beans. My wife loves it."

I scratched my head. "I was looking for something more in the way of vitamins, if you know what I mean."

The man closed his eyes and nodded. "I very do."

He reached under the counter and produced a packet of pills, two orange gel-caps. The label read "STACKER 2."

"This are my favorite. Perfect for staying awake and remaining healthy."

"No, no, I need those *other* pills. The ones that help you, you know..." I shot a fist under my forearm.

The man nodded solemnly as he reached down and ruffled a world of tin packets, sticking out his tongue as he felt around. There was a genius to the way he sorted through the scramble of substances, his eyes cringing as indicators as his fingers got closer to his target. He looked like a symphony master conducting the final part of his opus, the mad scramble before the bow. His fist finally emerged, triumphant from the hunt. He let go of one packet at a time, letting them hit the counter in a series of clacking, plasticky thuds.

The doors jingled, causing me to suck air uneasily through my teeth. A grizzled road worker entered the store, carrying his previous conversation inside. He moved with the stretched-out manner of a cowboy, like the ground in front of him was exclusively his and no one else's. His cheek stuck out with food as he chewed, revealing itself by scent as sausage as he got closer. He wore a blue PECO jumpsuit and a pair of rubber yellow boots. The boots were caked in dry asphalt. He had one of those Bluetooth headsets and was talking into the air around him. Me and the cashier stood idly, human fixtures in his world of open conversation.

"Yeah. I know, they're the worst, but hey," he said. "Ugh. Let me call you back—actually just hold on." He slapped a fifty on the counter. "On six."

The man's gaze lingered on the array of boner pills, the sight of which seemingly hit him in the gut, forcing him to emit a judgmental gust of air. He reached into his pocket and produced a foil-wrapped sandwich. Sausage, egg, and cheese on an unnaturally shiny bagel. He unwrapped it just enough to take a bite and carried on with his conversation, milling around me and the cashier in a way I found to be disorienting. The man spoke boldly to himself as if he were utterly alone and comfortable. I imagined that the person he was speaking to was doing the same as him, dominating a public space by means of hands-free communication, leaving a wake of unsettled reality behind him. This was a sinister lack of boundary, the polar evil to bullet-proof glass.

"I'll tell ya what we need to do—" the man said through a mouthful of egg as he finally walked off, "—is open a fuckin' gash statshion."

The bells jangled as the door opened and shut. The man's voice became an unintelligible ping of white noise, blending with the pale ambiance of cold morning.

The cashier, having finished watching the PECO man leave, returned to our deal.

"Rhino-7 is good, but this? The Rhino-8? It is even better. This ones, the Wicked Intentions? Wears off fast but is good for quick sneaky times if you know what I am saying to you. But *this*," he said, tapping his finger down on the last packet. "This is called the S-W-A-G. It is the strongest, most potent medicine of all."

"Swag?"

He scratched the packet against the skin of his hand while he looked furtively around the store. "No. S-W-A-G. It stands for sex with grudge. Look," he said, showing me the packet. On the back of the plastic sleeve were separate illustrations with directions for each scenario.

The first drawing was labeled "1 to HURT IT" and displayed a stick figure woman lying under a stick figure man. Her little arms covered her head in a manner that suggested she was plenty worn out from having been proficiently sexed.

The second drawing was labeled "2 to KILL IT" and showed the same stick figure woman lying on her back with her arms reached out in panic as a flame engulfed the region of her crotch. The stick figure man stood over his partner, triumphantly flexing his biceps toward her fiery nethers.

The cashier leaned and whispered behind his hand. He was still holding the packet of S-W-A-G. "After my wife's mother died she was very sad; very upset and wanted no sex for a very long time. I begged her nightly. I said please many times, even bought her chocolate covered raisins—still, there was nothing. Then one time after a long night shift, I took the S-W-A-G-sex-with-grudge and made her be awake. I cried out to her, begging her to crumble my erection. A man my age so firm and taut in the pants? Surely I'd suffer a chest attack of the heart."

"What happened?"

The man leaned over the counter, grunting in a belly pressure whisper. He was so close to my ear that I could hear the saliva working in his mouth. "Hand release," he said.

I took a twenty out of my pocket and slapped it onto the counter. "Sold."

He slid an e-cigarette forward on top of the S.W.A.G.

"Maybe this too, the vanilla flavored e-juice will help you as well. Only for $10.99, just for you."

I held the E-Cig in my hands. It was made out of a hard smooth material. Either plastic or metal, I couldn't tell. I pulled the picture of Clay out of my pocket. "Any chance this was the guy who robbed you?"

The man twisted his face as he pushed the picture away. "Please, no. That man is far too ugly to be a thief. That is simply the face of a rapist." The man gestured for a second and bent down behind the counter. He rose slowly, solemnly placing a small cardboard box on the glass in front of me.

"What's that?" I asked.

"It's a taser, for you to shock the rapist when you find him."

"I don't have that kind of money."

The cashier slid the S-W-A-G, the E-cig, and the Taser forward. His eyes darted arithmetically around in his head. "My grandson bought this taser from a Persian hookah shop owner who I simply cannot stand. I confiscated it last week when I found—but everything combined, I can give you here for twenty dollars flat. An unheard-of deal."

I stroked my chin in consideration. "How about ten?

"Fifteen. And also, I will keep an eye out for the rapist. It is my regret that his face has attached to my memory. I will see him always when I close my eyes."

I pushed the twenty toward him. "You drive a hard bargain."

The man snatched the bill and made change. "We are also making headway on the thief," he said, cracking a roll of quarters into his tray.

"Really? What kind?"

"We have learned he is of a gang."

"A gang? Around here?"

"Yes, they call themselves the Roxborough Indians. They have special clothes made and everything. And I think I know the boy. I see his father from time-to-time."

"What's his father drive?" I asked, intrigued.

"A black truck, a very loud one. He cursed me once for not having diesel pump and then I get and he never comes back. He also has called me a nigger twice."

I took my taser, my S-W-A-G, and my E-cig and put them in one of the plastic bags hanging off a hook from his display. I slipped the packets that John left out of my pocket and set them on his nude counter.

"Is this what the thief took?"

The cashier looked at me with awe. "My sir! Yes! How do you find?"

"The kid I'm looking for—"

"The rapist?"

"I think he's mixed up with the leader of the gang who stole from you."

The man held the salvia packet, inspecting it in the light. He pinched the bottom of the foil and turned it over. Something that looked like cooking spices fell into his hand. He squeezed the herbs and let them fall softly back into the packet. "I try this once, the Salvia 40x. Me and my wife's anniversary, we smoked it through a hookah. I do not recommend. Very, very strange."

"Give me my twenty back and I'll shock the thief when I find him."

"Where?"

"I don't know, wherever I find him."

"No, I meant on his body. I want you to shock his genitals, and instead of money I will give you one free canister of mango E-juice. The girls love it."

"Eh, keep it. I gotta go."

***

Most of the mess had been cleaned by the time I got there. Just the charred remains of useless crap remained—blankets with singed edges, melted bags of chips, warped soda bottles, a stretched-out shirt, a perfectly undisturbed hairbrush with its tag still intact, and a plastic bag filled with other plastic shopping bags. A shopping cart leaned appropriately in the direction of its missing wheel. The glow of the morning was gone, the peace and magic faded. The sky and air were serious now, official blue of the early afternoon.

A rough-looking guy about two decades younger than me was there scavenging, grubbing butts and other nonsense off the ground. I kicked a chunk of brick to get his attention. He froze and turned around, unhappy about my presence.

"Hey, guy, I'm not a cop if that's what you're worried about. Just out here looking for someone. Sent on behalf of their concerned parents, that's all." I took the picture out of my wallet. "Name's Clay, you seen him?"

The guy inched toward me, his wet sneakers bubbling with every step. He was wearing tight, ragged dungarees with a matching denim jacket. His denim ensemble was faded, bleached by time into the color of a salted road, everything blotched of multi-colored paint. He put his foot up on a half cinderblock, a miniature ruin, and wet his mustache. "I ain't no junkie," he said, flashing a bottle of Wild Irish Rose.

"I didn't assume you were."

"Whaddaya back here lookin' to get your dick sucked or something'? Cause I ain't the one. I'll crack your head, pal."

"Truth be told, I'm always in the market for a good hummer, though not from you. Nothing personal."

"You think you're better than me?"

"Unfortunately, I barely am."

"I know."

I squinted. "What the hell's that supposed to mean?"

The man spit through brown teeth and smiled. "I believe you knew my ex-wife, RIP."

"*Jesus...*"

"Yup, Barry McPhearson. Livin', breathin', and kickin' ass."

I spit on the ground. "You *coward*!"

"Fuck you, kid toucher."

Blood rushed to my head. Tears formed in my eyes. "She was seventeen!"

"Sixteen, actually."

A chunky green military helicopter flew overhead and drowned our conversation in the noise of its double blades. Barry adjusted his crotch and looked up, cupping his forehead with a dirty hand.

"CH-47 Chinook, right there," he beamed, oddly proud. "Used to help build those suckers at the Boeing plant down there in Chester. Sheet metal union. Goddamn, that was sweet, going to bed knowin' I built some shit they'd use in war. Fuckin' kicked ass."

"What I did was *wrong*, diabolically selfish. I was in a troubled marriage, sexually frustrated to the point of oblivion, and, goddammit, I was weak. An opportunity presented itself, and I fooled around—"

Barry snapped out of his daydream. "Fooled around? You ate'r pussy, Ed."

My shoulders dropped. "Yes...yes, I did. I ate a seventeen—"

"Sixteen."

"Ok, I ate a sixteen—I swear she was seventeen—eh, what's it matter? I did it. And guess what? I owned up to my actions. Faced the consequences. And I, flawed as I am, at least *tried* to be there for the people I loved, and sure, they shut me out, but fuck! I was *there*. What about you Barry? Huh?"

Barry's eyes followed the dot of remaining helicopter in the sky, squinting to drink in every second of its momentary existence. Once it was gone he dug into his jacket and pulled out his Irish Rose. He cracked the cap and drank half of it, licking his teeth. His face was weathered, wrinkles spidering across like dried up rivers, a big boozer's nose standing out red and porous. The man had had a rough paper route, I could tell. Weak winds sent an empty donut wrapper tumbling behind Barry's sneaker as he twisted the lid back on his bottle, a little tighter than necessary, and put it back in his pocket. "I ain't makin' no excuses, but my life's been far from a picnic—not like *you* give a shit, but I had a rough time comin' up and by the time I was married, I was a fuckin' mess. All strung out on smack and uppers. Shit was bad, ya know? Tryin' to stay straight on crooked tracks." He spit again. "So, I figured I'd go clean myself up, come back. But...I met a girl. Right there in one of those group homes."

I snorted. "That's it? That's your excuse?"

"Oh, *fuck off!* She was *nice* to me, Eddie. Plus, I'd never hit her or cheated on her before, so there wasn't that *negativity*, that bitter resentment I was always used to. It was *good*, everythin' about it."

"So you had a little side-piece. So what?"

Barry laughed to himself and shook his head. "It ain't a sidepiece if ya knock her up." He slid the bottle back out and took the cap off. He put the bottle to his lips but didn't take a sip. He just held it there, moving it in a circle around his mouth as he spoke. "Pulled another whole couple of grubby little kids up outta that one, and then—" he looked sorrowfully up at the sky. "Goddamn bitch got hit by a bus."

"Christ! Who?"

"My ex. One of her casino chips rolled out into the street. She followed it out between two parked cars and ka-blam. Lived on support for two more weeks and then I pulled the plug and split for awhile. Kept tellin' myself I was gonna go back, make right with everyone, Lynne, Brenda, Manny, and Luisa. But the days just passed and it all got away from me. It just...went away. Off into a neverendin' tomorrow."

I took my hat off and shook it out. There was a twig in there, digging against my head. "Wait so you left your *other* family too?"

Barry sipped his wine. "Better than molesetin' em." He put the bottle back in his jacket and looked at the sky where the helicopter had been. His face was fixed in a resilient grin, showcasing his corn-colored teeth. It twitched and faded. He looked like he was about to cry. "Fuck was I supposed to do?" he asked the clouds. "Knock? Hey, girls! Daddy's home!" Barry drained the contents of his bottle and hurled it over the fence onto the train tracks. The bottle went through a dead bush and shattered. "I don't know the first thing about either of them, other than their mother's dead. I remember the obituary. Cried like a fuckin' baby when I saw it in the paper. My new girl and kids damn near put me on depression pills. I couldn't tell them anything, it was *eatin'* me."

"Well, for starters, Lynne—she's your oldest, right?—from what I can tell, she's been having a hard time with the drugs and whatnot, so that's no good, and Brenda, well, I don't know that she's got the cleanest of noses, but I can tell she's trying, *trying* to keep the whole thing, or what's left, at least, together. She's a good girl tangled in a fucking mess."

Barry wiped his eyes.

We watched a school of dead leaves blow across the train tracks as Barry nodded at his thoughts.

"Yup, she's fierce. Just like her mother. A good and bad quality in a woman. And Lynne, although I hate to say it, she's always been a fuck up. It's weird how you can tell, even when they're little." He reached into his jacket then remembered he'd finished the wine. "Lemme see that picture again."

I pulled the picture of Clay back out of my jacket.

"I seen him. He don't look like that though. He's uglier in real life, with those, what are those things called? Reggae hair?"

"Dreadlocks."

"Yup. He's got the bread-locks," Barry said, lifting his leg to let out a disastrously wet fart. "Haven't really seen much of him since what's-his-name came back here and fucked him up, fucked this whole place up, really, almost sent us all up in flames."

"What guy?"

"You know him. Fuckin' shit! What's his fuckin' name? I *know* you know him—"

Two police officers came out from the trees carrying coffee. One of them shouted, "Hey! You guys can't be back here!"

Barry tore ass across the marbleized earth, running in a drunk, shoe-slapping sprint.

One of the officers, coffee in hand, ran behind Barry goading him. "C'mere you old drunk!"

Barry crashed face down in the ground, clinging to the metal chain link fence that separated the park from the train tracks. The officer walked over and poured some hot coffee on his back.

The other officer looked at me. "C'mon old man. Get lost."

Joel

The bag of frozen muffins ached on my thigh as I shivered through the woods behind Brenda's. I parted the prickly branches of a wild raspberry bush and stepped through to a trail. Sleep-deprived and cold as I was, there was a reinvigorated lightness to my step. I was still floating off the double morning orgasm that unexpectedly ended by consoling the crying Brenda. The stuff she told me was sad for sure, but it didn't really disprove my point.

Everything around me was frozen. Icicles hung from dead branches, refracting light from the rising sun in multicolored shimmers. The trees reached upward, skeletal and haunted. It was like time itself had been stopped by the cold temps in a perfect mystical moment. I fantasized briefly about my dad leaving my family. I think I would have liked it. Panic surged as I remembered the watch. *Where did I put it?* The question hung heavy on my head, intensifying the soft morning light into a nuisance. A pebble bounced off the tree next to me. And then another. The throws got shorter, leading toward a towering mess of thorns and plants and trees. Some of it looked like dead poison ivy.

I approached with caution. Parting only the plants I was certain wouldn't give me a rash.

The bush-tower shook, birthing a solemn Fig out from its prickly womb. Finger to his lips, he led me through his little hobbit world and into a clearing. It wasn't big, maybe ten-feet wide in diameter. In the left corner of the clearing stood the crumbly, dilapidated remains of a cottage. The mortar between the stones was reduced to dry powder and flaked off. I could have pushed it over if I wanted. Cigarette butts, guts of exploded fireworks, beer and energy drink cans, all were littered on the ground. Fig kicked an empty can of Coors Original out of his way and sat on a flipped over 5-gallon bucket.

He looked at me.

I looked at him.

"Well?" he asked as if it were obvious.

"Well, what? You're the one who brought me back here."

"Did ya get any pussy?"

"Fig—"

"I need to know what kind of guy I'm working with before we move on."

"Jesus Christ! Fine, yeah,—Actually, wait, have *you* ever gotten any pussy before?"

"Not directly, I—"

"Nope, changed my mind. I don't even want to hear this." I stomped an energy drink can, flattening it on the ground. "Seriously, dude, what were you doing in my yard?"

Fig pulled a pack of matches out of his pocket. He lit one and used it to light the whole pack, holding it as long as he could before throwing it on the ground. The flame quickly faded into grey, sulfury smoke. "Stealing your trash."

"Why?"

"For my dad, dummy. He was right behind your wall when we were talking. That's why I gave you signals."

"I knew you were giving me signals!"

"Yeah, then I signaled you with the rocks too, led you to my fort."

"Yeah that was pretty good—so wait...why's your dad want my trash?"

"He thinks you're planning his demise."

"Oh, shit, the *video*."

"What video?"

"Did you fucking tell him I grow weed?!"

"Wait, what video?"

I gripped his hoodie, jacking him up against a tree. "Fig!"

"Get off me, faggot!"

"Did you?"

"No, you fucking dick! But maybe now I will since you're turning on me like a goddamn asshole."

I let go of his sweatshirt. His neck was red and scratched from where I grabbed him, the collar of his hoodie hung stretched and loose.

"Sorry, dude, I'm just fucked up about the trash thing. Caught me off guard."

"Who cares," he muttered as he adjusted his shirt. "It's just trash."

"It's not, though—"

A large dripping icicle fell from a high branch and took a few others with it. Most of them exploded on the branches, but one of them staked the ground next to the cottage. I grabbed Fig's forearms and moved him out of the way, even though they were nowhere near hitting us.

Seeing we were safe, Fig pushed away. "Get off. And what's this video you're talking about?"

"Nope, not till you get my trash back."

"I gotta leave for my meet in like five minutes. I left the basement window—"

Fig's eyes caught something. I looked down. The bag of muffins had fallen out of my jacket pocket and was lying in the dirt. All four of them. Fig crouched. I crouched.

"Wait a minute. I'm going to give them to you. I just need—"

Fig swooped down and snagged the bag and began backpedaling away. "Better hurry up and get it while my dad's away at my wrestling meet. You only have a couple hours."

Muffins tucked to his chest, he lowered his head, blasting through the thorns like a power running back.

"Just a quarter muffin!" I called after him. "Trust me. Fig!"

A shaking bush was all that remained of him. I kicked Fig's bucket and started to make my way back through the thorns.

Brenda

I sat in the kitchen, eating a fresh PB&J. Joel had given me some grape jelly that morning before I left his house. My first bite was perfect. The bread was soft and fresh. A glob of crunchy peanut butter swirled with an oozing pocket of jelly. I washed my perfect bite down with a sip of ice cold two-percent. It was orgasmic. Nothing could bother me. Not the wallpaper, the carpet, my sister—

Lynne popped her head into the kitchen, flashing a big, coked-out smile. She looked like the cat from Alice and Wonderland.

"Bren-daaaaa," she beamed musically. The storm door swung open and shut, rattling against the wood. A hushed mix of voices filled the living room.

"Who's here?" I asked, realizing I didn't have a bra on.

"Clay and Donny. And-guess-what-they-haaaaaave," she sang shrilly, each word ascending up a musical scale.

Lynne squirmed with delight, knowing I was about to be in possession of a fuck-ton of opiates. She rubbed her wet, coke-runny nose and wiped it on her tank top. A glob of jelly fell from my finger onto my plate. I dipped a corner of my sandwich and smeared the jelly back onto my bread.

An ass crack was all I could see of my sister as she dug through the bottom of the fridge. Her crack was hidden in a way, camouflaged by the lumpy terrain of her lower back. Beer cans rolled and thundered as she opened the drawer that was supposed to be for vegetables. One of the cans slipped as she stood up, but she caught it against her stomach, causing it to jiggle. It reminded me of gravy after a day in the fridge. The way it turns into that gross, meaty jello.

"And what are you all smiley about, Miss Thing?" she playfully interrogated, setting the beers down on the table to tickle me. "Did somebody fuck their gay-boy, weirdo neighbor? Huh? Huh?"

I laughed and pushed her away. "You're a nut!"

"Oh, my little Brenda-bunny's in luh-huv!" she squealed, clasping her hands by her face and fluttering her eyelids.

"Please, I just needed to get laid."

Lynne's eyes glistened as she smiled. She made a fist to check her nails, moving her body to a song inside her head. "Uh-*huh*." Her gaze fell on me and softened "Well, he must've done something right."

"Yeah—gave me a jar of jelly."

Lynne laughed and hugged her trio of beers. She started to walk into the living room but stopped and turned around. She put the beers back down, stamping the table with a new set of wet rings. She leaned forward and stared at the wall. "Know what would be cool?"

I licked my fingers. "What?"

She squeezed her eyes like she was trying to project a dream onto the cabinets. "To move somewhere. Like Texas or Alaska. Just...go."

"And do what?"

"I don't know. Get a job and just...I don't know." Lynne sighed and picked the beers up as she wiggled her way back into the living room.

"C'mon Bren. They need to talk to you."

The cry feeling came back. It fizzled at the bottom of my throat.

Clay milled behind Donny, leaning on a couch and looking around. He had one of those caveman faces. Big and wrong and ugly. Tennis-ball hair for a beard. He wore those patchwork hippy pants, the wide-legged corduroy ones and a tattered Grateful Dead shirt over a long sleeve thermal that used to be white. His hair was wild, some of it dreaded, some not. A piece of soiled gauze covered the back of his head. He had bags under his eyes that perspired. Wet little beads, like warts made of water.

He approached to introduce himself, a little more poised than I'd have expected. "Clay. And I take it you already know Donny here." He stuck out his hand.

"Yeah. Sup, Donny."

Clay's hand was soft and moist when we shook.

Donny squeezed Lynne from behind and kissed her ear, pulling her down with him as he sat on the couch. Lynne crashed down on his lap, somehow supported by his bony legs. Donny's top half emerged out from behind my sister, straining in a sad crunch toward the table. He grabbed a beer and tossed it to Clay. Donny grabbed another for himself and opened it with his face disgustingly close to the can. A little genie of vapor rose from the freshly cracked beer, barely able to escape before Donny jolted the can up and chugged.

"You were a huge help to us, me and Donny here," said Clay, setting his unopened beer on my coffee table. He reached into the little messenger bag that sat limp near his feet. It was beaten and dirty, made of denim, corduroy, and canvas and had a ton of ugly little pins on it, unknown bands and other weird shit. Clay pulled three prescription bottles out of his bag and set them on the table. "Those are 30s. I got a hundred there and another hundred coming after we get what we need from your neighbor over there."

I opened one of the bottles and tilted it. A gang of small blue pills spilled neatly into my palm. These were the ones Lynne had before. Smooth and blue with m-30 stamped in the middle. Pure oxycodone. They didn't have acetaminophen like percs so you could take a bunch of them without having to worry about frying your liver. They were legit.

I tipped the pills back into the bottle, listening to them rattle as they hit. "Cool, so give me the other two hundred and you'll get the video."

Clay smiled, showing me his buttery, disgusting teeth. A brown stripe ran across the front two and up into his gums, like an upside down Nike sign. He looked at Donny and laughed. "You're right, man, she is tough." He turned back to me. "I'll tell you what, take this hundred and then, no, no hear me out, then I'll agree to deal *exclusively* with you. Twenty-five cents a milligram all the way up."

My phone buzzed in my pocket. I silenced it. "How many can you do?"

"How many do you want?"

"A thousand."

"A *thousand* thirties?"

"Yeah."

Clay turned to consult with Donny, a bit shocked to see his partner sucking on Lynne's neck as he rubbed her belly from behind, rounding up to her breasts. Clay cleared his throat.

Donny squeezed my sister's tit for good measure and brushed her to the side. "Bro, no way she could cover that. That's like, that's like a lot of fuckin' money."

Clay nodded in agreement. "Yeah, seventy-five hundred. And just to be clear, I don't front anything. You'd need all the cash up front."

"Ok."

"You *sure* you can cover that? I don't need it tonight. I just need to know I'm not wasting my time."

My phone buzzed again. It was Joel. He'd called me like six times. I ignored it.

"Everything okay?" Clay asked, suspiciously eyeing my phone.

Lynne called out from the couch, "It's probably gay boy wantin' some round two of his little Brenny-bun—"

Donny grabbed Lynne's pussy over her jeans and she smacked his hand, letting out a delighted giggle. "Donn-eeeee! Oh my God!"

"You know what?" I said, cramming my phone back into my jean pocket. "I think you're full of shit. You can't get a thousand thirties. No one can. Unless you got a connect with a delivery guy, which I've only seen once, and it got busted immediately. So, what the fuck are you really doing here?"

Lynne pushed Donny off and sipped her beer, watching intently. Even Donny seemed a little tense. Clay opened his eyes and sighed, shaking his head.

"Actually, there *is* a way to get a thousand thirties. All you need to do is be assaulted by some crazy psycho and have him try to burn you alive. Then you steal a doctor's pad at the hospital and write scripts for whatever you want. Even without that, I'm more than plugged-in. I know girls who fuck doctors and can get them to write whatever— point is, I can make you *a lot* of money, thousands of dollars at a time, and I plan to. Just, Brenda, please, please don't ever come at me like that ever again. Please. I really...I really don't like that."

Lynne, seizing an opportunity to cut the tension and get high for free, opened one of the bottles and dumped some pills onto the coffee table. "My fee for hooking it up!" She took each pill, one-by-one, and placed it under her driver's license, blasting it with the rusty pliers.

Clay tucked a strand of hair behind his ear and arched an eyebrow at me, a subtle *do-we-have-a-deal* look.

I nodded.

Lynne divvied the blue powder into four neat little piles. She motioned for me to join them, but I declined, opting to linger awkwardly instead. Clay and Donny went down and snorted theirs. Lynne did both hers and mine and then ran to the sink. She'd snorted so much she was gagging.

Clay wiped his nose with a tie-dye handkerchief, folding it neatly before he put it back into his pocket. "The video, please, before we get too carried away."

I took my phone out and held it up to them. "Here it is. Want me to play it?"

Donny clapped his hands. "Hell yeah, bro! Hook it up to the TV. There's a way to do that. You need this cable thing that connects the internet or somethin'."

Clay motioned for Donny to relax while keeping his eyes on mine, his piercing pale blue eyes. They were sadly beautiful, highlighting the flaws of his horrible face.

"We will *not* be hooking it up to the TV. Just scroll it, can you do that? Like a fast-forward feature? And please, no volume."

"You got a phone?"

"No. Donny, let me—thank you. Here, use his. I know the number."

"First, you gotta download this app."

Clay's blue eyes narrowed into icicles. "App?"

"Yeah, it's double encrypted."

"Encrypted against *who* exactly?"

"Look, what you guys do with the video is *your* business. I'm not getting *my* phone number tied up in it. Just download the app."

Clay turned to Donny. "You ever heard of this app before?"

Donny took his leg out between Lynne's thighs and stood up, popping his shoulders like an old-school gangster. "Let me uh...let me see" He grabbed his phone. "Oh yeah, this dude I used to fuck with had something like this. Asian dude. Said it's uh—what's that called again?"

"Encrypted?"

"Yeah! But I couldn't tell. Never needed any special glasses or anything to read the messages so I don't know."

Clay shook his head. "Fine, just send it."

"Cool," I said, heading over to the table to grab my pills. "Feel free to watch it after I send it. Just to make sure I'm not fucking around or whatever. I just, you know—"

Clay touched my hand lightly. It made my blood run cold. "I totally understand."

Lynne crushed some more pills and slid me another bump. A tiny one.

"Here ya go, Brenda."

"Nah, I'm good."

"Oh, *c'mon*." Lynne picked a pill off the table and tossed it on my lap. "At least pop one if you don't want to rail it. Have some fucking fun, ya tightass."

Clay and Donny went back to the floor, kneeling in front of the table. Clay took some pills out of his own bottle and dumped them back into mine, the one that Lynne opened. "You should probably put these out of reach. Just to be safe." He smiled, a weird jack-o-lantern smile.

I put the bottle in my purse and set it down next to my foot. The little blue pill Lynne had thrown me rolled between the sofa cushions. I dug it out. It was small. Blue and smooth—speckled actually as I looked closer. It was actually *white* with a million blue flecks. Flavor-blast-crystal-looking things. I figured I could do *one*. Just to shut them up. I didn't want Clay thinking I was a narc or anything. Plus, it was only thirty milligrams.

Fig

Parents wearing fleeces cheered from the bleachers as Chuck Morgan got his ass kicked by some kid from the Kensington Jaguars. It was ridiculous. The kid looked like a crack baby. Skinny body, watermelon head, big bulging eyes, an alien crawling over Chuck with ease and pinning him to the mat. I made a mental note to tell Chuck to quit and went back to hating Joel. Fucking *Joel*. The piece of shit ripped me off. I'd eaten an entire muffin and here forty five minutes later felt nothing. Wasn't high at all. And to make things worse, I was up soon. The match after next.

I ripped my button-ups off and jogged over near the snack bar to warm up. I needed to get myself pumped. There was a spot between the bleachers where I'd go and think about how shitty my life was while I jumped around to get loose. I'd think about my Mom, about how my dad told me that she left our family to smoke crack with niggers in the projects. I'd think about how much I hated crack and niggers and the towelheads who gave my dad stress disorder over in the Middle East.

Coach Rusnak motored toward me from the bench. I noticed how his arms always chugged by his sides when he moved, reminding me of a train.

"The hell you doin, kid?"

"Getting ready."

He spun me around and strapped my headgear tight, buttoning it at my chin. His face looked *so* old.

"Getting ready? You're on now, dinkus!"

I stepped out on the mat. The lights were bright, brighter than normal. And whiter. Very white. The foam felt extra squishy, so much that I could feel it depress under every step I took. The numbers on the scoreboard, the giant red numbers, blinked and reset. Everything going to 8's before 0. I saw the guy in charge of the scoreboard. His big belly seemed concentrated in the middle of his pleated khakis, pressing against the big plastic table where he was working. He fidgeted with a little box and the board blinked again. The round was set to three minutes. I felt, for the first time ever, ruled by numbers.

It was an away match so we didn't have a lot of people cheering on our side—which was good. Made me feel like a bad guy. The kid I was wrestling, a skinny redheaded dildo from Delaware who went to some rich school near Wilmington, walked out on the mat to greet me. His forehead was crunched and intense. He bit down on his mouth guard and pumped his fists together, spit misting in the impossibly white lights that shone down through metal cages, protection from basketballs, I guess. I looked through him, past all the bullshit snarling and intimidation, into the center of his eyes. It was all there. The fear and softness. The movie nights with his parents, expensive furniture, trips to Europe and other gay countries like it. I saw a little bitch-made momma's boy who was about to enter *my* world, the world of a warrior, the world of a guy who channeled Indian spirits and got stabbed by his dad.

Next thing I see is my dad high up in the bleachers. He looked old too, just like coach, lost in a swirl of ancient looking parents. How was I just noticing this? How *old* everyone was. Sad-looking. My dad stood and gave me a double-thumbs up. I nodded as a five-hundred pound thought dropped from the top of my head, out of nowhere, like the wrestling moves the night before.

Time=Sadness

The ref waved his hand in my face. "Yo, kid, you ready?"

I had no idea how long I'd been standing there, not a clue. The idea of time itself felt odd, like a theory. The scoreboard was huge and important. I wanted to get on my knees and worship it, watch it flash and reset in square zero-eights. Zero-eight, wasn't that the symbol for infinity? I could hear my dad and Coach Rusnak yelling but couldn't make out the words or *meaning* of what they were saying. They were so far away. The only people of importance were the angry ginger, the ref, and me. The other two, ref and ginger, looked at me weird, like they wanted to ask me a question but didn't know what.

A whistle pierced the air. The pissed-off redhead got down on all fours. He looked up and said, "C'mon!"

It occurred to me for the first time that wrestling was kinda gay, at least the way the matches started out. I got down and knelt around him, careful not to get too close. I usually put a bunch of weight on the guy's back when I started but didn't want to touch this kid. I didn't want anything to do with him really. I just knelt there with my hand barely on him, which felt even gayer somehow. Another whistle blew and the kid knocked my limp hand off and stood. He seemed perplexed, frozen in his own confusion. The place exploded with angry screams as the ginger grabbed me by the neck and whipped me around.

The coaches, the parents, everyone freaked as the ginger locked up with me. I stood my ground but was feeling weird, like my legs were made of stone. The yells and cheers sounded like they were coming from a thousand yards away. I heard Coach Rusnak from the bleachers.

"Get low, kid! Get lowwww!" he belted from the bottom of his gut.

I tried, but everything was moving so slow. Me. The ginger. Time. The ginger went for my legs and slammed me on the mat. He pinned my shoulders down for a two-count but I kicked out. I wriggled loose and popped back up on my feet, thrilled by the speed of my instinct, how my body knew exactly what to do even though I was thinking about something else. There wasn't much time left on the clock and the ginger was up five-nothing.

The kid, who was now smiling behind his mouthguard, came back at me and tightened his hands around my waist. He had me from behind which was bad, the worst possible position next to being mounted on the ground. I saw my dad in the stands, slamming his fists into his thighs and yelling. His screams blended into the swirl of the parents around him, the ocean of old and desperate sadness, the past crying out against the future which was me and the ginger. We were them but in the future.

The ginger, who still had me from behind swung me around. He was giving it everything but couldn't get me off my feet.

I looked at the clock again. The round was almost over.

My dad screamed again. This time I heard him.

"Goddammit, Figgy, get 'im!"

I dug my hands into his armpits, and I shit you not, tickled the ginger. He cried out, loosening his grip. We locked up again, face-to-face. His skin was the color of his hair. I spit out of the bottom of my mouth guard and hit him in the eyes, gripping him from the belly. Spit flew from his furious ginger mouth as he torqued his bodyweight to the left. I resisted the other way—not too hard, just enough to let him know I wasn't going that way. I let him push to the right, and then pushed to the left. He went a little harder to the right and I pushed back again. He pushed again, this time with every spec of might in his little freckled body, and I pulled, grabbing his spandex and lifting him into the air. A camera flashed somewhere. The ginger was upside down and I had left my feet. We floated in a silent tumble as the crowd joined in a wave of noise, a suspenseful, "Ohhhhhh."

The kid let out a horrible groan as his back slammed down on the mat.

I looked up at the clock while I laid on him, pinning both his shoulders to the floor. The ref was so stunned with the takedown that he didn't even count to three. The clock ran out and the buzzer sounded. Coach Rusnak went ballistic, locomoting his way out onto the mats. The ginger wheezed on the floor. Everyone was quiet except for my dad. He stood at the top of the bleachers with both fists in the air, his arms outstretched and shaped like a V.

"Wooo!"

Back on the sideline, my dad squeezed my shoulders in a torturous massage as Coach Rusnak ruffled my hair.

"Hoo *boy*!" whispered Rusnak. "Kid doesn't know what *day* it is." He squeezed his rolled-up bunch of papers in excitement and did something gross with his mouth.

We stood and watched as my opponent got medical attention from Carl Delaney's mom, who was a nurse.

Both sides cheered for the injured ginger as his coach and Mrs. Delaney lifted him to his feet and helped him to the bench. I slipped out of my dad's death massage and rotated my shoulder like I was working out an injury so he'd get off me.

My dad covered his mouth with the back of his hand and whispered to Coach. "Whatta pussy." Coach Rusnak packed a lip and gave some to my dad. "Really gave old-Red there a good lickin'," said Rusnak, as he adjusted the lump of Skoal with his tongue.

"A *good* lickin'," echoed my dad as he pinched from the tin and packed himself a lip.

The two men broke off into a conversation about other lickins they'd seen before. My stomach growled, stopping Rusnak's story about a Mexican he met in the Navy. My dad dug into his pocket and pulled out a glob of wrinkled ones wrapped in receipts with coins stuffed inside them. A nickel fell on the ground, flipping in slow-motion as it floated to the mat. It didn't bounce when it landed. It just stopped. I picked it up.

My dad elbowed Rusnak. "What can this little machine eat? I don't want to give him nothin' that's gonna mess him up."

I held the nickel in my hand, trying to figure out how I'd feel if my face was on money.

Rusnak reached into the front pocket of his fleece and gave me two small packets with lightning bolts on them. It reminded me of the shit I stole from the gas station. I grabbed the packets awkwardly. My hand was already busy with the nickel. It was sweating too. My hands always sweat like crazy if I hold a coin. Maybe something to do with holding a dead guy's head, I thought.

"What's this?"

Rusnak spoke to my dad instead of me for some reason. "Energy cream. It's good. Look," he pointed to the packet. "It says right there, B vitamins."

My dad nodded his head in approval. "That's a good healthy snack, Fig. I think it's also got some of that taurine in there too. Check it out."

Rusnak nodded, staring over the crowd of parents.

I tore one of the packets open with my teeth and squeezed the gel into my mouth. It tasted like chalk. "Whus Taur-ee?" I asked, with a mouthful of energy jizz.

A whistle blew. Another match began. Scott Schmidt versus some kid from Maryland.

My dad shrugged and looked at Rusnak.

Coach, keeping his eyes on the ongoing match said, "Eh, it's some shit the Asians extracted from plants or something—control in the wrists, Schmitty!—uh, what's that stuff called? Jinko Galoba? Like that stuff."

My dad nodded his head, "Those chinks do know a lot about health, Figgy. They got *a lot* of ancient secrets."

A parent, younger guy about Joel's age, jumped down from the second row of bleachers to the spot where I warmed up. He shook out his knee and came towards us. His smile grew as he got closer, big perfect white teeth with a silver canine. His nose was crooked, like it'd been broken a bunch of times, and he was wearing a Next Gen MMA shirt. He looked like a friendly Russian gangster.

"Man, I'm sorry to interrupt but is that your son?" he asked, smiling. "I mean, wow, that was something else."

I tried saying thanks, but my mouth was full of purple goop.

Mr. Rusnak smiled at the guy and nodded. "Which one of these critters is yours?"

"Afraid I'm just here with my son. Up there in the bleachers with his mom," he said pointing. "He's only in fourth grade so he's still got a while. Name's Rob by the way." He extended an arm to my dad. My dad ignored his offer to shake and squeezed my shoulders. "He gets it from his old man. Right, Figgy?" He put me in a headlock and gave me a noogie, pulling me in front of him.

The purple goop started hardening in my mouth, condensing into a mucousy putty, slowly taking on the shape of a turd. It was happening all over again. The blur of grass and kicks and yells, the feeling of that cold horrible nugget on my tongue, biting down into the creamy center. All I could smell or taste was *shit*.

I bent forward and retched on the sideline. The purple energy turd rolled out of my mouth, glistening under the gymnasium's bright lights. My dad grabbed the back of my shirt. "The hell's a-matter with you?" He turned to Coach Rusnak. "Coach?"

Rob bent down and picked up the energy packet. "You guys didn't give him this, did you? Stuff's gnarly, full of caffeine and a bunch of other crap."

My dad scoffed. "What, are you like the Surgeon General or somethin'?"

Rob pulled a banana out of his hoodie pocket and my dad smacked it to the ground. It hit with a wet splat and flattened on the mat.

"What the fuck are you givin' him? Huh?"

Rob was confused. "I'm sorry. Is he allergic?"

"No, I just don't like strangers offerin' shit to my kid. It's creepy. Child molester-like. Go back to your own kid—*if* that's even him."

Rob put his hands up and backed away, looking more amused than angry, but still a little pissed.

Coach spoke up in my dad's defense. "Guy's a veteran, bud. Show some class."

"What the fuck's that supposed to mean?" asked my dad.

"You know, just like, show some respect. That's all."

Rob nodded and backed away, still processing what'd happened. He walked back up the bleachers and rejoined his wife and kid. His wife tried to ask him a question and he shook his head.

I tapped my dad. "I'm gonna go sit with my team."

My dad, who was now fully staring at Rob and his family, nodded without looking.

My stomach growled as I dipped out the double doors and headed back to the lockers for another muffin.

Joel

The wind kicked up, bullying me from behind. I bent forward and puffed my cheeks in an internal scream, protesting the bitter gust. I was standing behind Brenda's. Somewhere in the grey area between the woods and her backyard, where the grass devolved into other, more primordial forms of weeds, stingers of bare feet and possible rash-inducers, woody stalks with ugly flowers; breakers of weed-whacker string.

The unmistakable sound of a laugh came from her house, interrupting my brief and sinister reverie among the more barbaric plants. The laugh was shrill, definitely not Brenda's. I checked my phone again to see if she'd called back.

Nope.

I fled to the woods, letting nature swallow my miserable existence. Fuck her. The manipulative bitch. She was just using me for the video so why did I care anyway? I didn't need her advice. The sky loomed, a murky vaporous ocean filled with muscular dark clouds. One of the goonish clouds parted, letting the sun sting my eyes between the cold rattling branches. I wanted to reach up and rip it out of the sky. Throw it at Brenda's house.

I jogged militantly along a little path of trampled earth where wild raspberries grow in the summer. The plants were dead, reduced to brown, berry-less stems bent sorrowfully toward what was left of the snow. Certain parts of the ground were wet, making fart-like sounds when I stepped.

I thrashed through a row of dead bushes and stopped at the bottom of a hill to get my breath. There at the top was Cork's towering retainage wall. Intimidating metal cages stacked on top of one another, filled to the brim with football-sized chunks of blue stone and modified concrete. Apparently, the earth around John's house had been moving and he didn't like it. That was the kind of guy I was dealing with. A guy who built walls to hold the earth. A brutal master of the terrain.

I hooked my hands in the freezing chain-link cages and climbed. A rascal piece of metal snagged my jacket and tore a hole. I wiggled myself loose, almost falling, but stabilized. Eight feet off the ground, and four to go. I held my jacket's cotton entrails from spilling out as I continued up the wobbly cage-wall.

I pulled myself up into his yard on my belly, lying like a hesitant alligator in his short stretch of wild grass, the stuff outside his fence, the same alien grass as Brenda's. There were no neighbors in sight, no noise. The sky darkened, casting a welcome shadow over the entire street. Poisonous-looking clouds stacked dramatically in the sky. Wind kicked up and bent the trees. It smelled like it could snow, the space-linen scent of the future's frozen precipitation.

John's fence was short, easier to go over than under. Standing at a whopping four feet, it was a total non-fortification. A bunch of bulky cuts of uneven timber that rested in slotted concrete holders shaped like mini-tombstones. Still on the lookout for neighbors, I spilled over and crawled around the perimeter of the yard, making sure to stay within his decorative landscaping for cover.

I emerged out from beneath a raindrop maple, pushing out from its umbrella of sagged branches, its kaleidoscopic dome, and ducked under a barren burning bush. I crept through thick, straw-colored winter grass, trampled some invasive deadnettle and cracked through brittle sedum. I rolled three times across the grass and crawled over to his basement.

I peered in the window through cupped hands. A million different tools and gadgets and not one out of place. Everything contained neatly in or on racks, shelves, five-gallon buckets, metal boxes, milk crates, hooks, bungees, hooks with bungees, etc. It was immaculate. I used my sleeve to wipe my breath off the glass and re-cupped my hands.

There was my trash bag. Slumped against a ladder, next to a table saw and several different types of post-hole diggers.

The glass was cold on my palms as I pushed up, wincing at the window's vinyl shriek. I stuck my head in and was instantly assaulted by basement smells—wet cement and mold, general dank and dinge. My feet flailed behind as the weight of my body crushed my gut against the windowsill.

I untied the bags and spread the trash on the ground. Crinkled wrappers, broken eggshells, slimy paper towels, and banana peels laid innocently on Cork's damp floor. Kicking through my trash, I found cloning gel, some trimmings, and a bottle of PK-Boost.

Knocks rattled the storm door upstairs. Its rusted, creaky springs cried. My heart thudded in my throat as the knocker knocked again, this time delivering a new set of particularly nasty bangs to the actual front door, the wood one.

And then there was quiet.

I waited, frozen in a petrified silence. The knocks came again, forcing me to my knees in prayer. The cement was harshly textured, rough on them. Sock-shredding properties for sure.

"God, if you exist, please let me get out of here. I'll go to church. I'll start donating to those late-night commercials with the sad kids, I'll—"

The springs of the storm door let out a metallic wail and shut. I chalked the whole thing up to a mailman or one of those religious black lady trios who went door to door handing out pamphlets about the apocalypse. Already kneeling, I scooped the non-incriminating trash back into the bag and tied it up. I needed something to put my other stuff in—my bad stuff, but it was hard to see. The dark sky somehow muted the light inside, putting the basement into an old black and white movie.

John's system of organization evolved as I went further. The hooks, straps, and shelves split into buckets full of every type of hardware imaginable—nuts, bolts, joist hangers, screws, anchors, toggle bolts, hex bolts, machine screws, and a bunch of other stuff I didn't recognize—every possible size and metric contained within a network of buckets, cups, and coffee cans.

A table caught my eye. It was tucked into the corner of the wall, hidden under the steps. Nails protruded hellishly out of its smashed, splintery surface granting it the effect of a medieval torture device. On top of the table sat two milk crates full of sanding pads, of course organized by grit rating. Inside the crates, tucked between the 80 and 60-grit pads was a manila envelope. The envelope was old and water-stained, thin and dried by time. I slid it out, handling it with the delicacy of a dead leaf, and carefully peeked inside.

There was a stack of pictures. Pictures of John and a red-headed woman. Polaroids at first. John and the girl, sitting on a tire swing. John was smiling hopefully, she was not. The girl's hair a stormy network of outrageous red curls. Her face was sharp and angular, with a glint in her eyes that suggested mischief, vague promises of sex. Her top quality wasn't her looks—she was by no means ugly, but also no belle of the ball—instead, it rested in her pornographic aura, the ease in which her presence dissolved into the fantasies of men.

The couple aged as I flipped through the photos. Got married, had a kid.

A shot of them on their honeymoon: Cork wearing khaki shorts, a Hawaiian shirt, and sandals, holding a Coors Light in his left hand with an arm around his wife. She looked spectacular. Sunkissed and smiling in a patterned sundress with a green Larimar pendant hanging over her summer-freckled chest. The surf was frozen behind them in a misty crash.

The next picture—drastically un-Caribbean—flashed a few years forward: it was of the three of them—John, wife, and the baby Fig, all at a summertime cookout. They seemed cramped in a tiny-looking backyard. The yard was mostly hardened dirt, lunar and sad with a goatee of weeds and grass. Behind them was a cratered cement driveway. A landing strip of camouflage-colored grass ran alongside. Both John and his wife had gained noteworthy amounts of weight in their faces, both of their cheeks puffy and fixed in forced grimaces on what appeared to be a scorcher of a day judging by the ages of the old men in the background who allowed themselves the luxury of wearing shorts outdoors. The brave, short-pantsed elders sat in plastic lawn chairs, sipping Budweisers, seemingly oblivious to the fact they were in frame. The baby Fig reached toward the camera crying with outstretched arms and kicking feet.

Next picture: mom sitting cross-legged in a cushionless patio chair, her back resting against those dirty, rubber straps with Fig on her lap. There was a cig burning in an ashtray on the glass table behind them. She was caught in a blink, angling her shoulder to hold Fig's attention toward the lens. Fig, caught in mid-squirm, pointed his finger over the glass table. The smoke from the cig streamed around his face, rising from the metropolis of empty cans and bottles. Some of the cans stood straight while others were pinched in the middle, leaning like old ruins.

Folded neatly behind the pictures were papers—family court documents, driver's license photos, criminal records, unintelligible letters scrawled in inks of various colors, and finally an address and a name.

Donna B. Winters
4137 Beechwood Lane,
Wilmington, Delaware

Someone rapped on the window. Horrible thuds on glass. I stuffed the pictures back into the envelope, tearing it as I pushed it into my pocket. They rapped again. I ran to the steps and stopped. My heart performed an unwanted drum solo in my chest.

The window slid open, revealing Eddie Hayden's elderly face. He looked pissed in a way old people shouldn't. "The hell you doing?"

"Uh, I, uh..." I was frozen.

"Open the door!"

I obeyed, frantically moving through the shadowy basement toward the light of the window, relieved on some level it was Eddie and not

John, though disappointed it wasn't Brenda. I slid a coffee can of roofing nails out of the way and opened up. Eddie pushed while I opened, lending an effort against the stubborn vinyl weather stripping as it protested across the cement floor. Eddie stepped inside, blowing in his leathery hands.

"How'd you figure to come in here?" he asked.

"What?"

Eddie pointed at the trash with his eyes. "You heard me. Who told you?" He followed behind as I located a box of contractor bags and stuffed my things inside.

"No one *told* me. I was up this morning—"

"What time?"

"Huh?"

"What time?"

"I don't know, five? Maybe five thirty? I heard someone banging around my yard and saw Fig grabbing my trash. Cork was standing right there. It was early."

Eddie remained skeptical. "And what would a guy like you be doing up at such a respectable hour?"

"Guy like? I went to a party for my parents and came home a little early. Had some company over—"

"Company? Like Clay and Donny?"

"I don't even know those guys!"

"Apparently you do."

"I mean, I know they exist and are part of some evil hippy gang. You know they threatened me, right?"

"How?"

I leaned against a six-foot ladder that was chained to a bigger ladder. The sun peeked out from the clouds, adding color back into the basement. Eddie's cheeks flushed from the heat of the house.

"They wanted a video."

"Yeah, I heard."

"How?"

"I know everything, kid. Like how you've been following Cork around on behalf of Clay. Taking videos for his gang."

"What? Dude, no. I was jogging in the park. I didn't know he was going to be there."

"Park? What park?"

"The park from the video. Where he was beating up Clay before the fire? You saw it right?"

The old man's eyes narrowed. "*What?*" Eddie looked at his feet and grumbled. He dug one of his spotted hands into the massive bucket of change, a rusted coffee can that sat heavily on a makeshift table comprised of a door resting on two metal sawhorses. He plucked a quarter, twirling it between his knuckles as he silently chuckled in what looked like admiration. After a moment of twirling, he tossed the coin back into the bucket where it rattled the others. "Son of a *bitch*."

Eddie

I eyed Cork's can of change. Must've been damn near a hundred dollars in there. I was mad, pissed as hell, but a small part of me wanted to laugh. OSHA video? Of course that wasn't the case. How could I have been so thick? "Call him," I commanded. "Call him right now."

"Who? John?"

"No, Clay, call Clay."

"I don't have his number."

"Oh, right. He doesn't have a phone."

"Wait, how'd—"

"Where'd you meet him? Where's he hang?"

"How do you know so much about him?"

"I'll ask the questions, thank you!"

"Seriously?"

"Don't be a ninny."

Joel swung the mostly empty bag by his feet, scuffling it on the floor. "Look, I've only ever met Donny."

"Where?"

"At Brenda's"

"What? What were *you* doing with her?

"Uh..."

"Christ." I rested my forehead in the meat of my palm, between my index and my thumb. The poor girl. Running with the likes of this mope since she was born. Blame it on that no-good dad of hers. Chump-zero.

"You and her?"

"Yeah, why? What's so bad about that?"

"Eh."

"What?"

I kicked his bag with my velcro sneakers, jostling the empty containers inside. Joel pulled it away from my foot and squared his posture. I felt around my hip for my revolver.

"*You*, of all people, calling *my* character into question. Funny."

"Funny how?" I said, gripping my gun.

Joel lifted his bag, knocking out the excess air as he twisted it shut and swung it over his shoulder. "Considering you're a *sex offender* and all."

I clutched my fists and stepped toward him. "Where the hell did you get that from?"

"Um, the internet? Right off the Megan's law website. I search it every time I move. Curiosity more than anything."

"Who the hell's Megan?"

"I don't know. Some girl they named it after."

"Does it have my picture on there?"

"No, just your name and the charge."

I put a hand to the wall, moving it off just as fast. It was cold and damp and nasty.

"Does it at least mention she was *seventeen*?"

"Are you serious?"

I spit on the floor. "Christ."

Joel pulled the bag up high on his shoulder headed toward the door. I blocked him.

"Wait, Joel is it?"

"Yeah, now move."

"I think we can help each other here."

"No thanks, I'm all good on candy."

I stood in front of the door and locked it for effect. The cement was darkened where I spit. I rubbed it in with my foot and spread it around.

"Wonder what John would do if he found out you were down here? What with those guys threatening his boy and all? Whew, it could get *real* ugly for you."

"Who's threatening Fig?"
"Your boys, Clay and Co."
"They're *not* my boys."

"Said they were gonna poison him with drugs if John didn't play ball—then again who knows? Maybe he's making this all up."

Joel's eyes moved around in thought. "Yeah, probably not. That's kinda their thing."
"Whose thing?"
"Evil hippies. Mega dosing their enemies on—wait John was on *acid* last night? I mean, he was acting weird, but not like—"
"He claims they gave him something else. Dah-rawr-rah?"
"Datura? Ugh."

"I'll be honest. I had no idea this Clay kid was such a son of a bitch when I agreed to work with his parents. They made him seem, I don't know, like a little junkie or something. But apparently he's tied in—"

"Yeah, with some serious people, I know. Wait—what do you mean *working with his parents*?"
"I'm a private investigator. Hired by his dad. The family's loaded beyond comprehension. Talking beaucoup bucks."
"How'd you get past the, uh, you know?"
"What the background check? Eh, I got in before all the computers and what not. Back before everyone's lives became grocery store

tabloids—But this Clay thing is bigger than I thought, and I'm realizing now that I might be a bit too close to it. Can't see the edges, you know? I'm tangled. You, me, John, Clay and Brenda. It's like a, what's it called?" I snapped my fingers trying to think of the word.

"A knot of circumstance?"

"Hey, yeah. I like that, but no. This is more of a...Mexican ball-grab, that's it! And at its center, deep in its ugly, twisted nexus—is the tape. Think about it. It's what links us all. You to me, John to Clay, Brenda to you—*but* if you help *me* get to Clay, I can see to it that *he* goes away. And then, like magic, your problems with John, with me, your little thing with Brenda, it'll all just float away."

"Clay doesn't even have the tape."

"What?"

Joel folded his arms across his chest. He seemed to be feeling his oats. "I had Brenda send it in an app. Set it to disappear after five minutes. So, yeah, he's a total non-factor."

"What the devil is an app?"

Joel seemed confused. "An app? It's an application. Like something extra your phone can do besides call people. I'm just gonna fess up to John. Tell him what happened and how I took care of it."

I picked a penny out of the coffee can and rolled it in my fingers. 1943, older than me by a year. God, these things used to be so *valuable*. And now? Worthless scraps. A cruel joke for poor hands. And why? Why do things keep getting so expensive? Why can't things just cost the same?

I touched the wall again, remembered it was wet and pulled away. "And what makes you think John'll buy your little story about apps? You're in bed with Clay, as far as he's concerned."

"So what should I do then?"

"Send *me* a copy of the video."

"What?"

"Oh, don't be so dense!"

"I'm not being dense! I just don't see how giving *you* the video helps me in any way."

I dropped the penny back into the coffee can. Its sound was absorbed by all the other coins, a sort of chainmail slither. "Lives are at stake and all you can think about is yourself."

"Pretty much."

"Going from that angle, the you-being-a-self-centered-lump-of-worthless-dough-in-an-otherwise-interconnected-network-of-humanity angle, picture this very likely and real scenario: John finds Clay and kills him, possibly Donny too. And then what? A big murder investigation? Do you really want to be in the middle of that? Having those homicide detectives sniffing between the dotted lines of your toilet paper?"

Joel hemmed and hawed, scratching the back of his neck. I could see he was thinking.

"Or you can give *me* the video like I said before, and I'll use it to persuade John *not* to kill those zeros. I'll tell him the thing about the app and how I worked with Brenda to set that all up. That way I have enough time to get Clay back to his folks and convince Donny to disappear for a while. The whole thing'll just—" I flew my hand over and around Joel's head, "*schoo.*"

"Fine, but that's it. I'm deleting it off my phone. You'll be the last one with it. Well, you and maybe Brenda, but I'll talk to her."

"I bet you will," I said, smiling.

Joel put his bag down and pulled out his phone. The clouds had settled back in the sky, greying the room again.

"What the hell are you doing?"

"Giving you the tape. What's your number?"

"No. Send it to my email. I don't trust the phone. Not with this *app* business. And let me see it, the whole thing."

Joel sighed and clicked on the screen of his phone.

Amazing times, I thought. Videos and pictures flying about the world around us. Ghosts of information settling in our brains, our breasts, our throats. I wondered if that's what these newfangled cancers were? Pictures and videos absorbed by people's flesh, the body unable to express them, too old to understand.

Joel played me the video. He apologized for the shakiness and quality, but I thought it was excellent. There it was, clear as day: John Cork giving my buddy Clay a 1970's ass kicking. Absolutely dominating the boy who, in all honesty, wasn't as small and sickly as I'd imagined. Clay flying into the fiery oil drum and John roasting his head. It was sick. Twisted. Captured by a device that was supposed to be used for communication. This was it, I thought. This was the new communication.

"What's your email address?" Joel asked, getting his phone ready to take my info.

"Eddie at—you ready for the rest?—A-O-L-dot-com."

"Dude."

"What?"

"That's crazy." Joel, shaking his head in wonder about my email, grabbed his bag and opened the door. He stopped, half-lit by the cloudy sun and turned around. "Do you think Brenda's using me?"

I laughed, scraping the sole of my shoe over the cement. "Yes."

The door closed behind him.

I watched the kid tumble awkwardly through the yard, the bag flapping in the wind behind his back as he went. He moved through John's plants, destroying them with uncoordinated rolls and tumbles. He popped over the fence like a sheep and went off into the woods beyond John's wall.

Joel's bag of trash leaned lumpily against a ladder.

I pulsed with voyeuristic excitement as I kicked it over, spreading its contents carefully with one grey sneaker, making sure to avoid the banana peels for good measure. The feeling that overtook me was a queer one, a new fetish blossoming in the bowels of my wickedness.

Viewing a person's trash was the next best thing to seeing them naked—in fact, it was almost the same. Parts of them blown into tissues and napkins, hairs on razors, exterior layers of the foods they put inside themselves. It was nudity deconstructed. If only it were Brenda's or Lynne's. Blood flowed into my member as I thought about the sister's *combined* trash, about Brenda *using* Joel.

I snatched the bucket of change and left.

Brenda

Folds of syrupy light dripped through the blinds, brightening Clay's scraggly beard. I'd been inspecting him all afternoon, looking for a sign of attractiveness, trying to convince myself he wasn't *that* ugly. And there was something about him, a sense of class I felt drawn to. A prism beamed through the window, a little rainbow square that danced on the carpet. Someone's crystal wind chime, if I had to guess.

"Where's my sister?"

Clay shrugged.

I wanted to touch him, but in a motherly way. Touch and nurture him. I wanted to nurture everybody. I wanted to have a baby so I could touch someone all the time.

I was high.

I'd popped the pill Lynne gave me and snorted another not long after. A mistake, but *fuck*. I felt great. I was *so comfortable*. My couch, my rock-hard, piece-of-shit Ikea sofa, felt like a waterbed. And I was floating above it. Everything was perfect, or so I thought until hearing the mattress squeaking above.

Clay lifted his head and grinned widely, "I think they're upstairs."

"Gross."

The coils squeaked deeper, the rusty, springy notes held longer, in a way that made me believe Lynne was on top, crushing Donny. Some of Clay's loose hairs fell to his shoulder as he sat up. The grin still plastered on his face.

"What?" I asked, now smiling myself.

He shook his head. "It's—I'm just happy is all. Glad we could come to an agreement." Clay yawned and shook his face. He reached into his pocket and took out a little baggie. He dumped half the bag out onto the table and chopped it up into two little lines.

The coils stopped for a good ten seconds, then started back up.

I cringed. "Ugh. Probably just switched positions."

Clay pulled his hair back and sniffed his line up, motioning for me to do the next. "What do you think? Doggy, perhaps?"

"Ew, gross. That literally just made me see Lynne's butthole in my mind."

Blood rushed to my head as I sat up. My vision wasn't blurry, it was more frosted, like a film over my eyes. The pressure of the floor felt good against my socks. It felt *right* in some kind of weird way.

I knelt on my rug, enjoying the floor's solidity as I bent to snort the line. It had been awhile and I was excited to do some coke. My fingers felt wonderful against my nose, my proper dainty nose. I felt like a princess, the way my body was all light and floaty.

I sniffed the line and gagged.

It wasn't coke.

"What the fuck was that?" I asked, slightly panicked, smacking my mouth to figure out what I'd just tasted.

"K," said Clay, finally opening his beer.

The inside of my head rang—or, more like whooshed. Like seashells held against my ear but louder. I couldn't see in fluid motion if that makes sense, more like frames of time, like the world was an oncoming train. Clay talked excitedly. I couldn't hear him, but I don't think he cared. He wasn't worried about me. In fact, he looked happy, happy I was falling apart. My eyes got heavy, impossibly heavy, and started to shut. It was like I was being vacuumed out of existence. I needed to *open my eyes.*

But when I opened them it just got worse. The room split into layers, cards shuffling in and out of view, falling into a drain of some kind—"*I am a human female*," I thought.

Everything went black.

***

I woke up crushed. Literally.

Clay was on top of me, moaning as he climbed my body. His breath was hot on my face, beyond bad. The mechanical glow of streetlights replaced the folds of syrup from before. Their sterile glow stopped at the end of my couch, just enough to spotlight his horrible mask of a face as it hovered above. His wet, disgusting teeth gnashed as he forced me down. I opened my mouth to scream, but his hand was already covering it.

I bit him, his foul, vinegary skin.

"Easy," he whispered. His breath smelled like bad eggs.

I bucked my knee towards his balls, but he blocked it with a shin. Clay spun his legs off the couch and shoved me in the gut, knocking the wind out of me. I gasped, flailing my free arm off the couch. The cold metal pliers brushed against my hand. I grabbed them and swung. He blocked my arm at the elbow but wasn't quick enough. The large pliers clunked wonderfully against his skull.

He let go of my mouth and I screamed.

Clay, holding his head with one hand, shoved his palm back over my mouth, instantly swelling my lips, and kneed me in the arm, the one with the pliers, holding it down so I couldn't hit him again. The metallic taste of blood filled my mouth as Clay began to choke me, harder and harder. The streetlights slowly faded into a swarm of little dots as he kissed the top of my head, shushing me. Tears streaked my cheeks as I screamed into his palm.

Deep whooping barks came from out of the kitchen. I thought I was hallucinating, but then I saw him, saw Roger moving through the slants of light coming in from the windows. Strings of saliva swung from his snarling mouth as his jaws snapped, missing Clay's leg by an inch.

"No! Bad! Stop!" Clay screamed and kicked wildly.

Roger coiled on his hind legs and lunged again, this time biting Clay's arm. Clay snatched the pliers out of my frozen hands and turned around. Maybe it was all the drugs, but I swear I saw it, how Roger closed his eyes in acceptance as Clay raised the tool and hammered on his skull.

It hit with a horrible, cracking thud.

Donny came stumbling down the steps and pulled my gun out of his waistband. "Gimme your phone! Slide it forward. And the purse! Clay, get her purse."

Clay ignored him. He was busy beating Roger's head into mush. There was a disgusting wetness to the noise that made Donny cover his mouth. He was holding Clay's messenger bag over his shoulder. It was bulky and full.

"Dude, let's go!"

Donny rattled Clay's bag and threw it to him. Clay caught it with his good hand and draped the bad one by his side. I looked down at the floor by the couch and saw my purse was missing.

"Yo! What the fuck?" I screamed.

Donny shoved the gun in my face. It wasn't pressed against my head but I could feel it, the cold metal tapping me and going away, tap and away...Donny was on the verge of dipping out, swaying back and forth all fucked up.

"Dude, lay out some of that K. Guhhead, a big fat line."

"What?"

"For her, dude! So she doesn't follow us."

Clay moved his shitty dreads out of his face and reached in his pocket. He pulled out his little bag and dumped a gagger on the table. Donny jabbed my brain stem with the revolver. Roger's legs were still moving. Twitching like a stomped bug.

"Guhhead!"

Tears dropped, wetting the K as I snorted it. My nostril burned as chunks of ketamine paste hit the back of my throat. I stopped halfway through the line and gagged. The gun again. It tasted like a coin in my mouth. I collapsed in tears against the table and ruined the rest of the K. It didn't matter. I'd snorted enough. The world was inside of a car wash. Everything blurred by liquid. Wet spidery webs of liquid light.

Clay pushed Donny. Donny pointed upstairs.

I fought to stay awake, horrified at the idea of waking up with Clay on top of me again. But it was too late. The shit was kicking in. I thought about Lynne, wondering where the fuck she was. The couch shook as Donny ripped the pillows out from under me and stacked them on Roger's head. Clay nodded.

Donny pushed the barrel against the pillow and looked away.

I closed my eyes.

Fig

My dad was livid in the truck. Punching the steering wheel, cutting people off, screaming—it was bad. I was also super high from the second muffin. It was the second highest I'd ever been next to the salvia at that point.

He took a hard left, gluing me to the passenger side door as the tune of Ol' Susana echoed in my head. It was the song Rusnak whistled while we stood and watched as my dad got the call that sent him into orbit. The call that made him lean against his truck and say, *no, get out,* and *you're kiddin'* a hundred times while massaging the back of his neck. Every thirty seconds Coach would stop whistling Ol' Susana. He'd wink at me and start back up. It was fucking bizarre.

My dad hit a pothole and *snapped.*

"MOTHERFUCKER!"

My chin dropped as the truck sank and rocketed upward. I stuck my arms out, assuming something of a bull rider position. It felt like we kept going up, like we were flying. I glanced out the window to see how high up we were. The road underneath the truck was a blur, looking like a channel my dad didn't pay for. The tires were on the ground.

I did that thing where I softened my voice; the way kids do when they're in trouble but need something. "Dad? What's the matter?" I was trying my best not to sound high. My voice, along with Ol' Sue and now the Hokey Pokey, echoed in my head. Everything looked thick and blurrily colorful like my eyes were open underwater.

My dad gripped the wheel and stared ahead. "Nothin'," he said, finally looking over. "Everythin' cool with you?"

His question hung like smoke, filling the truck, absorbing all the breathable air. I wanted to tell him everything, let him into all my thoughts. And then maybe he'd tell *me* everything. Maybe we'd figure it all out. Maybe it was just that simple.

His eyes moved around me, flickering through streaks of orange light.

I changed my mind. I didn't want to tell him *anything*. In fact, I never wanted to talk ever again. I'd be silent forever. People would eventually think I was retarded and leave me alone. My dad would have to stop hitting me and everything.

The pressure of his stare was too intense.

"Who, me?" I squeaked out.

"Who the hell do ya think?"

The oncoming cars looked slow from far away, like they were barely moving. But then they'd get close and go so fast, *vwoom,* like they were blasting into hyperspace. I looked out the window at the road again, at how the lines and everything merged into one thing, a sliding blur. We were going too fast for colors.

My dad gripped the collar of my sweatshirt. "The hell's a-matter with you, Figgy?"

"I think I miss mom sometimes."

My dad screeched the tires as he took a right, totally blowing a stop sign. It alerted some fat guy who was smoking a cigarette on his porch. The guy walked down the steps, fanning his hands in an effort to tell my dad to slow down.

My dad gave him the finger and sped up. "Yeah, well, she doesn't miss you, so fuck her."

We pulled up to the house.

My dad jammed his shifter into park and we rocked to a stop. Mr. Hayden was standing outside our yard. Something about his face looked shady, weirder than usual. He opened my door and offered to help me out, grabbing me with his gross hands. They felt like they were made out of ball skin.

"Hey there, champ!" He said, gripping my shoulder as I slid past him. My dad smacked the back of my head. "Go wash your ass."

I jogged to the front door, happy to get away. If there was one thing I was figuring out, it was that I didn't like to be high around my dad. He was too serious. I thought about that, about being serious as I tried to open the door. The knob was stuck. It wouldn't work.

Then I heard my Dad.

"Hey, Dumbass."

I turned my head. His big fat ring flew toward me, wings of keys fanned out, jingling in the air. Why so many keys? Why did anyone need access to so many doors? It was like he was secretly a janitor or something. I caught them, thank God. They would have broken my nose.

***

I laid in bed after my shower feeling refreshed. My mind was on sweatpants. I'd just slid my naked body into a clean pair of Russells fresh out the dryer. They were perfect, the way I imagined a vagina would feel. Why would anyone ever wear anything *besides* sweatpants? It didn't make sense. It was stupid. I vowed to myself, then and there, that I'd never get a job that forced me to wear any other kind of pants—especially not dress pants. They were the worst. So gross and slippery.

Running through all the possible options of sweatpants jobs in my head: "*Coach, gym teacher, construction, trash man, NFL...*"

The basement door opened outside my window. I heard the mumble of my dad and Mr. Hayden talking out back. My lights were out so they couldn't see me. I cracked the window to listen.

Eddie

John's outside lighting was a bit much, a big stadium set up. Total halogen overkill. If anything, it only deepened the darkness beyond. John was furious, kicking the ground as he spoke, shredding the frozen earth like ice cream out of the freezer that wasn't ready for a spoon. I squinted in the light, illuminated in John's super glow, blocking what I could with my hand.

"Calm down? I'm talkin' about my house, Eddie. My personal sanctuary violated like I'm some kinda bitch. And my change? Fuckin' took my *change*? Took forever to save that up!" His boot dug hard with a final kick, neatly scalping the lawn.

The sky looked cold. Black and shiny and clean. Dotted pulsing stars and a red blinking light. A satellite maybe. My breath hung in the air, floating over to John's breath, merging and fading in the light. A pool of nervous saliva accumulated in my mouth. I swallowed, relishing it like whiskey. It had been a while since I felt anything, let alone genuine thrill. Life against the edge of death. Everything was brightened, every thought and word magnified in resolution.

I had Cork right where I wanted him. Angry and out of sorts.

"Look, Johnny, I know you're upset. Hell, I'd be too. But we gotta get to the head of the snake. The rest will slither away."

John spit in disagreement.

I put my hands in my pockets and looked to the woods. The moon was a sliver, a toenail in the sky. The rest of its dark rock was traced and visible. John being agitated was good. I wanted him emotional and irrational. But, I had to let him cool out. Couldn't press him.

He kicked the ground again. "Fuckin' had him too."

"How so?" I asked.

"The trash bags! Had all kinds of incriminatin' shit in them. Fertilizers, trimmings—"

"And you're sure you saw them in there?"

John clenched his jaw. He looked like he was about to blast me. "Yes."

"Slick son of—"

John held up a fist, signaling me to be quiet as he moved toward the fence, silently stalking as he looked into the woods. His lips puckered in concentration. He crept over this fence and peered off the top of his retaining wall into the darkness of the woods, standing at the limit of his floodlights. He signaled again, using his hand like an arrow and pointed me back toward the basement as he leapt soundlessly off his wall.

"John! *John!*" I whispered loudly.

A hush fell over, a ringing silence. Imaginary blotches of purple danced in my compromised vision. I heard a bush about two houses down crackle, snapping and shaking, the sounds animals make in the woods. John came thrashing out of the tree line, dragging someone behind him. He marched uphill, through his neighbor's yard, pushing his wobbly-legged prisoner forward. Cork got to his own fence and threw the guy over, slamming him down on the frozen grass. They looked like fighting shadows.

I jogged over. "Now calm down there, John. Don't do anything—"

"The fuck you doin' creepin' round my house? Was that Joel with you? Huh? Answer me!" Cork ragdolled the guy by his shirt.

"I have no idea what you're talking about, just let me go," said the guy in his grips.

John lifted and slammed him again, knocking the hood off his face. I couldn't believe it. "Clay?"

He was curled in the fetal, clutching a little messenger bag to his chest while he nursed his left arm. He was *terrified*. "No, no! Please! I'll give it back I promise!"

John hopped the fence and grabbed Clay's head, holding it in the radiant lighting. I pulled the picture out of my pocket to compare.

Uglier. But still him. Clay had one of those hateable faces, one where the top lip hangs over the bottom in a sneering beak. Something about it reminded me of the French.

John pushed me out of the way

Clay looked up, holding his ribs. "Please!" he cried, showing us his arm. "I'm hurt. I'll do anything. Just don't—"

Cork grabbed him by the throat and choked him. "Tryin' to get my Figgy, huh?"

I tugged John's jacket. "Easy! Gotta bring him back in one piece."

John let go.

Clay fondled his neck like he was checking if it still worked. "I was walking in the woods and got lost."

John kicked his bad arm.

"Arghh!"

"Bullshit! There was someone else with you, I heard him. Was it Joel?"

Clay crumbled against the fence in agony and gripped his arm. His hand looked lifeless and white. He took his good arm and adjusted the bag on his shoulder.

John kicked it. "What's in here?"

Clay shrugged and shook his head. "Clothes and shit."

John bent down and snatched the bag. He unzipped it and dumped it on the ground. A few pharmacy bottles fell, along with one of those bank bags, the coin purses they give business owners. Inside the bank bag were two fat wads of cash in rubber bands. A good deal of change from the looks of it.

John gave the bag another good shake and a syringe fell out. I stopped one of the pharmacy bottles from rolling away with my foot.

John nudged the syringe with his boot. "*Jesus*. You know there's a bad batch floating around, right? It's in the paper. Already killed a few people out in Marcus Hook. They say it's cut with *fent-ta-nal* or some shit."

"It's for steroids."

"Yeah, okay, Arnold."

"Listen, Clay, just give the man what he wants so I can get you out of here. Your family's looking for you. Worried sick."

"What do you mean?" he asked, voice cracking and upset.

John kicked him in the stomach. "Was that shit for Joel?"

"*Unngf*! It's medicine! I have a prescription and everything."

John laughed, jabbing a thumb toward Clay. "You believe this kid?"

I picked up one of the pill bottles. "Technically, he's not lying."

"What?"

"See? Says his name right here. I just wonder how he got so many."

My legs quaked as I squatted down to open Clay's bag. The slope in John's yard was ridiculous, a goddamn ski hill. I dug around, careful not to jab myself on hypos and felt something, some plastic tubes. "What the hell are these?" I asked, holding them up.

Clay rubbed his ribs.

John tapped my arm with the back of his hand. "Careful Eddie. These kids got all kinds of drugs these days. It's crazy."

"They're not *drugs*," said Clay, with a bit of condescending edge.

"Yeah, okay."

"Here, I'll show you," he said, reaching out.

I handed him the thing.

John lifted a boot to Clay's face. "Try *anything* and I'll stomp you—"

Clay bent the tube. It cracked and glowed neon green. He handed it back to me. "It's a glow-stick."

"The hell do you do with these? I asked.

Clay shrugged. "I dunno. Usually, people dance with them, or just, like, rage out."

"How old are you?" asked John.

"Twenty-eight."

John's eyes opened wide, puckering his lips in an airy whistle. "*Dancin'*? Phew."

I picked up the pill bottles and read the labels, one-by-one, using the glowstick to see. "Interesting…"

"What is?" asked John.

"His prescriptions—same pills, but from different doctors."

Clay scampered on all fours, trying to make a break for it. John took a good step and kicked him in the side.

I picked the stacks of cash off the ground and fanned through them. "Got to be what? About ten grand here, would you say?"

John eyed up the cash. "I'd say."

Clay got his breath back. "Those pills are all in my name. They are my legal property, and so is the cash. This, what you guys are doing right now, is technically strong-armed robbery."

John slapped Clay across the back of the head, sending his face into the cratered dirt.

"There's a strong arm for ya."

"Alright, take it easy." I set the pills down and picked up his bag. "Well, they are in your name. No denying that."

"Don't tell me you're believin' this!"

"Well, it's true, John. Though I wonder… I wonder how he pulled it off."

John bent down and gripped Clay by the collar of his hoodie. "I'm gonna give you one chance. How'd you—"

I undid all the zippers and shook it the bag. A prescription pad fell out. "And there it is."

"How'd this dinkus get his grubby little fingers on a doctor book?"

"Well, and correct me if I'm wrong here, Clay, but my guess is that after the thing down at the park…"

John stiffened up.

"…after getting beat up or what have you, you went to the hospital and stole that pad—"

Clay held his bad arm up, inspecting it from different angles.

"I didn't get *beat up*. I was viciously attacked…by a fucking *lunatic*. And guess what?"

John Cork squatted down next to Clay's face. "Where's the tape?"

Clay snapped his head away in refusal, looking toward the woods. We all stood there, steaming in the cold.

Clay puckered his oddly shaped lips and shook his head. "I dunno."

John snatched Clay's bad arm and pushed up his sleeve. His arm was a scatterplot of swollen puncture wounds. Some of them bad too. Could see his fatty tissue and everything. John took one of his pinecones of a finger and plunged the tip into the worst looking wound. He squeezed Clay's mouth with his other hand.

Clay writhed maniacally, eye's bulging in visceral shock.

"Where is it?!"

A frustrated tear rolled down the side of Clay's cheek.

"Huh?"

John pulled his fingertip out of the cut and wiped it in the dirt. Clay snatched his arm back and winced at the sky, fighting his tears.

"I-I don't have it."

Cork gripped his arm.

"Donny does! I don't have a phone."

John pulled his phone out. "Now ya do. Call him."

Clay looked at me, baffled by John's stupidity. "Really? Off an unknown number after being snatched out of the woods by a maniac? You really think he's gonna come?"

I stepped up. "Kid's got a point, John. Let me get him back to his dad. That way, at least one of them is out of the picture. Then we get Donny." I turned to Clay. "What's his last name?"

"Falcone."

John shook his head, "No fucking way. I'm taping this worm to a fucking chair until I get that tape and if I don't get it by sunrise he's dead."

"Johnny! Listen to yourself."

Clay shrugged. "He's not gonna come here!"

John squatted to pack the spilled contents back into Clay's bag.

"If he wants to see all of this again he will."

"Ah, c'mon John. Why not just keep the money and forget it? I mean, all this over an OSHA fine?"

Clay piped up. "*OSHA fine?*

John held a finger out to both of us. "Shut up! Both of you."

"Cut the bullshit, Johnny, I've seen the real video."

"Whaddya mean *real* video?"

"It wasn't of you on a roof, it was you attacking this kid and starting a fire. And guess what, John? Guess who else has the video? Yup. That's right. And if I don't get him back I swear—argh!"

John grabbed my jacket and drove me up the hill. My sneakers slipped on the grass and we fell. He kneed me in the thigh. A solid, meaty thud.

"You traitorous old fuck—!"

"Dad! Look out!" Figgy screamed out the window.

Clay jumped on John's back and held him in a chokehold. He popped a vial of liquid out of his breast pocket and splashed it in John's mouth and eyes.

"Pfft! What the-what the *fuck*?" John stumbled back.

Clay went for the messenger satchel, trying to pull it off Cork, who was now blind. He batted him to the ground. Ropes of saliva hung from John's mouth as he pulled a knife out of his pocket and ripped it through the air. "I'll fuckin' kill you! Both of yas—Pfffft!"

I dove out of the blade's way and landed on the ground, gripping a tit of frozen lawn to keep me from rolling down the hill. Clay, watching the movements of the knife, sprung up and punched John in the boys. John went down to a knee, swinging his little blade around like a madman. Clay ripped the bag from John's grasp. He swung it over his shoulder and ran toward the woods.

I reached for his ankle to trip him, but he jumped right over me.

John

Dirt crumbled against my eyelids. Worm dirt. The cottage cheese stuff they make diggin' around. I stood up. Gave my hands another good wipe and held my eyes open, standin' toward the wind. Let 'em tear up, clean themselves out. A little trick my old man taught me to get sawdust out the eyes.

Eddie hobbled over, his little shoes squeakin' on a snow patch. "You can still get him!"

The wind changed, hittin' the back of my head. Cold and snappy. True polar air, I thought. Doesn't have to carry the scent of all the shit it travels over. Straight from the north. Doesn't touch any of those equator countries.

Eddie squeaked away hissin'.

"Go back inside!"

"Who go back inside?"

"Fig!"

Somethin' plastic grazed my face. I pushed it away and swung an elbow at nothin'. "Get offa me!" Eddie's arm hair brushed my cheek. He squirted somethin' in my eye. I staggered back.

"Gaa! You old shit!" I swung. Thudded him a good one.

Eddie's shoes squeaked and he crashed to the ground. I heard him wheezin'. A crunched, grated moan.

"The hell was that?"

"*Hup*, It's Visine. I'm trying to help you."

The streetlights arced in neon smears as I continued to open and shut my eyes, working the world back into existence through a mechanical opening and shutting of the lids. It felt weird, these maintenance blinks. Reminded me of the bowling alley mechanic, the poor fuck who twists wrenches behind the fire of bowling balls, cannonballs really. Jesus, just the idea. Two ships lined up and firin' away. Wood crackin' under the force of a sixteen-pound Spaldin' and bustin' some thoughtless grunt in the belly as he bent over the starboard and falls like a turd into the white-capped water, swallowed up by the sea with a fuckin' bowlin' ball half-inside his gut draggin' him to the bottom. I bet that guy, that mechanic doesn't even sleep. He lays his head down and all he can hear is the thunder crack of that ball against the pins.

God, the sky. Black and starry. Make a man believe-in-God-and-angels kinda thing. I staggered into my fence and watched the trees shake and rumble, every bush and blade of thawed grass movin' in unison, shakin' like wet dogs in slow motion. I was rooted firmly. Hell, the earth under my feet was *mine*, with the papers to prove it inside. These were my lands and I'd kill to defend them. I finally understood that.

Eddie fought his collar from blowin' up around his neck. He was on his side in the fetal position clutchin' his shoulder. His lips pressed into the frozen dirt as he cursed the ground, same ground I was standin' on and owned. I could have shot him if I wanted to. Said he was trespassin' and shot him right down.

"God take me now." He whined as he kicked his little sneakers and hammered his fists. "Please." He had given up, writhin' loony in an elderly tantrum. He reminded me of one of those dark creatures at the bottom of the ocean, somethin' that tries to wriggle its way back into the sand.

"What'd you say about my boy, Eddie?"

Eddie sat up on his ass. His eyes soured in pain as he rolled his shoulder with caution, testin' it. He spied somethin' on the ground and picked it up. The vial, tinted green or blue, I couldn't tell. He had it clutched in his little turtle-skin hand. He shot the other one up for a lift to his feet.

I lifted him up. Not turtle skin, more like the kind of skin that forms right after a cut. That smooth scar tissue.

"Watch the shoulder!"

"Shut up."

He stood, knees bent as he rotated his joint. The bottle was pinched in his goblin fingers, spinning as he continued to rehab himself. There was somethin' fucked up about seein' an old man in grass-stained khakis. The way sweat glistened on his old dead skin. Dinosaur skin. Skin like a lizard.

"Any idea what this is?"

"Somethin' that shouldn't be in my eyes if I had to guess."

Eddie shook his head. "I'm serious."

"Oh you're serious now, huh?"

Eddie called into the woods. "Pssst! Fig!"

"Jesus, Eddie, you don't have to cry."

"Crying?"

"Yeah, cryin'. You're cryin' right now."

A Luke Bryan song was playin' from somewhere. The one he did with that white rapper whose name I forced myself to forget, just—I don't know, I stopped listenin' to Luke since then. Never forgave him, and now it was playin' at some low hum from every direction around me.

"*This is how we roll-oo-ohh-oh-oh oh ohhhh ohhh!*"

Eddie stopped cryin'. His face settled into a hateful smile, a devil smile, one that didn't show any teeth. "You okay there, Johnny?"

"I don't believe in anything," I answered, realizin' I was walkin' up my hill. I turned and looked. Eddie was a thousand feet away.

"John."

Teleportation is a bitch, I thought as I leaned against my house, feelin' the vinyl-sidin' bend under my weight. The plastic horrified me. It always did, I guess, somewhere in my head, but here it was now, front and center.

"We need to find your *boy*."

Eddie's musty breath hit my face. It lingered, warm and humid in my personal ozone layer, smelling like one of those white things that gets stuck in the throat. My house wasn't my house. It was a blueprint of my house, complete with cross sections, electrical plans, plumbing—the plastic was a shell for the blueprint and I could pull it off. All I had to do was rip the side off my house and it was gone.

"*This is how we roll-oo-ohh-oh-oh oh ohhhh ohhh!*"

Colors were bright, unbelievably sharp and focused. The trees, the grass, the snow, everythin', shaded in burnin' motion as I rolled down the hill. Just like I did when I was younger, wrappin' myself in the blur. I spent a lot of time spinnin' as a child, engulfed in a bouquet of hazy color. There was somethin' important about a spin, I decided, and chose to believe it.

Eddie was in every corner of my yard, convergin' from every angle and next thing I know I'm in my house, man's cock-eyed dream against nature. The TV was on. A blast of color and light and noise. I adjusted the zoom and deciphered the shapes to be professional wrestlin'. Men in bright underwear locked in a big meaty puzzle. The remote dangled dangerously off the arm of the couch. Touchin' it was out of the question. Changin' the channel was like a mortal sin. The one guy slammed on the canvas and bounced a little. Was the ring hard or soft? Sounded hard but looked soft. The *couch*. I believed in it. Spinnin' and a couch. It was in my head that wrestlin' was fake, but how? What did this mean? Fake as in didn't exist? Or fake as there bein' some outside force dictatin' the outcome of the match? Because what could be more real than that? Men destroyin' their bodies as some shadowy figure watches from above? And the people? The crowd, hootin' and hollerin, rallyin' behind some man in pink underwear because that's *their* man and the guy in the orange underwear needs to be slammed into the mat. Cause that's real, too. These were the true gladiators of our synthetic times, I decided. Warriors fighting in the honor of gas station snacks and energy drinks. The man in a suit watching and writing their fates, sacrificial lambs to turbo tax and mountain dew.

Spinnin', couch, pro-wrestlin'.

Eddie was back in my face again. "We have to get your *boy*."

This was it. Finally. Life in the Old Testament. Death and sons and revenge. Seein' burnin' bushes and outer space. Old men givin' me guidance and shit. All some fucked up package deal and I was in it.

God, couch, spinnin', pro-wrestlin', the man in a suit who owned and watched the matches, the people who held signs and screamed.

Eddie squeezed his hands in anger and breathed like he was trying to hurt himself. His old carbonated eyes glistened in the stale light of the TV.

"Remember, Eddie? When he told those women to cut that baby in half?"

"What?"

The remote fell when I smacked the couch. "That old, wily Jew was like, hey man, I'm fuckin' kiddin'. Don't cut that baby in half. Get out!"

Eddie paced the floor. He was missin' it. Missin' the whole thing. How it's all been here forever—how *we're* the things that change, the fallin' leaves in the equation, too crust-eyed to see the tree.

"*This is how we roll-oo-ohh-oh-oh oh ohhhh ohhh!*"

He told that bitch to cut a baby down the middle and share it.

Joel

I thought I heard someone yelling. I muted the TV and listened. Nothing.

Onscreen, a high-ranking official from the Church of Scientology, some weird space religion that I would've like to believe in, smiled at his interviewer. He re-crossed his legs and cupped his knee with two hands. Cocking his head, he smiled even deeper, like he was winning somehow.

Then I heard something. This time for sure. I killed the lights and parted the blinds.

Eddie was walking around the side of the house with a flashlight, his elbow bent at a perfect ninety degrees as he illuminated the night around him. He cupped his mouth to yell into the woods.

I cracked the window.

"Fig-gy! Fiiiiig!" Eddie called, spotlighting bushes and trees as he made his way around to the back of the house.

I grabbed my keys and headed outside.

It was a cold night, possibly the coldest of the year. More stars than usual in the sky and the moon was tiny, only a little sliver visible. Astronomy was one of those things I wanted to be into but never could. I just couldn't commit to studying space like that.

Eddie's flashlight swept the grass and blinded me, a dull sting to my eyes that had just adjusted to the dark as I came around the side of John's house. Though, I had made sure to stay on Brenda's territory in case he came out.

"Joel?"

"Fuck Eddie. Can you please?"

The light moved to the ground. Eddie's ghastly figure stood in the shadow, the outer edges of the flashlight's range. A shake in his hand caused the light to dance slightly.

"What's the matter with Fig?"

"Boy, some nerve, I'll tell you." Eddie motioned me into John's backyard.

"I'm cool."

"What? You worried about him?" he asked, pointing up through the wooden deck. "He's gone."

"Gone like?"

"Mentally. Whacked out. Your boy—you know he robbed Brenda?"

"Who did?"

"Clay."

Brenda's back door was wide open, flapping chillingly in the wind. A gust kicked up carrying a line of swirling leaves and a candy wrapper. Brenda's door bounced on the hinges and settled after the wind stopped. Eddie lowered his arm as a shield against the gust and reached into Cork's basement to turn on a light. The lights flicked on in that slow, liquidy way that fluorescent bulbs usually do, that purple magma start before really coming on. I followed him in.

Eddie handed me the flashlight. "Go find Fig. I'll go check on Brenda."

I pushed the flashlight back at him. "You go find Fig."

"I can't walk in those woods!"

Eddie rested his hand on the same shelf he had before, only something was missing. The *change bucket.*

"You piece of shit."

"Excuse me?"

Eddie looked down and then right back up. There was a tight, challenging look on his face, a bared teeth growl. "How dare you?"

I set the flashlight down on a milk crate full of heavy chains. The chains were covered in black soot and rust. Dotted with globs of blue gel. Hydraulic oil, I think.

"I bet if Fig was a jar of change, you'd have him back by now."

"Jesus, fine. *You* get Brenda. I'll try to see what I can."

***

Eddie watched me from John's basement. Arms folded, he leaned against the door frame. He was pissed, and I didn't want him to see me hesitate. I had to just walk in there. Into a dark environment through a flapping door without letting him see me flinch. My hesitation was something he could use against me. He *was* against me now, I was sure. And what about Cork? What did he mean *gone*?

I flicked the light on. No Roger on his bed of unwashed sheets and towels—actually, there weren't any sheets or towels either. Just a duo of laundry baskets overturned, neatly folded clothes spilled out from the sides. Maybe Roger escaped, I thought. Messed up the basement and took off. I hoped that was the case, prayed it was the simple misdeeds of a stray dog, simple animal vandalism, the beastly thrashings of a dumb and unconscious mind. I'm gonna knock these laundry baskets over and split, I thought, trying to channel the mind of Roger.

But that didn't explain the open door. It was a ball knob, not a handle. An impossible feat for even the brightest of dogs.

I stopped midway up the steps and dialed her number. The electronic rings pulsed in my ear. A step squeaked. Three times and voicemail.

"Brenda?" I called up the steps. "Everything ok?"

I walked up into the kitchen and flicked on another light. Another section of the mystery lit and conquered. More mess, chairs from the kitchen table overturned, fridge open. This, I thought, was a human mess.

I flicked the living room light on and immediately turned it off.

Roger had not destroyed the house. He was dead, entangled in a catatonic mess, a horrible spaghetti of domestic possessions, blankets, cushions, throw pillows and a blanket, wrapped around his bloody and very destroyed dog head. His hindquarters stuck out of the mess, poking up in different directions like he'd been killed in action.

Brenda mumbled into the bare fabric of the cushionless couch as her socked feet kicked down against the armrest. She was weeping silently.

Brenda

Joel stood over Roger's dead body, looking down at the dog's stiff hairy legs sticking up out of the blanket. A halo of dried blood fanned the carpet around his head.

I stood up and puked. All over the coffee table. Little chunks of bread and streaks of purple jelly stood out of it, making me want to throw up even more, something like nausea felt at a spiritual level.

My head rushed in a toxic swirl as I laid back down, stuck between things seeming painfully real and unreal at the same time, like I'd been pushed into a sort of middle, a betweenness. I laid on the bare fabric of the cushionless couch, crying into the crumbs and coins and hairs. And then there was this other thing, a whispered surge of emotion from the past, the time I got stung by a bee. I could feel it, the abject horror shooting through my young body as I screamed toward the house, feeling my blood run cold as the bee's venom crept through my veins. There was this sense of indignation, a violation by nature. It was all I could think of, that feeling, only now it was watered-down and stale, giving way to an unspeakably quiet frustration.

***

Roger was gone by the time I woke up. Every single light in the house was on, giving each and every object a sort of glowing edge. Everything with its unique jellybean of light. The souls of regular stuff. I watched Joel on his hands and knees as he scrubbed the carpet with some foamy white shit.

"Where'd you—?"

Joel dropped his sponge into the bucket of dirty liquid. It made a sound like running water. Like one of those indoor waterfall things. He snapped my dish gloves off his hands and hung them on the sides of the bucket.

"The basement. At least until the ground, you know, thaws or whatever." Joel patted the back of my head with clammy after-glove hands. I sensed a hesitation on his part and fought to ignore it.

"I know," he said softly.

I pulled my shoulder away and wiped my eyes. "Fucking assholes!"

"Clay did this?"

I nodded. "And Donny, those *motherfuckers.*" I wiped the snot from my nose and sat up on my feet. Crying was over. It was time to get my shit back and fuck those assholes up for killing my dog. Joel rubbed the back of my neck and I started crying again. I balled up and rolled into his arms.

"Here," he said, putting a brown napkin to my face.

I blew my nose, audibly filling the napkin. Joel got up and threw it in the trash. My house was fucked. The railing was broken, the TV was smashed. All the pictures and dolphins floating on the carpet. The *smell.* It was destroyed, beyond unlivable. The only thing left was the coffee table. Smeared with powder and covered in vomit. Clay's empty beer can sat on the very edge, sweaty with condensation.

I kicked it off the table.

"Hey!" said Joel as he scurried to pick it up.

"Look around, Joel, look around."

"Your sister's in bad shape."

"Lynne?"

My legs were still heavy from the K. Moving reactivated the swirl, the cloud of poisonous gases in my head. Moving through my wrecked house, I felt like I was walking through the apocalypse.

Joel turned around. We were halfway up the steps. "Why the fuck did you let those guys into your house?"

"Lynne did! They're like hippies. I didn't...I don't know."

Joel was serious. He looked at me dead-on. "Hippies are the *worst* fucking people in the world. They're just drug addicts who hide behind the veneer of acid, that fake utopia of...I don't know, whatever, but in reality, it's all bullshit, a big fat lie. The first chance they get, they'll fuck you, especially wooks like Clay."

"What's a wook?" I asked, holding my head. It was starting to hurt in waves, in womps and squeezes.

Joel opened my sister's door and stepped to the side like we were entering a five-star restaurant or something. I looked at him as I walked in, trying to let him know he was being an idiot, but he didn't say anything, he didn't even look at me.

Lynne's sheets hung off her bed and puddled on the carpet below. She was naked over the covers, slouched pale against the headrest with her head slumped to the right. Her eyes were glazed and half open, legs splayed. There was a needle sticking out of her left arm, below the aerobic band she'd used to tie off.

I ran over and slapped her face.

Joel cupped my shoulders. "Hey, it's okay." He took my hand and put it to her neck. Her pulse was slow but steady. "See?"

I punched Lynne in her head. "Fucking idiot!"

Joel pulled me off. "Look at me."

I refused.

"Are you okay to drive?"

"Yeah," I lied, glancing out Lynne's door, peering across the hall and into my own bedroom. All my shit was everywhere. My drawers were ransacked and dumped out. The mattress flipped. My clothes covered the entire floor.

Lynne's eyelids fluttered. Her body shook. I thought she looked blue, but it might have just been the light.

Joel

Brenda took the needle out of her sister's arm and set it on the nightstand. She pressed a shirt down to stop the blood. Lynne's skin was a sickly shade of blue, the color of veins. She laid there, horrible and naked, corpselike. The sides of her mouth shone with drool as her eyes twitched. It was as if she were relaying some unspeakable message from beyond. Brenda shook Lynne's head and slapped her. Lynne's breasts jiggled under the force of the blow. I couldn't help but notice them. They were huge and moving, triggering parts of my lizard brain, the evolutionary part trained to spot tits in the wild. Horrible.

Brenda let go of her sister and grabbed me.
"What the fuck do I do?"
"You gotta get her to the ER."
"You're not coming?"
"Brenda, listen—"
"We can't. They'll violate her."
"Huh?"
"Her parole."
"Oh."

Brenda chewed her finger as tears gathered in her eyes, little drops of water gaining critical mass and breaking off, falling onto the faded blue carpet as if abandoning the ship. Three tears, a sigh, and she wiped her face. It was all she allowed herself.
"I am *not* sending her to jail!"
"What about a halfway house?"
"They're even worse."
"How?"

Lynne's shallow breathing increased into quick rattling gasps. She shifted her head to the left and wheezed. Her hair was nice. I'd never noticed it before. It looked soft and shiny. Her roots were a reddish-brown. The blonde was a dye.

"Because—fuck, help me get her down—it's easy as shit to get drugs into those places. Easier than jail."

I helped Brenda scoop Lynne's doughy mass off the bed and onto the floor. She wasn't super heavy, just awkward to move since her body was entirely dead weight, inert and dependent. She felt like a giant butt.

Brenda put a finger to Lynne's neck and counted. "Seriously, the drugs in those places are out of control."

"I'm sure there's *some kind* of restriction—"

Brenda, at her wit's end, grabbed my ear and twisted.

"Joel, shut the fuck up!

I recoiled, freeing my ear from her crabby grasp.

"You have no idea what you're talking about!"

"Jesus Brenda—"

She gritted her teeth and pulled her hair. "Just, fuck! Listen, listen, you fucking *idiot*, those places—which your rich-boy princely little ass will never know anything about—those places allow people to drop *clothes* off to inmates. Think about it. Pills, packets of dope, whatever you can think of, stitched into sweatpants, sneakers, socks—*anything* you can imagine. And the guards, the fucking piece of shit guards who *should* be working fries at McDonald's, the ones who are *supposed* to be in charge of inspecting and making sure people aren't getting high, are bringing in drugs *too!* Now, Joel, please, please just shut the fuck up and help me! I need to get this shit out of her system."

Brenda's eyes were wet and blue and intense. They pierced mine in a way that told me she was right. She was utterly above me in this setting and we both knew it. She had the authority of oppression.

"Turn her on her side."

I did as she said, using extreme caution not to touch her unconscious sister's breasts, which was tough since they, like the rest of her body, hung freely. Brenda, I guess sensing my discomfort at seeing her unconscious sister's vagina, pulled a blanket off the bed, one of those southwestern woven design, and swaddled her lower half.

I touched Brenda's shoulder. "Hey, are *you* okay?"

"Joel—just..." The question froze Brenda in frustration, stopping her from the task of separating her sister's tits as Lynne lay on her side. I helped stabilize her sister, placing a knee against her back. Brenda gave up and let go of her sister's breasts, letting the one closest to the floor hit with a thud, pinning an empty bag of Cheetos to the carpet. The words "dangerously cheesy" reflected in the light of the ceiling fan above.

Brenda recomposed herself and went back at Lynne's breasts, spreading them out from her chest to either side.

"Here, keep them like this."

"What?"

Brenda grabbed my hands. "Jesus, Joel, not right now. Just please do this and don't be weird about it. Please?" She had gotten angry to the point of being nice.

I obeyed, trying not to look, or think about how Lynne's nipples were the biggest I'd ever seen, easily the size of a full potato chip.

Brenda handed me a small trashcan. "Keep this in front of her face."

"What are you doing?" I asked, spreading her sister's unruly breasts, trying to gain some form of non-perverted grip on the gelatinous folds of tissue.

Brenda ignored my question and took a step back. "Hold them out."

She swung her leg and kicked her sister in the solar plexus, catching the edge of my right index finger, which didn't hurt too bad thanks to her sister's generous levels of subcutaneous tissue, but I complained anyway, just because. "Ow, my finger!"

"Spread 'em, Joel!"

"Can't we use ammonia?"

Brenda took an extra step back and this time kicked *through* her sister, hitting the exact middle of her chest. Lynne's eyes bulged as she shot up, a true heroin Frankenstein bolting upright as she hurled into the trash can, puking so hard that it splashed out from the bottom. Some of it missed completely and got on my jeans. I was holding the can with my foot.

I sat in Lynne's room after the ordeal, alone and wondering if kicking her in the stomach was all that necessary since Lynne had *shot* the heroin. Then again, it had worked, so who knows. The shower was running down the hall. Brenda was rinsing Lynne with cold water. I figured it was best to stay in here. I'd already seen her sister's naked breasts and huge surprising bush, there was no need to be in the bathroom and see more. I'd about hit my limit on *not being weird* or whatever Brenda asked of me.

I picked up the empty bag of Cheetos. Tidying was a good idea. It would re-grant me the authority I had coming in here, back when I dragged a dead dog into the basement, thudding its dog head down a flight of stairs while Brenda slept on the couch, still high on whatever she'd been on. *Rich-boy?* Slightly better than gay boy, but still. The level of respect was too low and I had mentally checked out. My feelings for Brenda were gone, replaced with the curious detached view of an anthropologist sent to study a foreign population. A population I was better than, right? That was the point of anthropology. The subject of studying humans in the wild like animals. A cerebral conspiracy of humor.

Looking around for the trash can, I noticed something. The dolphins again. They were in Lynne's room as well, a ton of them sitting around, different colors, shapes, and sizes, just like downstairs, only more densely populated since the room was smaller.

Brenda mummy-walked her towel-wrapped sister back into the room. Lynne's hair was darkened with wetness and hung below her shoulders. I tried to help Brenda but ended up forming a sort of conga line. I detached, opting to prepare Lynne's bed instead and fluffed a pillow.

"Thanks." Brenda said, pulling the pillow out of my hand and stuffing it under Lynne's head.

She looked ghastly and pale, like a dead person breathing. It gave me that feeling, the one at every funeral I've ever been to. That sick fear of kneeling next to a dead, dressed up body that someone on salary schizophrenically washed and dressed, mumbling empty prayers under the ozone of ancient aftershaves and perfumes. Smiling at old ladies whose names escaped me.

"Does your sister always sleep on her back? Or is this more of an impromptu thing?"

"You know you can leave, right?" Brenda adjusted Lynne's hands and pulled a blanket over her sister. She looked at me, her eyes like two sad stones, and then turned away to peer out the window. Her hands fell softly on the dusty sill. But then she turned—an abrupt twist of the neck, and winced up at the ceiling. I think she was praying.

"You guys big fans of marine biology or something?" I asked.

"What?" she asked, still looking up.

I pointed to one of the glass dolphins. "You guys have like millions of these things. They're all over the place."

Brenda pumped a one-note laugh out of her nose. A hyper-sigh. "They were our mom's idea. Made her happy, I guess." Buried somewhere in her face was a shard of lost joy. "Whenever me or my sister were sad about something, usually about boys, or..." She paused. "Or whatever, our mom would go out and get us these dolphins. It was her way of, I don't know, trying to help?" Brenda looked around the room. "And I guess from the looks of it we were sad a lot." She chuckled at her feet, her face slowly curling back into an expression of emotional pain.

I touched her shoulder. "It's not dumb. It's really nice."

Brenda wiped her eyes and laughed weakly. "God, just the idea of her handing us these fucking things thinking it would make a difference...it's like...I don't know. It makes me feel dumb and hopeless."

"Why?"

"Thinking of her trying to relate like that. To try so hard and be so wildly unsuccessful."

"She loved you."

"Shut up. You didn't even know her."

"True, but there are a fuck ton of dolphins."

"Glass dolphins aren't *love*."

"True. Though maybe sometimes love gets lost in translation."

A gunshot echoed in the woods.

Fig

I had come into the woods with my Swiss-army knife figuring I'd poke the guy who attacked my dad, jab him right in the heart. But the gunshot scared the shit out of me. And I was freezing. Figured I'd go regroup and come back. Maybe light his house on fire or something.

A twig snapped, then another.

I was sure I heard it, the sounds of someone creeping through the woods. It got closer and closer. I breathed with my nostrils so they couldn't see my steam. Then it got quiet again. I made a break for it.

Twigs were snapping all around me as someone burst through the bushes.

We slammed into the ground and then rolled down the hill. I rushed to get up, but he already had me by the collar. The cold metal of a gun pressed against the back of my head.

"It's a fuckin' kid, bro!" he said laughing and threw me on the ground. "A fuckin' kid."

The guy that poisoned my dad stood there holding his arm while he studied my face.

"What are you doing?" he asked, spreading his fingers and squeezing his hand.

I looked at the other guy. He was wearing one of those big puffy jackets with fur around the hood. He had a line shaved in his one eyebrow. His tongue ring glistened as he smiled.

"None of your fucking business!"

The guy in the puffy coat grabbed me and I grabbed his wrist— knocking the gun out of his hand. The ugly one sprang for it but he was too late. I had already picked it up.

"Back up!" I said, jabbing the gun towards them. "Back the fuck up!".

The dude with the tongue ring crouched and backed away. He put his hands up and turned around. Cop sirens cried from up the street. I thought I saw the lights but wasn't sure.

"Give me the bag."

Tongue ring snatched the bag from the other guy and tossed it at my feet. "Fuck, man, take it, just go."

I aimed the gun at the ugly one and he just stood there. He wasn't scared like his friend. It was like he was thinking or something.

"This is for poisoning my dad."

I squeezed the trigger.

Click.

I squeezed again.

Click.

I picked the bag up and ran toward my fort. A nice-size rock caught me in the back but I kept going. The cop lights rolled at the top of the hill, changing the color of the sky in waves of red and blue. A rock flew over my shoulder and bounced off a tree. I was close, maybe five or ten feet away from my fort. Flashlights crisscrossed down the hill. People yelled. I swung the bag over my head and launched it over my fort's thorny wall and detoured up toward my yard.

Then the skinny kid closed in. He was a freak, a short little bottle rocket blasting up the hill behind me. I looked up at my yard. There was still the wall to climb. No way I'd get up it in time. I turned back around to go down but got snagged on something and went flying in the air. The sky spun as I rolled, bumping my elbows and knees on rocks and roots. I tried to scream but it was too late, tongue ring was all over me. He covered my mouth and snatched the gun. Whacked me in the temple with it.

Eddie

Their radios beeped and crackled as they crunched their way through the woods, swashbuckling the darkness with their flashlights, moving in rhythmic seriousness against the ghost of a heard gunshot. More cars came and then some left. People chatted and pointed.

Before long they were gone, taking their assemblage of lighting apparatuses with them.

Brenda slunk out of her basement some sixty feet away. Her arms were folded across her chest, pulling her sweater tight against her body. Joel was behind her, his hands outstretched above his head confused. He tried to massage Brenda's shoulders but she pulled away.

I whistled and waved them over.

They walked up John's wooden steps coming from the backyard. The deck was in good shape. Sturdy, but to my estimation, in need of a good staining. Parts of it were looking sun-beaten and grey. Surprising, knowing John and all.

Joel's hand was at the small of Brenda's back. He put it there as a way of telling her to stop, to let him open the little latch so they could move through the spring-loaded gate that blocked the stairs. Brenda stopped moving and grimaced at the moon, somehow irritated by Joel's kindness, or maybe at having to stop or just being cold. Who *knows?* Who knows what it is exactly that plagues the demented minds of beautiful women, frustrated empresses on their little patches of Earth?

"What's going on?" asked Brenda, as she settled back against Joel's chest.

"Gunshot," I said. "Figgy ran off into the woods shortly before."

"And where's his *dad?*" she asked indignantly, puffing a cheek's worth of steam.

She turned toward the sliding glass doors, snapping her vision away in shock, forcing it toward her feet, right at a sizable knot in the deck.

John stood naked against the glass door, his shoulders pinned back and posture perfect. His rather impressive member, bursting out of an eagle's nest of unruly pubes, mashed against the fogged glass, giving it a bloated and smushed effect like a hotdog on the end of a twelve pack against the plastic, which may have created an illusion of more girth than he actually had, but still, it was impressive. It was intensely colored, blood-rushed and red, marbleized with veins.

"Does he have a rubber band-?" asked Joel as he blocked Brenda with his body.

Sure enough, Joel was right. John had somehow fastened a red rubber band around the base of his unit, a deadly three-sixty pinch around the root. This came as a slight relief to my surprise, demystifying the aggression of John's flaccid penis—though it was still impressive, rubber band or no. And John wasn't just mashing his horn against the glass for the sake of showing off. No. He was engrossed in a task. Writing something in the fog of the glass, his own language of mystical runes with the oily smears of his finger. "I'm afraid he was forced to mouthwash with this. Got all in his eyes too." I pulled the little vial out of my jacket pocket and shook it.

"*Dude.*" Joel's jaw dropped.

Brenda turned her head and looked up at him. Her neck muscles flexed as she did this. Soft striations where her hair touched. Something like a ball of yarn. "What is it?"

Joel looked up at the sky, blown away to the point of smiling. "That's a *whole* vial of acid. John's on—a low estimation? Considering he probably didn't absorb *all* of it—at least twenty hits, ten at the absolute minimum. Though who knows? He could also be on *a hundred.*"

"Is that a lot?" she asked.

Joel shook his head and exhaled something that could have been a laugh. I looked over at John, who was trying to remove the rubber band from his penis, stretching it to a dangerously snap-able length.

"Oh my God," Brenda whispered into her hands. They were folded over her nose in a Virgin Mary-like way.

Joel opened the door and hopped away.

John stopped tugging. He put a hand through the door and retracted it back into the house. He was wild-eyed. The stuff beyond wonder. We watched, waving encouragingly as he stepped outside, one leg and then another, observing his body as if landing on an alien planet. The temperature disgusted him, baffled him. John retracted his arms into his chest and hunched forward.

Joel stepped up, hands outstretched as if to signal he came in peace.

"Hey, John, I'm gonna get that thing off you, okay?"

John stepped back. His skin was goose-pimpled and pale under his thick coat of body hair. He crossed his hands over his genitals and cowered.

"It's okay." Joel took another step and bent down. He nodded at me to lend support. "Grab the tip and stretch it out."

"Why on earth should I do that?"

"To thin it out. So I can get the band off."

"No. *You* hold the top. I'll take it off."

"What difference does it make?"

"The top's sensitive. I don't want to touch the sensitive part."

John gasped and bent forward.

Brenda, I guess annoyed, took it upon herself to address the situation. She already had the band looped around the tip and was digging her nail into the rubber as she stretched the band and broke it. John breathed in shivering puffs as Joel hovered like Brenda's little surgical assistant, trying to get that hot potato out of her hands.

Joel shot me a sideways look and headed down the steps. "Get him inside. I'm gonna go look for Fig."

***

John sat in his lazy boy recliner, stabbing the air with his remote as he mumbled. His eyes, which were beyond bug-eyed, seemed to vibrate in his skull. The sleeve of his robe—Brenda had somehow convinced him to put it on—rippled as he moved, dashing in grandiose sweeps like he was addressing a crowd. The robe was red, made out of this silky material. His ex-wife's if I had to guess.

I interlocked my fingers over my belly and leaned back on John's sofa. Sucker was *comfortable*. "Hopefully it's not permanent."

Brenda narrowed her eyes. "Who did this?"

I pulled a lever and the footrest lifted my feet as I went back even further, wishing I had a cigar. It would have made the whole thing. "One Clay Hayden. Your business partner, I hear."

It was like Brenda sucked all the saliva to the back of her mouth. That was the face she gave me.

"Video for the pills. Correct? Only you, with the help of old bong brains, of course, tricked him. Gave him a dud. But—" I chuckled "—and here's where it seems to get good in my mind, Clay and his minion threw a little rat of their own into the salad. A little snatch and grab?"

Brenda's face plunged into her hands and she cried.

"Oh come now, Brenda. I wasn't—"

"He tried to rape me!"

She wiped her face with the sleeve of her jacket. A trail of tears and snot glistened on the material, sparkling under John's eye-aching LED fixtures. I had planned on dimming them, but decided against it, what with this new revelation, figuring it to be wholly inappropriate.

"Who did?"

"My *business partner.* Asshole."

I pulled the lever and sprang up, out of the world of John's sofa, and headed to the kitchen. John was standing, fully in the throes of his oration. His right hand outstretched, palm up like he was holding the Hamlet skull. His pendulous member swung through the opening of the robe. It had grown comfortable in the heat.

"How did the heroes fall?" I thought I heard him whisper.

I tore three feet of paper towels off the tube and walked it back to Brenda, doing my best to ignore John and his nonsense, reveling in how much I liked *being* in his house. There was something about it, something utopian, about being able to turn up the heat, or tear long runs of paper products off the role and not bat an eye. It felt like I was rich.

Brenda's head was in her hands, elbows supported in her lap. She tugged her hair softly, pulling it up and then down, away from the middle.

"Here."

A bubble of snot emerged from her nostril and popped as she muttered thanks. I nodded and stood by as she emptied her sinuses into the paper towel. Once she was done, she folded it neatly and placed it by her feet. I offered to take it to the trash for her, show her I wasn't afraid to touch her mucus or anything else that came out of her. I wanted her to know that—that she was incapable of producing anything that made me squirm or feel dirty.

She stepped on it and told me not to touch it and I sat back down.

"*Thank God*, Roger was there..." Her voice began to trail into another high-pitched cry.

"Roger? The dog?"

"Yes," she whispered, out of breath from crying. "He saved me."

I scooted to the edge of my seat and folded my hands. "Where is he now? Is he okay?"

Her face crinkled and she shook her head.

Fig

Again, with the fucking duct-tape, wrapped around my whole body this time, my sides and arms, stiff and tight like one of those nutcracker things. I was in the back seat next to Clay. He was holding Donny's gun, opening the cylinder, spinning it, clicking it in and out as the car junked along I-95, aggravating my monster concussion headache.

"What the fuck!" I yelled, pushing against the tape. I felt like a worm.

Clay tapped the top of my head, the spot where he'd knocked me out with the gun. Donny grimaced in the mirror, smiling as he took a drag from his cig. My body rocked as Donny hit a bump. The tires rubbed and hummed against the undercarriage of the car.

Clay smacked Donny. "Watch the road!"

Donny took his eyes off the road to yell at Clay through the mirror. "I *am* watchin' it!"

Road signs trailed as we went under their big bars of steel. Blurs, extensions of the light and metal stretched as we passed the exit for the airport. I always got nervous around it, the exit for the airport. Sometimes when my dad was driving, he'd space out and we'd end up taking the exit, having to circle the terminals while he punched his wheel and freaked. And the cars around us would either be driving super slow or super fast, people pulling out and pulling in, everyone cutting each other off which only made him madder. One time we were passing through and I saw a lady crying. She stood with her luggage and leaned against a giant cement column. People walked right by her. She wasn't a bum or a crackhead, either. Just a normal lady crying at the airport. My dad used to punch the wheel till his knuckles bled.

"Let me go you faggots!"

Donny looked up in the mirror. "Clay."

Clay was looking out the window. "What?"

"You gonna let him call us that?"

Clay waved him off.

"Have you ever been on a plane?" he asked me.

I shook my head.

"Really?"

"My dad refuses to fly without his gun because of 9/11"

Donny's eyes reappeared in the rearview. "Yeah, but if you don't fly the terrorists win."

Clay shook his head. "Jesus, man."

"I'm serious bro. They want to switch us into Muslims. All of us." Donny puffed the last of his cig and cracked the window to toss it into the wind. He rolled it back up and lit another. He looked back in the mirror. "I saw a documentary about it and everything."

Clay waved the smoke from Donny's cigarette out of his face. "Lower your window."

The cigarette dangled from Donny's lip as he looked up into the mirror. He seemed hurt and then mad. "Why don't you lower yours? I'm just sayin'."

"Because I'm not—you know what? Fine. Keep your window up, fuck it."

Air rushed in as Donny cranked the window back down, his shoulder moving in little rolls as he squeaked the handle. The wind was cold and smelled like metal. He lifted his cig out the window and ashed it with the wind. He didn't tap or flick it or anything. It looked cool.

Clay tapped the spot on my head again.

"If your dad doesn't play ball we're *all* screwed, just know that. That this isn't me vs. you or anything like that. It might feel like that, but it's not."

Lights pulsed rhythmically out of the top of Donny's phone as it vibrated and rang. The ringtone was a song. I couldn't think of the name, but I knew it. He lifted it to his face and shot it back down into his lap.

"It's fuckin' Stan, bro! What do I tell him?"

Clay snatched the phone. "Yo." He said, deepening his voice, listening for a while and then said. "Nah, dude, not yet, but I think—actually, we definitely got you on that other thing. Talked to dude tonight. Lookin' like tomorrow." He nodded. "Yeah, we can do early."

Donny looked up in the mirror and bit his nail. He lifted his eyebrows up at Clay. Like, *are you sure?*

The roads were narrow and windy with big metal bumpers to keep people from falling off the edge. I think there was a creek on the other side of the rail, but it was dark and hard to tell. Donny took a left, bringing us onto a main road for a second then back onto an even darker and windier one than before. I saw a deer's eyes glow and then we turned again and went a quarter mile and pulled into an apartment complex. It was called Camelot Courts.

Donny's car whined as we chugged up the hill that led into the complex. There were about ten or fifteen brick buildings, all with sets of concrete steps leading up and into outside halls of doorways. A dumpster sat crooked in the lot, chair legs, magazines, a rolled-up carpet, and other trash stuck out of it. Most of the cars here looked like Donny's, dented and beaten up with sun-chewed spots on the paint.

A woman wearing a velour sweatsuit walked to the dumpster and threw a wet roll of paper towels into it. She was shaped like a tall egg. Her cig pulsed in orange glows as she walked back toward her house, holding her wet hand out in front of her.

Donny parked and turned around. "I don't know, bro—"

Clay placed Donny's phone on the middle console. "We don't have a choice."

"Yeah, I just don't know how I feel about this dude's *dad* showing up at our house with guns. Know what I'm sayin'?"

Clay watched as two black kids walked by the car, a boy and a girl about my age. The girl hit the boy on the head and ran away laughing. "I already told you, dude. He's a non-factor. Out on the edge of time and space. Plus, he doesn't even have to come. We'll have Lynne broker it through Brenda. We'll tell her she can have her bag or whatever."

"But we don't have it."

"She doesn't know that."

"And what if this dude's dad doesn't have any guns?"

I laughed. "My dad's got a ton of guns. Assault rifles, shotguns, shit with laser scopes. He's gonna show up and blast you pussies. Just let me go."

Clay smacked my head and I got dizzy.

Donny's phone rang again, lighting the car like a disco ball. He picked it up and studied the screen, cringing. "It's Lynne, bro. What do I tell her?"

"Just—let's get inside first."

Donny slumped in his seat and silenced the call. He turned his car off. "I'm not feelin' so hot bro."

Joel

I'm talking medieval levels of darkness. Pitch black. Plus, the woods were sloped, a downward pitch of trees and shrubs that felt like it was swallowing me as I moved in a cautious squat, grabbing branches to keep me from tumbling to my doom. It reminded me of childhood the way I was moving, using my body, the animalistic range of motion we forget once we start thinking about our bodies.

Shadows flittered, accompanied by rustling tricks of the wind. Trolls, fairies, sprites and genies—these things made sense. It's easy to judge when you can walk two feet and flick a light with a switch, but before then? There was just darkness. Twelve hours a day the lights went out and the world became a negative canvas, something for people to project their incessant bubbling terror onto and *see*.

I needed to get the hell out. Not just out of the woods, but this place. Things were starting to get really fucked up. I could feel it. I could *feel* the woods.

A bush rustled nearby.

My body strained under the ancient weight of nature, the massive looming death that surrounds a squirrel. All it took was the swoosh of grass, the plastic baggy swoosh brought on by another living entity in the dark.

I called for Fig and then sped back toward the house. Call it fear, or call it the mammalian duty to survive.

I stopped under John's wall and shivered. I needed to catch my breath before climbing it. The air had a bitter quality, a mint-in-the-mouth chill as if I were breathing the very essence of frostbite. I stuck my hands in my jacket and squeezed my fists. My cheeks puffed and I blew out all my air. I don't know why I did this. Instinct maybe? Maybe that's all it took. Fifteen minutes in the woods at night and I'd grown feral.

A hard gust blew, stripping skin cells from my neck and face as it rushed by. I gathered myself and bent against it, greeting it head on. The trees whistled and shook. I got lower and more compact, grabbing the chain-link metal cages of John's retention wall. They were painfully cold and metallic, lonely somehow, I thought. Then I got an idea. Something I could do with my weed. Something that could expedite my departure for sure. I could be gone in a day.

Opting out of climbing John's rock cage, I decided to walk around and up the hill toward his neighbors instead. Glowing windows came into view, first as blurs of light and then full, illuminated squares bouncing in the darkness as I walked, incandescent and inviting. I wondered, maybe that's what it's all about. Lights. Lumens. Fire. Beaming out from every corner of the world to safeguard us against threats both real and imagined. Shattering the unknown and unknowable. Perhaps the hydrogen bomb was our true destiny, going out in a perfect flash of knowing. I saw someone watching TV through their window, basking in the glow, the light.

Brenda

"Look at him." Eddie tapped my elbow.

John stood in the kitchen. His socks square on the tile. The tiles were like mock stone, made to look like a castle floor. A mix of grey, orange, and bluish slates laid in a way that made it hard to find a pattern. John opened a cabinet and shut it. He opened it again, this time closing it slowly.

I could still feel the spot on my elbow where Eddie had touched. It was like my body sucked it up or absorbed it. It made me feel sick and greasy.

Joel came in through the back door and slid it shut behind him. He rubbed the bottom of his sneakers on the thick, bristled mat and took his coat off. He had this look on his face, like he'd forgotten what he wanted to say.

"How's he doing?" he asked, shivering off the last of the cold.

Eddie held his hands out, "Where's Fig?"

John was opening two cabinets now, one with his right and one with his left. The one creaked and jumped at the hinge. He slid out the silverware drawer and pushed it back in. It was one of those silent things that closed itself.

Eddie tapped my arm again. "Don't you think it's strange?," he asked.

I moved my elbow, rubbing the spot he'd touched to cancel it out. "What is?"

"How they knew where to look. I figure you hid your money well. Everyone hides it. It's money, we hide it well, especially with, you know."

"He's playing games, Brenda. It's all angles with him." Joel said as he stomped through the kitchen, right past John as he was inspecting a fork, twirling it under the light.

The living room floor was beautiful. Original floorboards. The color of coffee with a dollop of cream. They had little nicks and gouges, jags and broken pieces darkened with absorbed stain, shiny and dull, flaws trapped behind layers of clear coat. It reminded me of somewhere a vampire would live in one of those shows. Time-forgotten.

Eddie blocked Joel with a spotty hand and swiveled in his seat.

"Call her. Call your sister. She knows where they are."

"Who?" asked Joel.

Joel's foot was on a spot that'd gotten repaired. I could tell because the wood went the other way, a little patch. There was drama in these floors, a splattered urgency about them, a loneliness I could feel and understand.

John rejoined us in the living room to study himself in a porthole mirror on the wall. He rubbed his hand along his face, grazing his coarse stubble. I couldn't hear the sound but knew it was there. I'd stroked faces before and heard it, the little hummingbird noise of facial hair. John could grow a beard, a nice full beard. He wasn't fat and had nice floors. His thermostat was digital and could be controlled remotely through a phone. Something shifted in me, the repulsion for John parted into a neutrality. I didn't exactly want him, but I also didn't *not*. Plus, I always found something attractive about people while they are intoxicated. Getting to see them almost naked in a way.

"Am I this?" John asked, absorbed in his reflection.

Eddie shrunk in his chair, clearly uncomfortable with the question, like it sucked the air out his body. Men like Eddie looked to guys like Joel for answers to stuff like this. Eddie really was an angle man. John was a floor man. And Joel was a guy who handled these questions.

John's beard scrunched and folded into something resembling one of those maps that show the height of mountains. Brown for mountains, green for grass and blue for the ocean. A three-color— actually four-color world. The lines were black. Supposedly they spaced the signs between states to make up for the lines on the map. I didn't believe it.

Eddie hiked his pants up even though he was sitting.

John's lips trembled as he stared into his reflection. His hands held his face, twisting into sad claws. The deeper he looked the more scrunched and distorted his face became, and the tighter his claws. Eddie, as if struck with a world-changing idea, stood up. Before saying anything, he looked around, rotating slowly and nodding, his hands out by his sides. The look on his face was approval. He was impressed, showing it with his entire body.

"You have a lot of nice *stuff*, John."

John looked deeper in the mirror and Eddie looked deeper into the stuff.

"Your thermostat has digital numbers? All I can do with mine is twist it. Twist it and hope it works. You know yours works. Know why? Because you select a clean digital number. I twist mine and feel superstitious."

John covered his face and moaned. He retched, a dry heave of air, breathing in and out real fast. Something I did at yoga once. I went on a groupon deal and really liked it but never did it again. Collecting himself, John looked back into the mirror, greeted by a reflection of his own horror. Eddie continued to inspect the house.

"Wait, is this not a real fireplace? Is that gas? Is that natural gas? I honestly can't tell if that flame is real or fake. Amazing."

John clung to his handrail. A dungeon slab of reclaimed wood he bolted into the wall with heavy brass fittings. The brass was aged and darkened. It's mascara-dark knots glistened with lacquer sheen. The bottom of the railing was fat and thinned toward the top. It was the shape of a rifle.

"You did well here, John. A lot of nice stuff."

My phone rang. It was Lynne.

Eddie

Brenda rose from the couch. There was a caterpillar-like quality to her walk, a sense of energy coming from the middle, a casual sashay powered by rump and stomach. She lifted the phone to her ear and crossed her arms.

John was falling apart, more and more, obliterated by his reflection. He was breathing heavily, dots of spit flying off his lips and onto the mirror. He seemed determined to *look*, but it was destroying him. He was losing this battle, whatever it was.

"Is that a new backsplash?" I asked. "I've never seen one like it."

Joel approached John. His steps were cautious and awkward, the opposite of Brenda's, more of a legs and arms movement. He slid his hand in his pocket and pulled out an old envelope. It was dry and thinned by time.

He held it out to John, "Here. John. Get out of the mirror. Check these out."

John whipped his head toward Joel. It was snake-like, quick and dangerous. I looked around, forcing myself to take inventory of his things. I wanted to consume their novelty, to enjoy them as much as possible. I focused on his floors, the island countertop in his kitchen— so much space and windows. I focused on the abundance of natural light that would be there in the morning, visualizing the realtor with her clients, the smooth and effortless transaction that would be the sale. John's chunk of time-swollen equity.

"Am I bein' tested?"

"If you want to be." Joel shrugged.

This toppled John. Knocked his breath out as he gripped the railing. Collapsing on it, merging into the wood. It was as if he were trying to seep into the cracks.

"My life is so goddamn *big*. How do we do it?"

"Do what?"

"Fit all these goddamn lives here? It's...We gotta be spirits. Otherwise...there's no way unless we're all ghosts."

Joel slid some pictures out of the envelope. "Hey, man, look. It's you. You're not a ghost."

John snatched them and let his body fall back against the stairs. He winced upon impact, though maybe it was the photos.

"That's me?"

Joel cleared his throat. "Uh, Yeah. I took them from your basement."

"You stole them?"

"I didn't *steal* them. I took them to look at. I was going to give them back, unlike Eddie. He stole your change, you know?"

"My change?"

"Yeah, your coins."

"Oh." John paused in thought. He didn't seem that bothered by either of us being in his house and taking from him.

I still could have kicked Joel in the head, though, the little snake.

"Why were you guys down there?"

Joel looked at me, asking with his eyebrows if I wanted to answer. I tightened my lips and shook my head.

"You stole my trash and I went down there to take it back."

"Why did I steal your trash?"

"To find out my secrets."

"But I already know your secrets. I know about the gas station boner pills. I found them."

"That wasn't mine."

"Those weren't boner pills either," I told him.

John looked me up and down. He swallowed his spit and shook his head.

"Look, John," I said, "You are the kind of guy who knows what goes on *behind* the walls of a house. You understand the idea of a *home*, unlike most people, who only live in them and pray, people like me who don't understand roof leaks and faulty sockets. All we can do is hope they're not broken until they are. And then we keep on like they're not. You know when stuff's broken and how to fix things and make them right."

"Why did you steal my change?"

There was light in Joel's eyes, a muted jovial smirk. I could have rolled him down a hill.

"Because I'm old and I'm poor. Reduced by circumstances beyond my control. Compressed by time into a thief and beggar. But if we can get Clay—"

John's limp penis emerged slowly from the middle of his robe, bashfully, like a bullfrog from under a rock. I watched it, the mess of skin unfolding from being stuck together.

"Um, but if we get Clay..." I said looking at the floor.

"Is that Fig's mom?" asked Joel.

John nodded into his hands. His nod continued and escalated into an unbalanced rocking motion. I thought to check on his crotch, figuring I could read his thoughts through it but decided against it. I'd already clocked enough viewing time on that thing and needed to sleep before I could clock any more.

"She's really pretty."

"She left me."

"Hey," I interjected. "You tried, but it's no easy task. A beautiful woman requires the same amount of time and attention as a publicly traded corporation. The same manpower and will, charts and plummeting graphs. If they leave, they leave. There's nothing you can do. It's like trying to control the stock market, impossible."

"You're *sorry*? He tried to fucking *rape* me, Lynne! Yeah? How'd he know then, huh? To lift the corner of the rug? How'd he know to lift it up? Oh so—let *you speak*? You have got to be fucking—*Lynne!*" Brenda screamed from the kitchen.

We heard something break, a high-pitched porcelain shatter. I went to go in and John raised his hand.

"I can repair anything she destroys."

"That's what you do, John, that is what you do."

"That old fruit bowl was a *mistake*. Oh Jesus!"

John gripped the sides of his head as he grappled with the idea.

"Why was it a mistake?" Joel was confused.

Our talk had been lowered to near whispers. There was a sense of respect for Brenda among us, as if she was some angry god storming above. John sat back on the steps. He seemed deeply calmed, the state of a man after sex he could be proud of. There was a look about his face, a dissolved smile that wasn't by any means obvious. A tired sort of giving up.

"Buyin' fruit and vegetables is a stress. Nothin' like a can. A can lasts forever, all that salt and everythin'. Produce, man, that stuff just dies."

"You don't even need to cook the stuff in cans," I offered, "It's good the way it is."

Brenda stormed back into the room, moving in angry little steps that I found delightful. There was still that centrifugal motion to her movements, only now sped up. She moved all the way to the door and came back as if on a catwalk to display her anger. The kitchen was filled with her emotion. I wanted to go in and feel it. I could pretend to wash my hands.

"She set it up," she said, smacking Joel on the chest. "She...ugh."

Joel tried to comfort her, but she pushed him away.

I inched toward her, making sure my shoulder was inside of the kitchen. "Did she happen to mention where they are?"

Joel stepped between us. "Would you stop thinking about your dumb fucking case for a second?"

"I'm not."

Brenda sat down and held her head, rocking back and forth. "They have him."

"Who?"

"Fig, they have Fig."

I stroked my face and looked at John. He was absent on the steps, mouth hung open in an expression that portrayed distance. I gripped the doorway's molding. My fingers were in the kitchen now too.

"Did she give an address? It's very important you tell me. So we can get back-up."

"Brenda, don't, he'll—"

"What? Call Clay's daddy?" I interrupted. "Damn right, I will. This is some big-time shit here."

Brenda shook her head as she spoke. "They said if I bring them John's guns, they'll give me my money and release Fig."

"No way they'll fork over ten grand for a couple of guns."

"Guns go for a lot of money on the black market, dude. You'd be surprised." Joel cut in.

"Surprised? I was a *cop*, you reefer-head."

"Wait, how'd you know about the money?" asked Brenda.

John closed his robe and stiffened up. He towered over us on the first step. He was already the tallest and now he was a monument, something to be toppled by ropes and angry hands in the future. But for now, here, he was in charge. We all felt it. Out of his mind and in charge. Brenda's eyes seemed to glisten. I wonder if Joel noticed.

"If they want my guns then...well...that's what it's gonna be. They can have them." John's voice was warbled when he spoke, but still authoritative. His hairy chest protruded from his robe, big square pecs that only a small portion of the world got. Barrel-chested and hairy with a no-nonsense donger.

John thumbed through a few more photos, placing the ones he viewed in the back of the stack. His breathing was sure now, an oceanic rise and fall that had replaced the spasms from before. A tear dropped silently down his cheek.

"I just want to see my boy. He's the only thing, the only thing I actually know."

I got my leg in the kitchen.

Fig

The apartment was disgusting, a gross two-bedroom square with tan carpets—desert camouflage with stains. Hard sticky ones. Like when I rubbed deodorant on the rug at my aunt's house and lit it on fire. The deodorant was flammable. I used to trace designs on things and light them. I burnt a dick into my aunt's carpet and my dad *fucked me up.*

The living room was up front, the first thing I saw walking in. They had plastic chairs for furniture and cushions from different sofas littered around the floor. One of the chairs was tipped over. There was a blanket over the pillows. It was a Chicago Bears blanket that was supposed to look like a football field when laid out flat, but was kicked over and folded in a way that only showed the end-zones and a little bit of the field, the fifty-yard line. Past the living room was a little kitchen. A tight squeeze, even if no one was in it. There was a small round table in the kitchen with no chairs pressed against the wall. The table blocked the oven, and there was a fire extinguisher on the counter. There was a scale on the table. Empty plastic baggies and razor blades on there too. Needles in the sink. An electric stove with "GE" written on the top in old-looking letters.

"Do you think he's gonna bring somethin' with him?" asked Donny.

Clay lifted the tipped-over plastic chair and sat it against the wall. He shoved me down into it. "Don't move."

Donny lingered for a second and tapped Clay. "Whaddya think? Should I call him?"

"Yeah, Donny. Just—fuck, man. Just—let's get ourselves right first." Clay put his foot near a plastic shopping bag full of trash and rubbed it. A plastic lid and straw were sticking out of the top. The straw was chewed, flat and wide.

"You know anyone that's good right now?" Donny scratched the back of his neck.

Clay stopped rustling the bag. "What? Where's the rest of our shit?"

Donny inhaled scared and painfully, like he was about to get hit in the stomach. "Fuckin Lynne, bro. She pigged out. Shot like *four* bags."

Clay leaned against the wall and slid down onto one of the sofa cushions. "There were *five* bags left, Donny."

Donny unzipped his coat and reached into one of the inside pockets. "Here." He pulled out a little white bag and tossed it onto Clay's lap.

Clay caught the bag and opened it. He looked seriously disappointed. "Blow? You think I want to do blow right now?"

"Well, fuck it, if you don't want it, give it back. I'm sick too, bro."

This made Clay laugh. He opened the bag of coke and dumped some onto a bent-up spoon he'd pulled out from somewhere in the blanket.

"C'mon man," said Donny. "Can't we just sniff it?"

Clay shook his head.

"Bro, I *hate* shooting coke. You *know* how I pass out."

Clay felt around his jacket and pulled out a syringe. He took the orange cap off and set it on my lap. It was cleaner than I thought it would be. I don't know why but I figured it'd be dirtier, caked in blood or something.

"Bro, just remembered." Donny snapped his fingers and jogged away.

The way he jogged reminded me of an athlete. That's what he naturally was. Donny looked like he'd be awesome at basketball, maybe football too. I felt kinda sorry for him, the fact that he wasn't playing sports.

Clay craned his neck to see into the hallway. Donny was still in the room, opening and shutting drawers. Clay dipped a little razor in Donny's bag and snorted some of the powder. Donny's door swung open, the sound of a loose, rattling knob and the squeak of the hinge.

The idea of them being roommates in this broken place made me feel cold.

Donny came heavy-footed down the short hallway and stopped at the little electrical panel. It was tiny, a quarter of the size of the one at my house. It bummed me out, how they barely had any electric.

"Fuckin' what's his face—Steve Rainer was supposed to grab these and got busted hoppin' a turnstile, bro." He forced laugh. "Can't believe I didn't tell you, dude. Totally forgot."

Donny smiled, waiting for Clay to smile back, but he didn't. He didn't even say anything. He just wiped his nose. After a few more seconds of Donny smiling and pretending not to have known about the pills, Clay, looking a bit irritated, set the spoon down on the blanket. Smoothing it out to make sure it'd stay flat, he got up and slowly made his way to his feet. Donny offered a hand but Clay didn't take it.

"Dude, I mean, wow! Like, sixteen thirties here the whole time and I had *no idea*. That's what kind of day it's been. We'll definitely look back on this day, bro."

Clay snatched the pills and walked into the kitchen. "Right."

Donny followed him in. "Fuck's that supposed to mean?"

They were out of my sight now, arguing in low mumbles as they banged around on the table.

The doorknob rattled, then a knock. Clay and Donny stopped arguing about the pills and started arguing about the door.

Donny came out from the kitchen slicking his hair back and shaking his head. He looked at me, almost like he was asking me if I knew who was outside. I must've given him a look that pissed him off because he flinched at me, raising his fists into his chest and flexing.

Clay poked his head out. "Who is it?"

Donny was flat against the door, squinting into the peephole. The way he was standing seemed to piss Clay off.

"Dude! Who is it?"

Donny adjusted his crotch and unlocked the door.

Lynne pulled her hood down and walked in. Her wet, black Reeboks glistened as she stood in the Chicago Bear's end zone. This was not a place where people worried about what they carried in on their shoes. No one worried about anything here from what it looked like. I thought about that, how worrying works, how it keeps the mess inside of us instead of out.

"Stan come through?" Lynne looked at the spoon.

Clay made a death mask at Donny. "Are you kidding me?"

"What? I didn't—Lynne what the—how do you know about Stan?"

Lynne darted her vision back and forth between the two of them and then looked at me. Her face bent in a sorry expression, like I'd deflated her or something.

"I swear, bro. I—"

Lynne shifted her weight to the left and crossed her arms. Her eyelids opened slowly, but impressively wide as her head angled to the right. Her movements were familiar. Her stance was a classic TV one, taken from all the angry women on daytime talk shows and courtroom dramas. She stood crooked and posed as if to confront a group of men about their potential fatherhood.

"What. The. Fuck."

Clay raised a hand to Lynne and turned away. "Get her out of here, Donny."

Donny wrapped his arms around Lynne, apologizing quietly as he led her toward the door. Lynne shoved him off and stamped toward me. Donny pulled her back. His arms dug into her stomach as he whispered into her ear, pleading. Clay was in the kitchen. I couldn't see him but heard him banging on the kitchen table. I figured he was in there losing his mind or something.

"My fuckin' sister knows, ya idiots!"

Donny's eyes bulged under the force of Lynne's weight as she collapsed on him. Clay came out of the kitchen holding the sandwich bag, shaking it so the blue powder settled to one corner. He bent down and picked the other bag up, the white powder, and mixed it with the blue, flicking the bag and shaking it.

Donny, who was still struggling with Lynne, sliding down the wall as she cried, cupped the side of his head, horrified at what Clay had done with his drugs.

Clay oozed down the wall opposite to them, back into the spot he was in before, watching as Donny nurtured Lynne, rocking her back and forth, and then he switched his attention to the spoon, fully focused in a way that seemed disgusting. His chin melted into his neck as he looked at it. His mouth hung open, wet and gross.

Lynne's boobs were bigger than Mrs. B's, but not by much.

"Here." Donny rolled a bottle of Sprite across the floor.

Clay, still with his chin tucked, looked at the bottle and dismissed it. "Get me some water."

Lynne did a football stance to get herself off the ground. She looked back at Donny as she picked the bottle up and took it to the kitchen. Clay lifted the spoon to his nose and sniffed some of the powder. Donny recoiled at the injustice.

"Bro!"

"Donny, don't even."

Clay lifted the spoon again, this time with more powder and sniffed it off. Lynne held the soda over the sink and let it glug out the bottle. The tap squeaked on and off and she came back into the living room, swirling the liquid, looking through the green plastic to inspect the water like she was some kind of chemist. Like she wasn't just filling a soda bottle with water.

"Just so you know," she said, "I am not okay with any of this."

Clay ignored Lynne as she sat back down against Donny, who looked like he had a big ass egg on his face. Clay pulled an orange-capped syringe out from one of the folds of the blanket and dipped it into the bottle. He shook his head and mumbled, took it out, and took the cap off. He dipped it back in and used it to suck up a tiny bit of water. He squirted it on the powder and mixed it around in the spoon.

Donny threw him a cig. Clay took the filter out and tore it into little pieces. He took one of the pieces and rolled it into a pea-sized ball and set it on his lap. Everyone was silent, watching as he did this. Clay's chin grew tighter and more crunched as his mouth hung open, wetter and more disgusting. He brushed his hair out of his face and stuck the piece of cotton onto the spoon and drew up the liquid. He held the needle to his eyes and flicked it, his tongue stuck out of the corner of his mouth.

Clay put the cap back on and threw it to Donny.

"Here, let her go first."

"We got three hypos! Why do we gotta share?"

"What's a little bodily fluid between star-crossed lovers like yourselves?"

Lynne narrowed her eyes at Clay and snatched the needle from Donny. She pulled the scrunchie out of her hair and rolled it up her arm. "C'mon, hold it."

Donny whispered something to her.

"I'll be fine, just fucking hold it."

Donny shot the stuff for Lynne. They sent it back to Clay and watched as he sucked it back up through the cotton. Donny took the needle and crunched against the wall in a shameful little ball, hiding himself from sight. He popped the needle out and sank against Lynne. Blood trickled down his arm, but he didn't care. Nobody cared. Which was the point, I guess. Lynne cuddled into Donny's chest as Donny rubbed her back for a moment, but his hand physically trailed off and fell against his body. They were sitting on the floor, in the middle of a big stain surrounded by trash.

Clay smiled and shook his head as he pulled some more of the liquid up with another needle. He capped it and set it down on the blanket.

Donny and Lynne were eye to eye, blurrily mumbling about love.

Clay looked at me and laughed, and I felt on his side for some reason.

He dumped some more of the powder on the spoon, just a little, and did the shit with the water and the cotton and sucked it up into another needle. Clay shot a string of liquid out the tip and onto the rug as he flicked it. A new stain formed where it hit.

Donny's eye's widened as Clay stood up behind me. I tried to turn around, but it was too late. Clay had me in a headlock. The needle hit my neck and then it got hot. I screamed, but his hand was over my mouth. He pulled the needle out and drove it back in. Then it felt hot again. I felt really scared, and then really good. Everyone looked far away and distorted like I was looking up from underwater.

Then I puked.

Joel

I sat there next to Brenda, watching her watch Eddie sleep, hearing the occasional thud of whatever John was doing upstairs.

I waved my hand over Eddies face and snapped a finger. He grumbled and scratched his leg.

"What are you doing?" Brenda asked.

"Shh. I got a plan. I can get rid of my shit. Possibly tomorrow. I'll have enough money for us to get the fuck out of here."

"*Us?*"

I grabbed my keys out of my pocket and twirled them. They spun faster and faster until finally coalescing in a blur of repeated motion.

"I'm gonna blast my weed with butane."

"Huh?"

"Look...I don't have time to explain. I know a place where I can get a ton of it, but it's closing soon. I gotta go now. We can talk later."

Brenda tugged her sweater around herself and looked back at Eddie. His head was arched back, drool glistening the corners of his mouth as he snored. He readjusted his arms and squirmed back into position, this time rolling onto his side.

***

My steering wheel was vibrating harder than usual—actually, it surpassed vibration. It was officially shaking now. I chalked it up to the temperature. Cold air always amplifies the knocks and rattles of any questionable car. My dad told me one of my cylinders was shot when I bought the truck. He said I was supposed to have four but only three were firing. Tire salesman. Thinks he's a mechanic.

Brenda shut the door and shivered to get warm. I cranked the heat but cold air blasted through the vents.

"Fuck!"

"What?"

"Heat's cold."

"Yeah, no shit. You just turned it on."

I hit a left and then a quick right. A cat darted out from under a car and scattered low to the ground. Its glowing eyes bounced up and into the cemetery. It was a black cat, too. A black cat creeping around a cemetery in the dead of winter. I tried not to think about it.

"I gotta use your basement."

"Why my basement? What's wrong with yours?"

"Look, Brenda. Do we have a deal or not?"

"Oh, so *that's* what this is?"

"What? What's *this*?

"Oh, please."

"Oh, please, what?

I took a left on Umbria and sped down the hill toward I-76. It was up ahead, the highway, its mass of halogen dots. A semi-realistic portrayal of cinematic hyper-speed that I sped to join into, gearing for the blend. My dots among the others.

"You're using me." She said out the window. "Just to use my basement."

"Wait, let me get this straight. So you, in your head, somehow think that *I'm* the user? God, it must be nice to be able to deceive yourself so thoroughly."

"Jesus, Joel. You're so...ugh." Brenda shook her head at whatever she was thinking and continued looking out the window.

"I'm so what? In touch with reality?"

She turned, only to jeer in mocking disbelief before returning her gaze to the outer world, her vision fleeing the car, out to the beckoning highway. My merge was coming. Light butterflies took over my stomach as I took the curve of the on-ramp, gearing to join the flow of traffic. I'd never gotten over the feeling, not since that first time I merged with my dad in the car. It seemed impossible. To assume that the whirling world of speed and metal would somehow absorb my presence without this horrible impact was almost too much to bear. All that math and physics, the odds of people paying attention and letting me *in*.

"Butane's pretty volatile. So—I figure I'd do it at your place since I still stand a chance at getting my deposit back, which thinking, in purely rational business terms, is more money for the getaway."

She turned back around, this time raising her eyebrows in a challenging manner.

"Okay yeah, since I live in a fucked-up piece-of-shit house we might as well just do it there and fuck it up more. Thanks."

The dots were everywhere in my mirror, leaving me no other choice than to speed up and force them to accept me. I closed my eyes and hit the gas.

I opened them a second later to Brenda checking herself in the mirror. My truck had safely merged into the mechanical horde.

"It's funny," she said.

"What is?"

"How you just *assume* I want to go. Let's pack up and follow Joel forever. Hitch right onto that train wreck of a life."

"If my life's a train wreck, yours is the apocalypse."

"Fuck you."

"Fine. Don't come. See if I care."

A tractor trailer womped its air breaks. I jammed mine. Traffic grinded to a halt. A couple of white pick-ups blew past us on the shoulder, the construction trucks that give themselves orange police lights for some reason. Such a weird authority to have.

"I guess we can forget it now anyway," I said, drumming my wheel. "This traffic fucks the whole idea."

"Where are you trying to get to? She asked, still looking out the window.

"South street."

"Take the next exit. We can cut through the park."

"The exit's a half mile up. We're stopped dead."

"Ride the shoulder."

I held my hand across Brenda's lap and signaled to the truck to let me over. He moved up. Brenda reached across and blared my horn. The driver jammed his brakes and looked down at us. Brenda gave him the finger.

"Go! Quick."

I jammed the gas and cut over to the shoulder, following in the wake of the construction sirens ahead. We got off the exit and went under an overpass.

"Take this left and follow King drive. It'll dump you onto Kelly and then onto the Parkway from there."

"I know where I am. And honestly Brenda. That's fine if you don't want to come. But I need to use your basement. I'll give you two thousand bucks *and*—ready? I'll let you stay at *my* house for the remainder of the lease. There's like four months left, which of course I'd pay before leaving."

"Four thousand."

"Thirty-five hundred."

Brenda fidgeted her fingers in her lap. "So what do you need from me?"

"Nothing. Just stay out of your house for a day or two and then, whatever, you can live your life however you see fit from there."

"Where in California are you going?"

I didn't say anything.

"Jesus, Joel. You don't even know do you?"

"I'll be fine," I assured her.

***

An electronic bell sounded when we walked in the store, a two-note song of mediocre commerce.

Doo-*doo.*

Better than those ringing bells but still tacky. Everything about this place was cheesy. Charged with that tongue-in-cheek caricature of stoner ethics. Racks of bowls, bongs, chillums, steamrollers, two expensive hookahs, and a gra-hookah sat up top out of arm's reach behind the cashier, admist a wall of different rolling papers, vape batteries, and grinders. The endless paraphernalia of smoking pot.

Roy, the manager of Tunnel Vision head shop, looked up from his phone and nodded. "Sup, dude," he said, sliding off his stool behind the counter.

Roy was a lanky redhead with a tri-colored goatee and bushy eyebrows that made him appear perpetually serious—which at the time, arced on his forehead at the sight of Brenda. She pulled her sweater shut in response. He was skinny to the point of concern. And he always wore oversized draping sweaters, ones made of unusually thin material, sheer garments that showcased his lack of mass, his protruding bony shoulders. He wore black skinny jeans and a pair of Chuck Taylor's that were drawn on with different color markers.

"Do you guys still have Isobutane?"

Roy pointed to a small display behind the counter. There were six tubes in a box with the top torn off along the perforated line.

"Is that all you have?"

"We might have some more in the basement." His eyes slid over toward Brenda and then back to me. "How many did you need?"

"All of them."

Roy adjusted his curtain-like sweater on his shoulders, kind of like Brenda, in a series of awkward shrugs. He seemed annoyed by my answer, its urgency and drama. It was above his authority as manager in some vague way.

"Hold on," he said, shaking his head as he ducked under the counter and headed toward the basement. The way he ducked was his response to my command. It was deft and expert. He breached the space under the counter with the full authority of an employee of the store, someone who ducked in and out of the space that other people, customers like us, couldn't. The sign he entered said: employees only. He shut the door behind him to preserve the illusion of having entered a sacred space reserved for people of his position. It was the best he could do, flexing his shard of power.

Brenda leafed through a rack of stoner-oriented T-shirts, stopping at one that was supposed to be a five-day forecast, with a weed-leaf sun surrounded by clouds in each individual box of the day calling for, of course, cloudy. There was another shirt that was supposed to look like a Jack Daniel's bottle, with that same scrawled cursive lettering, and instead of the trademark old no. 7 there was a big 420 with "Cannabis" in place of Jack Daniel's.

"How many of these do you have in your closet?"

"Please," I said, watching Roy emerge stony-faced from the basement, moving in a laborious trudge under the weight of a box of butane, displaying his strength.

"Dude we have like fifteen cases," he grunted, letting the box slam on the glass counter.

I pulled a wad of cash out of my pocket and counted eight hundred bucks, roughly one-quarter of my emergency cash stash, which was all I had left until I sold my weed.

"Here's eight-hundred. I'll even help you carry them up."

Roy paused, clutching his phone. "I don't even know if I'm allowed to sell someone that much. Hold on. Let me—"

I laid another two hundred bucks down. "A thousand, but I need them now."

Roy set his phone on the counter and wind-milled his arm in preparation for the task ahead, bending his legs in some sort of unidentifiable stretch.

"Fine, but it's gotta be quick. Everyone helps."

I tossed Brenda my keys. "Pull my truck up into the loading zone."

Brenda

The truck bounced. Joel was jumping around on the back bumper, sliding the boxes into order, laying them down on their sides so they weren't sticking up. Pointing, he counted the boxes twice and pulled out his phone. Probably to do some math.

The manager kid leaned against the building and lit a cigarette. He was exhausted from going up and down the stairs. Joel wasn't tired at all. He seemed the opposite. Like coked-out, all jittery and nervous. He shook the kid's hand and gave him some more money. The manager nodded, pocketing the bills as he tucked his smoking hand across his chest to catch his breath. He looked at me through the window. Joel turned and looked too. I pulled my sleeves over my hands and looked the other way. Something felt wrong. Deeply wrong. Like I was gonna die or something.

Joel wiped sweat from his face and started the truck. His smile faded as he looked at me. I was crunched against the door, stretching my sweater. I wanted to crawl inside of it, hide from this feeling, this spider-on-the-skin crawly feeling like I was about to be hit with a personal-sized asteroid, but there wasn't enough material. So, I stretched it some more and it ripped.

I cried into my sleeves.

Joel shifted the car into park.

"What's wrong?"

"I don't *know*," I warbled. "I feel like...like everything's wrong. *Everything.* Out of place, and I'm losing my mind, or dying, or about to explode. It's just *wrong.*"

Joel looked me over and shifted into drive. He pulled me into him and said, "Hold on."

***

We sat on a bench off Main Street overlooking the black choppy water. Parts along the bank were slushy, some spots fully frozen. Night clouds glowed grey, wisped around the sides of the full moon, like hands holding it in the sky, offering it up to whatever was above it.

Joel was trying not to shiver. I could tell. He'd given me his jacket, making a cape around my shoulders.

We huddled together on the uncomfortable bench. The part I was sitting on was cracked, bending under my butt and sagging. I pushed down thinking it would snap but it didn't. The air was so cold I could feel it in my mouth. A creamy feeling.

Joel had gotten us hot chocolate from Starbucks. I didn't want to drink mine. It felt too good on my hands. Warm.

"Better?"

I nodded and wiped my eyes, "What if it happens again?"

Joel picked a pebble up and tossed it into the river. "It's just your body processing your mega-fucked up day. Don't worry about it."

The street was crawling with people, the late-night migration between bars. Mostly the business earmuff crowd. Guys in dress clothes wearing heavy pea coats walking by, office workers. One of them looked over and said something neither of us could understand. He was too drunk.

"You guys, woo...aw man. You know?"

His friends laughed and pushed him down the street, cheering on whatever was happening. They took turns smacking their inebriated buddy in the ass, knocking him off course and laughing. They went and others came—people exactly like them. We continued watching the factory line of drunks in business casual as they stumbled by, yelling like idiots: Red-faced bankers, multiple-chinned mortgage brokers, salespeople with brutally gelled hair—scrambling up and down Main Street as they smacked each other on the backs and laughed uncomfortably. A jagged, desperate laugh that could have been a scream.

Joel pointed that out. How hard they laughed. He looked around, sipping his hot chocolate and shook his head. His mouth hung open, stuck in search of the right words.

"Why do they get so drunk?" I asked him.

"I don't know," he said. "I think it's just that whole office culture. That compression of lost freedom. Like when it's someone's birthday and they act like they're having *extra* fun just because it's their birthday. Did you ever see that? It happens at weddings too. It's instant depression when I see it."

"You think what we do is better?" I asked him.

"I mean, I'm glad I'm not them, but I don't know. My life kind of sucks too, I guess."

He squeezed me into him and we sat like that for a while, shoulder to shoulder as the warmth of our hot chocolates faded in our hands. We watched the nighttime bustle, the unofficial parade of weekend night desperation, the adult Easter egg hunt for meaning. Cops, drunken idiots, slow-walking old people, people walking dogs, and young girls dressed like it wasn't freezing, shuffling by. Our faces got closer as we sat, our cheeks finally touching and then turning as we met in a kiss. I bit his lip and he sighed. We exchanged face-murmurs, speaking in a language we created, stealing each other's air as we bit and tugged and pulled, like we were trying to rip physical mementos from each other. Joel breathed, and I breathed harder. He grabbed my thigh and I grabbed his dick. He bit my neck and I pulled his hair. The streams of people walking by only intensified our burst of passion, swirling the contents of my stomach into an abstract painting. I bit Joel's neck and whisper-begged him not to go. He kissed the top of my head and hugged me so hard I couldn't breathe.

I put my head down on his shoulder and he stroked my hair.

"You have really soft hair," he said, smelling it like a weirdo.

I pointed up to the sky. It was jet black with more stars than usual—or maybe they were just brighter. It's hard to tell since I don't have any reason to keep track of stuff like that.

A girl wearing a short skirt leaned over a railing and puked into the river while her friend held her hair.

"Is it true?" I asked.

"What?"

"How some of the stars are dead?"

My head bobbed on Joel's shoulder as he shrugged.

"Yeah, I mean, some of them are dead but you can still see them. It has to do with the way we perceive time. The light we see is travelling away from the body of a fallen star and it sits right there. A dot. A miracle and a dot. Who knows? Maybe our bodies do something similar.

"Weird," I replied.

"Wanna know what's even weirder?"

"What?"

"Some people believe that the universe, you know like the big bang?"

"I think so."

"It's a theory of creation, or story depending on how you look at it, that the universe came out of a big explosion in outer space, or just space, or nothing—whatever it was called. This great nothingness exploded into everything and that's why we're here."

"Seriously?"

"Yeah, it's what we're supposed to believe. Isn't that weird?"

"I've literally never thought about it."

Joel sipped his hot chocolate and then kissed the side of my nose and a little bit of my eye. I think he went for my cheek and missed.

"Some people believe that the big bang thing—the space explosion I mentioned? That it's happened an *infinite* amount of times. We're born, die, and then go back into the ground and eventually, like billions of years later the planet is destroyed and breaks apart into particles that float around as space dust until it happens again, billions, maybe trillions, maybe eternities later, that same blowing up of nothing that everyone's so hot about. We come back and live again. Same life and everything like nothing ever happened. It's supposedly what Déjà vu's about."

"Hmm," I said, sipping some of Joel's hot chocolate since it was somehow warmer than mine. "I guess that's kinda nice."

"You think so?"

"Yeah, like I'm temporarily together with everyone I've ever met. Like if we ever break up or stop dating or whatever this is, it's like you'll never get away. No one ever does."

Joel kissed my head. "Temporarily together forever."

Joel

The cases of butane squeaked and slid around my truck bed as I went up a hill. Brenda switched the heat to blow on our faces. I had it set to our feet. The faces setting always dried my eyes out, made me feel artificially tired.

I closed my vent.

"Isn't that stuff flammable?" she asked me, turning to watch it.

"Yeah, it's super flammable."

"So you left a bomb, basically, in the back of your truck while we sat and had hot chocolate?"

"It's no different than hairspray. Or liquor."

"Then why are you driving so slow?"

I gritted my teeth in a form of silent prayer, huddled over the wheel as a low-level rage coursed through my body. I hadn't had a girlfriend since college, but it was all coming back. That under-the-microscope feeling of the all-seeing female eye, its inspection of my ways, my driving, my speed, the thoughtless minutia of my life torn into the light and combed over in painstaking detail.

"I know you had a tough day, but can you please? Not right now."

"I'm just asking," she said looking out the window. "*God.*"

After I got the last case of butane loaded into her basement, I went around the house and cracked every window, enough to let out air but not be noticeable. I didn't want to tip off the neighbors. The outside of her house still looked normal, still unbroken. The inside, however, was another story. I tried not to look but couldn't help it. This was a place of broken things and spirits, the physical wreckage of a failed family strewn about.

I went back downstairs. Brenda was in the living room. She was standing which irked me for some reason, staring into Roger's blood splatter like it was a campfire. It was horrible, the blood dried on the carpet, the bits of paper towel stuck from my unsuccessful scrub. She rubbed her foot on the dried blood, wincing in disgust every time she felt it.

I picked a cushion up and put it back on the couch.

"Joel, don't."

"Why?"

"Just...Can you please not touch them. I don't want any of this stuff being touched right now. Not until I find my sister."

It made no sense. It made absolutely no sense, but it was law, Brenda's law, and I was a serf in her kingdom of emotional irrationality. I stood watching her gross herself out on the spot on the carpet and wondered if women had ever been in control of the world, and if so, what happened? What was the world like under their absolute rule? Are we under it now?

"Did she tell you where they are?"

Brenda nodded.

"Okay...and where is that exactly?"

She shrugged.

"Fuck, Brenda, will you stop?"

"Stop *what*?"

"This whole thing of just, I don't know, not answering and staring off into space. Where are they? Where's Fig?"

She turned and faced the steps. "Can you *please* stop yelling?"

The edges of my vision were blurry, tinged with a tunnel-like sense of unreality. Brenda stood and huffed. I huffed too. We huffed together until she was satisfied.

"They're in Brookhaven."

"*Brookhaven*?"

"It's about a half hour south on 95."

"I know where Brookhaven is. What's the address?"

"They didn't give me one. Said they'll tell me later, when they're ready."

"Ready for what? And when? Tonight?"

Brenda lifted her hands up and out as her lips quaked in a suckling frown. She shook, about to cry. Her lips. Those little smears of hot cocoa at the corners of her mouth. Fuck man. The picture of her as a smiling child lying crooked on the floor among the already sad pictures of the rest of her family. As if the levels of disarray were somehow insufficient. As if someone needed to scatter her framed photos, destroying her family's personal stash of happiness propaganda to prove a point. It sent me into a state of transcendent depression, making me understand why people might have tried to carve some rules into the rocks, to help people avoid this, the timeless mess of abject failure, all those people screaming crying as they died, exiting the world with the same all-encompassing fear and confusion they came in with.

I sat her down on the cushionless couch and knelt by her.

"You need to sleep."

Her eyes daggered.

"Jesus fucking Christ, all I'm saying is you need some rest. Shower up and relax. That way you're fresh when Lynne calls. And I'll set my shit up in the meantime."

She got up and headed toward the steps, a sleepy, knuckle-forward shuffle of the feet that signified exponential unfairness. The same narcoleptic walk of people who wear pajama pants to the drug store in broad daylight. The all-stars of clinical depression.

"Fine, wake me up when you're done."

"Can you please just sleep at my house? I don't want you in here while I do this."

"Are you seriously kicking me out?"

"For fuck's sake, Brenda. I am not *kicking* you out. This stuff's dangerous. I don't want you in here."

"I thought you said it wasn't, remember? You literally just said it wasn't dangerous."

I could only crunch forward, curling my arms around the top of my head like a monster in transition. My head was a volcano of mean thoughts, any of which, if verbalized, would have started a domestic brouhaha that could have gone on for days—years maybe. Stuff so mean and true and cutting that we would had to have gotten married, just so we could fight forever. The high-octane argument fuel of vocal combat that lasted after death, moving epigenetically through time in the shape of new bodies.

"I don't want to be *alone,* Joel."

"Okay fine. I'm heading over there anyway. I gotta strip the buds off my plants so I can freeze them here. You can go upstairs and go to bed. I'll be downstairs in the basement. Then I'll come get you when I'm done so you can come back with me."

"Fine," she said, twisting the toe of her shoe into the rug.

***

I was back in Brenda's basement with everything I needed. Trash bags of roughly cut weed, my butane, and a legion of Pyrex dishes littered on the floor around me. Something like twenty of them. Maybe thirty. Innocent fifteen by ten bakeware set to my evil purpose. I'd stopped at three different grocery stores to procure them, by myself thank God. Brenda was still sleeping. I figured she'd be pissed but whatever. I had to let her rest. Plus, I couldn't deal with her coming, tired, grumpy, and ever-questioning, shadowing me as an unwanted consultant on something she'd never done or even heard of. These places were sad enough without that. The twenty-four-hour Acme's and Shop-Rite's. I hated going after 11 pm, seeing the dark side of the grocery store, seeing the women who I assumed to be single mothers frantically stocking the shelves, feeding the sleepless pulse of commercial consumption. Just unnerving.

***

I pulled some of my weed out of the freezer and shut the door. Frosty trash bags of ground-up nug slush. The basement door was open, slightly ajar with a fan positioned in the gap. It was hooked up to an extension cord from the second floor, since the outlets down here were apparently broken minus the laundry hookup. A cloud of dust gathered and then blew outside, as the little Vornado bumped and rumbled on the cement

I stuffed the blast tube full of cold weed and pointed it over a Pyrex dish. Lining up the spray tip, I pushed down and blasted the butane through the tube. No rotten egg smell of propane. Just the same old basement must as before. Good, I thought, watching the amber goo drip out of the tube and into the dish. Really good.

The basement door opened and knocked over the fan.

Eddie smoothed his hands over his jacket as he walked in. The more he saw, the tighter his eyes got. Me, the dishes, the butane. He knew I was doing something fucked up. He just didn't know what.

"Good God! Are you making meth down here?"

I finished blasting the last of the can through the tube. We were both silent, watching the rush of syrupy goo drip into the dish. Eddie dialed something into his flip-phone and held it up, wiggling it in his hand.

"You know what number that is?"

"I can't read your screen from here."

Eddie scowled and moved closer. "How about now?"

"Nope." I knocked the spent weed out of the tube and packed it with more.

"It's 9-1-1 nimrod."

I kicked the empty can by my foot, sending it rolling in a u pattern. Eddie watched it until it stopped and held his phone out.

"Give me the address or I'll hit this little red button and end your little, whatever the hell this is."

"Green button."

"What?"

"The red button is for hanging up." I picked up another can and blasted it through the weed. "How about this?" I said, keeping my vision on the tube, "How about I finish up what I'm doing and then give you the address since I don't exactly trust you right now, you rotten old fuck."

"Rotten?"

"You're the shittiest old person I've ever met."

"You're scum."

"I'd kill myself if you were my grandpa."

"That's it, I'm dialing."

I looked up from the tube. "I'll beat your old ass before they get here, drag you into the woods, and bury you next to Roger."

Eddie pulled a taser out of his pocket and held it in the air. "Touch me and taste the voltage."

He thrust the taser in my direction and squeezed the trigger. Nothing happened, no spark or buzz or anything. I set the can down and watched as he shook it and smacked the side. I slid the tray out of the way and picked up another.

"You forget to charge it or something?"

Eddie dropped the taser and pulled out a gun. A black 9mm. He cocked his legs back in an official-looking split stance and aimed with two hands as he squinted behind it. "This one doesn't need *charging*."

I dropped the can in the weed syrup and scuttled back off the cooler I'd been sitting on. "You'll blow us up, you idiot!"

"What?"

I lifted my hands off my head and pointed at the cases of butane. "Dude!"

Eddie poked his gun forward. "The address. Now!"

"I'm spraying butane through the weed to make hash. If you fire your gun, we will explode."

Eddie nudged a case with his Velcro sneaker. "You *imbecile*!"

"Yeah, well, how about you lower the gun?"

Brenda pushed through the door, sliding the fallen Vornado a little further along the floor as she shivered in her sweater. Eddie tucked his gun into his side holster and backed away in an incoherent apology.

"Why didn't you wake me up?"

"This old piece of shit was just trying to get me to sell you out and give him the address."

"Don't listen to him, Brenda. He's a young snot nose running on pure stoner-hubris. He thinks he knows all. Don't listen to it."

I took my hoodie off and threw it to Brenda. She put it on over her sweater, popping her head through and fixing her hair.

"Joel doesn't have the address."

"Don't lie, young lady."

I blasted butane through some weed and they both stopped. Brenda was about to say something to Eddie. Something mean. Probably for calling her young lady, for playing the role of whatever he was trying to be. She had that look to her. Like she was about to go off. But they studied me instead, pausing their little spat to observe something new, something they'd never seen before. It made me think of something, like a theory on how novelty could help spread peace, but I forget.

The door flung open. John kicked the fan out of his way and stood in the entrance, shadowed in the dawn's early light. His outfit reminded me he was on acid. A bathrobe, thermal pants, two different colored socks with sandals, a towel over his head fastened with a tie and a vest with extra clips and twin guns at his side nestled in belt holsters. The overturned Vornado sent another cloud of dust off the floor and into one of my trays. I watched as flecks and hairs settled in my butane hash syrup.

"C'mon, John, fuck!"

"Really, John?" Eddie shook his head.

Brenda, in what looked like a two-step ballroom dance routine, went back and then over to get behind me. Her hands cupped my shoulders, those soft wispy fingers. Her breath wafted on my neck, her fruity halitosis. "Alright," she said. "Ready to go?"

Eddie

John stood pidgeon-toed and painfully self-conscious. His eye's darted as his fingers came alive, crawling by his sides in nervous wriggles. He chewed his cuticle and glanced around the room.

Joel's tray of drugs clanked on the cement floor as he set it down. John had mussed up his crack-goo or whatever he was making. He crouched by John and stood his fan back up, aiming the airflow outside. The grime from the bottom of his socks faded up around the sides. John paid Joel no mind. His hands were in the pockets of his Nativity Rambo outfit or whatever he was wearing.

"You can't go dressing like that, John," Joel told him.

"Why?" he asked sheepishly.

"You're one to talk," I said to Joel. "Gonna ruin your damn socks walking around like that."

Joel scoffed over his goo. He jammed a baster full of pot and blasted a can through it. John stood knock-kneed and looked at everything but the people in the basement, working the invisible Rubik's cube with his jittery fingers. The fan rattled and bumped on the cement floor. Worthless really.

"He's right," said Brenda. "John can't be coming in there dressed like a fucking sultan."

John fell under the weight of her words, his arms dangling forward as he bent over deflated. The extra clips bounced in defeat from the vest as he reached into his pocket and pulled out the pictures.

"I was just trying to look like him."

"You," Joel corrected without looking up. "Look like you. And where the hell did you see yourself dressed like that?" The goo dripped out and fell into the tray, gelling in with the stuff that was already there. I covered my nose with my shirt but then took it away. No one else was doing it.

John moved in a single motion-tantrum, a full-body stomp. "What the hell do I wear then? How do you guys know what to wear?"

I inspected my tan jacket and corduroy trousers, my Velcro sneaks and grey and red insulated socks. How *did* I know to wear this, I wondered? I looked around at Brenda and Joel. They seemed to be dressed alike, give or take the tightness of their clothes, a couple of sweatpantsed nobodies. Bums lost in their selfish love, standard losers of their loser generation, lost in a kind of vapid reflection, a world of unrelentingly meaningless desire. It depressed me tremendously. Everything. I was so close and all I could feel was the weight of my head. A sad elephant head on my ruined body. I thought to stop. To lie down face-first on the dirty cement floor and lick it. Eat all of Joel's meth paste and lay down forever, licking the dirt till I died.

***

The sky was still darkish but beginning to lighten up. None of the multicolored bands of light, just the old dome. Blacklight purple. An alarming glow to the end of the night, or beginning of the day, depending how you look at it, and I felt stuck, lost between shades of night and day in a never-ending twilight. The old familiar cloud crept back in. That eternal snooze button feeling. Everything pointless and dull.

 I watched from the driver's seat, feeling the erotic rumble of John's engine under my entire private area. The heat felt damn good, warming these old bird bones. The urge to cry passed across my mental horizon. That wet wheezing pressure.

John was in the passenger seat. He sat stone-faced and robotic, staring ahead like his vision stopped at the windshield. His outfit was laughable, almost costumish. He'd have to sit in the car while we did this. One look at him and people would be calling the police.

Brenda and Joel stood by the side of the truck arguing. Probably over who got to lick the bag. She stood with her weight shifted to the left and her arms folded across her chest. Her lips sucked in a low hum of anger. Joel was the opposite. He stood straight and tall, lankily explaining himself, reaching at the air around him to make a point, and then gripping his head in mental exhaustion. The window was up but I could hear them, their tinny noise, like I was listening through a can.

"Just admit that you're a pussy."

"What I'm doing is ten times more dangerous."

"Than driving in a car with a guy on acid and all his guns?"

"I need to finish this. So you can come with me."

Brenda shoved him in the chest with her fists. Joel crossed his arms and recoiled, absorbing the blow. The whole thing was exhilarating. The thought of her hitting me. I felt good and then blackly jealous. She could throw me down the steps and I'd die a happy man.

"You said you were *staying*!"

"What? When?"

Brenda waved him off and turned to get in the truck. She stopped, almost gasping, and got in. Curse John! If he wasn't so wacked he could drive. That way I could have ridden in the back with Brenda, be next to her for the ride, listen to all her problem, relish in all of her earthly dilemmas, her gush of feminine gloom, spoils of the day's negative scavengings.

"Fuel should be good," John said from the passenger.

I turned the heat up and adjusted the rearview to see Brenda. She started to put the seatbelt around herself and then abandoned the idea altogether. The idea of us killing ourselves together entered my mind. Maybe be buried in the same plot, her on top of me forever.

"Can I please have an address?" I asked, turning my neck as far as it would go toward her.

Fig

Denim-colored light hovered in the room, just enough to see what was going on. The electric outline of morning ghosts. Me and Lynne. She was laying on her side next to me, right in front of a plastic chair. The chair was tipped over. It looked like we spilled out of it. Spilt people. A mess on the floor. That would be a good way to describe us. She had come out from Donny's room at some point to try to mother me or something, but really, it was just turning me on. But then she started to cry and ruined it. I floated as she cried, still stuck together, the tape and all, but it was *alright*. I don't think either of us slept at all.

"Shh," she said as she stroked my hair.

She unraveled me out of the blanket and slid a razor down my center, cutting the tape with shaky hands. I angled my shoulder so it was touching her boobs and she didn't even care.

"I'm gonna get you home sweetie."

Donny came out of the room with a towel over his dick. He was surprisingly ripped, glowing like a creature in the laser tag light. I didn't say anything. I just watched him, feeling Lynne's belly push against my knees. Donny wasn't that bad of a guy.

"What the fuck?" he angrily whispered, wrapping the towel around his waist as he came closer. "Lynne."

She stopped cutting and turned around. Lynne had gotten more than halfway down. I was almost free.

"Shhh," She whispered back, a little louder than Donny.

I flexed as she cut a few more inches. Donny just stood and watched helplessly. He knew he couldn't do shit. He had tattoos. Normal stuff. Celtic cross on his arm, area code on his right chest, a couple Chinese words or letters, bible verse, and a picture of a goblin on his ribs.

The lights turned on. Everyone blinked, momentarily stung by the bulb. Clay emerged from the door wearing exactly what he'd been wearing that night, only without sneakers. His toes were long and hairy with jagged yellow nails. There was a layer of dirt on his feet, faded coal miner black around the sides. He trudged to the kitchen, holding his forearm up over his eyes.

Lynne crossed her legs and held the wall to stand. It was a slow movement, one that required effort. Donny rubbed his hair faster and harder as Lynne cracked her neck. The sharp metal gleamed between her knuckles, tucked into her sweaty fist.

"What you did was *wrong.*"

Clay leaned against the fridge and shook his head. His fingers drummed against the freezer. Little padded thuds. He looked sick, hungover, like he was about to throw up. "Get her the fuck out of here."

Lynne's back jiggled as she stepped forward, shortening the distance between her and Clay. Clay looked down as he fondled the metal nub that stuck out from the silverware drawer, the little nipple of a handle.

"How about *you* get the fuck outta here? Back to daddy's mansion." Lynne responded.

"Last chance, Donny."

Donny stepped up. He looked at Clay and Lynne, and stepped back, though still in his bulldog stance. Puffed-out chest with arms out wide. The towel was hanging by a thread. "What mansion?" he said.

"Donny."

The bright light, the mess of the apartment, my stomach and head, it was all starting to get to me. Whatever he gave me was wearing off and I felt sick. I swallowed my warm spit, felt it go down my throat and started to wiggle out of the tape. Slowly, so no one could see.

Lynne pointed her razored fist toward Clay but spoke to Donny. "You know Hardt's dry cleaners? That's him. His parents own it and live out on the Main Line."

"Bro, what's she talkin' about?" Donny readjusted his towel.

Clay flattened his palms on the counter and looked down. "If my parents have all this money then how come I'm living like this? In this shithole of an apartment? With *you*?"

Lynne rolled, not her eyes, but her entire head in an angry laugh, stepping back to take in what she'd just heard.

"See? See what I mean, Donny? With *you*! Meaning poor people."

Donny's eyes darted confused. He untucked the towel and pulled it tighter. The goblin on his stomach snarled as he did this, its cartoon forehead lumpy with muscle and rib.

"Open your eyes Donny. You're the fall guy. If shit goes down, his parent's team of lawyers are gonna get him off by pinning the shit on *you*. He's just a rich, spoiled brat who couldn't hack it in his elite little world and all he cares about is getting high. He is not your friend."

"Don't let her manipulate you, man. She's just jealous," Clay said.

Donny, holding the top of his towel with two hands now, turned and looked at me. I was slumped and crunched, a booger flicked on the wall. My chest and stomach were slimy, scuffed by the underside of tape. My skin was pink and clammy, water-pruned.

Lynne's phone rang in her pocket. Some fucking pop song. Donny was still looking at me. He had this hurt searching expression on his face, like he'd run from a monster and ended up in front of a cliff.

"Dude," I said, sitting up against the wall, "Clay owns you. The whole way here he bossed you and commanded you. I just thought like, wow, this dude's getting bitched and he just takes it?"

The silverware drawer rattled open. Clay sprang out of the kitchen holding a dirty steak knife. It had a black plastic handle and was rusty in spots.

"If you're not gonna get her out, then I will."

Lynne stepped toward Clay and rose her razor fist. "What you gonna do with that little thing, rich boy?"

"You're gonna let him attack your girlfriend?!" I yelled to Donny.

Clay scowled, mean mugging me from across the room. That gross ugly face of his. Fucking Jesus. "Shut your fucking mouth before I make you like your dad!"

Lynne took the opportunity to attack, slashing the air with her fist as she charged. Clay, seeing her approach, turned, almost into a fencer stance, which, in my head, proved Lynne right. He attacked her like a rich person would. Elegantly.

Donny jumped on Clay's back, pulling back on his inner elbows and restrict his range of stabbing.

"Get off, you fucking idiot!" Clay screamed.

Donny tore him backwards and Clay dropped the knife. It flipped and fell on the blade, sticking out of the carpet. One of those things you couldn't do if you tried a hundred times. I flexed my elbows to bust out of the tape, but only got one arm free. The rest of it went up on my shoulder like a Ms. America sash. Clay resorted to girlish little kicks to keep Lynne from slashing his face as Donny whipped Clay around and put himself between the two, begging her to stop.

I slid the rest of the tape off and crawled along the carpet, through the jungle of trash and empty bags, a field of crumbs and sticky spots and grabbed the knife. None of them saw me. I crawled back into the corner and wrapped the blanket around my shoulders.

Someone knocked on the door.

Everyone froze. Even me. The whole place was silent. Donny's phone buzzed and rattled on the counter. Lynne's stupid ringer went off again too.

Donny undid the latches and locks and slowly opened the door.

"Yo. Stan the man! Sup bro?"

A short, stumpy black guy, who also looked Mexican, stood at the entrance breathing steam. He looked over his shoulders. Like a reflex or something. Every five seconds. Kinda like how people check their mirrors while driving. He seemed annoyed and kinda scared. He swung a limp duffel in through the door as he pushed past Donny and came inside.

Brenda

The sun was coming up, peeking over the river. The sky around the sun was orange, bleeding out into red then purple then blue. I could count the stars left in the sky, rolling my neck to look up out the window. The moon was still out, chalky and traced. A plane flew low, headed to the airport. Red lights blinking on the tail. Billboards flashed as we drove by, ones for cancer, jewelry, Rod Stewart live in concert, something about drunk driving, a radio station, a rehab facility with a guy hugging his son, and an ad for a plastic surgeon, a guy in scrubs stretching a glove and smiling. I tried to remember the name. I wanted to see if they could do something about my wrinkles.

"She's not answering," I said, tucking the phone between my legs.

No one said anything. John was frozen in a trance and Eddie was splitting his attention between the phone and the road, trying to send a text.

"What are you doing?" I asked him.

"Sorry, sweetie, I had to," he said, dropping his phone into John's empty cup holder.

"Had to what?"

John snapped out of his stare and into a panic. "What's that *noise*?" he asked looking around.

Eddie reached across and grabbed his seatbelt. John watched as he clicked it in. The beeping stopped. I hadn't even noticed it. My head had that no-sleep feeling, like a blurry channel behind my eyes, that salt and pepper snow. I grabbed some Adderall out of my purse.

John pulled the slack out of his seatbelt and inspected it.

I rattled the pills in my hand and looked around for a half-drunken bottle of water before realizing I wasn't in Joel's car. This was John's truck. It smelled like Pep Boys. Grease, dust, and cherry air freshener. It was clean too. Not even any of that dusty grime trapped in the little cracks and crevices.

Eddie looked up in the mirror. "I sent Clay's dad a message. Had to."

"What about my bag?"

Eddie shrugged with his face.

John unbuckled his seatbelt and rolled into the back of the truck in an awkward, clunky somersault, kicking the interior ceiling with his sandals. Thank God he had the thermals on. I'd seen enough of his dick for a lifetime. Eddie held his arm out and swerved. Multiple cars honked. Some even held their horns. A bald man in an SUV sped by, screaming silently behind the window.

"What the hell, John!" Eddie yelled.

John leaned across my lap to look out the window. He held his eyes open with his hands and peered into the sun, the molten orange mound, growing out of the river. The fiery sky had started to fade to soft peach and the purple was almost gone, transformed into a pale blue.

"I need energy." John pulled his eyes open wider, moving his head as we drove along.

I chucked a pill down my throat and got two more out of my purse. "Here," I said, handing them to John.

John inspected them in his palm. He held them up to the sun and tossed them in his mouth. He chewed, sticking out his tongue in a choked expression. "These are *disgusting*."

"Come on up here," Eddie said into the mirror as he patted the passenger seat. At first I thought he was talking to John. He patted the seat again. "Just in case he starts thrashing around back there."

"*I'm good*," I replied.

We took the exit for 476 toward MacDade and went under an overpass, a jungle of curved concrete and metal, spitting us out onto a double-laned street in Ridley Park. We were in the suburbs, something like Roxborough but with more space. I had a couple customers out here, a couple kids that used to deal with Donny.

John tapped my arm. "Give me more of those sun pills."

Eddie looked up in the mirror to let me know he was watching, arching his eyebrows in a fatherly way. I dug into my purse and gave John three more.

"Damnit, Brenda! Knock it off!"

"Doesn't he look like a witch?' John said, fighting the taste of chewed Adderall. He swallowed and laughed.

Eddie sighed in the mirror as we slowed around the curve. A sign with an arrow bent to the left warned us to take the turn at twenty-five mph. Eddie was only going fifteen, confirming something about old people that I already suspected, how the world moves for them, faster and faster, until finally it's all one confusing blur.

Next thing I know, we're on this road running against a creek, with lines of dead trees bent toward the water, behind the dented guardrail. Eddie made a left and there we were. A big sign and everything: Camelot Court Apartments.

We had to drive up a hill to get into the complex. Real steep too, lined with gigantic rocks on either side. A small shitty mountain with an even shittier apartment complex on top of it.

John reached under my feet and grabbed his rifle case. His ass went up in the air as Eddie hit the brakes.

"No, no, no. John! Goddamnit!"

The gun case smacked Eddie in the head and he cursed us, throwing wild punches toward the back of the truck.

Backpack on his shoulders and rifle case in hand, John opened the door and, more or less, fell onto the stale asphalt, rolling unnecessarily like he'd jumped out of some military vehicle. Eddie jammed the brakes.

"Get back here!"

John scaled the rocky crag and disappeared into a thin stretch of trees, his robe streaming behind.

Eddie muttered and punched the gas. John's door swung shut.

The place, or apartments, or whatever, were odd looking. I think it was the parking lot. It was too big, like mall size. *Way* too much for the size of the complex. To the point where someone fucked up. The pavement was different colors too, some black and other parts a bluish purple with tarry repair patches spread between. Some of the patches were shiny and others weren't. And on the edges of the patchwork lot sat about ten buildings. All brick. With six units to each building. Rusted air conditioners jutted out the exterior and hung in sad angles.

Each apartment had its own balcony, even on the ground level, laughably fenced with plastic-looking rails and spindles. They were like baby gates for grownups. The buildings were labeled A,B,C,D,F,G— all the way to K.

Eddie hunched over the wheel as we crawled through the lot, searching for signs of John's flapping robe as we made our way toward building F.

Almost every other car had steam coming out of the exhaust, mostly vans and trucks, vehicles of burden with magnets of the person's name and company stuck on whatever side was less dented, shaking in a collective morning rumble. A leg stuck out of a white van. The side of it said: Tony B's Plumbing, No Job Too Small. Some of the cars looked like they were painted with a brush. There was even a golf cart for some reason.

Big trees towered behind the building, reaching like fifty feet above the roofs. They moved back and forth in the wind, their dead branches spread into the sky like veins, reaching and receding. The metal tip of an electrical pylon stood behind them. A red light blinking in the distance. Some industrial place or thing.

A woman came out onto her balcony, smacked her satellite dish and went inside.

"Are you even looking for him?" Eddie asked.

"Look." I pointed over at a parked car. An unmarked Crown Vic. It was tan, with two guys sitting up front, two cop-looking guys. Eddie shifted into park and looked out his window. "What the hell do those knuckleheads want?"

Another car pulled into the lot. A black Kia. Eddie's grumbling grew into a low growl. He took his phone out of the cup holder and dialed a number, slow one finger dials, careful not to push the wrong button. He sighed and looked up into the mirror. There was no emotion in his face, no expression I could read. Usually I could pick up, like, creepiness or something, but no. He just looked at me like I was a bush or plastic bag.

"Hey, Mr. Hardt, Eddie Hayden here with very good news. Very, very good news. Call me back at six, one, oh—holy fucking shit."

John

Time peeled open, deeper and newer as I moved between the moments, the fabric between seconds peelin' like an orange into now. My head bounced and reset. Every step did this. The reset. And I didn't mind. *So what*, I thought. Translate the cave paintings. Look them up. I bet that's what they say. *So what*. And that's how it's supposed to be.

Light. It came pourin' through the branches as they shook in a mesmerizin' sway. Hands of God himself puttin' a spell over the cursed brick hut, den of wickedness and sin. The trees were maybe six or seven hundred feet high and I was wretched and small. A tick on the back of somethin' bigger. So, I thanked the sky, its illusion of light and water, our merciful curtain against the satanic reality of death and outer space.

The sun had finally detached from the earth, free from its lava lamp grip, and stood full—a complete blazin' circle, three hundred sixty perfect degrees. I looked up through the barren branches, the sycamore's fingers, and stared, lettin' the sun obliterate my vision, blinkin' through the pain of pure light, the ache of seeing God, watchin' him grow and turn white until He was all I could see, shootin' off in a cross of light, beamin' into the four holy directions and spreadin' in the space between.

I could feel the parkin' lot, the pressure of my body on its back. It was me. The parkin' lot, and so were the trees and the sky and I was somethin', a mirrored reflection stretched in an infinite repeat, somethin' to show and be shown, somethin' to be osmosed. Things vibrated and flowed through me as I flowed through the world, flickerin' in and out of caring and not. Those cave painting and the Bible. Every page. Who cares?

I glanced back up at the sun, thinkin' how people said it was just a star.

Doctors with their pills and questions. Don't they know that *why* is just a feelin'. They try, but they can't never get rid of the thoughts. Know why? Because thoughts aren't in the head. They're only passin' through—and even if they were, just to entertain their theories, to think they can toggle some switches, flood my brain with every newfangled neuro-dopa-transa-whatever, they'd still be there, stickin' like gum on the sidewalk, memories survivin' the blast of whatever chemical power-wash those fuckin' white-coat nerds dream up. The arrogance of thinking their little pills could affect my soul.

Fig

Stan stood by the door and took us in: The towelled Donny, razor-knuckled Lynne, Clay being Clay, and me against the wall, looking like the Virgin Mary in the filthy Chicago Bears blanket. He didn't flinch. Didn't even bat an eye. I liked this about him. His certainty. The way he didn't allow himself to melt into our chaos. This was a guy who didn't ask himself questions. I admired that. I admired his deep sense of cool.

Clay stepped up in front of Donny, who was readjusting his towel. "Hey, sorry for, you know...rough night. Your gear's on its way, though. It'll be here soon."

Stan, with his neatly manicured hands, unzipped his limp duffel, and threw a sandwich bag of tan powder to Donny. The bag was wrapped in tape, sealed shut and somewhat solid. "Flush that shit. Now."

Donny caught the bag and looked at Clay, who stepped up again, this time even closer to the guy, who was peeking out of the blinds. His jeans had premade slits and fraying holes. He bought them like that. With holes and slits. His sneakers were five different colors.

"Cops right there, sitting in the lot," the guy explained, still looking out the window.

Donny sprung into the bathroom. The light and fan kicked on and the lid slammed open, the clank of cold porcelain. The handle jingled and the toilet gurgled and groaned. The door flung back open and Donny was rubbing his head again, stretching his face out with his hand.

"It's clogged."

"I don't give a fuck man! Ditch that shit. More just pulled up."

Clay leaned against the counter and bit his nails. "Give it to the kid."

The guy and Donny looked at each other in thought. Lynne stepped back and crossed her arms. Her hips shifted in disagreement.

"He's a minor. He won't get in trouble. Or..." Clay said looking around.

Donny and the guy looked down at their feet.

"You will *not.*" Lynne's hips shifted again, her face twisting in disgust.

"No one asked you anything," Clay told her.

"You are *not* putting drugs in his ass."

"Not *in* or up. Just, you know, a tuck. Between the cheeks." Clay explained.

Lynne's tongue searched her mouth. She was furious. The other two just sat there, sighing at their feet. I wrapped the blanket tighter and gripped the knife. I did not want drugs anywhere near my ass.

Lynne's tongue clicked with an idea. "I'll spread it in the carpet."

"What?"

"Yeah. I'll spread it in the carpet, vacuum it up later."

Stan shut the blinds and crouched to a knee. "Yo! Someone's comin'!"

Donny readjusted his towel and looked up. I think he was praying. Clay pushed Lynne out of the way and moved toward me. My hands sweated as I gripped the knife. The handle had ridges, things to help me squeeze it. This was good. Helped with the sweat. The sweat made me think about my dad, what he'd said about holding a coin. The knife was sharp and I was nauseous, thinking about that needle, the burning prick in my neck and that feeling after. The knife had teeth on the blade. I forget what that's called.

Clay pulled a pistol out of his pocket and put it to my head. "I don't care what you do with it. Hide it."

All I could hear was my heartbeat. The sloshy glug on the side of my neck. The rest was washed out noise, noise like the creeping light from before. Stuff you weren't supposed to see, things you weren't supposed to hear. My mouth watered. It would not stop producing spit. Like when you're about to throw up. How your mouth gets all wet and you just know.

Clay gripped my arm and shook me. The blanket fell off my shoulders and I moved, quick and dangerous. His eyes stretched with fear as I poked his stomach with the knife. The teeth on the blade were a problem, those little notches in the knife. They stopped me from stabbing him like I wanted to.

He hit me in the head and ripped the knife out of my hand. I wrapped myself in the blanket, kicking to keep him from getting me back.

The door cracked around the knob and flew open. Light flooded the apartment. I blocked my eyes with my arm and squatted, like some creature from a dark world, a figment of a bad dream where the person was waking up. I half-expected to dissolve into nothing, to be forgotten.

There were screams and footsteps by my head and I smelled Lynne's perfume as she snatched the bag off the ground and took off through Donny's bedroom. The window squeaked open and I could smell fresh air, the dead tree scent of winter. Grey smells.

Joel

I unraveled the t-shirt from my face and checked the thermostat. Sixty-eight, down three degrees, a good sign considering it had been about an hour. Plus, the temp would keep rising throughout the day. They were calling for upper forties, which eliminated the possibility of freezing pipes since I'd cut off the heater and the water heater. Couldn't risk the pilot kicking on and ka-booming the house.

There were two trays in Brenda's room, three in Lynne's, four in the bathroom because of the vent fan, two under the hood vent on the stove, and one, the last and final tray, smack dab on the kitchen table, next to a lightly cracked window like a cherry pie. All of them still had that look, that oily solvent rainbow, ridding themselves of butane one bubble at a time.

I walked aimlessly about the house, going from room-to-room to search for something I'd forgotten, a mistake I wasn't aware of. Everything was done. But I couldn't leave it. There was a magnetism to the house and its danger, its possible combustion.

***

The area around my parents' house has a certain smell. A scent of indigenous vegetation. Something that triggers the brain stem in this subtly piercing manner, giving us a brief taste, a window into when we were pure animals, before we drew the distinction between scent and memory. These streets were familiar and satisfying. The quaint optometrist, the orthodontist, all the houses in between, the beaming gas stations, health food store, all thawing upon my arrival, signaling to me that I was here, home, whatever that is.

Every yard had at least one tree. Massively old ones, Oaks and Red Maple. None of the weak saplings displayed in the minority of yards in Roxborough. This was a place of big personal trees where kids stayed indoors and didn't play outside. Here play was sanctioned and watched in forms of official leagues and games. One could even call it interaction.

I went up and down that hill, the one that tingled my groin if I was going fast enough. My parent's house was to the left, a white, two-story colonial, an unfenced front yard with two massive leaf piles under my dad's personal Box Elder, those trees with the little helicopter leaves that twirl to the ground. He had, and this pissed me off every time I saw it, a decorative bridge installed in the front yard. A structure that crossed nothing. Totally unnecessary and wholly stupid. The short driveway fed a two-car garage that my dad pulled into with exact and deliberate precision, using the camera function of his car to get in as far possible, pre-orgasmically gritting his teeth as he nosed up against the wall, pinning the beach chairs. That was the kind of guy he was, the type to ravenously enjoy every inch of available square footage in a garage.

The sound of my car door shutting echoed against the morning silence, most likely sending my mom and some of the neighbors out of their chairs and toward their windows. The people here were eerily attuned, natives to their digital landscape, to the ever-present vibration of soft noise, the rumblings of trash and delivery, the buzzing zoom of mail-carriers speeding away. These were a people who tracked packages with tenacity and fervor; people who followed the journey of a box between places.

The watch beat against my thigh, cold through the thin material of my jeans pocket. Three knocks and the door was open. No clicking of latches or heavy slides of metal. This was a land of unlocked doors.

My mom stuck her arms out and smiled, desperately pulling me into a hug. She was a short round woman with tawny hair. Her face was kind and approving, with a crinkle in her eyes that made me feel perfect. Her skin glowed from all the walks she did. Formal walks and marches against horrible diseases. The worse the disease the better and more crowded the walk. Cancer walks were her favorite. The suicide walk was another one she liked. It was at nighttime. She'd walk all night for suicide and finish at the art museum steps at sunrise. She'd come back and talk about how she met someone who'd been through a lot who was the nicest person and how it was such a sin. The cancer ones were a party, though. She really had fun at those. There were so many people there who'd been through so much and my mom would come home and shake her head and click her tongue until she passed out.

Certain aspects of the neighborhood were embedded in my mom, the same frozen in time and thawing upon my arrival feeling.

She hugged me again and took my coat. There was a closet at the bottom of the steps that was set up with a light that clicked on with the door. It was strictly for coats and jackets, one or two umbrellas but that was it. Leather dusters, beige pull-over windbreakers, trench coats, pea coats, official button-ups of Evermore tires, classic denim jackets, and a mysterious CGI Financial rain jacket that must've been left over from a party. There was a perfected subtlety to the way she put stuff on hangers, tilts and flicks of the wrist and the jacket was on the hanger and slid into the closet, lost in the shuffle of the others.

A bastard mitten lay on the ground next to the umbrellas.

"I need you to go through these jackets, hun. Whatever you want, you need to take."

"I'm good."

"It's a sin to have all these jackets."

"Whose mitten?"

She snatched the mitten off the ground, sliding it onto her hand as she clamped up and down as if to channel the original owner. "Maybe it's mine and I don't even know it. What a sin."

"I'm moving to California."

My mom's face puddled around the mitten as she smelled it, a look of abject fear and loss. Real horror. She held her hands in front of her body and breathed.

"Just—talk to your father. He wants to talk to you. Do you," my mom looked into the kitchen and mouthed the words, "have his watch?"

I nodded.

She winced and walked away.

I could already feel the pressure, the invisible strings, the centrifugal force of shared blood. One look was all it took. A single look from my mom and California turned to dust, broke off into the Pacific from my own internal earthquake. I thought of history's great men, Julius Cesar and Genghis Kahn, how they would have taken a sword to their mothers in their moment of disapproval.

My mom sniffled and opened the door to the basement, setting off on a quest for the other mitten. My chest caved. She'd die before she wasted a mitten, what with all these hungry kids and cancer and suicide. The problem with a single mitten was that it couldn't be donated, and to throw it out would be a waste. This left my poor mother trapped in the paradox of her modern morality, tortured by visions of a Siberian orphan with a single frost-bitten hand, preserving the mitten in a dusty plastic bin in his honor.

A mug clanked on the kitchen table. My dad's way of telling me to come in. Our communication had stooped to a language of clanks, sighs, eye-contactless handshakes, and ignored voicemails.

I walked through the hallway with my hands in my pockets, cowering in the presence of my father. He sat at the kitchen table, silent and upright as he read the news. His glasses rested low on his nose, rocking as he breathed. He breathed heavily. Not unhealthily, but prominently—like the air around him was exclusively his to consume. My father displayed an aura of carved esteem that I found intimidating. A person you assumed was awake before you.

He looked up from the paper, silent, as if I were something in a store that he was scanning for value. He wore a jeff cap, something new for him, and he wore it without fear or hesitation like he'd worn one forever. His decision to jeff cap was to be accepted and respected.

"Guess you heard, huh?"

"California?"

"Yeah."

He whipped the paper expertly, cracking a razor-straight crease down the middle of the real estate classifieds and erecting it between us. Part of me believed he didn't actually read the news, but only stared at it.

"I wanted to apologize—"

"I was going to give it to you anyway."

He turned to the next page and whipped it again. I took the watch out of my pocket and dropped it on the table. My dad peered out around the side of his paper and then set it down, ironing it with his hands.

"California, huh?"

"Yeah."

"So you can get stoned legally?"

"You're such a *dick*."

My dad took his glasses off and wiped them on his shirt. He adjusted his cap, tilting it slightly off-center and continued his rubbing of the news. The paper was flat, perfectly two-dimensional, obedient from a morning of hard whips and folds. He had it well-trained and broken down.

"*I'm* a dick? How?"

"Because! You're always acting better, better than me and mom."

"Joel—" he lifted the cap and scratched his head. "She really worries about you."

"You think I don't know that?"

He turned the page and folded the paper in half, pressing it flat against the table. This was the fun section, comics and word puzzles.

"Did you ever stop to consider that maybe, just maybe, I actually *am* better than you?"

"Why? Because you worked at Evermore for twenty years?"

He swirled a finger in his coffee and sucked it off. There were donuts on the table. A white box with no logo. A real donut place. An underground shop. Unbranded, astray from national logos or corporate ties. No board or trustees or stocks. I thought of that. People investing in crumbs of donuts around the country.

"Thirty."

He lifted the box and took one. A classic chocolate frosted. The donut was large and caked in layers of opaque sugary icing. Underground donuts were usually large, twice the size as national chains.

He held the box by the lid and dangled it toward me.

"No thanks."

"I'd pull up in that parking lot every morning and sit in my car. An industrial center, Joel. Have you spent much time in an industrial center? Of course you haven't. It would break you, the boredom, all the grey sameness, you couldn't handle it."

My dad folded the ends of his donut up as he bit down with a force of vengeance. His teeth sank into the spongy dough as he tore a piece off.

"And then my boss, *wooo*, Mr. Salerno. A champion among assholes. Worst boss I'd ever had. Mean too. Not by today's standards either. This was the seventies when assholes could use all their tools. I mean, Joel, the guy was red. You could see his anger. It was like he'd been holding his breath since he was born. Hairs, thick straw-like hairs coming out of his nose, shooting out diagonally. Fifteen years of that guy, Joel. Fifteen years of a red bald man with nose hairs breathing down my neck. Have you ever felt that? Felt the force of a man's dissatisfaction with life? In the seventies and some of the eighties? You couldn't imagine if you tried."

My dad lifted the donuts by the lid and shook them, imploring me to take one. It was ridiculous for me not to have one. An underground donut from a place with plain white boxes. I eyed a French cruller but declined in a show of force. My dad countered with a "suit-yourself" expression.

"Anyway, and I swear I'm not making this up, after fifteen years of that guy making my life hell, I watched him die."

"What?"

I considered taking the cruller. My dad caught my eyes and lifted the box. I reached in and tore it in half, the ultimate show of force. My dad hated when me and my mom did that. Just take the whole donut, he'd say. Who'd want to eat the other half?

He grimaced at the disemboweled cruller as he sipped his coffee. "He had my desk moved so we faced each other. So he could keep an eye on me," he paused and stared off, "And so one day I'm sitting at my desk, up to my neck in invoices, and I'm watching him through that smudged plexiglas window. We used to joke that his breath caused it. You know, the oily smudge? He had the worst coffee breath imaginable. This one black guy—shit I forget his name, funny guy, funny as hell—said the boss must've aged his coffee like wine and drank it. Coffee from nineteen forty-two, he said. You know, because his breath was so bad."

"Yeah, I get it."

My dad stopped and looked at me, not so much looking at me, more like channeling me to access the lost part of his brain. To thin the fog in his eyes.

He snapped his fingers. "Oh, and the only person Mr. Salerno hated worse than me was this other guy. Another black guy, only this guy was old—what the hell was his name? Not the guy who talked about his breath—well he hated him too I'm sure, but no, the other guy, the foreman of the factory. Everyone used to call him buffalo head—Ernie! I forget his last name. Reid maybe? Ernest Reid? Either way—Mr. Salerno used to call over there and *scream* at him. Joel, when I say scream, I mean *scream* at him. Degrading this man, basically a senior citizen, through a phone. That's a, you know, and so anyway, I'm watching him, seeing him all red-faced, vibrating jowls—" my dad bit his donut, pausing to chew and swallow. "And I'll never forget—" he swallowed again and sipped his coffee. "How he looked at me through that window. His eyebrows shot high on his head and he pointed at me like I was next. Waiting in line to incur his wrath. He inhaled one good time through those broomstick-hair nostrils and then it happened."

"What did?"

"Mr. Salerno had the big one."

"The big one?"

"Yup, dropped the phone and clutched his chest as he gasped behind the smudged plexiglas, looking up to the fluorescent light fixture, pleading, as if it were God. And we locked eyes, just briefly, but something in his face—" my dad laughed. "The hatred, Joel. You'd think he'd ask for help or something—but no. This guy used his last seconds on earth to scowl, to give me the look of his lemon-bit hatred. Furious till the bitter end. And that was that. He slumped over his desk and died. And you know what? Nothing changed. The copy machines kept humming, people kept chattering. The office ran just like it had before. For a good while too. I sat and watched, wondering if anyone would notice, until finally, Peggy, I think, came in. Looked like an escaped nun—Ernest White! Yup. White, not Reid. He was Ernest White."

My dad pushed the last of his donut into his mouth with a finger and looked out the window. We had a little window next to the kitchen table that he always made sure to sit in front of when he ate.

"What the *fuck*, dad? You let him die?"

He licked chocolate icing from the corner of his lip. "Sure did."

He sipped his coffee and grabbed another donut. A classic powdered jelly. "Fact of the matter is, Joel, you won't feel *fulfilled*. It won't all click in some breakthrough, chorus-of-angels moment. You work and then you die—and, just, you can only hope someone will show up and cry at your funeral." He bit down into the donut and caught the spurting jelly with his coffee hand. It had been at the ready.

"What?"

"Some people have funerals and no one goes, Joel. I've seen it."

"How could you know that unless you went?"

"Don't do that."

"Do what?"

My dad turned the page of the paper and smoothed it. I could quiz him on the news and he'd know nothing. The paper was merely a partition, a buffer against people talking to him. A fortified activity that couldn't be disturbed.

"Attack a man on semantics."

"So, that's the lesson? Work until I die?"

"You're missing the point."

"Pretty sure I'm not."

He spread the fallen jelly back onto the donut and took another bite. "It might not sound much to a bi-coastal entrepreneur like yourself, but I eventually ran that little place. Took over for Mr. Salerno."

"No, you took over for that other guy, the old man, remember? After his wife died."

He nodded. "Right, right. Forgot about Mr. Pierce. He was a decent man. You know what his wife died from?"

"What?"

"Brain tumor. She just keeled right over. Was vacuuming and then—"

I finished my cruller and took another half donut, one with internal chocolate frosting, spilling its guts as I tore it.

My dad watched and sighed. "Now who in their right mind is going to eat the other half of *that*?"

"Mom."

My dad looked out the window and shook his head. "Those last fifteen years at Evermore tires were something else. You know why?"

"Because you became the boss?"

"Because I stopped complaining and did the work. Took pride in it too."

"Yeah, well, that's pretty easy to do when everyone dies and you become the boss of the whole place."

"I killed the fantasy, Joel, occupied the actual real estate of my life for a change. Which wasn't much, right? A tire company in a bleak industrial complex. Four grey walls and a ceiling, watching a bunch of mopes bop around."

"Yup, one that you were the boss of after two deaths."

My dad took his glasses off and wiped the bridge of his nose. "I made it a point to find younger guys, guys who reminded me of myself when I first started, shell-shocked newlyweds staring vacantly at the walls, rocked by the tumbling doom of adulthood. I sought them out, Joel. Talked to them. Asked them about their plans, their families, their lives, hopes, dreams, fears—and goddammit, Joel, something happened in that place. Something spread. The walls stopped looking so grey, the copy machines became less noisy, the air cleaner, fresher, more breathable. That's what love is, Joel. That's what love does. It lightens the grey, lightens the air, eases the heart. And my fear for you, Joel, is that you'll never truly experience it." My dad picked his paper back off the table and put it back in front of his face.

"So you were bored, then people died, and then you became the boss and stopped being bored."

My dad folded the top half of the paper down so I could see his eyes. "How about I just get you a job at Evermore?"

I slid the watch toward him.

My dad lifted it off the paper and put it around his wrist. "Eighteen an hour to start plus benefits. A little late, but you could start working on that 401k of yours."

"I'm good."

"A lot of my co-worker's kids work there. You'd be surprised, how they, you know..."

"How they what?"

"Just how they put up with their nonsense. The chronic tardiness and attitude. That's the scourge of your generation, Joel. Dreams and nonsense. They were instilled in you. Your generation was indoctrinated in the unreal, awash in stickers that say things like special and superstar. I remember you coming home from school with those stickers and thinking, Christ."

"How many people had to die for that watch? Two? That's not bad."

My dad checked the time and whipped the paper, turning to the very end, the part about culture and TV. He definitely didn't read it, now I was convinced. He shook the paper and held it in front of his face. The Rolex glistened and went dull, blending in with the wood-paneling that went halfway up the wall.

Eddie

We were dazed by what we saw. Me, the fed, the dago cop and the Swede, all stood holding our johnsons in a collective stupor. People were out now, villagers of the complex, milling about their well-warmed up vehicles, stalling to get a glimpse of the spectacle, the immense gathering of authority outside of the F building.

A plumber pulled off in his van. His face floated behind the smudged glass of his window as he greedily absorbed us.

Another car pulled up, a white Denali truck. It parked sideways taking up three spots.

The short paisan cop puffed his arms out and stormed over. His partner, the Swede, reached to pull him back but missed.

"You old fuck!"

A man hopped out of the passenger side of the Denali and smoothed his suit. I immediately knew him. That caveman-ish face, awkward doughy build. He was shorter than Clay but had a similar demeanor, that of an elite. His eyes smiled with apprehension as he appraised the scene.

"Hey, Joe, easy," called the Swede after his partner.

I eyed the dago, "What are you bozos even doing down here? This is out of your jurisdiction."

The other guy came out of his Kia, a retired fed from the looks of it. He lit up a hot snack and approached Mr. Hardt. I placed the guy in his sixties, a man of John's size and grizzle, but with more of a belly. He shook hands with Mr. Hardt.

They crossed their arms across their chests and talked.

I approached them. "Mr. Hardt? Eddie Hayden."

A look spread across his face, a mixture of disgust and concern as he weakly shook my hand. He seemed largely uncomfortable, glancing back at the fed as if apologizing for my presence.

I greeted him as well.

"Eddie. I'm working for Mr. Hardt here."

"In what capacity?" asked the man, ditching his cigarette as he slid a new one out of his soft pack. His olive-skinned face hung loose and old, stress-aged, pocks and pits and dark hooded eyes. His nose was bulbous and pored like mine.

"Private investigation."

The dago grabbed my arm and whirled me around. "Beat it, ya old pervert!"

The Swede got between us like a hockey ref, backing his partner away from me.

"Easy, Joe. C'mon."

The fed exhaled a cloud of smoke and pointed up to the apartment with the lit tip of his cigarette. "And that guy who just blasted in there? He's with you?"

"He's been drugged with LSD."

"Drugged? By who?"

"Clay, Mr. Hardt's—"

"I know who Clay is. I've been employed by his father."

"In what capacity?"

Joe lurched forward and grabbed my shoulder. He spun me around and drove his knuckles in my stomach. "That's for the girl."

"Goddamnit, Joe."

The asphalt was cold, stinging my knees through my corduroy trousers. I got dizzy and could really taste the air. It took me back to the days of football in the park, the unexpected scent of earth and sweat as the other boys gathered and backed up to give air after the rattle-bang of a vicious spill or tackle or falling from a tree. I laid there, recovering from the out of body experience of immediate trauma and wondered if this was what having your life flash before your eyes was all about, all the hype and drama proving again to be utterly mild and meaningless. It's like words do a disservice to experience, in every aspect of life.

"Oh, you feeling tough? Hitting an old man like that?"

I couldn't see Brenda but could feel her standing near me, could hear the sound of her shoe scraping the cold asphalt against my ear. An untied lace grazed my cheek and I fought the urge to bite it, to suck it up into my mouth like a strand of pasta.

"He's a fucking *child molester.*"

I could breathe but chose not to. This injury was all I had, the right to be crumpled on the ground like an old tire in the woods, a drifting bag of fast food trash. I rubbed my face against the pavement, absorbing the glass and dust and pebbles, mopping up the general spall of a lot, the stuff reserved for the bottom of a shoe.

"What, the thing with the seventeen-year-old?"

The Fed spoke. "Yup. Elizabeth McPhearson was his most, for the lack of a better word, famous incident. But there were others. Numerous complaints of groping, flashing, and harassment from multiple women on his beat. Complaints from several hairdressers regarding a strategically-timed push of the head against their chests. The escaped mail order brides—"

I got on a knee, but Brenda was gone. The truck fired up and she peeled out. I saw her though. Her eyes. And that was it. The last of whatever I had left.

Joe smacked my arm out with his baton and I fell. The Swede pulled him away. I heard police cars pulling up, doors opening and shutting. Beeps of the radio. Mr. Hardt and the fed's voices got further and further away.

I laid there, feeling the weight of my gun on my hip. The earth smelled fresh, finally warmed up. Someone tried to help me and I pushed them away. Joe cackled, that hyena laugh ringing somewhere in the distance as he told the other cops who I was. It smelled like spring and I was on the ground. A carcass, the butt of some sick joke that guys like Joe reveled in and laughed at. I'd found Clay and this was my reward?

The sun was fully out now. Warm on my back and pleasant. The slight smell of a freshly weeded garden hung in the air. Tilled earth and dirt. Spring was just around the corner.

Fig

Blocking Clay's screaming charge, my dad diverted the knife away from himself and plunged it into Clay's stomach. He took the knife out and jammed it back in, ripping down and over, using his entire body to saw through Clay's flesh, fileting about an inch or two of skin until the blade bent and snapped. Blood spilled out of Clay's gut and soaked my dad. They both just stood there, mutually stupefied as they stared into each other's eyes, communicating through gasped expressions.

And then my dad threw up.

Donny held his hands out and looked down in a bow. His one knee raised, floating weakly toward the center of his chest as he mumbled apologies to the carpet. Stan pushed Donny out of the way and took off, down the hallway and out the same window as Lynne. His gun fell out his waistband and was lying on the carpet. It was little, one of those James Bond ones. All black and metal, about the size of my hand.

Clay's eye's flickered between short, lung-gurgling breaths as his weight crashed against my dad who stumbled back himself. An envelope slid out of his pocket and onto the floor. Pictures fell and fanned out, forming a disturbing family collage on the carpet. Clay's blood-soaked shirt clung tightly to his chest and shone as my dad stood him up against the wall, jamming the broken half of the knife into his chest near his heart.

Donny ran out the front door and was greeted by beeps and mega-phoned voices.

My dad's face broke when he saw me. It was the first and only time I ever saw him cry. A little can rolled in and the apartment filled with smoke. He picked it up and threw it outside, letting Clay fall face down onto the Chicago Bears blanket.

My dad picked his rifle up and put the barrel to my head.

"You want to kill me?!"

"Dad! Stop! No!"

"That's not what they fucking said!"

Clay coughed and wheezed. Then he went quiet. He breathed again but barely. More of a hiss. Like a leak or something. My dad, without hardly looking, turned his gun away from me and shot Clay in the head.

Another can rolled in. This time my throat got hot, like I was breathing in buffalo wings and my dad pushed me from behind, "Get the fuck out of here. Go!"

Clay's blood soaked through my shoe as I ran across the carpet, almost slipping on the pictures. The smoke had gotten so thick I could barely see, but swear I saw my dad wink at me. He put his back to the door and screamed, "Clear!"

I grabbed Stan's gun and hopped out the window. The ground came sooner and harder than I hoped, buckling my knees out and sending me into a somersault. Someone yelled as I rattled over the seven-foot chain link fence and jumped down into the rocky woods.

John

The sun was still up there, mirror-bright among the finger-painted clouds. It was gettin' warm out. The ground was givin' off a faint scent of thawed earth, that pondish smell of spring. A plane moved slow and tiny across the sky. Birds flew around it, miles below but looked like they were with it. The smell of fast food lingered, that greasy smell of beef and burnt plastic.

There were a whole lotta cops now, guns pointed and yellin'. One of the cops had gotten a megaphone and was usin' the hell out of it. Somethin' about a hostage situation.

I leaned against the rail and listened to the shouts and orders. It was plastic. Some weak PVC bullshit. It couldn't be trusted. Nothin' plastic could. Plastic is a lie.

Eddie was down on the ground, scramblin' around with that poopy-pants walk of his, hip-limpin' about the scene. A cop came out from around the back of the buildin' and yelled somethin' to the others. Two more cops joined him. They jogged away holdin' their belts. The megaphone guy blasted noise at me.

I saw the tip of my nose and stopped lookin'. I hated seeing that. Reminded me I had a face I couldn't see.

The megaphone guy told me to drop my weapon.

Eddie was lookin' pretty unnatural too. The way he left the crowd in a rush away from the action, throwin' his hands about all crazy.

The people's attention was split. Some checkin' out Eddie. Others on the cops, and some on me. I nodded and smiled as Eddie stormed across the lot toward a dumpster. Everyone was lookin'. Saw Donny down there, too. Not in handcuffs or anything. Just standin' with the cops.

The guy said somethin' about a final warnin'.

And so now everyone's lookin' at me, but I'm watchin' Eddie. Watchin' him feel around on one of those little dumpsters, a three-yard can with the plastic flaps on the top and sides about forty feet away, but it was hard to tell since I was so high up. Didn't want to fall for an optical illusion. Eddie slid the flap open and jumped in like it was his house. Fuckin' shut the flap and everythin'.

Gunshot. A horrible soundin' one too. The way it echoed in the can.

This blonde cop and some others rushed over, all holdin' their belts. The other cops were closer to me now. Right at the bottom of the steps. The guy with a megaphone did a signal with his hands.

I thought about that kid in the desert. The way his head splashed when they shot him.

Joel

I pulled onto Overlook and parked. An odd calm swept over me seeing the street, the houses, the trees, the usual scuttlebutt of trash and candy wrappers floating in their eco-system of forgotten things. It was familiar, just like the stuff around my parent's.

I felt expansive. The fact I had confronted my dad, the hash bubbling away in Brenda's. I had set a plan and was finally seeing something through.

The weather added to my mood. It was warm compared to what it'd been. Warm enough to smell things, like the cigarette someone had been smoking before I pulled up. The snow was gone, but left a dampness, a vague turtle tank scent.

Brenda came rumbling around the corner in John's truck. I heard the engine, saw the truck, and smelled the diesel. All in that order. The truck skidded with her angry turn of the wheel. She slammed to a stop and smacked the dash.

I didn't see Eddie or John—or Fig for that matter. No one was even outside. Just us. In a vacuum of two. Me and my truck and Brenda in John's. She was visibly upset, rocked by whatever she had seen. We sat like that, apart, trapped in the eerie silence of our respective vehicles.

An egg-shaped sparrow fluttered above a power line and attached magnetically to the wire. It vibrated its little body inside the feathers and let out a low-voltage kip-kip-zee rattle, an electric grasshopper noise that set off some other unseen birds.

I crossed the street and waved, but Brenda just stared forward. I bent into her field of vision and waved again so she'd have to respond.

Apparently she didn't.

The latch slapped embarrassingly out of my hand as I tried to open the door. I felt exposed, highlighted and vulnerable, centered in a spotlight of failure. I instinctively pulled again, letting the handle slap harder. I smacked the window. Brenda sighed and hit the unlock button, signaling a hush of internal metal.

I opened the door and got in.

Heat gushed out of the vents. Full fan, no defrost or feet. Brenda's bangs bobbed up and down like something on the surface of the water from the rush of hot, chassis-scented air. An olfactory glimpse of London in the twenties. This was the smell of grease and metal, heat that passed through carcinogenic fluids. Eye-watering forced air set to MAX, drowning out the bird warbles, the spirit of passing cars on streets beyond.

Brenda just sat there agape. She looked equal parts angry and entertained.

"Where is everyone?"

"I don't know," she said to the windshield.

I let my finger rest in the groove of the unlock button. "I talked to my dad. Told him my plan and everything."

"Joel, I just—"

"Was Fig there?"

Brenda clenched her jaw, shoring the structure of her face up against its imminent collapse, fighting against the shaky crush of wrinkles and lines that were slowly acquiring tracts of territory starting from her eyes and chin and meeting at her lips. She slumped over the wheel and sobbed into the faded leather.

Pretty soon I'd have the money to take care of Brenda. I felt good about that. Helping her back onto her feet. I planned on sharing it in total. No sense of hierarchy or order or debt or anything like that. Just two people, living off a small sum of currency like it was the land. Back to the basics. Neolithic values. Survival over actualization. Concerning ourselves only with heat and berries and meat and stories. We could raise a child and show them the way, gear the future toward being happy with the overwhelming abundance at their disposal, to settle, to enjoy a tangled mess of outdated phone chargers as the miracle they are, to relish in the worst and dumbest reality shows, reveling in the allergen laden rush of central air, the creeping breeze through a cracked window. It was all ours.

I gasped at the sight of Brenda's house. All the windows were closed, at least the ones I could see from where we sat. Her car. It was parked right out front.

"Call your sister."

Brenda ignored me, still crying.

I grabbed her shoulder and shook it.

The front of Brenda's house erupted in a thunderous flash and boom. Time stopped. Noise ceased. Brenda screamed and we ducked. Chunks of glass and wood sprayed across the windshield. Flames whooshed and receded, settling into the airy roast of fire.

Another explosion, a thunderclap out from the basement sending an arc of dust and projectiles out into the woods. A cathedral of needled flames stretched toward the sky and fell, revealing the heat-stripped remains of the house as it fell into instant dilapidation. Part of the roof toward the back, the area over Brenda's room, caved in, emitting a horrible cracking sound, layered by the faint squeaks of nails. It was like a thousand trees falling. Smoking shingles floated to the ground like apocalyptic feathers. Broken joists and two-by-fours stuck out of the caved roof.

A wave of morbidly excited neighbors approached the catastrophe, basking in the glow of fire. Some pointed and others covered their mouths as they gazed at the inferno, its hellish glowing dust. Another large piece of roof caved and they emitted a collective roller coaster *oooh* as the fire launched skyward.

Sirens harmonized in the distance. A shrieking metallic wail.

Lynne's soot-blackened face emerged from the second story window, coughing among a jet stream of dark smoke. She climbed out and straddled the sill. Screams erupted from the crowd. Brenda may or may not have been hitting me. I couldn't tell and didn't care. All I could do was watch as Lynne tipped her weight outward despite the screams, rotating her body on the sash of the window, the wood snapping and letting her go, falling between the space of life and death, free floating in her final seconds before impact.

Fig

A loud shush rose from behind a tree. Stan was crouched by a group of hanging vines with a finger to his lips. Three cop cars zoomed along the curve and up into the mouth of the apartment complex. I ducked behind a sticker bush and rolled down the hill. The creek trickled by in little sounds against the rocks. Peeing sounds.

A half hour passed and me and Stan didn't talk. Not a word to each other, which felt cool, like we were cowboys or something. We just looked at stuff, shrunk away from lights and sirens, wiped mud off our sneaks, and snuck glances at each other. Finally, someone came to pick him up. A Puerto Rican guy in a dented minivan with tiger-scraped Sunoco stickers forming a crooked line across the side of the car.

I tried to get in, but Stan locked the doors.

"C'mon man! I could work for you."

Stan said something in Spanish to the driver that made them both laugh. Then he said something else, something longer that drew a click and sigh out of the driver. He raised his butt off the seat and dug in his pocket. Stan said something else. More clicks and headshakes. The driver lifted his butt again and handed Stan a bunch of hundreds.

Stan peeled off five-hundred bucks and put it in my palm. "Get a cab. Walk. Do whatever you want. You can't come with me."

"Dude, just give me a ride."

Stan thought for a second and re-locked the doors. "Wait here. I call you a cab. And clean your sneaks man. Got blood and papers and shit stuck to you."

The sky glowed red on the top of the hill, dyed in the spinning light of sirens. I pulled the paper off my shoe and wiped my sneakers in the dirt. I almost lost my breath when I read it, the blood-stained typed up-paper. My mom, Donna Sommers, her phone number, address and everything.

A black and yellow cab pulled up to the stop sign at the end of the street and idled. The driver wore one of those turban things and swiveled his head to look around. He probably never picked someone up out of the woods before.

I tapped the back window. He couldn't speak enough English to say it, but I could tell he was like, who are you? Who is this kid from the woods?

Another rush of cop cars and an ambulance blew past and rounded the bend headed up to the apartments.

I held a hundred dollar bill up to his window and he unlocked the door.

He watched me in the mirror as I got in, his eyes rising slowly to meet mine.

"Where do you go?"

I pointed to the address on the paper, covering the blood spot with my hand, and he put it in his GPS.

"Is it far?" I asked.

"Eh, not bad."

***

I woke up in a panic, kicking toward the guy as he shook my shoulder, totally forgetting what had happened and where I was.

"Pay now, you are here."

"I already fucking paid"

"No, different." He pointed at the meter. Sixty-seven dollars and forty-three cents.

"Fucking dickhead."

The man raised his knee and turned in his seat to face me. "Who is dickhead?"

I couldn't talk. If I talked, I would have cried. I reached into my pocket and grabbed another hundred, muttering in a weak voice as the cabbie watched with his haunted raccoon eyes. He stooped down and lifted his shirt to show me his knife. It looked like a mini-sword, curved with a gold and white handle that sat in a leather holster.

"See this? I carry this always to protect trouble. It is part of my belief."

I pulled the gun out of my pocket and held it in my lap. The man nodded at it and tucked his shirt back in. He didn't seem scared or upset, just respectful of the fact.

I looked around. The houses here were just like the ones in my old neighborhood only they weren't right next to each other, touching like they were on Overlook. They stood alone and had yards that were a little bigger than mine. Not by much, but a definite difference.

"Which house is it again?"

"There, 4137." He pointed to the shittiest house on the street. A squat, brick bungalow with moss and mold growing out of the mortar.

The yard was a sea of wet, unraked leaves. Vines climbed the west side of the house. They withered up along the chimney and stopped at the vinyl A-frame section that looked like a second-floor add-on. Leaves stuck up out of the gutter and paint peeled off the shutters. One of the shutters was red and the rest were black; another was missing.

"How much to buy from you?"

"The house?"

"No, the gun. It is very mini. I like it."

"Gun for the knife." I spit on the street. A dry foamy spit that got taken by the wind. It felt good. Out here doing business with this man. The cold transaction of weapons between strangers. Guns and knives.

The man smiled politely. "I simply cannot."

***

Black and green spots of algae stained the cement walkway along with dried bird shit and who knows what else. A big broken chunk of cement jutted out of the ground, lifted by an exposed root from a leaning Chinese stinkball tree.

I took a deep breath and knocked on the door. The gun swayed in my pocket. It felt cold against my leg. Made me know it was there.

Footsteps shuffled inside of the house, the distinct scraping sound of slippers, a light patter back and forth, toward and away from the door. After a few seconds of silence, things clicked and unlatched and it finally opened—just a little. Enough so I could see her face, her big head of curly hair, hairline receding hard in the front—which I didn't even know could happen to a woman. She had a big brown wart on her chin and a few small ones around her eye that moved every time she blinked.

"May I help you?" she asked.

"I'm looking for my mom but I don't think you're her."

"Well, I sure don't remember giving birth to you," she said opening the door. "What's your mother's name? Maybe I can help."

"Donna," I said, "Her name's Donna Cork, or at least it was...she got divorced a while back."

"Oh, God! Are you her—her *Jimmy*? Please! Come in. Have a seat, sweetie. I know your mother very well."

The place was disgusting. It was like Clay and Donny's place, only someone tried to clean it once a month and gave up halfway through. Everything smelled like football pads, or maybe a birdcage. It was also crammed full of shit, bulk paper towels and toilet paper, cases of soda and beer, boxes of variety snack packs. And there was mail *everywhere*. It was like she collected it.

The lady clasped the side of her face, oblivious to the mess. Her eyes sparkled with a happy wetness.

"We used to work together," she said, blowing her nose. "For quite some time actually, over at the Dairy Queen off the Kirkwood highway. I was still getting my teaching degree and, well, your mom was getting her affairs in order, let's just say."

"The affair she had on my dad?"

"Oh no! *No*." She frowned amused. "How about this? You tell me what you know about her and I'll fill in the rest. 'kay? Name's Linda by the way." She motioned for me to sit.

I plopped down on her shitty brown couch. It was full of cat hair and pretzel crumbs and was probably the most uncomfortable thing I'd ever sat on. I could feel the springs or whatever was in there. "Um...she had red hair and freckles and was nice to me and her name is Donna...that's pretty much it."

"Uh, huh. And did your father ever talk to you about her?"

"Yeah."

"And what did he say?"

"That she left us to go smoke crack with niggers in the projects."

"Jimmy! *Please.* I—" The lady sighed. "What *really* happened was your mother met a nice black man. He was a doctor and your father was abusing her—"

"Who, Larry?"

"Yes, actually. Yeah, that's his name. How did you know?"

"He wasn't a doctor, he was the mailman. My dad wanted to kill him."

"Oh...but...she told me he was...Well, any-hoo, your mother was just getting out of Gander Hill—"

"What's that?"

"It's a correctional facility, sweetie."

"Like jail?"

"Your mother had issues, sweetie. Substance abuse issues and she got into some trouble."

"Wait, so my mom actually *was* smoking crack with—"

The door opened. A kid about nine or ten years old ran inside, schoolbag and lunch box jiggling, and crashed into Linda's knee. He was really tan and retarded from what I could tell.

"Xander!" She squealed, reaching out to hug him.

A short, fat, black guy came strolling in, flipping through the mail. He noticed me and stopped. "Tell him we're not interested. Don't need no more magazines subscriptions or any shit like that."

"It's Donna's son, Maurice!"

"Crazy ass Donna?"

"Maurice!'

Maurice turned to me. "I didn't mean nothing by it. She was just...a real lively lady."

"Yeah," I said. "Apparently she's a crackhead or something."

Maurice's eyebrows rose slowly, fully controlled under a well-trained cool, an apparent master of impromptu family gatherings and surprises. He motioned Linda into the kitchen with a single flick of his shiny, bald head.

They disappeared through the door, leaving me alone with Xander. I only had one retarded kid in my school and I never really talked to him so I didn't know what to do.

"Hey, buddy, you like the Power Rangers?" I asked pointing to his shirt and pants and schoolbag.

"I like wrestling," he said, smiling and stretched his arms toward me. His hard plastic lunchbox rattled against his schoolbag as he came for my legs. I instinctively stuffed his take down and backed up. Xander pushed himself up off the floor and into a sprinter's stance. His head tilted upward revealing a devilish smile, something like an invitation to Xander Land.

"Dude, stop. I don't want to wrestle you."

"Too bad," he said in a weird voice, something he'd no doubt gotten from some corny show and had practiced in the mirror. His eyes rolled up, half visible under his brow as his face fixed in a playfully menacing grin, the part where the bad guy sees that the good guy's been practicing and is ready to show him a few tricks of his own. It was like he learned everything he knew from TV.

I wondered how many retarded kids had been called to the dark side through television?

Xander charged. His Power Rangers lunchbox banged my elbow and his hard head drilled me in the gut. Falling back, I hooked his elbows and swung him around and pinned him onto the couch. Xander kicked and wriggled under me. He was having the time of his life.

***

The next day I got to meet my mom.

The agreed spot was TGI Friday's in New Castle Delaware. It was in a shopping center off the side of a two-lane highway. Next to the shopping center was a place that sold mulch and big rocks for people to put into their yard. They had a huge statue of Paul Bunyan outside.

Linda pulled into the lot and unbuckled her seat belt. She twisted her body to address me. Her face was round and bulged at the cheeks. She was the kind of person who looked sad, even when they tried to smile.

"Here," she said, smiling and holding out ten bucks. "Just in case."

"In case of what?"

"Just in case."

"I'm good."

She stuck the ten in my chest. "Take it."

A gust of wind rocked the car and stopped. There were only three other cars in the parking lot. A few seagulls too. It was nice out. Clear blue sky and mildly warm sun but was colder than the day before. It'd gotten windy. I crushed the ten down into my pocket with the three hundred dollars.

"You should sign Xander up for wrestling."

"Oh? What makes you say that?"

"Because he loves it. We wrestled the whole time you and Maurice were arguing in the kitchen. We only stopped because I remembered my gun."

"Gun?"

"Yeah. I got a gun. A little one. I stole it off a Puerto Rican yesterday. Are they Black or Mexican? Do you know?"

"Give me the gun."

"Why? It's mine. I have the right to bear it."

Linda scratched the side of her head and pulled her hair. She breathed, in and out through her nose and placed her hands down on her lap and looked out the windshield. Two seagulls fought over a piece of bread. A car drove past and they flew away, leaving it torn on the ground. The sky was perfectly blue.

"I'm not going to shoot people at my school with it. I just want to have it."

"The reason Xander doesn't wrestle is because we can't afford it. Let me sell the gun. That way Xander can wrestle

I gave her the ten back and another hundred on top of it. She held the money in the claws of her hands. Her mouth hung open. She was baffled.

"That should cover his gear."

"Give me the gun."

"I don't have one. I was just kidding."

***

I pushed through the doors into TGI Fridays, past the claw game and a machine that sold stickers and temporary tattoos. My elbow pulsed from getting knocked against the door. Linda had taken me to Xander-land over the gun and won. She jacked me up with those big meaty forearms and wrestled it out of my pocket. Afterwards she cried and apologized and tried to give me back my money. I told her to keep it. I had a bunch more in the fort and could buy a new gun anyway. I walked past the hostess. She didn't look or say anything. She just popped her gum and stared into her phone, probably at something dumb, I thought as I entered the restaurant floor, scanning for possible moms.

The place was sad and mostly empty, open looking and dumb. There was this older couple sitting at a booth with their canes resting against the table silently gorging on a sampler platter, eating it like they'd caught it in the wild. They were both so fat that their stomachs touched the table. The guy had suspenders on and his wife had hairs growing out of her chin. Not a lot, about five or six. The woman stopped shoving fries in her face as I walked by, following me with her eyes while her husband sucked his milkshake like a mosquito.

Diagonal past the old fats were these two black ladies. They were Muslim, wearing the foot clan outfit and all. They had a little boy with them. He was wearing a white altar boy costume with one of those Aladdin hats. He was crying and carrying on and the one lady, who I'm guessing was his mother, smacked his hand and told him to stop.

I recognized my mom as soon as I saw her. She was sitting in a booth alone. The cushion was bright red and shot high over her head, making her look like the Queen from Alice in Wonderland. There was a crack in the seat that oozed chewed-up yellow foam and rubbed against her reddish-blond hair. The static made little strands stick up. It made her look crazy.

Our eyes met.

At first she looked at me like I was just a regular person, someone else's kid. And then she realized. I saw it. Her whole face change, turned a dial and all of a sudden she became my mom. A smile took her face, slowly spreading, all the way up to her eyes and forehead, crashing down into a confused, sorry frown. A tear ran down her cheek and she wiped it away. She laughed and covered her mouth with the back of her hand. Her shoulders shook.

I felt a strange twinge of pride for my dad and then realized it was my mom and blocked it out of my head. She got up out of the booth and hugged me, almost squeezing me to death. My mom's tits weren't as big as Mrs. B's but were definitely bigger than our school nurse's, who had high B's or maybe a C. I pulled my body away as I hugged her, out of respect.

"Oh my Gawd! Get in here! Hug your mother!" she said, squeezing me all the way into her.

I got a better look at her once I broke free. She was still standing there, bent over and gawking. She had tight, faded jeans and wore a tighter tank top that showed ample cleavage, big hoop earrings, and a ton of make-up. She was dressed like the girls from my school. The girls who—there was no way around it—my mom was dressed like a slut, a forty-year-old, teenage slut.

I tried my best to keep my eyes off her freckly quaking tits as I helped her back to her seat. They kept shaking and wiggling while she cried from across the booth. I thought about Brian, how I finally understood his dilemma and wholeheartedly regretted all the stuff I said to him about Mrs. B. I had no idea how weird it was to have a hot mom. I just didn't know.

Her lips quivered when she stared into my eyes. "Please tell me you're not mad at *meeee...*" Her voice trailed off into a high pitch squeal as she broke down crying into her folded hands. She stared at me from across the table with tears streaming down her cheeks, leaking out of her eyes. "*Oh, Jimmy.*"

The waiter came out, a young black kid with a neck tattoo, probably just out of high school if I had to guess. He spun an empty tray between his hands and hesitated. "Y'all need more time?" he asked, arching both eyebrows.

My mom picked her face up out of her hands and took a deep inhale. "I'll have a Long Island please."

"Can I have a burger and fries?" I added.

We looked at each other. Neither of us had anything to say. My mom took her hand off the table and squeezed it between her thighs. They were shaking. And she wore *so much* makeup, more than the girls in my class who had acne. In the right light, I could see some of the spots where it caked around her wrinkles. It reminded me of the stuff my dad used to skim plaster walls, all the cracks and divots before he painted. I always thought it was gross when girls caked that shit on, a huge turn-off far as I was concerned—all very good news in terms of knocking the hot mom thing down a peg.

The waiter set her Long Island on the table. It was dripping with condensation. My mom nodded and pulled the drink in toward herself, devastating the soggy black napkin underneath. She leaned forward and sucked half the glass down through her straw. I flagged the waiter down right as he turned back toward the kitchen.

"Hey, sorry, can I get a strawberry shake?"

"No prob."

My mom's drink continued to drop as she eyed me from across the table, finally letting the straw out of her mouth to take a breath. She let out a deep ahh and wiped her nose with the back of her thumb and reached for my hands. I let her hold them but didn't like it. I didn't want people to think we were some weirdo-bible family who prayed in public before meals. I did another quick scan around the restaurant, realizing I had nothing to worry about. Still the same two tables from before: the Black Muslims and the old fat couple.

"You keep crying into your drink like that, we'll be here all night."

My mom was confused. "Huh?"

"No, I mean, like your tears are gonna keep filling up your drink and it'll never end. You'll just have to keep drinking it forever—it was a joke."

My mom's face dropped. "Jesus, Jimmy, that so sad."

I looked back over at the old fat couple. The guy was staring at us. I stared back thinking he'd stop looking, but he just stared more. My mom's drink was gone and she was looking for our waiter, her hand raised slightly and her face fixed like she knew the answer to a question.

The waiter popped out of the industrial kitchen door but instantly turned around and went back in, throwing his hands up like he forgot something. I saw his head through the little porthole window. He was probably talking to the chef, maybe bossing all the Mexicans around that my dad told me were in the backs of restaurants. I wondered about that, if he got to boss all the Mexicans. My mom rested her chin on her fist and looked at me, but her eyes kept moving around the room, scanning for that waiter.

"So," I asked, "Where you been?"

My mom dropped a finger over her empty glass as the waiter reached over us to set my burger down. I took a bite and chewed, watching her eyes follow our waiter to the bar.

"Mom."

She squeezed my hands and pouted, like that was supposed to be her answer. I pulled away and took another bite of my burger, realizing I'd forgot to ask for mustard. The waiter set my mom's drink on the table and she slid it to the side, like she was making a statement by not sipping it immediately and grabbed my hands again.

"There was a lot going on when you were little. A whole lot. Your dad came home from the war and he was all messed up."

"What war?"

"Iraq."

"Was that even a real war?"

"Of course it was, Jimmy. People died."

Another black napkin devastated as my mom slid her drink toward herself. I guess she felt like she proved her point by not drinking it right away.

"I'm serious, Jimmy. He was never the same."

She had two straws going now, crushing her long island.

"He got discharged, or fired I guess, depending on how you look at it, and I don't know what for, he wouldn't say, but one day he just showed up at the house, he said they canned him and he was fucking— excuse me, love. He was so mean after that. You were two at the time and he wouldn't even look at you. It was like you weren't there. And he was hitting me. All the time just beating me." She kept her eyes up while she sipped her drink to let me know she had more to say.

"I get that, but that was like ten years ago. You left when I was what, three?"

Her big fake ring smacked the table.

"I didn't *leave*. I was put out. By your father."

"After you cheated on him, right?"

My mom held her head in her hands and massaged her temples. Our waiter came out.

"How's that burger, big dog?"

I nodded without looking. I'm pretty sure he saw my mom crying and walked away.

"He was beating me!"

"Yeah, well, guess who he started beating after you left?"

Her red hair spilled over the table. The few pieces that were touching the foam stuck up and floated above the mess. She was a broken down fantasy, a drunk crackhead who couldn't own up to the fact that she ditched me.

She lifted her head off the table and slid her drink away. Spider legs of mascara dripped from her eyes. "You want to know why I didn't come get you? You really wanna know?"

I shrugged and bit into my burger. "I don't think it matters at this point, but yeah, go ahead."

My mom gave me one of those how-could-you looks. I ignored her and took another bite as she continued.

"Your father, the guy who used to beat me and abuse me mentally, you know him? Anyway, he told me—he told me that if I ever tried to get in touch with you that...that he'd kill me." She took a sip of her drink and waited for me to respond.

I finished chewing and swallowed my burger. Then I took a fry and dipped it in ketchup. The waiter gave me my milkshake and apologized for forgetting it. I'd forgotten about it too. I sucked my milkshake down, just like my mom did with her Long Island. I kept drinking it until I got brain freeze. Once my headache went away I ate the rest of my burger and got up.

***

I stood outside of TGI Friday's with absolutely no idea what to do. The weather cleared a little. The wind died and I could feel the sun. I was wearing the sweatshirt Linda gave me since my clothes were all dirty. It was her son's. It had the name of the special retarded school that he went to written across the chest. I wanted to ditch it so bad. I didn't want people to think I was retarded too.

The fat couple I saw earlier came walking out. The man was holding his back like it hurt and his wife stared ahead like a zombie, fumbling through her purse. I ducked behind a Subaru so they couldn't see me. I don't know why, I just didn't want them to. I picked up a little piece of gravel and threw it. Nothing that would hurt them, just a little tiny piece they probably wouldn't feel. It bounced off the back of the guy's white sneaker but he didn't even notice. I felt stupid right after I did it.

I watched as the fat couple pulled off into the stream of traffic. The woman's arms rose to the ceiling of the car. I think she was upset or something, probably had to shit. Steam puttered out of the exhaust and they merged. They weren't as big as that lady I saw on the show about fat people getting craned out of their houses, but they weren't far away from it either. There was definitely a crane, somewhere, waiting in some parking lot of their fat futures, dying to hoist them embarrassingly out of their homes and into some, I guess, specialized warehouse for the extreme obese. A home for the hoisted where they got hooked to tubes and fluids and watched movies. I wondered what they'd be arguing about. What do people who are dangerously fat think and argue about? What is there to say?

For a second it started to get away from me. My thoughts, spinning off into a rush, a blur of unidentifiable feelings—an accelerating mistake. That's the feeling I got. A fast unraveling.

I gripped my pocket, feeling the single hundred-dollar bill. I had enough money to get home and a fortune waiting for me once I did. Eddie said there was ten thousand dollars in the bag and some pills. I could sell the pills and buy a motorcycle. I'd have a house, a motorcycle, sweatpants, ten thousand bucks, and all my dad's stuff.

I was set for life.

Epilogue

Brenda

My black pants are dusted with flour and my hands stink like ham. The flour is from one of the rolls, the sourdough, I think. Not sure whose idea that was, to sprinkle a flavorless powder onto a roll, but I'm certain it's a bad one. I specialize in putting the meat on. The person on my right cuts the rolls. The person to my left puts the cheese on. Together we are the line team and make a little more than the cashiers since we work with knives in what they call a fast-paced, challenging environment. Line team member. That's my official title.

It's finally warm outside. Somewhere between spring and summer. Mowers buzzing and birds singing. The smell is everywhere. Gasoline and cut grass and the smoggy mixed fuel of weed whackers.

Everything echoes, almost like I am living in a seashell or guitar. There's new recessed lighting in the ceiling and the walls are painted yellow. I picked the color—Concord Ivory. It's soft, not too bright. I'd read somewhere that yellow was supposed to make you happy.

My keys bang and slide across my coffee table, one of those cheap Ikea ones made from wine corks. The old one was totally toasted. Pretty much everything was. The whole house fit into two dumpsters and the ashes were swept away. Lynne had been so high on heroin that she probably didn't feel much of the burning alive and falling. They think she might have been OD-ed and jolted up out of some kind of subconscious instinct. She died an hour later in the hospital. She was totally braindead. I had to pull a plug.

I push the power button on the remote, and by the time I sit and curl up on the couch, the TV is on. It takes a second for these new TVs to come on for some reason. It's a smart TV. One that hooks up to the internet, but I don't know how to do that so I just watch regular cable on it. One of the girls on the line team claims to be good with stuff like TVs and computers and said she can come set it up so I can save the money on cable, but I don't really care. I'd probably cry if she came in here.

Just in time for *The Bachelor*. The season has been good and tonight is the finale. A small part of me was excited about it all day, holding on to the little glimmer of hope the season had given me. It's the first sign of anything in a long time, and yeah, it's kinda shitty that *The Bachelor* finale is the only good thing in my life, but fuck, it's *something*. And I see these girls, Melissa, the sweet down-home country bumpkin, Brandy, the east coast in-your-face-city bitch with a touch of class, Braxton, the black hippy chick, and a girl from Venezuela who won a beauty pageant but doesn't have a personality. She's more of a hot robot trained to say certain things like God and family, and the girls are all lined up and waiting for the verdict and all I can think about is Joel, how he hates this show and everything I watch, how he's such a pompous dick about TV. And I still stink like ham and am picking up a little buffalo chicken.

I reach into my pocket and hold the bag of pills, rubbing the tablets through the smooth plastic of the bag. Nothing crazy. Just a few Xanax and a 10-mg Roxicodone. I bought them a while back, the night after my sister's funeral, which is kind of fucked up but whatever. Months gone by and here they still are. It feels powerful to have them and not do them. Joel would have been proud, but also fuck him. I don't need his approval for shit.

I'm strongly considering pursuing a lesbian relationship with the girl at my work who's good with computers, though I don't know how to go about doing that.

I take a quarter out of my pocket and hold it. Fuck Joel. The quarter crushes the pills in the bag no problem. Me and my sister used to do mixtures like this. We called them "cocktails." I can get a little fucked up, a little buzzed, something to celebrate the verdict that's coming after the commercial break. I'm an adult with a job in a brand new house. If I was shooting dope like Lynne, then yeah, that would be bad.

Plus, Lynne's birthday was the day before. May 23rd. I feel like she'd have appreciated me doing a little cocktail for her.

I shake the bag a little, flicking it here and there to mix the powders. Flicking the bag reminds me of that game, the board game with the dice trapped in a bubble that you push down on. I laid a little line out on the table. A taste. Basically nothing. And smile about Lynne, about how she'd have snorted this whole pile.

A dirt bike screams prepubescently down the street and stops in front of the house. The motor sounds shrill and out of breath, and then it goes off. I can still hear the weed-whackers and push mowers, the mosquito-ish buzz of lawn equipment.

I wipe the powder off the table and put it into the bag.

Keys jangle against the door and it opens. Fig's a lot quicker with the door. He's carrying two packages in his arms and kicking another. He looks like shit, too. Bagged eyes, skinny—it's hard to tell from seeing him every day, but he looks like he was losing weight, a lot of it. Maybe he's still depressed about his dad. His mom too, apparently.

"What'd you get now?" I ask, wiping the powdered smudge off the table.

Fig kicks the one box and it slides across the floor. No concern for the hardwood.

"One of these is for you."

I pause the TV and walk over. Pausing live TV is something I can do now. The only thing that could possibly trump the verdict is a package. Not junk mail, or some credit card bullshit. A real package. A box and everything.

The TV screen is frozen on the hot robot's face in what could be a perfume ad. I move past Fig and look outside, over at Cork's bushes—they are full of butterflies. Big ones with black and orange wings, tiny flying tigers buzzing around his yard.

"When can I move back there?"

I shrug.

"You see that new Indian family that moved into Eddy's?"

"The guy with the thing on his head?"

"Yeah, did you know they all carry knives in holsters? It's part of their religion."

"Huh?"

"Yeah, they can't cut their hair and have to carry knives. It's fuckin' awesome."

I eye Fig's packages. "Where are you getting all this shit from?"

"From colleges. They send me stuff so I'll wrestle there. It happens all the time."

I pick the box up and shake it for a clue. No noise, but the box is light. I figure some distant relative heard and sent a candle or something.

The return label reads:

SCI Pittsburgh

Inmate # 406-435

Pittsburg, PA 15233

Styrofoam peanuts spill out as I pull a smaller box out of the bigger one. I kick the first box out of the way. The little peanut things fly everywhere. I open the smaller box, cutting the tape with my nail, pushing through the peanuts until I feel it. I grip it tight and pull it out. It's heavy and wrapped in brown paper—a shitload of paper, way too much. I twist it and ripped the paper, finally getting it open, but jerk too hard on the last tear.

A big beautiful glass dolphin sails out from my grip. All I can do is stand there and watch helplessly as it nosedives toward my brand-new hardwood floors.

Manufactured by Amazon.ca
Acheson, AB